American Pie

Also by Michael Lee West

She Flew the Coop
Crazy Ladies

American Pie

A NOVEL

Michael Lee West

HarperPerennial
A Division of HarperCollins*Publishers*

First HarperPerennial edition published 1997.

Designed by Caitlin Daniels

The Library of Congress has catalogued the hardcover edition as follows:

West, Michael Lee.
   American pie : a novel / Michael Lee West. — 1st ed.
     p. cm.
   ISBN 0-06-018357-8
   I. Title.
  PS3573.E8244A8   1996
  813'.54—dc20   96-20899

ISBN 0-06-098433-3 (pbk.)

00 01 ❖/RRD 10 9

In memory of my father

Work and pray, live on hay,
You'll get pie in the sky when you die.
—Joe Hill, *The Preacher and the Slave*

PRELUDE

BAJA CALIFORNIA
■ ■ ■ ■ ■ ■ ■ ■ ■ ■ ■

December 29, 1995

FREDDIE

I was diving off the coast of Punta Eugenia, in the cool blue waters above Isla Natividad, when a grey whale plowed through a kelp bed. It moved like a train bearing down on a weedy cross-roads. I thought I wouldn't have time to get out of the way, but at the last possible second, the whale veered 90 degrees, rising at a slant. I looked up and saw forty feet of living tissue, lungs the size of a Volkswagen, a 250-pound heart beating nine times a minute. I'd been all over the world and seen thousands of whales, but I never really stopped being awestruck. That was a little amazing when you considered my career—I'm a cetalogist, specializing in the study of *Eschrichtius gibbosus*, the grey whale.

My husband, Dr. Sam Espy, studied whales, too, but he was about twenty feet above me, sitting in a borrowed boat with his blond assistant. The only way I could reach him was through telepathy, but I was firmly rooted in the scientific world. Although I was born in Tallulah, Tennessee, I no longer considered myself "from" the South—that realm of fantastic cooks, ancestor worshipers, prejudiced fools, and eccentric ladies who took to their beds for decades.

Now I lived on the West Coast in a little seaside town named Dewey, due north of San Francisco. Every November Sam and I braved the California current to Baja, specifically the 28th Parallel, to the lagoons in and around Guerrero Negro, where the grey whales gather from December until March, to breed and give birth. The rest of the year we lived in Dewey, where Sam's dad, Mackie, owned a sheep ranch. Our whale-watching delighted the residents. They loved to tell tourists how we bought and converted a secondhand tuna boat for the price of a double-wide trailer. It had been dry-docked for a while, but it was seaworthy, with a solid wooden hull, the same as Jacques Cousteau's old mine sweeper. The folks in Dewey always pointed this out to the tourists, adding that John Wayne had a mine sweep, bought for a song and refurbished into a swanky yacht. Sam named the tuna boat *Miss Freddie,* and while the town looked on admiringly, I smashed a bottle of good California champagne against the bow.

Now I was close enough to see lice around the whale's eye, all etched with lice. Greys aren't sonic like toothed whales, but this one knew I was here. Only about ten percent of the greys in Baja are "friendlies"—they'll seek you out in the lagoons. I didn't know about this one, but I decided to swim for a closer look. The whale, sensing my approach, shot forward, and the giant fluke slapped down inches from my face, parting the water with such force that it lifted me out of the kelp. The blast knocked the regulator out of my mouth. For a moment I saw nothing but bubbles spinning away from me. The plush side of a rock loomed up. I threw out my hands, but I couldn't avoid the rock; I crashed into it, grazing my forehead, then drifted backward in the current. I was dimly aware of my mask spiraling down toward the kelp. A little to the right, a rocky slope disappeared into a thousand shades of blue.

Right about then I seemed to lose time. A tight sensation spread through my chest. With a start, I realized I was holding my breath; I frantically groped for the regulator, fit it into my mouth, and sucked in air. I stared anxiously at the exhaled oxygen as it rose in large, flattened bubbles. The surface was dappled and wavering, its radiance partially obscured by the curved hull of the boat, and I thought this is what heaven must look like when you die.

I shook my head to clear it, and water swirled around me, cool and effervescent, the way champagne feels when you swallow it straight from the bottle. A plume of red spun out, feathering in the water. It looked like spilled ink. I felt a little stunned, but I knew I was in fairly shallow water because colors began to disappear at twenty-five feet. Reds and oranges leave first; by the time you reach one hundred feet, all that remains is blue. I ran my fingers through the ink; then I slowly realized that it wasn't ink, it was blood. Every diver in the world, dazed or not, knew what that meant—what it attracted. Sharks, I thought, turning 180 degrees. Oh, my god, *sharks*. I didn't see anything ominous in the murky blue, but those shadows could be anything. On the way down to Baja, we had seen a macerated seal—no doubt the work of a great white. Although I had shared other waters with predatory fish, mainly tigers and blues, it wasn't in the presence of blood; a shark can detect a single drop in thirty gallons of water. I didn't have to think twice about it; I began digging through the water, screaming bubbles all the way to the surface.

By the time Sam and his assistant, Nina VanHook, dragged me onto the boat, I was sobbing. "Oh, my *god*, Freddie. What the hell happened?" Sam straddled me, peering down into my face. It was a relief to look into those sweet, almond-shaped eyes, the irises flecked green. His hair was cropped even shorter than mine, and the bright Baja sun was turning it sherry-colored. I opened my mouth wide, fully expecting to say something like, Thank god you saved me. Instead, I reached for the side of the boat and pulled myself up, thinking I might have to retch into the water. I couldn't help it; this was a family trait: vomiting during a crisis. After Mother died, my sisters and I couldn't stop gagging. I remembered crowding around the commode, bumping heads with Eleanor and Jo-Nell. Our grandmother, Minerva

Pray, who hadn't inherited the regurgitation gene, solved the problem by handing out Tupperware bowls, a different color for each sister.

"Freddie, were you too deep?" Sam was saying. He sounded every inch the scientist, but I thought I heard real fear in his voice. He faced Nina VanHook. "Could she have decompressed?"

"In these waters?" said Nina. "Decompensate is more like it." She had chin-length blond hair, sooty at the roots, permed within an inch of its life; she wore a loose T-shirt over her bikini. From the bottom of the boat, I gazed up at her. She was a graduate student at Scripps, my old alma mater, and she'd just turned twenty-three—that made her six years younger than my baby sister, Jo-Nell. I felt very sad. At thirty-three I was too old to be having conniption fits, in a boat or anywhere else.

"Maybe she just freaked out," Nina was saying. "It happens."

I tried not to look at the girl—and she really was just a girl. What did she know about life? I thought about saying something just a little crazy: Look, I didn't panic down there, I got bit. See the mark? *Infectó un mosquito. Comprende?* I knew she'd already made up her mind about me. Well, fine. I'd composed an unflattering picture of her, too. She probably drank raspberry mineral water because the bottle was cute; and I hated the way she measured distances in kilometers. I myself stuck to the American mile.

"Freddie? *Freddie*," Sam was saying. "Look at me, honey. Look at me. You didn't get spooked by a shark, did you?"

"Shark?" Nina spat out the word, then crossed her arms. "You've got to be kidding."

Sam ignored her and said, "Honey, what did you see down there? And what scraped your head?" He gingerly lifted my bangs. I have very short hair, with weird, wispy bangs. I licked my lips, waiting for the nausea to pass.

"I think she must have swallowed her tongue or something," said Nina.

"No, she just needs to get her breath." Sam patted my arm. I hated when people talked about me like I wasn't there. I shut my eyes, straining to collect myself; before I could admit the truth or even shape my lips into a *W* and say *whale*, it was just a whale, Sam touched my forehead. His fingers felt sharp and cold, and I worried that they might draw out the truth. I knew he wouldn't understand what I'd done. I myself barely understood it. I saw a whale and misjudged the situation, I could tell him. For just a second I'd forgotten the subtle interactions between greys and humans—it's never wise to make the first move with something sixteen meters long. Suddenly I understood why people told white lies. They served as little lifeboats, keeping you afloat, out of dangerous waters.

"She's really bleeding. Look at this." He pushed back my bangs. "Something happened down there." He unzipped my wet suit, and my left breast tumbled out. Then he began searching my midsection for lacerations.

"Oh, she's all right, Sam."

"Freddie? Listen, I know you're dazed, but try to focus. Okay?" He leaned forward, frowning with concern. "What did you see? A shark? Was it a hammerhead?"

"I really doubt it," said Nina. "They're so shy. They won't come near Aqua-Lung bubbles. Maybe she *thought* it was a shark. Sometimes groupers can look menacing."

"*I know the difference*," I said through my teeth.

"Of course she does," Sam said. Nina gazed down at me, her lips moving slightly as though she were whispering a secret to herself. She was backlit by the smudged outline of Punta Eugenia, where the spiny mountains plunge into the water. From here it looked desolate, exactly how you'd imagine a desert to be, although up close it is poignantly alive. Sometimes I took early morning walks, and it seemed to me that the sand had a memory, recording the movements of every passing animal, from the swish marks left by a night-hunting lizard to dimples of a trotting fox. I would step over the jetsam from cruise

ships and the northern cities, and head straight for the flotsam.
I picked up figs, giant Ferguson cones, diminutive hatchet
shells. Some foggy mornings I followed a coyote's pug marks or
a jackrabbit's dots-and-dashes. Once I found a dolphin half-
buried at the tide line. By late morning I'd give up. That was
when a persistent wind pushed down from the northwest,
blowing until sunset, working on the nerves.

"It wasn't a goddamn grouper," I said.

"Okay, okay." Nina held up both hands. "You don't have to
get hostile."

"I'm not." I began trembling. I wanted her to know that I
hadn't always studied whales. About a million years ago I had
gone to medical school in Memphis, even if I hadn't lasted
beyond my second year. My grades had been decent, and I
wasn't squeamish during dissections. I had been expelled for
something preventable and regrettable—I stole a cadaver's gallbladder and heart. It's the truth. For a hundred dollars I broke
into the lab, using a passkey, and purloined the organs for a couple of first-year students who were failing anatomy. Just as I set
the organs into a Playmate cooler, two security guards caught
me. They aimed their guns and everything. I dropped to my
knees, and the cooler tipped over. The organs slid across the
floor, between one of the guard's splayed legs.

"Could it have been a blue shark, Freddie?" he asked.

"What makes you think it was a shark?" Nina asked with a
freezing stare.

"She's been diving for years." Sam's voice sounded oddly
apologetic. He tucked one arm protectively under my neck, lifting me several inches. "She knows what she's doing."

"If you insist." Nina wiped her nose with the back of her
hand. She stared down at me. "Take a deep breath and tell us
what happened, okay?"

I wanted to rise up and slap her silly; instead I out-and-out lied.
"T-t-t-tiger sh-sh-shark," I said, my voice obscured by Sam's arm.

"No way." Nina stepped backward, laughing uncertainly. "I don't believe it. I'm going down there." She sat down, squeezing her feet into flippers. She grabbed a mask, then spit onto the glass, vigorously rubbing it with her fingers. Next, she shrugged on a tank and fit the regulator into her mouth. I glanced over at Sam, wondering if he would allow her to dive alone, but he made no move to stop her. I was glad. He rocked on his heels, thoughtfully watching her climb up on the edge of the boat, her back to the water. She turned, raised her thumb. Sam lifted his, too, stabbing it into the air. She grinned around the respirator, then fell backward into the water. In my mind's eye, I saw her passing through layers of red and orange, into the purest blue. She would kick through blood, into colder water. There was no shark, of course, and probably no whale, just a field of kelp, the kind they harvest in southern California.

Sam pressed a napkin to my forehead. "Here, you're still bleeding. I shouldn't have let you dive alone."

"Oh, forget it." I peeled off the napkin and looked at it. My blood was astonishingly red, brighter than a chili pepper. This amazed me. I had always thought of myself as a pale, anemic sort of person. "Do I need stitches?"

"For a scratch?" He grinned and patted my knee. "I don't think so, babe."

"I'm seeing double," I said, my voice rising.

"Stop worrying," he said.

"I'm not." We both knew it was the truth: I worried. I came from a long line of fretful women, the kind that made people crazy. When my grandmother was young, she claimed to be something of a clairvoyant. If she dreamed someone died, they usually did. She'd been raised on the Bible, in which magic is part of the natural world—water into wine, the fishes and the loaves, heal the sick, raise the dead. Still, she found her visions alarming. My sisters ran the family bakery—a seat-of-the-pants operation that would have worried anyone. Jo-Nell believed fretting was stupid, yet she indulged herself in horoscopes and palm readings; once she ran up a two-hundred-dollar phone bill, calling Dionne Warwick's psychic network. Eleanor and I were plain old worriers. When we were growing up in Tallulah, our high school team was called the Warriors. Eleanor mono- grammed our glee club sweaters, and her fingers made a Freudian slip, transposing the *A*'s to *O*'s, and the *O*'s to *E*'s, dropping the *S*'s altogether. Naturally, we stood out, the only WORRIERS in the whole twenty-member chorus.

Now Sam leaned over the rail, and the whole boat listed to the left. He was poised over the water, as if to throw himself into it, searching for Nina's bubbles. I felt a sinking in my chest, something Minerva would call a Sign, and I wished I had never left Dewey. I thought back to this morning when we had walked down to the dock. We'd planned a morning of diving, followed by lunch on the bow and a cruise around the point. I'd assumed it was just the two of us. When I saw Nina waiting on the bow, I tried to hide my disappointment. She stood up and waved. "I brought avocados for later," she called. "I even brought a bikini. See?" She pulled up her blouse, revealing a series of lurid green strings.

"How fitting." Sam smiled, and I noticed his slightly crooked eyetooth. That tooth seemed like family to me. We had been married seven years, that proverbial itchy season, but I couldn't imagine myself with another man. We had been together so long that a kind of metallurgy had occurred, our souls melding like iron and brass. One molecule inseparable from the other. At least, it seemed that way to me.

Now I listened to Nina's bubbles, the soft *gulp-gulp* of air. Her flippers smacked against the side of the boat, and she made a gargling noise. "See anything?" Sam called down.

"Nope. Just Freddie's mask. It was a bitch to find in all that kelp." She tossed it up to Sam, and he caught it with one hand. She pulled off her flippers, making soft grunting sounds, then heaved them into the boat; they bounced on the blue fiberglass bottom, spraying water onto my wet suit; I braced for the shocking cold, but I was surprised to feel nothing. I was insulated against all extremes. Sam handed the mask to me, then turned to assist Nina, who was climbing up on the motor. They clasped hands, then leaned backward, pulling in opposite directions. For a second it was impossible to tell if they were coming together or apart.

TALLULAH, TENNESSEE

■ ■ ■ ■ ■ ■ ■ ■ ■ ■ ■ ■

December 1995–January 1996

JO-NELL

I was sitting at the Starlight Lounge, where every hour was happy hour—the best kind of place for an optimist like me. It sat on the Pennington County line, just a mile past the railroad crossing, a squatty building outlined in a crooked string of Christmas lights. Even though it was almost New Year's, when everyone in town was swigging champagne, the lounge's lights burned year-round. It wasn't the Opryland Hotel, but Tallulah, Tennessee, was a far cry from Nashville.

I sat at the far end of the bar, sipping my third, or maybe it was my fourth, tequila sunrise. Lord, I loved that drink. I had me a buzz, and it was making me flirt with a green-eyed cowboy. Tequila *always* goes straight to my head. I told the cowboy a joke, and he told me his name was Jesse, that he was born right here in Tallulah, Tennessee. I didn't tell him I was, too, because then he might place me—Pennington County had been named after my stepdaddy's people, but the whole clan was dead, so it wasn't doing them any good. Me, I was a McBroom, not rich or locally famous, although sometimes I lied to men. I was damn good at making up stories, but I wasn't sure what to tell this guy. He had nice hands and a nice smile; from the way he kept buying drinks, he must've had a nice job, too. Liquor wasn't cheap at the Starlight.

"Hey, gal. Tell me another joke," Jesse asked, nudging my arm.

"Okay, here's an oldie." I licked salt from a pretzel. "Why does the wind blow from west to east in Arkansas?"

"It *does*? Why?" Jesse scratched his head and opened his eyes wide, as if I was Bill Hall on Channel 4, describing a meteorological phenomenon.

"Because Tennessee sucks." I grinned around the pretzel, then bit down hard, scattering salty bits onto my tongue.

"I love a woman with a sense of humor," Jesse said, putting one hand over his heart. "In fact, I love women, period."

"*All* of them?" I leaned toward him, my blond hair swinging.

"I guess," he said, swallowing hard.

"Well, I don't know if that's good or bad."

"No?" He looked troubled.

"See, I've got this theory about love."

"A what?" He blinked, looking more alarmed than ever.

"A theory." I sipped my tequila sunrise. "You know what that is?"

"Uh-uh." He shook his head.

"Well, this is my theory. I think love's a muscle. And it needs plenty of exercise."

"Honey, you come to the right man." He grinned, then hoisted his belt, letting his thumb rest on the buckle. It was pure silver with a sunburst design. "I got something that'll put the NordicTrack to shame."

"I was thinking of a more gentle exertion." I cupped one hand and flexed my fingers. I looked up at the cowboy and smiled. "Like this."

"Hell, I'll drink to that." Watching my fingers, he swallowed hard and tugged on his hat. Then he signaled the skinny waitress and ordered another round of tequila sunrises.

"You read my mind." I picked up the basket of pretzels, shaking them. "All that salt was making me thirsty, I guess."

"Me, too," said the cowboy.

"But you haven't eaten a thing!"

"Shoot, I get full looking at you."

I tapped one red fingernail against my chin. I had this built-in radar against flattery; I called it my shit detector. Right about now, a siren was going off inside my head. I squinted my eyes and said, "Full of what?"

"I don't know. Good stuff." He ducked his head, grinning. He seemed pretty innocent, and I relaxed. I found myself returning his smile. A long, whimpering love ballad started playing on the jukebox, and he slid his palm over my knee. The shit detector began blaring again. I stopped smiling and stared down at his hand—the short stubby fingers, white against my faded Levi's, with a gold horseshoe ring jutting up from his pinkie. The bar was a little too warm; smoke hung in the air, and the music was too loud. In about two seconds I'd have to move his hand or he'd get the wrong idea. That was how these cowboys were—buy you a few drinks, then they were ready to pounce. It's pay-back time, baby. Peel off them jeans, turn down your bed, and light the light. Even if you were ready, too, you had to pretend you weren't. You had to play hard-to-get. Sometimes it was a real bummer being female.

"Getting a little grabby, aren't you?" I playfully slapped the back of his wrist, but he kept holding on to my thigh, digging his fingers into my jeans. My third husband used to slap me around some. I felt my face redden. "Hey, that hurts. Don't you manhandle *me*."

"Manhandle? You ain't one of them impersonators, are you?" Jesse released my leg. He smiled and pushed back his hat. His forehead was damp and shiny, and I wondered if he was prematurely bald, like Garth Brooks. I had always heard that bald men made the best lovers—all that testosterone, I guess. Unfortunately, I did not have me any firsthand experience with baldies.

"Course not." I drew back, pretending to be offended. "Are you?"

"Want me to check?" He started to unbuckle his belt. It made a jangling sound, and I saw a flash of fuchsia underwear. This affected me deeply, honest to god. He seemed real young, but he had the most beautiful green eyes. I didn't know how young, because I'd never been good at guessing ages. In fact, I'd never been good at anything except attracting men and baking pies. My specialty was lemon meringue. I was raised to believe that all lemon pies were not created equal. They were like men—some were too sweet, others too sour; if you weren't careful, they'd leave a bad taste in your mouth. Most all would sweat without refrigeration.

Me, I adored pies, but men have been my undoing. *Unlucky in love*, my fortune cookies always said. And on my palm, my life line was hidden by a childhood scar. Not a good sign, if you asked me. I had been married three times—once widowed, twice divorced. In between I'd gone with doctors, lawyers, and bankers. Bankers were cheapskates; doctors were too tired to make good lovers; and lawyers were political and paranoid, honest to god, always worrying that their wives were having them tailed. They worried you'd hold a press conference like Gennifer Flowers did. But I would never try to ruin a man's reputation—hell, I'd try to help it along. Vote for this man, I'd say. He could run the entire country with his tongue.

"Go ahead," I told Jesse, tossing my head. "Take off your pants. I've seen a penis before."

From the bar, a man called, "Ain't *that* the truth. She seen mine. In fact, we run out of rubbers one night and had to use trash bags."

I whirled around. Laughing at me was a man with curly blond hair and a thick mustache. Goddamn, I thought. I knew how old that clown was—Dickie Johnson was a twenty-two-year-old roofer, barely old enough to drink, and he screwed with his socks on, dirty crew socks with Nike stamped on the ankles. He knew a little too much about me, so I unzipped my purse and took out my keys.

"You stay out of this, Dickie," I said, my eyes narrowed. "I'm old enough to be your mother."

"Then give me some titty milk, like you done that night at the Winona Motel. Remember that, sugarpie?" Dickie laughed and puckered his lips, making sucking noises. A couple of men with gold chains and sideburns snickered. Jesse pulled down his hat, slouching in his chair.

"First, change your diaper." I stood up, twirling my car keys menacingly. "Because you're full of shit." The men at the bar laughed again, jabbing Dickie with their elbows. In a minute, I thought, they'd all start exchanging stories. Sometimes it just didn't pay to leave home. I tossed down the rest of my drink, grimacing at the sweetness. Then I blew Jesse a kiss. I hated to leave, just when I'd gotten something stirred up, but I didn't have a choice. I strutted out of the bar, stepping out of the door into the chilly December night.

The sky was blacker than usual—no moon, no stars. My breath hung in the air. Behind me, I heard a blast of music. I turned and saw Jesse standing in the door, propping it open with his boot, all backlit by the Christmas lights. He was hiding something behind his back. Over his shoulder, way deep into the bar, I saw the skinny waitress feeding quarters into the jukebox. After a minute Roseanne Cash started singing "My Baby Thinks He's a Train."

"One for the road?" said Jesse. He swung out his arm, producing a tequila sunrise in a tall plastic cup. "Ta-da!"

"No, thanks," I said, wrinkling my nose. "I've got a long drive home."

"Aw, I done ordered it for you. I even got the bartender to put it in a take-out cup, and you know that's against the law."

"Well . . ." I hesitated, but the drink glowed like a jewel in his hand. What the hell, I thought, and walked toward it, tottering slightly. Roseanne Cash's voice seeped through the open door, crooning about trains and failed love. I'm like that song, I thought. And not too different from a train—fast, solid, and eye-catching. Unstoppable. I was wearing high heels and jeans, a lethal combination with tequila. All my life I'd heard that high heels would break your arches and tilt your womb, leaving you flat-footed and sterile—two undesirable conditions, whether you're a bride or a bird dog. I was neither. At twenty-nine, I was fresh out of husbands, and the last time I checked, I didn't have a tail, even though I knew men thought otherwise.

"Thanks," I said. I plucked the cup from Jesse's hand and took a dainty sip.

"Don't mention it." He hooked one hand in his belt loop, glancing at me sideways. "Hey, can I see you again?"

"Sure."

"When?" He shifted his eyes, then licked his lips.

"How about tomorrow evening? We can meet here, at the Starlight. Then we'll just see how it goes." I gave him my prettiest smile, the one that made me a local beauty queen, and then I walked over to my yellow Volkswagen. I had bought it at a garage sale, my favorite haunt for vintage clothing and used appliances. It's amazing what people throw away. They don't value used or damaged goods, but that's lucky for me.

"Hey," Jesse called. "What's your name?"

"Jo-Nell."

"That's a pretty name. Ain't you gone give me just one kiss, Jo-Nell, baby?"

"Come here, then." I leaned against my car, waiting for him to walk over to me. His boots made a crunching sound in the gravel. He slid his arms around my shoulders, drawing me close, pulling me into the V of his legs. Oh, god, he smelled good. Like tequila and Doublemint gum and man-sweat. I tried not to breathe too fast, tried not to spill the drink down his back. As he bent over to kiss me, I felt the painful edge of his silver belt buckle, pressing hard into my stomach. His tongue slipped between my teeth, and I tasted tequila. I opened my lips, as if I was drinking him—a sweet, tangy man. When he started to push against me, I pulled away—less is more with a man.

Smiling up at him, I pushed back my hair. Because of the kissing, it was all tangled, and my sweater had fallen off one shoulder. With one finger Jesse pulled it up. "There you go," he said, letting his hand linger on my collarbone. "Promise you'll be here tomorrow?"

"Would I lie?" I smiled, then climbed into my Volkswagen, tucking the drink between my legs. My car was a real hoot—round and squatty like a yellow bell pepper, with the seats covered in wrinkly vinyl. When the motor cranked, it sputtered like a go-cart, with a hollow, tinny sound. I shifted into first gear and drove to the edge of the gravel lot. Then I glanced up in the rearview mirror. Jesse was still staring, his breath white and frayed against the dark sky. That was youth for you, I thought, chewing on my lip. Passion with a capital P. It occurred to me that I was making a mistake, that I should stop the car and beckon him inside. We could make love in the backseat, folding ourselves like two accordions; or else we could get a room at the motel. Hell, we didn't even have to make love just yet—we could just sit in the car, with the heater blowing against our feet. The thought of finding a man who would actually talk to me, as opposed to screw me, made me hit the brake. When I looked into the side mirror, Jesse was already walking back inside the Starlight. The door swung shut behind him.

Oh, well, I thought. *Que sera sera*. That was my motto. Whatever will be will be. Anyhow, I had promised to meet Jerry Kirby at Waffle House, to pay him for a lid of dope I'd bought last month. I had clean forgot about Jerry. He was the type who'd drive straight over to my house and bang on the door, waking Minerva and Eleanor. If I hurried, maybe I could get to the Waffle House before he stormed off.

I angled the car onto the road and drove down the black highway. My headlights made two pale circles on the asphalt. I

knew this road better in daylight when it was all hemmed in by
board fences, strings of barbed wire, giant round bales of fescue
hay. Tonight the pastures looked evil. Why, anything could be
out there. Flying saucers with little green men, all dressed in tinfoil, performing cattle mutilations. Honest to god, that would
just be my luck.

Thinking about the aliens made me shiver just the least. I
turned up the radio. An oldie was playing, "Spirit in the Sky." If
that song didn't have a sixties beat, it would be creepy; but I
sang along, tapping one fingernail against the steering wheel. I
am not a skittish person—everybody says I have balls for a
woman—but I couldn't help but feel scared. The highway was
in the sticks, miles from town. If only I'd asked the green-eyed
cowboy to come along. I remembered how he'd kissed me, and
I squirmed. I would have asked him to come along, but it wasn't
like I had any place to go.

I lived in my childhood home with my grandmother and
Eleanor, my freaking old maid sister. Freddie, my other sister,
ran away to California eight years ago. You couldn't blame her.
She was the first McBroom to get any education—a bachelor's
in chemistry, two years of medical school, and two master's
degrees in marine biology. She sent us pictures of her redwood
house overlooking this great big bay, where she lived with her
husband, a boy genius. His full name was Dr. Sam Espy. He was
not the sort of doctor who could write prescriptions for
Valium—I learned that real fast. He was a Ph.D. I thought
maybe that stood for Piled Hip Deep.

Eleanor was a high school graduate like me. She was eight
years older than me, but she seemed like Minerva's age, always
running to Senior Citizens and the nursing home, stuffing the station wagon full of old ladies. She loved to throw Tupperware parties. But when it came time for me to entertain, which usually
involved men, Eleanor would get upset. (She was afraid they
might be burglars.) That young man at the Starlight, Jesse, was

the type to give her a heart attack, even though he seemed prosperous. His boots were real snakeskin, with brown leather inserts. Two hundred dollars a pair at Western Outlet on Highway 231.

Keeping those boots in my mind, I sped down the road, gripping the tequila sunrise between my legs. When the car hit a bump, the liquor splashed onto my jeans. The coolness seeped into my crotch. Goddammit, I thought. If that stain didn't dry by the time I got home, Eleanor would say it was from something else. As if she knew from actual experience—ha! "Stay away from me," she'd cry, waving her hands. "No telling what kind of nasty disease you're harboring. And don't try and tell me you caught it from a toilet seat! Why can't you stop carousing and just settle down?"

Damn, it's not like I haven't tried. I had always counted on having a husband and children. A cute brick house with a brass cherub weathervane. An herb garden full of chives and chervil. Sometimes I saw myself living in a mini-manse with wrought-iron gates and dark green tennis courts—listen, I could get used to ostentation in a heartbeat. All by myself I wasn't much, but with a rich husband I could have been somebody. Maybe even the Martha Stewart of Tallulah, Tennessee. On account of my interest in the food industry, I read her magazine; I kept up like a regular person would. If I had a rich husband, why, I'd stuff my Thanksgiving turkey with sun-dried tomatoes, porcino mushrooms, and fresh rosemary; or I could even stuff it with cornbread and prosciutto—something I couldn't even begin to pronounce. I could just see me asking the butcher. With a bundle of money, I could host me an annual New Year's open house with champagne punch and four types of caviar; on Halloween I'd carve pumpkins to look like old men and space invaders; Christmas wouldn't be Christmas without a live poinsettia tree, like the ones at Opryland, and a front yard filled with teeny white lights. Hell, I'd be so stylish I'd put Martha herself to shame.

Of course, I didn't get my chance to be anything but a floozy. My biological clock had more life in it than Eleanor's, but even so, cowboys were getting harder to find. I might never have me a child, much less an honest-to-god husband. All the men in my life kept dying or running away, leaving me stuck at the bakery, cooking side by side with Eleanor. The bakery wasn't even a bona fide bakery—the sign out front said FRED'S DOUGHNUTS in great big red letters. That was my daddy's idea, Fred McBroom, but he died when I was just a teeny-tiny baby, changing the course of all our lives. I didn't have a memory of him, but Minerva told me that in the olden days, Fred's Doughnuts was a hangout for merchants and lawyers; now it was nothing more than a dingy, early morning place where contractors and auto parts salesmen gathered for coffee and frosted bear claws. We didn't even serve cappuccino. I had some trendy ideas of a chalkboard menu, live daisies on the tables. The sign out front would be hand-painted, AMERICAN PIE—BAKERY & TEAROOM. I told Eleanor we could draw students and faculty from the little college, not to mention the new people who were moving into town. "If it's such a good idea," she told me, "then why hasn't anyone else tried it?"

"They have," I said. "In other places. We can be the first one in Tallulah to serve focaccia—"

"Is that Italian for the F-word?"

"No, it's a freaking flat bread," I snapped. "We can serve it with fresh basil and sea salt. And we can serve Gorgonzola with honey."

"Gorgon*what?*"

"It's a cheese, an Italian cheese."

"You should move to Italy, since you like it so much. I'm sure all this foreign food will be a real big hit in this town." Eleanor rolled her pale yellow eyes. "These people don't even know what goat cheese is. They think Parmesan comes in a green Kraft can."

"We'll teach them."

"We'll go bankrupt."

"Not if we buy in bulk. Then we can turn a profit."

"We can't even sell our nice, normal doughnuts!"

"That's because they're so ordinary. Oh, Eleanor, don't you ever have any dreams?"

"No, just visions. And I feel one coming on." Eleanor spread her big, freckled hands. "I see a black-and-white checkerboard floor. Classical music playing in the background. Your personal favorite—what's that guy's name? Ravel."

"Yes, yes." I nodded. "Go on."

"Menus as long and complex as your marital history."

"I don't know what you mean," I said, narrowing my eyes. The truth is I have been married so many times my name sounds like a law firm—Jo-Nell McBroom Hill Bailey Johnson. After the last divorce, I took back my maiden name, McBroom, but I still felt the weight of all those other men. My first husband, Bobby Hill, died when a watermelon truck accidentally dumped its contents into his red Mustang convertible. Husband number two, Ed Bailey, beat the shit out of me, and number three, Jordy Johnson, was a no-good run-around. Nowadays, all I want is someone who will pay me a little attention. Hell, I ain't asking for love. Just a decent man. If there is anyone in the world like that, I wish they'd write—Ms. Jo-Nell McBroom, c/o Fred's Doughnut Shop, Tallulah, Tennessee 38502.

The Volkswagen was chugging along in fourth gear, racing over the rough-paved road. I turned up the radio, Crash Test Dummies were singing that silly humming song. My headlights swept over painted white letters—RRX. I was just a little too woozy to think what it meant, so I just reached between my legs for the drink. It felt cold against the back of my throat. Right about then my breath could've lit fires. I was feeling the buzz again, and it reminded me of the cowboy. Just for a split second,

I was happy, and I thought my turn would come. I barely noticed the railroad tracks coming up—a big mistake.

The train whistle shrieked, and I did, too. Both sounds hung in the air like notes from a church organ. Then I saw the train. It was so close I saw pieces of the engineer: eyes peeled back like two hard-boiled eggs, a cigarette crimped in his mouth, the tip glowing orange. *Oh, my god*, I thought. *He's going to hit me!* I crushed the plastic cup, splashing the tequila down the front of my blouse. Then I stepped hard on the gas. For just a moment, I thought I might outrun the train, but time seemed to fold back on itself. From the second I'd left the bar, my clock had started running backward—now it was approaching zero. With one hand, I yanked the wheel, hoping to veer off into the ditch, but the train caught my left rear fender. The whistle blew again. Then I heard an awful screech—metal against metal, or maybe it was me, yelling my head off. The whole car lurched forward, and I fell against the door, all pressed up against the glass like a goldfish. I looked down and saw gravel, iron, tracks. Red sparks rained up, instantly turning to ash. The whistle went straight to my bones, a curved sound like needle-nose pliers. I knew then I was going to die.

It must've all happened in seconds, but it seemed to last hours. The Volkswagen's front tires popped off the track, digging into the gravel, then suddenly it flipped around, spinning away from the tracks. My door popped open and ripped off its hinges. I tried to hang on to the steering wheel, but my body was too heavy. The wheel came off in my hands, and I flew out into the dark. I had always heard that if you fell from a high place, like a skyscraper, your heart would stop beating a split second before you hit the ground. But this was a train wreck, not the Life & Casualty Building in downtown Nashville. I longed for an honest-to-god vision: Jesus, angels, tunnel of light. I didn't see a damn thing. I guessed it was all a big fat lie— dying and going up to heaven was not like winning an all-expense-paid vacation on a Princess cruise. Your whole life didn't flash before you. All I saw was the last thirty minutes: the man I left back at the Starlight—his palm on my leg, his boot wedged in the door, the drink gripped in his hand, held up against the night like an offering.

MINERVA PRAY

When the midnight train passed through downtown Tallulah, it stirred me from a fine dream: I was mowing my yard, twenty full acres that sloped into Church Creek. In the dream I wore me a sleeveless A-line dress, turquoise with white rickrack, the latest style from the 1949 Sears Roebuck catalogue. The sun poured over my shoulders. It seemed salty, buttery, like something you'd brush over corn. Every time the mower hit a rock, my upper arms shook like turkey wattle. Which only went to show that I was born old, but I was getting younger all the time.

The train whistle blew again, and the dream fell away. I lay real still in the featherbed, trying to hear my push mower and smell the fresh-cut grass. I couldn't hear nothing but my own heart pumping and the train just a-rattling. Me, I was a good dreamer, but sometimes I had trouble remembering them in the morning. Bits and pieces would leap up, flashing like a trout in the Caney Fork. I would try to lure it back, but child, that river is deep. You can't see the bottom if you tried.

In the olden days, when I couldn't fall asleep, I counted boxcars in my mind the way some people counted sheep. I liked how the whistle blew at every crossroads and how the cars shuffled like an empty roller coaster. In my mind's eye, I scooted along with the train as it rushed over Maple Hill Road, Horn Springs, Cairo Bend. Pennington County was hemmed in by three rivers—the Cumberland, Limestone, and Caney Fork. Back in them days, railroad trestles was built up high over these rivers. The town of Tallulah was hard to get to, my Lord, the road was steep and twisty. In them days you could only reach it by ferry. Now you have to cross that high, green bridge, known to the locals as Lover's Leap. It was built by the Corps of Engineers in 1946, five years after Amos and I came to town. Some mornings it looked ghostly, a wispy green arch supported by the fog, and other times you just knew it was going to collapse. The bridge led to Tallulah proper, a town sprouting out of the cliffs like a bag of Magic Rocks, spearing up overnight in river water. Not too far from the square was Church Creek, where my grassy yard began. I lived in a white frame house on a hill, two wood gliders on the front porch. This was where I rocked my girl Ruthie after we left Texas. She was a sickly thing. Back then, I craved for the Lord to let just one of my babies live. I'd already buried two in Mount Olive, Texas, near the Guadalupe River. Amos said that Tallulah, Tennessee, was bound to be lucky for us, because his favorite actress was Tallulah Bankhead. He just knew we'd find luck, but believing something don't make it true.

If I ever had me any great-grandchildren, which didn't look likely, I would spin out a story of Texas, about two sisters who married two brothers. Hattie and me was the sisters; Amos and Burl was the brothers. I was seventeen, and Hattie was eighteen-and-a-half. It was a double wedding at the First Baptist Church on Limestone Road, and we filled up that little white building on both sides, spilling out into the street. We picked November 15, 1932, the year Mount Olive was electrified. If my Amos was still alive, we would be married sixty-three years this year. Say what you want, but that's a long time, child. To this day, I won't look at another man—in my heart I am still married. Last Wednesday, an old geezer with a beard tried to talk to me at the post office. (Well, I'd just had my hair done.) I stood in line, playing like I was deaf.

No sooner had I drifted back to the dream, cutting my grass and dividing the wild ferns, when another sound pulled me back to the bedroom. Someone was on the front porch, just a-banging on the door; or else I was dreaming they was. My mind skidded just a bit. I couldn't remember if this was the house on Church Creek or the one before that, on Petty Gap Road, in Mount Olive, Texas. No, this was Eleanor and Jo-Nell's house on River Street, a yellow clapboard with bottle-green shutters, although the paint was flaking like crisp onion skin. The house had been tearing itself apart for twenty-nine years, after all the deaths started happening.

A house will do that after a tragedy—fall to pieces on you. It's no different, really, than a worn-out body, full of hairline cracks and broken foundations, frayed wires and clogged pipes. You no sooner get one thing fixed and something else breaks down.

The knocking was more frantic now. Whoever was standing on the porch was bound to be freezing. If it was a burglar, maybe he'd smash through the glass. If it was one of Jo-Nell's suitors, I hoped he'd just leave, but the banging noise went on and on. I thought to myself, *Why, they're bound to break the door in half*. I could see it happening, sure I could. "Eleanor?" I cried, my voice full of rust. "Jo-Nell? Child, somebody get the door!"

No answer. Just the train wailing its ghost song. I was full awake now. I crept out of bed and pulled on my pink robe. Then I strained to listen. The knocking had stopped. I held my breath and listened again. A man cursed, and his footsteps shuffled down the sidewalk. A car door creaked open, then slammed. A second later, an engine revved up, then whined as the car backed out of the driveway. Still wearing my robe, I sat down on the bed, then settled back in the deep feather pillows—goose feather pillows I'd brung from Texas. I drew in a deep breath, trying to smell my yard back at Church Creek. Sometimes it smelled oniony like I was growing a salad, not a lawn.

Just let me rest, I thought. Just let me rest here a spell.

I have had dreams that came true—dreams where people died. Once, I dreamed that I was dressing for my mama's funeral, and I woke up just a-crying. My sister Hattie said if you told a dream the next morning, it wouldn't come true. You had to eat breakfast before you told. "I dreamed that Mama died," I told Hattie, over sausage and eggs. "And I was just a-digging through the chifforobe, trying to find me a black dress." Four days later, Mama keeled over in the kitchen, just as she reached to take a peach pie from the oven. Pie crust and syrup went everywhere. Later, when I went to the chifforobe and pulled out a black dress, my fingers shook so bad, I couldn't do up the buttons, just like in my dream. Hattie said, "Minerva, don't you go dreaming about me, girl." And the night before Jo-Nell's first husband died, I dreamed of watermelons. They were all mashed up on the road, and I was gathering the rinds in my apron to make jelly.

Now I shut my eyes and let my mind drift. Just let me drift, child. I fly back to Church Creek, where the grass has growed knee-high. It's so tall it tickles my legs; it's so tall it chokes the push mower and katydids fuss from the weeds. A flock of blue jays wheel in the air. Way, way off in the distance, the train whistle plays me a hymn, one of my favorites, "Bringing in the Sheaves." I've got my dress rolled up, tucked into my waistband. The sun is shining and I'm humming.

JO-NELL

It took forever for me to hit the ground. Minutes, hours, years. Hell, I didn't know how many. I'd just been hit by a train so naturally I was a tad confused. At least I had on clean underwear—hot-pink bikini pants with lace and teeny white bows. That was a good thing. If I was dead, which I strongly suspected, at least they'd know I was a quality person when they stripped me down at the funeral home.

On the other hand, I might not be dead. Doris Day got hit by a train and lived—why not me? Surely this was a Sign. I have always been into signs. I was a Libra, the scales, and according to Patric Walker's forecast in *TV Guide*, I would have made a damn good lawyer.

When I finally hit the earth, it was softer than I ever imagined and smelled of fescue hay. It took me a minute to realize that I *had* landed in hay, a great pile of it. That was a relief, because I could have ended up in a tree. Or splattered on the highway. You saw stuff like that all the time on the news, or in Eleanor's scrapbook (more on which later). It took me another minute to do a quick inventory—just to see if I was hurt real bad. My whole left side was throbbing, and I was scared to move it. What if I tore something loose?

I cracked open one eyelid, then the other. All around me was hay and a cold black sky. I stared down at my toes—they were all there, thank god, ten beautiful toes, the nails painted Antique Garnet. When I fell from the sky, I'd lost my high heels—*if* I *had* fallen, *if* this wasn't a dream. (For all I knew, it was a fucking nightmare.) I couldn't help but wonder if it was the kind of dream that was full of portents—warning me to slow down, to watch where I'm going, to prepare for a personal (or maybe even financial) derailment. I have had weirder dreams before.

I was hurting something awful, like my left leg had come undone at the root. Even with all the pain, I was really and truly alive. It was a freaking miracle, honest-to-god, like Dorothy tapping her ruby slippers three times or Jimmy Stewart on the bridge, getting another chance at life, or even the baby in the barn—little Lord Jesus on a bale of hay. There were miracles and parables galore in the Bible, not that I believed any of it. Another good place was black-and-white movies on A&E. It paid to be cultured, just as long as you didn't start growing bacteria.

Somewhere in the darkness I heard a screeching sound and wind scraping through the bare trees. It was the train trying to stop. It sounded awful, like in *Terminator*, when Linda Hamilton crushed Arnold's head, and his red eye s-l-o-w-l-y blinked out. God, that was gross. Everybody at the movie house clapped except me. I was too creeped out; my date had to carry me to his trailer and feed me beer and barbecue potato chips. Honest to god. See, I was the sort of child who believed in ghosts, fairies, and Santa Claus. For years I wore me a crucifix in case Bela Lugosi tried to suck my blood. Now, I wasn't nearly so superstitious—no, I left all that to Eleanor and Minerva—but I knew the world was full of unsolved mysteries. All you had to do was watch cable TV. On some channel or another you could see Robert Stack walking out of the mist in a trench coat, talking about abductions, haunted houses, and whatnot. And it wasn't just in America; weird things happened in England, too. My Led Zeppelin boxed set featured crop circles on the cover. Sure, they could be made by hoaxers, but personally I thought it was spaceships. I read all about it in the *National Enquirer*, what Eleanor buys to fill her scrapbook. She collects gruesome and/or weird stories, like ax murders and Amtrak derailments and dwarfs who get accidentally sucked up by department store escalators. These store-bought tragedies soothed Eleanor in a perverse way, Lord knew why. She spent whole evenings snipping the paper, pasting stories like MAN DREAMS HE IS A BIRD—WAKES UP ON A TELEPHONE POLE. Wouldn't it be a hoot if she bought an *Enquirer* and found a story about a train wreck in Guess Where, starring Guess Who?

I lifted my head just the least. Somewhere over by the trees were circles of light. I didn't know if it was radiance from the hereafter or the railroad men, sweeping their Eveready flashlights through the fog. The L&N came through Tallulah every single night, and I guessed it was the one that hit me. Where there are trains, there are men, and I was not fit to be seen. I wanted to straighten my sweater (it was all balled up under my armpits). When I went to pull it down, I somehow moved my leg. The pain brought tears to my eyes. I just had to leave it be. Normally, I wouldn't let nobody see me barefoot, unless I'd had a recent pedicure. My motto was never let a man see you look bad. It was best to strike a pretty pose. Not that it had ever got *me* nowhere. Men came and went like so many trains. They came and left me flat on my back, trying to remember what-all happened.

The lights bobbed up and down, cutting through the dark. I didn't know the cause of all that god-awful brightness, but I sincerely hoped it did not belong to little green men, the kind that drove spaceships. I could see me getting whisked away to the planet Uranus. *Your-anus*, I'd tell everybody later. *Get it?* Behind the flashlights were men's voices, so loud and countrified, I wanted to cry. And they were looking for me—searching for the victim, I heard one man say. The victim is bound to be here somewhere.

Way off in the distance I heard a siren, and I guessed it was coming for me. I was glad because my entire body was starting to throb—if I had an FM radio, I could have made good time to Iron Butterfly. I knew for a fact that paramedics brought black Hefty bags to accident scenes. This was so they could carry you off in pieces and innocent bystanders wouldn't vomit. Right about now those medics were probably thinking, Damn, a train wreck. I sure wish I hadn't of eat that pork barbecue for supper. Well, look here, I'd tell them. It's not my damn fault. When it comes to the Saturday night shift, it is smart to work on an empty stomach. Any fool knows that. On weekends, the natives of Tallulah got restless—drinking, smoking a little weed, looking for love in all the wrong places. Hell, I probably knew half the men on the rescue squad. (To tell the truth, I'd slept with ninety percent of them.) Who would have dreamed they'd be spread out in the dark with trash bags, trying to put me back together so Eleanor could throw a decent funeral.

I guess I must have passed out. When I came to, I was floating in space, moving down a long, white tunnel. Above me was one of them acoustic ceilings, the kind that has fifty holes per square inch, all hemmed in by a metal grid. You would think spaceships had prettier ceilings, but beggars couldn't be choosers. I ended up in a room, all surrounded by hooded men. They weren't green, but they came in assorted colors—blond and brunette, pink-cheeked and gray-eyed. Two were bearded. A couple looked like butchy women, but I didn't know for sure. Two wore earrings. Every single one was dressed in a pure white robe, and I thought to myself, Girl, there's a logical explanation for all this. They're either nurses or angels. Although on a recent *X-Files*, the flesh-eating aliens wore white silk jumpsuits. That's how they could recognize each other. This whole situation reminded me of when the house fell on the witch in *The Wizard of Oz*. Damn, that had to hurt—you know? I had fallen from the sky, too, but instead of being surrounded by Munchkins, I got me a bunch of fucking choirboys.

It just didn't seem fair.

"Don't move, miss," one of the choirboys said, reaching down to adjust the sheet on my leg. This was the sort of thing a man said after he stuck a gun in your ribs and asked for your purse; but this choirboy seemed harmless. I figured he would probably have to cut off my jeans—and they were name-brand Levi's I'd bought at Cissy Alsup's garage sale. Now that she'd stopped being a whore and married a doctor, she was floating in money. She had the best sales in town.

If I only had known I was going to end up on a cot, I would have worn my short wool dress, royal-blue plaid, the one I bought at Goodwill for five dollars. It showed off my legs like nobody's business, and it had been a long time since I'd had an audience—at least a day or two. (The green-eyed cowboy at the Starlight didn't count.) As I thought of him, it came to me that I needed a house of my own. Failing that, I supposed a double-wide trailer would do. I was so freaking tired of living with Mama's old drop-leaf cherry tables and the rose-backed chairs and lace doilies you had to iron. Things that Eleanor called antiques. If I ever got my own place, I'd fix it up real pretty. I'd drive to Pier 1 in Nashville and buy me some wicker chairs. I'd buy me a futon and hang matchstick blinds in all the windows. Teeny white candles would burn all night long. I'd put Bruce Springsteen on the CD player and listen to him sing about tunnels of love. Lord knew when I'd get enough money for all that.

Another choirboy reached up and squeezed a clear bag of fluid, like what I'd seen on TV. I had learned a lot about malpractice from shows like *ER* and *Chicago Hope*, although nobody here could hold a candle to George Clooney. "Let's get her hooked up to a monitor," one of them shouted. I couldn't see his face. It could have been honest-to-god *God* for all I knew, which subdued me just the least. If He could read my thoughts, I was done for, flat-out *done for*. He'd send me straight to hell, or else put me in a coma.

"Get a stat CBC, SMAC, and blood gasses," He called. "Stat KUB and total spine."

I didn't know what the hell he was talking about—I wasn't a bowl of alphabet soup. The dudes in the white coats hovered, telling me to hang on. Well, I'd try, even though it was easier to close my eyes and catnap. My mind whirled faster than Tweety Bird, it was faster than the train. It was easy to feel confused. Of course, it was. Still, if this *was* heaven, the men angels looked like drag queens. Although they really could have been aliens, just not green ones, abducting me to some ultra-fast UFO for a galactic gang-bang. That would be far out; that would be a hoot. Whatever the hell this was—life or death or science fiction—it was soft and numb and starched white, with the initials TCD stamped on the sheets. This could have meant several things, from Tallulah Civil Defense to This Cunt's Dead.

I sincerely hoped I woke up soon. It would be a cold, sunny morning. Over a breakfast of sausage, scrambled eggs, and biscuits, all drizzled with sorghum, I would tell Minerva and Eleanor about my dream—hit by a train, the midnight L&N, and rescued by space aliens/choirboys. It seemed so real, I'd say. Honest to god.

MINERVA PRAY

Just when I got back to sleep, the phone rang. I didn't know if it had anything to do with that banging I heard earlier, but something told me it was trouble. I got a shivery feeling in my bones. You live to be my age, and as long as your mind don't wander, you get a feel for things. I climbed out of bed and shuffled down the hall, my bare feet skating across the pine floor. A tightness moved through my chest, and I started breathing fast.

The phone sat on a rickety table, and the bell put me in mind of the dinger in my kitchen, letting me know when my pies was done. "Hello?" I said, then held my breath. I heard a thousand voices talking at once, across all the years and miles of my life, each one telling me of a fresh tragedy.

"Is this the McBroom residence?" asked a deep-voiced man.

For just a second I had to think. McBroom? No, ain't none of them here. They died off years ago. There's just me, Minerva Pray, and the granddaughters. Then of course it all came back to me. McBroom was my daughter's married name: Ruthie married Fred in 1957. Not a great big wedding, mind you, but there was a three-layer cake with roses (Fred, who was a fine baker, made it hisself). There was pink punch, assorted mints, and a rose-and-baby's-breath corsage. Now, all these years later, ain't nothing left of Ruthie and Fred except this house, the doughnut shop, and the three daughters. There was even less trace of

Ruthie's second husband, that old, no-good Wyatt Pennington. Eleanor was the only one who went by McBroom (she's an old maid, if you got to know the truth). Freddie was married, living far, far away. And Jo-Nell had herself a whole slew of last names, like buttons in a sewing box.

"Ma'am? You still there?" said the deep-voiced man. "Hello?"

"Yes, I'm here." I sighed and wondered if he'd been the one knocking at the door earlier. I sat down in the slipper chair, leaning one elbow on the rickety table. I sure hated it when my mind wandered. The older I got the more it roamed; it put me in mind of them cattle in Texas where each steer needs 150 acres just to survive. Can you feature that? It wasn't like I had me a big brain—shoot no. Mine was just dry and dark and dusty. Like a great big ranch at midnight, or an attic without a light. Sometimes you just lost your place was all. The past was a hundred-watt light bulb. It never went dark. I remembered more than I wanted to. I was born and reared in Mount Olive, Texas, but I had lived in Tennessee so long it felt like home. And the roof over my head was bought and paid for by Fred McBroom.

"You've reached the McBrooms'," I said into the phone, nodding curtly, as if the caller could see me.

"To who am I speakin', ma'am?" said the man.

"Minerva Pray," I told him. "My daughter was a Pray, then a McBroom. She was a Pennington for a few years, then she was almost a Crenshaw—do you remember Mr. Peter from the dime store? He sold baby ducks and chickens at Easter? They were engaged to be married. Anyway, he moved away, and then my daughter died . . . well, to make a long story short, I've nearbout raised the girls."

"Yes, ma'am," said the man. He cleared his throat, and I could hear him spitting. "You see, ma'am, this is Hoyt P. Calhoun from the Tennessee Highway Patrol? And I'm afraid I've got some bad news."

All right, I thought. Hit me with it. I squeezed the phone until my knuckles popped. In the seconds before Hoyt P. Calhoun told me what was what, I racked my brain, trying to beat him to the punch. Trying to feature what sort of news he was aiming to tell. Listen, I could tell you about the bad. I could tell you about crop failures and flu epidemics and world wars and burying little children in the cold, cold ground. I had always heard that the devil couldn't stand for folks to be happy, so he had to stir up the pot, adding fistfuls of cayenne and poison. Got to add his share of torment and heartbreak.

"Ma'am, is Jo-Nell McBroom your . . . daughter?"

"Granddaughter," I croaked. My old head started shaking, and it hurt to breathe. Wasn't Jo-Nell home? I couldn't remember hearing her little Volkswagen drive up. Sometimes she made a ruckus, turning on all the lights, whirring the blender, calling people on the phone. If the noise was loud enough to wake Eleanor, she would thunder down the stairs and start a fight. "Oh, Lord," I said into the phone. "What's happened?"

"She's been in a accident, ma'am."

"Accident!"

"There's no cause for panic, ma'am," Hoyt P. Calhoun said hastily. "Far's I know she's alive. Even so, you need to get on down to Tallulah General. She's at the emergency room."

"I'll be right there," I said. My knee started jerking up and down. If somebody had walked in and give me a thousand dollars to stop shimming that leg, I couldn't have done it. My mind seemed to shrivel, with one thought stampeding around and around: She's going to die she's going to die. I dropped the phone into my lap, but I didn't reach to pick it up. The flannel gown was stretched between my knees like a blue flowered ditch. I just sat there for a spell, jiggling the phone like it was a baby. So many questions and I had not asked Mr. Calhoun a single one. I thought about calling him back to ask what kind of accident. Did she run her little Volkswagen into a tree? Had somebody whopped her in the head with a beer bottle? (For years now Eleanor has been predicting this.) But I did not know Mr. Calhoun from Adam, much less his telephone number. I could see him in a patrol car, his belly wedged up along the steering wheel, saying 10-4 into the little black microphone. Then he'd spit into a Styrofoam coffee cup from the Minute Market.

From Eleanor's room came slow, shuffling noises, the kind that old, finicky women make, and I knew she was getting up. A minute later she stood in the doorway, her big freckled hand clutching the neck of her robe. "Who was that on the phone?" she asked, squinting in the bright light.

"The police." I picked up the receiver and laid it back on the hook. "I got to get to the hospital. Jo-Nell's been in a accident."

"Oh, Lord." Eleanor's eyebrows slanted together. "Is she hurt bad?"

"Bad enough for the po-lice to call."

"I'll just throw on some clothes, then." She eased back into her bedroom, and I eased back into mine. My fingers were too stiff to manage any buttons, so I just slipped on my best Sunday dress. When I went to pull on my support hose, my fingernails clawed through the nylon. The fresh runs made a zipping noise, but I didn't care. I stepped out of my room, tucking a pocketbook over my arm. From the hallway, I saw Eleanor sitting on her bed, tugging on fleece-lined boots. It was bad luck to put a hat or shoes on the bed, but I didn't say a word.

She was Ruthie's firstborn, which explained a lot. When you made a cake for the very first time, you couldn't expect perfection.

"I was just thinking," she said. "Maybe this is nothing but a little DUI, a minor run-in with the law. We both know what a drinker she is. This was bound to happen."

"The police talked like it was serious," I said.

"They always do, Minerva. To them jaywalking is a crime."

"Then why did they take her to the emergency room?"

"Why, to sober her up. Or get a blood test. It's a state law for drunk drivers. Or else it ought to be."

"We don't know she was drinking."

"The police don't call in the middle of the night just to chat, Minerva."

This was true. As I rubbed the pit of my stomach, I said, "I have a bad feeling right here."

"Maybe it's food poisoning," she suggested. She pulled on her other boot, grunting with the effort. "I told you that mayonnaise was old, but no, you just *had* to make chicken salad."

In the faint bedroom light her eyes looked pure yellow, the same color of my sister's, who died last August in Texas. Hattie had softer ways, even if she didn't like to travel, claiming that Tennessee was too far north. She liked to stay put. It was she who coined that phrase about if life gives you lemons, make lemonade, but I think a tourist overheard her and stole it. "I hope it makes them happy and rich," Hattie said in her sweet voice, but I myself was hopping mad. That is just how life is—you do something good and then it's stole from you. Just like it was never yours to start with.

Not only did Eleanor have my sister's eyes, she didn't like to travel. Call her a homebody, but I called it plain weird. I will say this for Eleanor—at the drop of a hat she'd have a tea party for my widow friends. She'd fill the dining room table with desserts: coconut layer cake, petit fours, teeny-tiny lemon tarts, and a few savories, like cheese straws. A few years ago she sold Avon and did a right brisk business. Then she got tired of going door-to-door. She would have made somebody a good wife, but that just wasn't in the cards. The poor thing didn't have no boyfriends or girlfriends—just me, Jo-Nell, and the widows. At first I thought she was shy; then I realized it was something deeper. She was a tall girl, nearly six foot; by the time she was fifteen she'd reached her full height. Instead of standing up

straight, she slouched over, hugging her arms to her chest. Me
and Ruthie bought her a back brace, one that had the *Good
Housekeeping* seal, but Eleanor refused to wear it. After a while,
her personality became hunched over, like she had bad posture
of the soul. The only time she brightened up was with the old
ladies—with them she had personality plus.

I tried to get her out of the house. I'd circle things in the newspaper, like a Young Democrats meeting or square dancing
lessons. "Why, I'm not interested in that!" she'd say. "But
Eleanor," I'd say, "there's more to life than this house, the
doughnut shop, and a bunch of widow women." "My life suits
me fine," she said, then lowered her eyebrows. I blamed a lot on
daytime television. She watched too much *Ricki Lake* and *Maury*
(she fixed the VCR so it would tape all her shows while she was
at the doughnut shop). I blamed the rest on cruel twists of fate.
Some way or another, Eleanor had got the idea that a crime
wave was heading straight for Tallulah, and she had a scrapbook to prove it. She showed me an article that claimed a violent crime happened in America every seventeen seconds. "And
mostly the culprits are men," she pointed out. She was even suspicious of poor old Brother Stowe, the Baptist minister, whose
picture hung in my bathroom. "Take it down," she always
begged me. "His eyes follow me wherever I go. I can't do my
business with him watching." I asked Jo-Nell what she thought,
and she said she didn't care, she was used to men looking at her
naked body. I refused to remove Brother Stowe's picture. I never
felt he was looking at me; I kindly felt his presence would keep
a old lady from falling in the bathtub, but I told Eleanor that if
it bothered her, just drape some toilet paper across the frame.
"Why don't you just turn the other cheek?" Jo-Nell suggested,
then fell over laughing, but I don't think Eleanor got it.

When we got to Tallulah General, I saw three police cars in the
U-shaped emergency driveway. A couple of officers were

milling about, but nobody stepped forward and claimed to be
Hoyt P. Calhoun. Once we got inside the hospital, we followed
signs to an aqua waiting room, which featured a TV hanging
from the ceiling and row after row of scratchy plaid chairs, like
what you see in a movie theater. The entire room was empty. It
faced double doors that led to a sealed-up room. NO ADMIT-
TANCE, a sign said in red letters. EMERGENCY PERSONNEL ONLY. Me
and Eleanor were all alone; I couldn't help but wonder why.
Didn't nobody ever get sick after midnight in Tallulah?

Eleanor made herself right at home, digging through the old
Redbooks. I sat down across from her and gazed up at the TV,
ready to watch the world traipse by every thirty minutes on
CNN. "I just can't sit here." Eleanor stood up. "I've got to see
what's going on."

I said nothing. Me, I been in enough hospitals, including this
one, to know a few things. Nurses are bossy, and they like to
keep you in the dark. When my sister Hattie lay dying in Texas,
the nurses marched in and out of that room like cruise direc-
tors—time to eat, time to wash, time to roll down to X-ray. The
one thing they missed was Hattie's time to die.

Eleanor slogged up to the doors and pushed a red knob that
said STAND BACK—MECHANICAL DOORS. There was a hissing sound,
then the doors gaped open. She leaped back, startled, then darted
on through. Her shoulders were hunched over like she had a
Pyrex bowl on her back. I didn't know where she got her timid-
ness from—the Prays or the McBrooms—but she'd got her tallness
from my Amos. He stood almost six feet, four inches.

Not three minutes later the double doors whooshed open,
and out came Eleanor, her eyes flashing yellow fire. "Something
bad must be happening," she said. "People are running around
and shouting. Rolling in scary-looking machines. I got chased
out. They wouldn't tell me doodly squat."

"Did you see Jo-Nell anywhere?"

"No, and believe me, I tried. The nurses had the nerve to ask if I was immediate family. You can't get much more immediate than a sister, I told them." She chewed her thumbnail. "I mean, really. Couldn't they see the family resemblance? But they still made me leave."

I felt sorry for her, all hunched over like Mrs. Bailey from the nursing home—they say she didn't have enough calcium in her bones. I knew that Eleanor's problem wasn't a lack of milk. Being ugly had took a toll. Then losing her mama and daddy just finished her off. Plus, it didn't help that her sisters were pretty. Jo-Nell was a born flirt, and Freddie was a genius; like most geniuses, Freddie had moved to greener pastures. I thought of her as a long-lost grandchild, one with a California area code. I had never seen them whales of hers, but I could feature the attraction. I myself liked great big things, too. I always thought I'd get back to Texas—it was just something I dreamed about. It was where my history lived, along with my blessings and my sorrows.

Well, you stay where you are needed. You go through the motions. You wake up with the roosters, make coffee, water your violets, bake a prune cake, watch the six o'clock news, say good night. They say life can survive in the most unlikely places. Back in the seventies, the girls fixed a greenhouse window. Freddie grew a plant that didn't have no roots or dirt, a bromeliad or some such. She told me that wheat kernels were recently found in Egypt. They had been put there thousands of years ago. Somebody planted them and you know what? They grew. And I heard Dan Rather say that there might be life on Mars, all froze up in the rocks. I believe that the weakest thing can be strong, whether it's wheat or a person. You just have to wait until the conditions are right.

A tired-looking doctor stepped out of the sealed doors, trailed by two stout nurses. When Eleanor saw him coming, she opened her pocketbook and pulled out two Kleenexes, handing one to me.

"I'm sorry it's taken so long," the doctor said, taking a sheaf of papers from a nurse. He did not look more than twenty, with his styled black hair and broad, oily face. "I'm Dr. Granstead, Ms. McBroom's orthopedic surgeon?" He shook my hand, then glanced down at the papers. "Ms. McBroom has a fractured hip and femur. But don't get your hopes up. These are just her orthopedic injuries."

"What happened to her?" Eleanor gaped up at him.

"Ms. McBroom is lucky to be alive." The doctor frowned. "In fact, she might have sustained more severe injuries. Her blood pressure and hematocrit keep dropping, which makes me think she's bleeding internally. A ruptured spleen, most likely. I've consulted a general surgeon. And I'm certain she has a concussion, maybe even cerebral edema. There's no neurosurgeon on staff here, but if she shows any neurological deficits at all, I'll ship her to Nashville."

"Is she going to be all right?" I twisted the Kleenex.

"She's critical," said the doctor.

"Well, good Lord," said Eleanor, waving one hand. "Don't pay attention to her. She's always been critical, especially of me. Sarcastic, too. It's just best to overlook it."

The doctor blinked.

"She won't die, will she?" My chest tightened.

"Not if I can help it." He gave me a shrewd stare. "The sooner we get her into surgery, the better."

"Surgery?" Eleanor gaped up at him.

"Her bones need reduction—that means setting, possibly pinned. A plastic hip isn't out of the question. Can one of you sign these forms?"

"They're just routine permission slips," said one of the hefty nurses.

"I guess I can. I'm her granny," I said, standing up. While I scratched out my name, the doctor studied the TV, which was playing one of them all-night news stations. A plane had

crashed in South America, and the strangest thought hit me—
more people probably suffered from curses than they ever realized. They just went through their lives thinking bad things
came in threes—stopped-up toilets, plane crashes, heart attacks,
wrecks.

"She ain't going to come out of this, is she?" I looked up into
his eyes. The ballpoint pen fell out of my fingers and hit the tile
floor. One of the fat nurses squatted down to get it, and I could
hear her pantyhose creaking like dry wood. One more pound on
you, I thought, and you'll bust. It was probably a good thing
that she worked in emergency.

"I'll do my best," said the doctor, dragging his eyes from the
TV, "but still, you might want to make the necessary calls. As far
as train wrecks go, it wasn't a bad accident. She's probably the
luckiest woman alive. Still, her prognosis is still grim. I know
that's confusing."

"Well, yes," said Eleanor. Then she sat up straight. "What do
you mean, train wreck?"

"I thought you knew. Her car was hit by a train." His eyes
switched from me to Eleanor, as if he was measuring how much
he should tell us.

Eleanor covered her mouth with her hands. She rocked back
and forth.

"Hit by a—" I couldn't say the word. I sagged back to the
chair, and my old leg started twitching again. The doctor gazed
up at the TV, rustling his papers. He was itching to take Jo-Nell
into surgery and cut her open. In the old days, Dr. Chili
Manning would have took my heartbeat, the tips of his fingers
drawing everything from my wrist. Do you need a sedative, old
girl? he would have asked. Just to take the edge off this train
wreck. He was an old-timey GP, what they don't make no more.
Before he moved away to Florida, he warned me about this
breed of new, young doctors. He said they practiced medicine
by the books. They need a million-dollar machine to tell you if

your heart is beating a hair too fast. His own son, Jackson, was a baby doctor in this very hospital, and he use to date Freddie. I say "date," but they were once engaged to be married. She was real closemouthed about why they broke up. Before I got to the bottom of it, she'd left for California. I suspect it had to do with her getting kicked out of medical school.

"How did she get hit by a train?" cried Eleanor, opening her eyes wide.

"You'll have to ask the police," he said. "I'll speak to you again after surgery."

He turned on his heels and left, rushing through the double doors. The nurses scuttled after him. As the doors shut, Eleanor stuck out her tongue. "What a twerp," she said. "And he looks *just* like that surgeon on *Days of Our Lives*, and he turned out to be a butcher."

"Honey, this ain't no soap opera," I said. "It's real life."

"Don't remind me." She picked up a *People* and began thumbing through it.

"What time is it in California?" I said, opening my purse, digging for loose quarters.

"Why?" Eleanor shot me a suspicious look. She lowered the magazine.

"We need to call Freddie," I said.

"What's the use? She's not there, remember? She's in Baja. We'll just have to wait until Western Union can send a telegram."

"I hate breaking bad news through a telegram," I said.

"I hate breaking the news, period." Her eyes turned a sour yellow, the color of kosher pickle juice. She slumped over and burst into tears.

"Oh, honey," I said, moving to the chair beside her. I tried to think of all the right things to say about families pulling together, but my mind drew a blank. I didn't want to alarm her, but I couldn't help but wonder if the family curse had been revived.

I blamed myself for getting it started. Hattie was too good to believe in such, even though she sat wide-eyed when Mam use to tell us legends of old Texas—lost travelers, mysterious disappearances, murders, and ghosts. We loved them tales better than Mam's peach cobbler, what won a blue ribbon nineteen years in a row at the Brabham County Fair. I just never thought it would come down to this—laying to rest everybody I loved. One by one they was snatched from me. Everybody said not to grieve, that my loved ones were in a better place, but how did they know? Had they been to heaven and back? I took death hard—took it personal. Found it just as mysterious as them shut emergency room doors.

Such as life, I thought, shutting my eyes. If Jo-Nell were here she'd say, No, you've got it all wrong. You mean Life sucks, not Such as life. While I ain't a crude woman, I got to admit that Jo-Nell could always make me laugh. And sometimes laughter is a blessing. It heals the soul, even as it clears the sinuses and bladder. At my age, even with the leaks, this can be a good thing.

FREDDIE

Sam and I were staying at the Hotel Mirabel, in the heart of Guerrero Negro, and all night long I kept dreaming about the whale. I saw myself spinning helplessly into the rock, losing my mask. Once, I woke up gasping, and Sam put his arms around me. "Shhh, it's all right," he said, kissing my hair.

"But I can't breathe," I said.

"Yes, you can. It's a dream," he told me. He picked up my hand and kissed it. "Nothing but a dream."

I rolled over, dragging his hand along. He pressed against me, tucking his legs behind my knees. His body felt warm—I could feel the heat radiate through my nightgown. I wanted to say, Sam, I have these fears. Make them go away. I wanted him to understand that I came from a long line of women who worried. The condition had completely skipped over Jo-Nell, but it had turned Eleanor into a cautious woman who kept up with crime statistics. Me, I just suffered from free-floating worry. Every fall, when Sam and I left for Baja, I fretted about currents, shallow harbors, storms, tidal waves, drug smugglers, and funny knocks in the diesel engine. I had a list of reasonable (if unlikely) fears, which included the dangers of swimming in the ocean at night, the dangers of driving in fog, the dangers of *E. coli* in beef and salmonella in shellfish.

Most of all, I worried about my marriage. Sam and I shared

the same bed, careers, and political views, but we were sometimes divided by picayune details. I was the sort of person who
loathed clutter. It made me crazy—a throwback to childhood
chaos, I supposed, because my mother, Ruthie, accumulated
many strange things before she died. She kept sour-mash
whiskey in Listerine bottles, hidden in empty shoe boxes. The
kitchen was full of old mayonnaise jars, brown paper sacks, and
newspapers. They were heaped along the walls, spilling into the
dining room. The newspapers were saved for the spare bedroom,
where Mother's pet parakeets flew around wildly, perching on
curtain rods and occasionally smashing into the windows. A
thick, slightly damp layer of papers lined the floor. The air was
full of dumb, furry moths that hatched out of the birdseed.

I grew into the sort of woman who craved order, a reaction
formation, no doubt. I saw no reason to change. A life without
clutter was a life that didn't drive you crazy. My desk was aus-
tere, a shining expanse of rosewood. I opened my mail over the
trash can, and I was always threatening to alphabetize the
kitchen pantry—the tamari sauce next to the toilet paper,
tortellini, and truffles. That sort of thing. My grandmother col-
lected salt and pepper shakers from Occupied Japan, but I accumulated nothing. Curiously enough, I was not Spartan when it
came to food. I adored eating red meat seven days a week,
preferably fried or barbecued, with an ice cream chaser—two
scoops of Baskin-Robbins chocolate peanut butter. More than
anything in the world I liked to sit around doing nothing—literally sitting at the window, watching the light move back and
forth across Tomales Bay.

Sam liked activity, and he moved in a messy vortex. His desk
was an old roll-top, the cubbyholes jammed with old American
Express bills, photographs of whales, unopened letters from
Publisher's Clearinghouse, and even grocery store receipts. He
was forever gathering souvenirs from his dives, mainly abalone
shells, which served as receptacles for paper clips and rubber

bands. His bedside table was littered with scientific journals, cetalogy texts, back issues of *Time* and the *New Republic*. For a scientist, he was handy around the house. He regrouted the kitchen tile, unclogged the bathroom sink, and patched hairline cracks in the ceiling. He counted sheep with Mr. Espy and participated in the annual round-up. Small engine repair was his métier, and the folks in Dewey were always asking him to look at their outboards.

I was crazy about the guy. He was brilliant, energetic, versatile, quirky, meticulous. He was also (I thought) a bit of an extremist. When it came to culinary matters, it wasn't enough for him to be a simple vegetarian. No, he had to be a vegan, eschewing all animal products, including milk, eggs, and cheese. He refused to eat an innocent-looking cole slaw if he suspected the dressing contained mayonnaise. Me, I couldn't imagine a world without baby back ribs, Caesar salad, and lemon meringue pie. Sam lived on spinach salads, lentils, and steamed kale; vegan cottage cheese, made from tofu, cider, and nutritional yeast; yogurt from a soya milk starter culture. Whenever we were in Mexico, he practically starved. "It's not a matter of what you sacrifice," he always said. "It's what you discover along the way."

For Sam, food was politics. Whales had been virtually hunted to extinction, and he wanted his lifestyle to promote the environment, if not a more humane, caring world. He was an animal rights activist, wearing plastic belts and tennis shoes to black-tie dinners. He didn't wear leather, silk, or wool, and he flat-out refused to eat honey. Although he was not a violent person, he fantasized about spraying mink coats with lime-green Day-Glo. Back in Dewey, one corner of our kitchen was dedicated to recycling, and he would painstakingly sift through the bins, weeding out my careless mistakes. "For a compulsively neat person," he'd say, "why can't you keep the plastics out of the organics?"

Although I didn't say anything, it seemed like a clear sign of passive aggression. I didn't know how many couples fought about food, but at one time our kitchen was a war zone. Since I'd grown up around lifelong bakers, I longed to make Sam a decent birthday cake, but it was impossible with his dietary restrictions. Once, I made him a "cake" out of a tofu brick, with a single candle. Because I had presented it in a mean-spirited style, calling him a fringe element, he began filling the house with Williams-Sonoma catalogues. I imagined great stacks of them falling over and crushing us; death would be instantaneous.

I try not to think about this very much, but about two years ago Sam fell desperately in love with another woman. It's the truth. I say desperately because it meets Webster's definition: extremely intense, rash, being beyond, or almost beyond, hope: causing despair. The woman was my age, but we were nothing alike. She was a blonde, blue-eyed lactovegetarian, a painter from San Francisco. Her name was Andrea, and she had two small daughters from a previous marriage. In my mind's eye, I always saw her throwing strained yogurt onto a blank canvas, while the children hovered in the background chewing bean sprouts. I imagined the woman's long, thin arms circling Sam's neck, her fingers crusted with burnt umber.

I do not know what made him vulnerable to her—to this day it is a blind spot in our relationship. If I knew, I could fix it, but even Sam seems to have suffered a selective memory loss. Me, I'd like to blame food, but it's not that simple. A tofu birthday cake doesn't wreck a marriage; but if you cut the tofu into lewd shapes, you are probably asking for trouble. Looking back, I think we stopped being kind to each other. And we had become competitors—who was more ecologically correct, Sam or Freddie? Who was the brightest scientist? Who could recognize the most whales by sight? Love cannot be sustained under these conditions, any more than yeast will proof in cold water.

In a curious way, losing Sam made him all the more valuable. I called my sisters long distance, admitting I wanted him back.

"There's something fishy about a man who studies whales for a living," Eleanor said.

"If there's one thing I know it's a cheating heart," said Jo-Nell. "My advice is: Keep a suitcase packed. Because mark my words, he *will do it again*."

I myself had been worried about the same thing. He had lied and shattered my trust—why should I be forgiving? Still, because of the whales, our careers were conjoined; we were like Siamese twins sharing the same brain. My sisters suggested that I'd been beaten down by the infidelity, scarred by it, but that just wasn't true. I wasn't intimidated, just keenly aware of the fragility of love.

The night Sam came back to me, I opened a bottle of pinot noir, a Beaulieu Vineyard 1993. While I poured the wine, he said he knew he'd acted horribly, but he loved me, and that was the bottom line. Me, I was wondering about the painter (had she thrown him out? or was Sam telling the truth—that he'd left her for *me*?). I sipped the wine, breathing in the raspberry-cherry aromas. Then I told him I would not stay married to an unfaithful man. Two strikes and you're out. That was *my* bottom line. Sam said he understood, that he only had one strike, and if I'd just take him back he'd be the model husband. He wanted a chance to show how much he loved me. I was a little dizzy from the wine, but I said, "Do you know what love is?"

"Not till I lost it," he said.

I wasn't sure if he meant me or the painter, but he swore up and down that it was me. Then, after a bit more wine, we got slap-happy drunk. (We were not big drinkers.) It seemed clear that people in love lived in constant jeopardy. They were either making love or making each other crazy. We opened another bottle of wine. He toasted my brown eyes, and I toasted his tofu, vowing to never desiccate it again. It seemed like a decent beginning. I took him to my bed and back into my life, but still, I worried.

Now I felt Sam's breath on my neck. His hand slid over my hip, and he said, "You asleep?"

"Uh-uh."

"Me, either." His lips moved down my neck. Then he tugged at my nightgown. "Can this come off?"

A little while later, I rolled over in bed, and dangled my feet over the side, Sam's side. I wasn't concerned about anything—not my so-called diving accident, not the lactovegetarian painter or Nina or anything. I was looking forward to having breakfast with him, and my mind refused to take the day any further.

I stood up slowly. On the opposite wall, a large iguana was stalking a fly. As much as I loved Sam and the whales, as much as I wanted to save them both from predators, I wasn't crazy about the Hotel Mirabel. It wasn't the best place in Guerrero Negro, but it was clean and affordable—a crumbling yellow stucco building where hot water was available from seven A.M. until one P.M. The courtyard was filled with sand and prickly pears, a scraggly palm, and a wall of red bougainvillea where lizards slept upside-down in the shade. A single almond tree slanted between two stone picnic tables, where we sometimes ate a late supper. Inside our room was a black telephone, which we were obliged to rent from the Mirabel. Taped onto the receiver were numbers for the Red Cross, the Oceanographic Institute, and the attorney for Protection of Tourists.

Sometimes I thought about calling that last number, lodging an anonymous complaint. Help me, I would say in Spanish. My love life is in danger. It needs camouflage, it needs preservation. I felt this keenly, because Nina VanHook's room was on the opposite end of the small, U-shaped courtyard. She liked to walk around with the curtains pulled open, revealing a compact body, with push-up bras and lacy panties, all in lollipop colors. I felt ashamed of my sensible white step-ins, bought in bulk at JCPenney. The only thing I could do, short of revamping my wardrobe, was to keep our curtains drawn.

Now I looked over at Sam. He was stepping into cutoff jeans, drawing them up over his thighs. He glanced back at me. "I told Nina we'd go to the Magdalena Cafe at seven o'clock."

"That's too early." I flopped back on the bed, draping one hand over my eyes. "Come back to bed."

"Breakfast at the Magdalena is a Sunday morning tradition," he said. "Besides, we've got work to do." He reached under the sheet and plucked out my foot, pinching my big toe. "I thought you had a craving for *huevos con chorizo*."

I didn't have anything but an unreasonable urge to call home and tell my sisters the truth—that I'd stupidly risked my life by (1) diving alone, and (2) aggravating a forty-foot whale. My sisters were loyal—they'd blame everything on Sam and Nina. "Get rid of the bitch," Jo-Nell would say. But I wasn't good at that sort of thing. I was always underestimating my foes. Years ago, when I lived in Memphis, I had a mouse in my kitchen. No big deal, I thought. I set a trap with Velveeta, all the while dreading the sickening thud, but the damn mouse dragged off the trap, cheese and all.

Ten minutes later, the three of us were walking down Avenida Baja California, a two-lane road in the center of Guerrero Negro. It was four blocks west of the salt company's headquarters—Exportadora de Sal. We stepped past the little post office, past Marcelo's bus station and coffee shop, and the peach-colored Motel Gámez. About five hundred yards from the post office was a little hut—the telegraph office. Normally it was closed on Sunday, but a girl with rumpled brown hair came running out, waving a paper. I recognized her as the waitress from the Magdalena Cafe—the owner's youngest daughter, Luz Martínez.

I stopped to stare. Nina strode ahead of me, asking Sam if we could take the Zodiac into the lagoon. She had high hopes of filming a cow-and-calf pair underwater. Sam seemed to consider this; he reached behind his glasses and rubbed his eyes. I knew what he was thinking: It's a cloudy day; visibility will be nil. Before he could answer, Luz Martínez cried, *"Señor Espy!"* She was breathless by the time she reached us, and the paper was crumpled in her fist.

"Trágico," said Luz, laying one hand against her cheek. She exhaled a stream of peppery air, all laced with mint and cilantro. Then she thrust the paper into my hands and said, *"Telégrafos."*

I unfolded it, then squinted down and read:

COME HOME STOP BAD TROUBLE STOP JONELL HIT BY
TRAIN STOP CRITICAL CONDITION STOP NOT EXPECTED
TO LIVE STOP LOVE ELEANOR STOP

"Who's Jonell?" said Nina, reading over my shoulder. She pronounced it as one word, all mashed together. I thought about correcting her, but I wasn't sure I could speak. My mind filled with a lurid scene—an old-timey locomotive slamming into a yea-big car.

"Her sister," Sam said, putting one arm around me.

"Her sister was hit by a freaking train?" Nina blinked. "Jesus."

I looked up at Sam and pushed the telegram into his hands. My head started throbbing and I thought I might have to sit down in the sandy street, my head tucked beneath my legs. I gripped his arm, waiting for him to read, hoping he'd tell me I misunderstood—*trenza* instead of *tren*. Luz Martínez touched my head, her fingers skipping over the choppy hair. With a stricken look she said, *"Lo siento mucho."*

"God, Freddie," said Sam, pulling me against his chest. "I'm sorry, too."

"Maybe it's a mistake?" I asked him. "Maybe the translation is wrong."

"We'll call your sister." He turned to Luz, then pointed toward the cafe. *"Me permite usar el teléfono?"*

"*Si, señor.*" She grabbed his arm, tugging him forward. "*Por aquí.*"

Inside the Magdalena Cafe, I gripped the old black telephone, listening to Eleanor talk. The scent of cilantro was making me dizzy. I kept touching the crusty scab over my left eyebrow. Eleanor's voice sounded far away, like the noise inside a conch.

"What's her condition?" I said. "Is she in a coma?"

"I don't know. She's in a deep, deep sleep. The doctor says it's from the surgery, that knockout medicine they had to give her."

"Surgery?"

"You'd think she would've broke every bone in her body, but she got lucky. All that she hurt was her hip and leg—her left one, I think. They've already fixed that." Eleanor's voice crackled over the wire. "But now they're thinking her spleen is busted. If it is, they'll have to go in and take it out. Freddie, I'm just beside myself with worry. She's already lost too much blood. I offered to give her some of mine, but she's B positive and I'm A negative."

"I'm B positive," I said.

"Well, that's a relief." She paused. "I know about livers and kidneys, but I don't know much about spleens. In fact, I didn't know I had one. What exactly does it do?"

"It's a filter for the blood." I briefly shut my eyes, trying to imagine Jo-Nell with a giant scar running down the length of her abdomen, like a red zipper. Once they opened her up, what other injuries would the surgeons find?

"She was hit by the midnight Nashville-Eastern," Eleanor was saying in a surprisingly calm voice. "At least, I *think* it was the Nashville-Eastern, but it could've been the L&N. This real shady lawyer called us up and said we ought to sue. He said once you hear the train's whistle, you have twenty-five seconds until impact. That's not very long, is it?"

Twenty-five seconds? I thought, awestruck. Did Jo-Nell have time to feel anything but surprise? I pictured Jo-Nell's soul lifting up and out of the car, circling like a bird, vanishing to blue.

"Well, I guess you'll be coming home?" said Eleanor.

"Yes, yes. Of course." I shut my eyes, hearing my own voice echoing. I'd always heard it was a trademark of the Pray-McBrooms—a Southern thing, repeating yourself over and over. Now I wondered if it was something greater, maybe a neuro-logical reaction, the body's way of handling a shock, helping you adjust to something strange and awful. "But I don't know when I'll get out of Baja. See, there's no real airport in Guerrero Negro, just a dirt strip."

"Isn't that dangerous?"

"No," I said, but I really wasn't sure. The closest airport was La Paz, about five hundred miles southeast. I'd only seen prop planes land at Laguna San Ignacio, mostly drug runners/census-takers, but I'd heard of crashes in the desert. "It's going to take some juggling. Or some bribing. But I'll be there."

"Then—" Eleanor broke off, sounding exasperated. "How will I know when to expect you?"

"I'll call from the airport."

"But how will you get from Nashville to Tallulah?"

"You can't pick me up?"

"Well, I could, I guess. The doctor says it's still touch-and-go with Jo-Nell." She paused, breathing into the phone. "Well, wait a second, there's this new limousine shuttle that a customer was telling me about. Some are limos, but most are just real nice vans. But that's what they call it. A limousine shuttle. But don't worry—it's not high-priced."

"It comes to Tallulah?"

"And all the little towns between Nashville and Knoxville. Lebanon, Carthage, Cookeville. Isn't that modern?"

"Sure. I'll phone when I get to Tallulah."

"Will you be coming alone?"

"Probably." I sighed, then glanced over at Sam. "Is Minerva there? Can I talk to her?"

"She's at the hospital, waiting to corner the doctors. Jo-Nell's got three surgeons, a brain man, a blood man, and one to check out her lungs so she won't get clots. I didn't know we had this many doctors at Tallulah General. In fact, that's where I'm headed right this very second. I've got three of Minerva's friends with me now, and we're running late. But Freddie?"

"Yes?"

"Be careful."

After Eleanor hung up, I still cupped the phone to my ear, listening to the strange Mexican dial tone. While most people ended conversations with "Good-bye," my sister always warned everyone to be careful, as if such cautions could prevent a catastrophe. I thought of all the times our mother and grandmother had issued similar caveats, as if they were trying to ward off danger the only way they knew. I hung up the receiver, then glanced over at the table where Sam and Nina were sitting. Spread out between them were plates—milk and *huevos rancheros* for Nina; wheat toast, jalapeño jelly, and bottled papaya juice for Sam; an untouched plate of *huevos con chorizo* was waiting for me, but I didn't think I could eat anything. As I walked over to the table, Nina was saying, "Damn, a train wreck. How perfectly awful. I guess Freddie will be leaving, huh?"

MINERVA PRAY

Not six hours after Jo-Nell got out of surgery, they had to take her back and remove her spleen. It was risky, the doctors said. I sat in the waiting room, staring out the narrow window, aiming my prayers at the sky. Eleanor missed the whole thing—she was sleeping in a maroon plastic armchair. With her head tipped back, she looked just like her daddy and all the McBrooms. They were strong-chinned people but weak in the nose and cheeks. Eleanor had some weak places in her personality, too. She had always been a fretful soul, but she got worse after Ruthie died. It was like she was always waiting for another bad thing to happen. I noticed that she wouldn't go nowhere in a car by herself, but I didn't say a word. Just sat back and watched. If it hadn't been for the doughnut shop, I think she would have stayed cooped up on River Street. On her days off, she'd watch TV, the cook shows on Discovery Channel, *Martha Stewart Living*, and *The Young and the Restless*. She'd break for lunch, fix herself a mayonnaise sandwich, then she'd catch *One Life to Live*. The rest of the day would be spent cooking and pasting things into her scrapbook. All of this time, mind you, she'd be running around in her nightgown. On weekends she'd forget to shave her legs and more than hair grew in.

I worried about her. On *Good Morning, America,* I heard a lady doctor talk about a disease called angora phobia. I thought maybe it was a fear of wool sweaters, but the doctor said it was where you can't leave the house. It started out where you could go to about five or six safe places, but after a while it turned you into a recluse. Some people got to where they couldn't set foot out of the house, not even if it was on fire.

Afraid this would happen to Eleanor, I worked me out a plan. I talked her into driving me to Senior Citizens. After we got there, I made her play bingo and Rook. Then I told all the ladies that me and Eleanor were going to the sale at Big Lots. "How many people want to go with us?" I asked. Eleanor was too kindhearted to say no to a bunch of old ladies. And that's how it started. Now, she won't go anywhere without a couple of wid- ows tagging along. On Saturday afternoons, soon as the bakery closed, me and her filled up the old station wagon with senior citizens. She'd take us anyplace we asked, as long as we didn't leave Tallulah proper. That is where she drew the line.

After a long time, one of the doctors—I didn't catch his name—took me out into the hall. He wore a green cap, and red hair fuzzed out over his ears; a paper mask dangled from his neck. I tried to read his face. His mouth was drawed down in the corners, and his forehead was lowered over his eyes—it was the look of a plumber who's about to tell you that tree roots have growed into your cast-iron pipes, that it's too late for Roto- rooter.

"She's lost her spleen," said the doctor, "but everything else looks pretty good."

"She's alive?" I grabbed his arm.

"Yes." He patted my hand. "She's a strong girl."

"When can I see her?"

"Now." He pointed to a set of doors that said ICU. I went by myself—didn't see no point in waking Eleanor just yet. I knocked at the doors, and a boy-nurse took me to a tiny room with glass walls. Jo-Nell was asleep, and tubes were poking out of her everywhere. A huge gauzy bandage, stained red and brown at the edges, was taped to her belly. Her face was washed-out, like they had pumped her full of Clorox rather than blood. I didn't think it was possible to be that pale and live.

"Sorry, she still hasn't come out of the anesthesia," said the boy-nurse.

"Oh, honey, it's not your fault," I said, but I was thinking it was mine, flat-out mine.

FREDDIE

At sunrise, I caught a flight to La Paz with a pilot who made census reports on the whales. The plane was a rickety twin-engine Cessna—more mosquito than plane. One wing had been patched with something that suspiciously resembled tinfoil. Although I occasionally had to make census reports myself, I despised flying in small planes, but I didn't have time to worry about it—the Cessna was the quickest way out of Baja. It seemed to me that I was good at checking out of tough situations, like they were disappointing hotels. I had moved to California to recover from a failed career and a smashed romance; now that I was going home, I couldn't help but wonder if I'd been running from something else, like my strange and harrowing Southern childhood.

At the edge of the dirt runway, I stood on my toes, my arms around Sam. Our noses were almost touching. He stuck out his tongue and licked a damp place on my cheek. "I'll miss you," he said.

"Then come with me," I said, but I knew it was useless. He wouldn't leave the whales. And leaving him with Nina filled me with nameless dread.

"Can't." Sam shrugged.

"Not even for a few days?" *Not even for an emergency*, I thought.

"I can't."

"I know." I lifted my chin and kissed him good-bye. "You be careful."

"I'll try."

As I ran over to the plane, I wasn't sure if I was warning Sam or myself—maybe it was the same thing. My sister had just been hit by a train, and I hadn't had a single premonition. Eleanor hadn't mentioned one, either. I wondered if the family curse had been revived. (Minerva always swore there really was one.)

Once inside the plane, I glanced at the pilot, wondering about his qualifications. He was holding a tiny flashlight between his teeth. The light was aimed at a clipboard. He scribbled furiously in Spanish, now and then touching dials and switches. He sighed deeply and I thought I smelled day-old whiskey—at least, I hoped it was old. The lights of the plane came on with a blast, shining on two coyotes beside a creosote bush. Their corneas reflected red in the glaring lights, then they turned and loped off into the desert. Straight ahead was a paved airstrip that dropped off suddenly into dirt. The propellers sputtered, then began revolving.

"Ready?" said the pilot, and I nodded. He was wearing a white, short-sleeved shirt with black-and-gold trim. He looked more like a maître d'. *Someone will take your order, señorita.* Margarita, sangria, tequila, or drink of the day, Plane Crash in the Desert. It's a real trip, minus the killer headache. Directly in front of the pilot, a light was blinking, and on another dial, a little needle swept around and around. The propellers sputtered, then began revolving, moving like bobbins on an old Singer. I pictured the pilot mashing pedals, feeding material into the needle. When the plane began taxiing, I leaned back. It careened down the strip on patched wheels, gathering speed. Every rock and hole shook it, sending alarming tremors through the framework. The pilot cursed in Spanish and English, snapping switches. With some effort, the plane rose from the end of the dirt runway, rattling and shuddering, its wake flattening the creosote.

Once we were airborne, the pilot stopped cursing. His expression turned grave as he made intricate adjustments to the instruments. I pressed close to my window, leaving a circle of moisture on the thick glass. I looked down and saw Sam, the borrowed Jeep, the sweep of desert. Behind him the sky was packed with purple clouds, and the dunes were humped together, the color of wet concrete. I hated to think that it would soon be daylight, with the whole, lonesome Mexican day stretching out in front of him. The plane tilted, and I saw a great sweep of blue, the Laguna Mañuala, blending darkly into the Pacific. Then the plane tipped in the other direction, toward the east, shifting over the salt flats. As we curved toward the desert, light broke through the clouds. Somewhere above us, America was waking up to coffee and the Sunday paper. All through the different time zones, people were looking forward to croissants and biscuits, maybe a leisurely morning in bed, but I was heading straight into chaos. I had a terrible premonition that I would never see this place again—that I was losing Sam and Baja and the whales—but I was a failure in the omen department. I had never predicted a single momentous event in my life.

"You want to have a drink in La Paz?" the pilot shouted over the loud engine. He lowered his eyelids.

"What?" I shouted, pretending I couldn't hear. I didn't want to have as much as a glass of water with this man. I just wanted to reach La Paz in one piece. I tried to think how to answer without offending him. If I accepted, he might get the wrong idea— assuming a drink meant I was attracted to him; he might not pay attention to the fuel gauge or a blinking light. On the other hand, if I declined he might feel offended and crash the plane anyway. In both scenarios I imagined him ignoring the panel of switches and gauges, with the plane missing the airport runway, nose-diving into the exact junction where the Sea of Cortez bleeds into the Pacific.

"I don't drink!" I yelled over the engine noise, trying to look innocent.

"No?" He wiggled his eyebrows. "Maybe you should, eh? Your face is long, señorita."

"It ought to be. My sister's not expected to live," I yelled. After a few seconds I added, "She got hit by a train."

"Tren?" His eyes popped open. With one hand, he crossed himself.

"I may be going home to her funeral," I said. The pilot shook his head, as if the motion would make me hush. Although we were headed south, I kept thinking of the wind behind us, pushing down from California. To the north, the San Andreas Fault cut at a slant, above the mouth of the Rio Colorado, dropping under the Sea of Cortez. When you lived in the Far West, you were always aware of that crooked line. The Tomales Bay, better known as home, was probably created by an earthquake. Eleanor called California the land of calamities, but I thought Tennessee was the land of disasters. I'd had enough happen to me there.

I felt at home in colder waters. Dewey was rural, but not backward—in some ways it was like my hometown in Tennessee, minus the ocean and old-time religion. My favorite haunt was a white frame gas-and-grocery store, the Honeydew, where a blue tick hound slept on a bench. Inside you could buy chicken liver pâté, capers, raspberry and thyme vinegars, and fresh sourdough bread—life's minor luxuries.

Back in Tallulah, unless things had changed considerably, you couldn't even get bow-tie pasta. I always believed that my years in rural Tennessee had prepared me for the Third World atmosphere of Baja. Every year, after we arrived in Mexico, Sam anchored the boat at a commercial fishing dock. In addition to the government regulations, it was difficult bringing a tuna boat into the lagoon, since it was blocked by a huge sandbar. All excursions had to be planned by the winds and tides. Sam was one of the few scientists allowed to anchor here, because he had a talent with machines. Once, he repaired a fisherman's engine with a paper clip, earning the man's respect; another time he discovered a cracked rotary button in a distributor. With his pocket knife he whittled pieces of wood and somehow affixed them with fishing line to the button, so that it would hit on all sides.

I tried living on the boat, but it made me pine for things I normally never thought about, like indoor plumbing and eighteenth-century novels. The boat dock reeked of shrimp and gasoline. Over by the Pemex pump, sand sharks hung upside down from a giant hook, red intestines spilling onto the dock. Once, I was running down the dock, trying to catch up with Sam, and I skidded in blood. I fell down, bruising my ribs. That night Sam found us a seedy motel room on Malarrimo Beach. Water bugs skated along the tile floor. The walls were painted sour green, and all night it sloughed off the walls. I woke up with green flecks in my hair, in the creases of my knees and elbows. We slept on a mattress that had crunched every time we rolled over. On the battered table was a hot plate, kettle, tin of tea, and a bag of pistachios—compliments of the management. A square glass ashtray was already full of pink shells.

Unfortunately the mattress was crawling with lice. We woke up in agony, itching ourselves with anything we could find— toothpicks, pistachio shells, even the rough green walls. Sam dug in his suitcase and produced a bottle of generic Kwell. As we rubbed on the pearly lotion, he said it could have been worse. If we had been born in another century, before the discovery of Kwell, we might have itched ourselves to death. And if we'd been in another field, say, ornithology, we might have encountered cannibals and tropical diseases in New Guinea— the favored habitat for the Greater and Lesser Birds of Paradise. Scabies, he said, was simply part of the adventure.

Now the plane hit an air pocket and plunged several feet. I screamed, and the pilot eyed me, lifting one crooked eyebrow. "I'm not scared," I said, but I gripped the torn vinyl seat. He laughed. We were flying over the desert now, and even in the dusky light, the plane cast a shadow over an arroyo full of marsh grasses and boulders. If we crashed and survived, which didn't seem likely, there would be no place to hide. I pictured the plane, the metal bent at angles, with a plume of smoke rising, the pilot circling like a coyote. I squeezed my eyes shut and thought of Sam's dad, Mr. Espy, counting sheep; his Australian Heeler, Daisy, ran in a wide circle, nipping at a ewe's hind leg. I thought of Eleanor, preparing for the worst, laying out Jo-Nell's silver earrings, a black dress, and white net gloves. Last of all, I allowed myself to think of Sam driving back to the Mirabel, where Nina was waiting with a fresh bottle of tequila, no doubt wearing her string bikini.

The plane hit another pocket, and my eyes blinked open. I pinched my seat, digging my fingernails into the vinyl fabric. I didn't know if I disliked this plane because it was puny, or because it was taking me someplace I hated. All those years ago, after I left Tennessee, I promised myself that I wouldn't return. When my sisters and Minerva begged me to come home for Christmas, I always blamed my career. It was the whales that drew me to Baja every December, I told them, half-believing it myself. A dark, ugly part of me was happy to have an excuse— something exotic, beyond their comprehension. I told myself that hundreds, maybe thousands of people left the bosom of their families and never looked back.

I wanted to blame the pilot, but I couldn't. My sister's fluky accident was taking me away from Sam and the whales. Yet aberrations were part of my life—you might even say they had shaped it: I met Sam after I stole the organs in Memphis.

The day I got tossed out of medical school, I caught a Trailways, and by suppertime, I was back in Tallulah. Despite my disgrace, my little family was overjoyed to see me. Minerva opened up her freezer and pulled out chicken soup and pecan brownies. Jo-Nell set the table with the silver, all decorated with majestic *P*'s, an inheritance from Mama's second marriage. Eleanor stripped my old bed, laying out crisp eyelet linens that smelled of lemon sachet. "Don't you worry. You can work at the doughnut shop with us," Jo-Nell said.

"I'll teach you to make jelly rolls," said Eleanor.

"I hear the telephone company is hiring," said Minerva.

I didn't know how to tell them I was moving on. In the first place, I didn't know where I was going—I just knew that I had exhausted all of my options. I had two years of medical school behind me, and a degree in chemistry, yet I'd been so determined to be a doctor that I'd failed to get a teaching certificate. I had what my baby sister Jo-Nell would call a B.S. in Bullshit. That night, I took out a World Book and found a United States map. With my eyes closed, I mashed my finger to the page. I blinked and saw that I'd picked the Mendocino coast, a few inches above San Francisco. I thought it was a fateful choice. The Wild West was the granddaddy of all legends—the great American dream.

The next morning, while Minerva and sisters stood on the front porch, I packed my real daddy's old Valiant. "Make her stop, Minerva," said Jo-Nell, tears streaming down her face.

"She won't leave," Eleanor said, watching me stuff the trunk with faded Levi's. "She won't go. She's too scared to drive all the way across the country."

"I'm not, either." I leaned over, gathering another stack of Levi's.

"Stop packing that damn car and look at me," Jo-Nell cried.

"What?" I turned around.

"You're just a baby," said Minerva, drawing Jo-Nell close, but I knew she was talking to me.

"It's not safe on the road," said Eleanor. "What if that old car breaks down? It never has run right."

"I can't stay here."

"Why not?"

I didn't answer. I leaned over and scooped up a pile of garage-sale blouses.

"Chicken!" Eleanor cried.

"She's not; she's just upset," said Jo-Nell. She raced down the steps and tackled me around the waist. "Please, please, please don't go."

I reached down and gently pulled her up. "Don't cry," I said, touching her cheek with one finger. "Your mascara is running."

She laughed and wiped her face. "I mean it. Don't go."

"Look, it's no big deal." I shrugged. "I'll be back."

"Promise?"

"You bet."

"Swear it."

"I swear."

It was a promise I would never keep. I'd planned to keep driving until I reached Mendocino or my car died, whichever came first. Right off the bat, I saw that the West wasn't like the South. Even their taste buds seemed different. In a way, I felt as if I had traveled to another country. Here, they put avocados on their BLTs, and their chowders were thick and abundantly clammy. I stopped at a place that advertised something called soba noodle salad with lemon wasabi dressing and shiitake mushrooms. At one cafe, a sign said: CHILI DOGS—SO HOT THE BUN HURTS. I'd ordered an omelette at Fog City Diner, and it was oozing with jalapeños, avocados, bacon, Monterey Jack cheese, and sour cream. I thought of the doughnut shop back home. We offered glazed and jelly doughnuts. Sometimes my sisters went out on a culinary limb and made chocolate or caramel icings. City Cafe began offering omelettes in 1979. They were filled with Kraft cheddar, then doubled over like pale yellow flounders. If anyone in Tallulah knew that this wasn't a genuine omelette, they never said. It was enough, I supposed, to eat something with an exotic name. In many ways I saw myself as a refugee from small-mindedness and my own stupid mistakes. If Mendocino proved to be like Tallulah, I'd drive further north. Anyway, I had already reconciled myself to Alaska and the Northern Lights.

When I crossed the Golden Gate, I took a twisty road over Mount Tamalpais. I had long views over the bay. The radio kept playing Cat Stevens, singing "Wild World." It was a cool, foggy summer day. Now and then, through gaps in the fog, I caught glimpses of the Pacific. The water seemed to rise up into the sky, folding back on itself. I had never seen anything like this, ever. I prayed the car would drop dead in Marin County, but it kept on puttering. I nearly wrecked a couple of times, slowing down to take in the views of the bay—the windswept, grassy hills angling toward the water. From here, San Francisco looked like faded shoe boxes, all backlit by skyscrapers. I actually got out of the Valiant and kicked the tires, hoping they'd explode. I only succeeded in stubbing my toe, so I climbed back into the car and continued to drive. It never occurred to me to stop or turn back toward San Francisco. The car earned its name, undaunted by the hairpin curves, courageously passing the logging trucks. I predicted we'd make it all the way to Spokane, maybe even Alaska.

My transmission went out somewhere near the Point Reyes National Seashore. After the dark ribbon of smoke cleared, I got out of the car and stepped into a cloud. At first I thought it was from my transmission, but it smelled of the sea. Out of the fog came a soft chirping and the ring of buoys. I climbed on the hood of the Valiant. On both sides, the road dropped off dramatically into a deep mist. I didn't know where I was, but I hoped it wasn't a small town. If it was, I'd just have to get my car repaired and then keep driving. Another Tallulah was bound to exist, teeny in every sort of way, and I had no intention of being trapped like that again. I hated living in a place where everyone knew your most intimate secrets, sometimes long before you did.

A black Jeep stopped, and a man with an auburn ponytail rolled down his window. I noticed his bumper sticker said I ❤ WHALES. I slid down the Valiant's hood and walked over to him. "You sightseeing or hitchhiking?" he said, glancing at my car.

"My car broke down."

"Need a lift?" He reached across the seat to open the passenger door.

I just stared, chewing the inside of my lip. Although Eleanor had warned me about the crazies in California, this guy looked quite normal; but still, I didn't know. "Is there a town close by?" I said, conscious of my accent.

"Sure, we're about three miles from Dewey. I live there, by the way."

The fog cleared. I looked all around and saw a grassy valley, full of California bay trees, huckleberry bushes, and grazing cows. A high ridge was half-hidden by low clouds. The man saw me staring up, and he said, "That's Mount Whittenberg."

"Great. Who are you?" I was pretending to be tough, just in case he was a weirdo.

"Oh, sorry. I'm Sam Espy." He leaned across the seat and held out his hand.

"Freddie McBroom." We shook hands. I climbed into his car, careful not to dislodge his notebooks and binoculars. I picked up a book, *Oceanic Field Guide to Whales*. There on the crumbly Pacific coast, high above the cold, shark-infested ocean, and the discreetly hidden San Andreas Fault, I collided with my destiny.

For a long time after I moved to California, I felt guilty—as if I'd abandoned Minerva and my sisters. I always pictured them in domestic scenes, clipping coupons, freezing chicken bones for stock, crimping their lives at the edges like a fluted pie crust. I felt guilty, like I should have worked at the doughnut shop. Instead I was photographing whales, kayaking, trout fishing at the Russian River, flying off to Japan to protest commercial whaling, sailing around the Galapagos Islands, where sperm whales haven't been hunted since Charles Darwin's time. I didn't want to live in Tennessee, but I still worried that Minerva might fall down the narrow, squirrely staircase and no one would hear her cries. I worried that Eleanor and Jo-Nell didn't have a drop of insurance on the doughnut shop—if it burned to the ground, they would be destitute.

I kept imagining the train crashing into Jo-Nell's car; a broken hip seemed minor. Maybe the doctors didn't yet know all that was wrong—crushed vertebrae, fractured skull and pelvis, transected aorta. Eleanor hadn't mentioned anything else, but it didn't take a degree in pathology to know what a train did to a body. When Jo-Nell and I were little we used to lay pennies on the tracks, crouching in the weeds, waiting for the L&N to flatten them. I couldn't help but worry that I was heading to a funeral. Still, I was the one who seemed dead. My heart felt cold and still. I couldn't feel it beating inside my chest. I thought maybe it had shrunk to the size of a pimento.

MINERVA PRAY

Me and Eleanor practically moved into Tallulah General, bringing a coffeepot, packets of Sweet'n Low, and plastic spoons. Down the hall were these machines that spit out thick bitter coffee, and it cost a fortune. So we set up a camp in the ICU waiting room, bringing in afghans and feather pillows. I could see why it was called that—we was waiting for our girl to wake up and tell everybody to go to hell. Leave it to my baby granddaughter to make a joke out of her accident. She had natural-born humor, and I could not imagine this world without her. God? I wanted to say. Ain't You satisfied? Ain't You done took enough?

I depended on Jo-Nell. She was the one who drove me to Nashville when I got cataracts. (The eye doctor took it off with a laser gun.) And she took me to Texas last August after my sister Hattie fell and broke her pelvis. As best I can piece it together, Hattie got up at daylight and walked out to feed the chickens. It had come a hard rain the night before, which was fairly unusual west of the 98th Meridian. Hattie was clucking to her chickens, tiptoeing around in her slippers. She skidded in the mud and fell over backward. The hens babbled around her. Right away, she knew she'd broke something—heard it snap, heard it crack in two.

Well, Hattie lay there, all surrounded by mud and Startena,

staring up at the dry blue sky. The old windmill, what Amos put up in 1937 for $420, spun around and around. The hens clucked softly, pecking around her white socks and slippers. A jackrabbit nearly ran over her; it zigzagged across the yard, ears folded back, then shot off across the dewy thicket. She did not begin to worry until a buzzard came to roost in a dead mesquite. She would have liked to wave her arms at him, but it hurt to move. "Git," she told the buzzard but it didn't budge. It just stared down at her, as if to say, Maybe I shouldn't fool with you. You skinny old thing you. Ain't much of a meal, not more than a chicken wing.

The mailman found her a little before noon and called 911. We had no kin to speak of—Hattie was childless—but she had a big church family in Mount Olive. A lady from her Sunday school class dialed my number and held the phone to Hattie's face. "I have fell and broke my pelvis," she said in that hoarse little voice of hers. "Broke it clean in two."

"I'll be there as soon as I can," I told her.

"You're too old to be on the road," she said.

"I'm only seventy-nine."

"Pshaw. Eighty, but who's counting?"

"I'm coming," I said. "I'll be there directly."

"Well, it ain't serious," she said. "Dr. Danvers says I'll be good as new in six weeks."

"Happy to hear it," I said. "But until that day comes, I'm waiting on you hand and foot."

"Pshaw," she said again. Then, in a much smaller voice, she said, "Minerva? It'll be good to have you home again."

I explained the situation to Jo-Nell, and she said, "Sure, I'll drive you. When do you want to leave?"

"Today," I said. "But what about the bakery? Won't Eleanor be shorthanded?"

"Fred's Doughnut shop isn't a big operation, Minerva. She won't make birthday cakes without a deposit these days. And we only sell four kinds of doughnuts. She can make them in her sleep."

I asked Winnie Daniels to stay with Eleanor, just to keep her company and all. Then me and Jo-Nell took off in her yellow Volkswagen. It took two days and a night to reach Mount Olive. We went straight to the hospital. Hattie was laying up in a bed, with her white hair sticking up in tufts. "Mam?" she said, looking at me questioningly. "Should I fix cornbread or biscuits?"

From a straight-backed chair, a little gray-headed woman leaned forward. She wore a starched cotton dress all strewn with yellow flowers. "She's out of her head," the woman told us.

"Are you a nurse?" asked Jo-Nell.

"No, honey. I'm Myra Hoffsteader. I go to church with Hattie? The ladies in our Sunday school class been taking turns setting with her. Lord knows, she's set with all of us at one time or another. You must be her sister."

"I'm Minerva Pray."

"She talks about you all the time."

"This here is my granddaughter, Jo-Nell."

"Pleased to meet you all," said Myra. "Even though it's under sad circumstances."

"When did she get so confused?" I asked.

"Late last night," said Myra.

"Has the doctor been by to see her?" I rubbed Hattie's wrist. "She's on fire."

"Yes, he has, honey," said Myra. "Dr. Danvers says he don't understand it. She was fine yesterday. But now she can't shake this fever."

"Hattie?" I picked up her hand. Her bones felt smaller than I remembered, like quail bones. She was hot and dry, making me think of when my babies use to run fevers.

"The bull has broke loose from the pen!" she hollered, looking at me with burning eyes. "Hurry, it'll get Josie."

"It's just the fever," Myra said, eyeing Hattie. "She don't

know what she's saying. Yesterday she was setting up and writing out recipes for Labor Day. Every year for as long as I can remember, she's fixed Dr. Pepper Baked Beans for the church supper. She was worried that this broke pelvis would keep her from cooking. She give me the recipes and made me promise I'd cook the beans."

"Hattie?" I said. "It's me, Minerva." I laid her hot hand between my two cool ones. She opened one eye, stared at Jo-Nell, and croaked, "I know what you done, Josie. But I won't tell your ma. You left the jar off the prickle pear jam and ants got in."

"Poor little thing," said Myra. She walked over to the foot of the bed.

"The jam is ruint," said Hattie. Her eyes filled. "When them ants get in, you can't make it right. You might as well throw it out and start fresh. Josie? Do you understand what I'm trying to say?"

"I'm so sorry," Jo-Nell told Hattie, humoring her. "I won't do it again."

"That's all right." Hattie winked. "We'll just open another jar, and who'll be the wiser."

We drove out to the Pray ranch, a rough-cut limestone house with a deep post and beam porch. The porch was all covered with grape vines, and ripe concords drifted down the railing. Way out in the yard, I saw an overturned Maxwell House can, with chicken feed scattered everywhere. There were skid marks in the mud where Hattie had fallen, which made my eyes water. She had lived all this time by herself, and she could have been with me. I felt robbed, and I wondered if Hattie did, too.

"I'm hungry?" said Jo-Nell.

"Well, come on inside." I opened the screen door. "Let's see what I can rustle up."

In the kitchen, I gathered poblano chiles, cheese, green onions, and tortillas. Jo-Nell found a jar of homemade salsa and pot beans. "Heat you some olive oil in that skillet," I told her, "and give me them pot beans. The secret is mashing them a little at a time."

"What for?" Jo-Nell looked inside the pot and wrinkled her nose.

"Why, for nachos, child. The best you ever eat. And quesadillas, too." I just hoped I wasn't too old to digest everything. Jo-Nell watched me mash the beans, then she drifted off, moving in the front room. I could see her fingering the plantation desk with the wavy glass doors and green felt drawer. Quilts were heaped on every sofa, chair, and bed. They were made from scraps, bits and pieces of our lives—baby dresses, our husbands' old plaid shirts, calico dresses that got wore out from so much washing. Jo-Nell turned away from the quilts and fingered the Mexican cupboards. In one of the closets, she took out Burl's old chaps, and said, "These are bitching! And this place is so far out."

"Well, it *is* a ranch," I reminded her. "You've got hundreds of acres between you and the next neighbor."

"No, I meant it's cool. Neat." She sat down at the table. "It even smells different from Tennessee."

"That's just jalapeño cheese," I said, ladling up the salsa.

She just smiled. Behind her the deep, greenish-blue windows looked cool and thick, as if they were filling with creek water. "Did you like living here, Minerva?"

"Oh, honey. I don't remember. That was so long ago. Years ago." I sighed, thinking it all seemed real distant, like I was remembering somebody else's life, or dreaming somebody else's dream.

"I love it here," she said. "How'd you ever leave Texas, Minerva?"

"I just did."

"I don't think I could have."

"Well, you do what you have to." I set the plate of nachos in front of her. I felt a powerful need to change the subject. "Eat up, child," I said, "before you shrivel up to nothing."

How did I ever leave Texas? I'll tell you why: My heart was broke, and I thought a change of scene might heal it, might turn my luck around. They say a person should never make hard and fast decisions when they are in a grief state, but I use to do it all the time, just all the time. After Freddie went to medical school in Memphis, she explained it to me. "It's fight or flight," she said. "It's the body's reaction to stress."

That made sense to me. Long ago all the fight had gone out of me; it's nobody's wonder that I was left with the flighty. It took a long time to wear me down, though. I had started out a feisty woman. Like I said before, me and Hattie married the Pray brothers in a double ceremony. My husband Amos, being the eldest, lived on the ranch; Hattie and Burl lived in town, up over the post office. My first child came in 1934, the tenth of January, and the doctor said your baby is stuck in the birth canal. I sat up in the bed and looked him square in the eye.

"Say again?" I said. I myself had saw pictures of canals— them ones in Venice and the one that was dug in Panama. Then a pain gripped me, way deep in my back, and I didn't hear what Dr. Danvers said. I lay there writhing in the narrow bed, tended by Hattie, barely hearing their voices. It seemed to me that the doctor was all wrong—my body wasn't no canal; no, my baby was like them tiny ships in a bottle, Lord knows how it got there, but it was trapped for all time unless you broke the glass.

Amos Jr. was born, and I said to myself, one child is surely enough. No more babies will come out of my little canal. No more ships in a bottle. Then, in the late summer of 19 and 37, I skipped my woman's time, and I thought: The Lord knows more than me. If He sees every sparrow fall, He must surely see me. I would love this child as much as my little Amos Jr. Big Amos said he was ready to have a whole slew of kids. Hell, yes, he told me. We'll fill this house up to the rafters!

A week later we went to a barbecue at Round Lick Ranch; I was setting in the shade with Lucy Jane VanHoosier and Martha Tillman. We was eating Alberta peach ice cream, and the ladies got to squinting at me really funny-like. Lucy Jane said to me, "Child, your face is all broke out."

"You've caught them German measles that's going around," said Martha.

"I don't feel sick." I rubbed my hand over my face. It felt rough, like a fine nettle rash.

"Maybe you just got a allergy to them peaches," said Lucy Jane.

"I never had one before," I said.

"Then it could be too much sun."

"No, it's the measles," said Martha. "Wait three days and see if it's still there. Then you'll know."

"It's just the heat," I said. "Nothing in the world but the heat."

My baby was a girl, born real easy, with soft brownish-blond hair that waved across her little head. I named her Josephine, because I read it in the San Antonio society pages. Turned out she was stone deaf. A real beautiful child, but you could not reason with her. Smart—I knowed Josie was smart—but how can you behave when you can't hear your mama's voice or the sound of a rattlesnake or thunder? You don't see danger until it slaps you upside the head. I had to watch her like a hawk because she was always slipping off to wade in Frog Creek, what empties into the Guadalupe River. She'd climb up in the henhouse and fall asleep. You could cry out her name till you was hoarse, and she never knew. Amos said we should've named her Wanda because she was a wanderer, but you don't know these things in advance.

In between chasing after Josie and Amos Jr. and helping out at the ranch, I got wore down. Three years later, worn out to my soul, I had me another baby girl on January 27, 1941. She was so little I could fit her in a shoe box, on account of me being skinny. I named her Ruthie, after Mam's mama, and we was all relieved when she could hear a pin drop fifty yards away.

During them hard Depression years, we made do. Burl and Hattie moved back to the ranch. They wasn't blessed with children but we all still had high hopes. The government came and taught Burl how to prune fruit trees, and Hattie did what she could around the ranch. It was hard, hard times. We thought for a while that Amos might have to go with the CCC to build Lake Brownwood, but he didn't have to. We burnt the nettles off prickly pears and fed them to the cattle; I made gravy from flour, milk, and drippings, and we mopped it up with hot biscuits. We milked twenty cows by hand, by the light of a kerosene lamp that was ordered from Sears, Roebuck. In the hot kitchen we peeled and boiled peaches until the sweat poured down our faces and backs. The wood stove seemed like it might catch the walls on fire. Me and Hattie would run out into the yard and sit under the cottonwoods, fanning ourselves with our aprons.

I will just tell you the truth, the people who settled hill country were not big plantation folks that was run out of the South after the Civil War. No, they was small, poor farmers. They didn't have a thing to lose, so they put up signs on their fences—GTT, GONE TO TEXAS. The Prays come from Louisiana and Tennessee, and my people, the Murrays, come from Alabama. All of us was hardy stock, folks not use to pampering. I did not worry my head about no family curses. There wasn't no time. Anyhow, the whole state of Texas, all of America, was having a run of bad luck. And like everybody else, I put my trust in Jesus and FDR.

Then spring arrived, bringing with it a stream of warmish, dirty air, and my babies come down with high fevers. Hattie and I took turns rocking them. Amos Jr.'s throat was so raw, he could not drink milk, and Josie just spit hers out on the floor.

Only the baby, Ruthie, seemed caught up in the long, hard sleep of the newborn. Now and then she'd wake up squalling, red-faced and sore-mouthed, but my titty milk seemed to go down like silky medicine. The doctor called it scarlatina. Said it was making the rounds. Said there was nothing to do but wait it out.

On the eleventh day, Josie was almost well—toddling around the room, with nothing more than a loose cough. The baby's fever had broke. Amos Jr. was still hot and flushed, too weak to climb out of his bed. He asked me for a spoonful of ice, and of course there was none to be had. I would have sold my soul to get my baby some ice. Amos was out counting cattle, so Burl hitched up the wagon and rode into town to the ice house. I'll bring back a whole block, he promised. While he was gone Little Amos started jerking all over. His teeth locked, and his eyes rolled back inside his head. Then he was still. When Burl showed up with the ice, it was too late.

While Hattie prepared Amos Jr.'s body for the funeral, I lay me down on the bed and cried. I will not get over this, I thought. I can't get past the heartbreak. I heard the screen door creak open and slam shut, as people came bringing food. Sometimes they slipped into my dark room and told me they was sorry, so very very sorry. If I needed anything, just let them know.

I wanted to shake them and cry, What I need is Little Amos! You give my boy back to me. But it wasn't their fault. The real shame was mine. Some of these women had lost babies and grandbabies, and I'd tell Hattie, We'd better catch a chicken and fry it for so-and-so. I was just going through the motions. Bringing food after a death was something you did without thinking. Then you went right back to your own life. And I had my own, sweet family all together under one roof. Somebody else's tragedy had nothing to do with me.

Now, despite my grief, a little bit of the world had opened up, showing me some hard secrets. After a longish time, I got up off my bed, pinned up my hair, and went out to greet the mourners.

In them days we laid out the dead at home, right in the living room—ain't that funny? Laying the dead in a living room. Ladies from Mount Olive and Brabham County filled the house. They worked my kitchen like it was a fine restaurant in San Antonio. Everybody talked at once. My mind skipped like a little bird, yet it was a comfort to have these women near me. They poured tea and swept up crumbs and brought out endless platters of chicken and biscuits; pinto beans and cherry salads; fig preserves and gingerbread pigs. Somebody brought a Corsicana fruit cake and laid out the slices on a pink glass plate. I felt as if these women were holding me up, carrying me along, and I thought, Minerva Pray, you will not get past losing Amos Jr., but you will live on to help somebody else. I wondered if that's how a heart healed.

The screen door opened and closed a thousand times. When nobody was looking, Josie wandered out of the house. She ran past the yard grass, through the shallow part of Frog Creek. She strode across some white rocks, the tail of her nightgown dripping behind her, and headed toward the broom weeds, where the hens sometimes nested. We knew this because we followed her trail. By the time we spotted her, she was standing in Mr. VanHoosier's pasture, where the old bull had broke loose from the fencing. He was sunning hisself, twirling his tail, switching black flies from his back.

Josie knelt to pick bluebonnets, and Amos clapped his hands. "Josie!" he hollered.

She never looked up.

He clapped again, and a covey of bobwhites tore out of the bushes. Amos and the bull took off running for Josie at the same time. I screamed out her name, Josie Josie Josie, but it wasn't no use. She was knocked up into the sky—arms thrown out, her white nightgown billowing. When Amos darted out to gather her up, the bull tried to run him down, too. I tried to help, but the women grabbed my arms and said, "No, Minerva!" Burl reached out to grab me, but I sank down to one knee. The Lord was not suppose to send more trouble than you could stand, but He must not been paying attention. Amos dove under a fence and scooped up Josie. I broke loose from the women and ran. Blood was streaming from Josie's nose and ears. I wiped it away with the hem of my dress, but it came right back.

Amos lowered his head to her chest. "Her heart is beating," he said. He pushed back his bangs. His hand came back bloody, and I saw that he'd cut his forehead; and it would leave a scar for the rest of his life.

We got her to the house and laid her on the bed. The neighbors fluttered around us, bringing washcloths and pans of water. Someone rode to town for the doctor. Baby Ruthie cried out for her milk, but it had dried up inside me. One of the women made her a sugar tit. Ruthie made little, greedy sucking sounds, stopping now and then to let out a wail, but my milk never come down.

"Open your eyes, Josie," I said. Amos put his hand on my shoulder. Before the doctor got there, she stopped breathing, but her heart kept on beating. I could hear it flutter around the room like a trapped bird. I thought maybe it was her soul, trying to find a way out. There was nothing left to do but open the door and set it free.

I lost my faith. It had run dry, just like my breast milk. The Lord seemed vengeful, taking away my babies, and I was through worshiping Him. He didn't deserve it. I told the preacher that Jesus was a no-good bastard.

"Don't you say that," the preacher hissed. "If you curse Him, He'll curse you."

"He already has." I looked into the preacher's eyes. They were pale gray and lashless. I knew he didn't understand. He and his missus didn't have no children.

I wasn't the only one with a hurt soul. Down at Liberty Bank, Amos heard about a sorghum mill in Tennessee that was hiring.

It was horse-powered, he said, and made 125 gallons a day. He asked me if I thought I could stand to leave Mount Olive. Yes, I thought. Yes, I could stand it. As long as it wasn't forever. As long as Hattie was keeping watch at the graveyard. As long as we knew the way home.

Tallulah, Tennessee, was on the Highland Rim, a river town full of rocky cliffs and dark ravines. That October the hills caught flame and the leaves gathered in deep drifts like smoldering ashes. We lived up the road from the mill, and sweet smoke hung over the trees. The furnaces glowed all night long, and the air was cold and cloudy, like something clabbered. Sometimes of a Saturday night, fiddle music would start up as the farmers waited their "time to make." Sad-eyed coon dogs would throw back their heads and yowl. In November, when the men butchered hogs, these same dogs fought over the pigs' feet.

I began to see that the South was not all one country. Rather, it was divided up like a dessert tray—pralines, divinity, fruit cake, sour grape pie. When strangers came to Mount Olive, hill country folks would say, Where're you from? Come on in and set a while; but when strangers came to Tallulah, the folks eyed them with caution and said, Why are you here? When are you leaving? The women in Tennessee were not like the women of my Texas, although they got riled if you pointed this out. They were quiet and standoffish, didn't mingle, and surrounded themselves with family. It didn't take me long to see that I'd exchanged one kind of lonesome for another. Sometimes I dreamed of Texas—dreamed I was wading in bluebonnets and sunflowers. I dreamed of our old water trough, all deep and black, with green scum growing in the corners. I dreamed of hot weedy pastures and no rainfall in weeks. I dreamed of milk buckets that needed straining, and Hattie pouring it through the cheesecloth. I'd wake up in a cold sweat, thinking I could smell the cedar sap oozing.

When the first snowfall came, I held little Ruthie up to the window and pointed at the flakes drifting down like goose feathers. I was so grateful that she was alive, even though this place was cold and hard in all sorts of ways. It seemed like another country, but in a way I was glad. I thought maybe God could not find me.

The next morning, when Jo-Nell and I got to the hospital, Hattie was in a stupor, talking to the ghosts of the Pray brothers. "Come here and set with me, Burl," she told the wall, then patted the crisp white sheet. "You, too, Amos."

Sometimes she argued with Mam, saying, "I will *too* have me a double wedding." Once she sang a lullaby to Ruthie, or maybe it was Josie. Then her voice broke off and she took a bone-deep chill. She passed to her reward a little after sunset without ever knowing I was here.

Me and Jo-Nell left and drove over to Mount Olive Funeral Home. We circled the courthouse square, with its mulberries and sycamores, the wood benches facing the street, where old men spit and whittled. We passed the pool hall, which I did not remember, and the Blue Mesa Diner, which I did. Before Fred McBroom died, he took all of us to Texas for a little vacation. He drove the station wagon, with Jo-Nell sitting in a car seat. I played license plate tag and I Spy with Freddie and Eleanor. As a special treat, Hattie took us out to lunch at the Blue Mesa. Beside the cash register was a stuffed Alaska brown bear and a moose head. On the lunch counter were four big jars where you could buy whole jalapeño peppers, pickled onions, pickled tomatoes, and pickled eggs. We ate chicken fried steak with pepper gravy, mashed potatoes, turnip greens, jalapeño corn-bread sticks. Then everybody ate two big helpings of Blue Bell ice cream.

Now Jo-Nell slowed down in front of the funeral home. "Just pass it by," I said, waving my hand. "I ain't ready to pick out no coffin." She drove on back to the ranch and we puttered around, trying to decide what dress to bury Hattie in. Before we could open her closet, the driveway filled up with cars and trucks. Just like in the olden days, women walked up to the house with food. The kitchen counters lined up with Pyrex dishes: macaroni and cheese; black beans and pinto beans; jars of pico de gallo, corn and tomato relish; jalapeño and prickly pear jellies; peach and gooseberry preserves. Strange women with kind eyes tied on aprons, set out platters of bone-in country ham, chicken fajitas, tamales, chili nachos. They set out yeast rolls, cole slaw, meat loaf, stuffed peppers, guacamole, chess pie, and pink Jell-O salads with crushed pineapple and marshmallows. They ushered the minister and his wife around the table. They handed plates to wrinkly, sad-faced men and old, old ladies smelling of sachet and talcum. Get you some of this fried chicken, the women would say. And don't forget that pepper-glazed ham. They would stand back, as if food was all they were offering. Their light, hushed voices seemed to conjure voices from the past—conversations that were old and dusty, spoken in this room and all the rooms of my life.

Like I said before, I myself had served food to the bereaved, but deep down I kindly thought it was silly. The truly heartbroke can't eat a bite. Then, after I got to know about death, it dawned on me that you have to think of the others—friends, neighbors, second cousins, nephews. People who are saddened but not crushed by the loss. They need shoring up, too, and food is the best way. Life goes on. The living must eat and breathe. After a while, you come to your senses. It sets in real gradual, without your noticing. After a while, you'll catch a whiff of a roast beef sandwich, made with sweet pickles and mustard, and you'll think, Maybe just a bite.

This is how the soul heals. It thaws out bit by bit, the way the ground warms after a hard winter. You notice the sun or hear the whippoorwill calling across the flats. You sweep your porch, go drink your coffee in the shade of the trumpet vines. You have days where you want to lay down and die, but what you learn is this: As long as there's somebody left on this earth who loves you, it's reason enough to stay alive. You don't give in to your broke heart—you just let the wide, cracked spaces fill up again.

This was a lesson you couldn't teach to other people. Either Ruthie had never learned it or she was too sick-hearted to care. I thought the Lord really did move in mysterious ways. Maybe He Himself couldn't figure it out. He'd took all three of my babies, then He turned right around and gave me the same number of grandchildren to raise. They say He doesn't close one door without opening another, but sometimes I wish He'd just mind His own business.

The day we left Texas, Jo-Nell was up at daylight, drinking coffee on the vine-covered porch. She looked out into the live oaks. I carried my coffee cup and stood beside her, just gazing out over the wavy grass. Someone, I don't know who, had planted a pecan tree, but it bore thick, black pods with bitter nuts. Lavender verbena and spiky mullein bloomed near the old pump house. Three magpies passed over the mesquite. They flew over the little graveyard, cawing into the red blaze of morning. The people I loved were disappearing from my life. Amos, Little Amos, Josie, Burl, Hattie. Ruthie. It seemed like an era was gone. All my young years, even my joys and hardships, were gone in a gully wash.

It was time I went back to Tennessee. I had my graves to tend. I had Brother Stowe's picture in the bathroom, and I talked to him every morning. But even so, as I stood there with Jo-Nell, I thought how good it would be to just stay put at the ranch. Get me a coon dog and live out my life under this streaky blue sky. I should have come back when Hattie was still alive, but that chance had come and gone. I put my hand on Jo-Nell's arm and said, "We'll come back here sometime, you and me."

"We can? You mean, you're not selling it?"

"Oh, I couldn't do that."

"I'm glad." Her eyes lit up, all blue flame, like pilot lights. She'd got those eyes from her daddy—the McBrooms had the prettiest blue eyes. And you would never guess her to be a day over twenty, but she was twenty-nine. Like all the Prays, she carried her age well. Me, I was a Pray by marriage, and we Murrays aged fast. Traveling was hard on my poor body. I didn't know if I'd have the strength to leave Mount Olive, but once I did, chances were I'd stay put. Old is old. People don't like to think a body can wear out, but child, anything can. No matter if it's a faucet or a hot water heater or a heart. Sometimes you can wear the love right out of yourself, and the life, too.

"You look at home here," I said, sipping my coffee.

"Maybe I am." She sighed. "I hate to say this, but I think I've used up Tallulah."

"How, child?"

"Well, I've got a lot of admirers, but they're all male." She raised her shoulders. "That's not a bad thing, except it's caused every single woman in Tallulah to hate my guts."

"Oh, honey, they don't."

"Minerva, I could tell you things that would curl your toes, but I won't." She smiled, then took a sip of coffee. "I'd just like a fresh start, in a place where nobody knows me. I've got flirt-ing down pat—I know men love me. But I'd like to have some women friends, too. Sometimes I watch you and your widow friends, and it seems so cozy."

"Well, sometimes they get on my nerves," I said.

"I guess." She laughed. "I want it all, Minerva. Lots of friends and lovers. And no bad reputation following me around. God, I wish we lived here. In Tallulah, I'm a branded woman, but in Mount Olive I'd be Hattie's great-niece. It'd be like a second chance, wouldn't it, Minerva?"

"Well, this house ain't going nowhere," I said, but deep down, I hoped she didn't aim to move here. A family ought to stay together, or at least within driving distance. I'd already lost Freddie to California. They say a fault line runs through that state, but personally I thought it had too many people. The sheer weight, if nothing else, would be its downfall. I saw why people chose to live in a land-locked place—they just hoped to escape high water. But I knew better: No matter where you go, the past floods back. You can try like the dickens, but you can't escape fate.

JO-NELL

A hospital was one hell of a place to be sick. There were more nurses than doctors—so guess who was running the show? You could bet your ass it wasn't the bone doctor. Hell no, it was the bone nurse, who couldn't wait to get home and soak her aching feet and watch *Dr. Quinn, Medicine Woman*. Since I myself didn't have a TV, I had a lot of time to think; and I thought I might be going crazy.

When I first woke up, I didn't know what decade it was. I was half-expecting to see the men walking around in leisure suits. A doctor told me I had an honest-to-God broke hip, along with a broke leg. As if that wasn't enough, they had cut me open down the middle, the way you split a watermelon, and scooped out my insides. I was full of thread, metal staples, and a plastic hip; it was made of the same stuff that lines frying pans. I felt like Mrs. Frankenstein—a fucking freak.

"Will I have a scar on my hip?" I asked him.

"A *scar*?" He blinked; his eyes were a colorless hazel, with teeny pupils, the kind that drug addicts have. "You'll be lucky to walk without a limp. I should think a scar is rather moot."

"Mute?" I cried. "Don't tell me I'm gonna lose my goddamn voice, too!"

He threw back his head and laughed. Then he put his hand

on my arm. "You've got spirit," he said. "That's good. You'll
need it to get well."

"You got any pull around here?" I smiled. See, I have these
dimples that drive men wild—I take their fingers and fit them
in the holes.

"Some." His hand was still on my arm. "I was chief of staff
last year."

"Then can I have a TV in here? See, I'm a little bored, and I
thought I could pass the time with Home Shopping Network.
Although HBO wouldn't be half-bad."

"Soon," he said, dragging his hand away. "Real soon."

I wasn't sure if he meant the TV or something else. He
stepped out of the room, sucking in his stomach. I took stock of
the situation. An ICU was no love nest. All around me were
freaking machines that recorded my every fart. I was connected
to a cardiac monitor that showed my heartbeat, what the
nurses called the QRS complex. Like it was a mental problem.
Clear fluids dripped into the backs of my hands. A plastic
catheter was wedged between my legs, draining hot pee from
my insides, filling an amber-colored bag. The bag was hooked
to the metal bed, for all the world to see and smell. Just outside
my room was a shiny red chest, better known as a crash cart. It
was full of long needles, adrenaline, and electric paddles that
could restart a heart, if need be, as if it were no more than a
stopped battery. Once a shift, the nurses counted the vials and
tested the voltage; they marked everything down on a clipboard. They said it was a rule, in case any morphine turned up
missing.

Every few minutes, the nurses busted into my cubicle like
they owned the joint, telling me to turn, cough, and deep
breathe. They even made me stand up. "I've got a broke hip," I
screeched. "Leave me alone, you leeches!"

"You don't want phlebitis, do you?" said a boy-nurse. His
name was Dwayne, a skinny, effeminate man. Not my type at all.

"I'll show you what fleabite-us is." I balled up my fist and stared him down.

"Here," he said, shoving a plastic doohickey into my hands. "This is called an incentive spirometer. You breathe into it. Try to make the little ball go all the way to the top."

"What's the point?" I said, waving the machine away.

"You want a collapsed lung?" He clucked like a hen, picking his way around my bed, fingering the shiny objects like they were something good to eat.

"Kiss my ass, and I'll think about it."

"Ooooh, is that a promise?" he said, then slithered out of my room. As soon as he was gone, I was sorry. All day and all night I couldn't do a damn thing but lay in the metal bed, gripping the trapeze bar when the nurses brought my bedpan. They called me an uncooperative patient—I raised hell when they made me stand up, putting actual weight on my freaking leg. I'd beg them to lay me down, just leave me be. Just let me lay. "You are not a hen," said one of the smart-ass nurses. Dwayne said if I was a pork roast, I'd be browned on one side. If I was a hamburger, I'd be burnt. I myself felt like a piece of marinating beef. That was a real depressing thought. Most of the time I tried not to think what I had become. The nurses called it prone and supine. Belly up and face down. I called it a pain in the ass.

I was too busted up to enjoy the drama of being On the Brink—a modern-day version of that old malady known as Taking to One's Bed. That's what women did in the olden days. Minerva told me all about it. This is why I was upset. All my life, if I was going to Take to My Bed, I wanted to do it in style. A four-poster canopy bed would be nice, with gauzy mosquito netting and piles of eyelet pillows. I myself believed that antique beds are the best places to have sex or a nervous breakdown. The old beds were made, literally, by the menfolks—to impress and entice us ladies. I think that's sweet. If a man goes to the trouble to carve hearts and rice plants on your bedposts, the least you can do is fuck him.

Instead of a bona fide sickbed, I had this awful metal thing that ran on motors. If somebody wanted to, they could fold me up into a C. I'd be stuck, like a pearl in a oyster shell. The only thing that made up for being hospitalized was the cute doctors, but even better was the gossip. Hospitals were hotbeds for scandal, perversions, and malpractice. It was amazing what you could learn by listening. In the past forty-eight hours, even though I was on the "critical list," I had paid attention. I knew more than I cared to about my freaking keepers. My bone man, Dr. Granstead, had a million degrees, a wife, two daughters, and a condo in Hilton Head. He was a Presbyterian and played golf every Thursday—two ball with his wife. My day nurse, Janice, had a crush on Dr. Granstead; unfortunately, Dwayne did, too.

I knew that Dwayne had himself a spotted dog named Mutton Chops that he swore could turn back flips; the other male nurse, Ronnie, was divorced, but he wasn't any fun. A regular guy, Dwayne called him. Every weekend, he drove a four-wheeler in the country and bet on college football (his brother was a no-good bookie). He was dating a divorced respiratory therapist named Judy Sue Jenkins, a thirty-two-year-old mother of two.

When the nurses left me alone, I had plenty of time to listen to the operators paging doctors, administrators, and janitors. The voices streamed out from the ceiling at regular intervals. Once you cracked the codes you could figure out what was happening all over the damn place. Stat meant Do It Right Now, and Code Blue meant somebody had croaked. When they called for housekeeping, it generally meant somebody puked on the floor.

Minerva and Eleanor's voices came at intervals, too. About once an hour they came into my cubicle, a cold, gray-colored room, and stood beside my bed. Minerva was the closest thing I had to a mother. Sometimes I dreamed she'd died; and once I dreamed she was a turnip. That time I woke up hysterical. Crying my eyes out. I had to put sliced cucumbers on my face to get the puffiness out.

"Jo-Nell, can I get you anything?" Minerva asked. I knew she was just dying to bring me a chess pie, or maybe a cream cheese brownie, but it was against the rules.

"Everything's fine at the doughnut shop," Eleanor said. "I hired me a woman to run the cash register—you remember Earlene Wauford? She used to work at Kmart? Billy Wauford's widow?"

"Tell her about the flowers," said Minerva.

"Oh, they're beautiful." Eleanor clapped her hands together. "And I've never seen so many."

"You could open a florist," said Minerva.

"The nurses won't let us bring them in here, so I had them sent to the house," Eleanor told me.

"But who sent them?" I asked Eleanor.

"Just about every man you've ever dated."

"Even the Starlight Lounge sent a mum basket," said Minerva.

"It's so cute. It has candy canes sticking out everywhere." Eleanor crooked her finger. "And the bow says EAT ME. It's wrote out in gold glitter. Isn't that just precious?"

"Darling," I said, then briefly shut my eyes.

"Did I tell you that Freddie called?" said Eleanor. "She's on her way to Tennessee."

"You mean she's leaving those whales for me?" I laughed. "Then I must be on my deathbed."

"Well, you came close," said Eleanor.

I stared at the ceiling. Next, Eleanor would start in about regional disasters, working her way up to the national and global. This was her hobby, along with TV shows. She liked to watch the Discovery Channel because she hoped it would make her smarter. All it seemed to do was make her fret. She said the glaciers were melting, the Colorado River was shrinking, and African elephants were being slaughtered for their ivory. In short, the planet was hanging by a fucking thread. I told her she should stop watching that Discovery Channel if it upset her so much. "It's a wonderful network," she said. "It's like *A Current Affair*, only for animals. Who's stalking who, who's running wild, who's extinct and who's the flavor-of-the-month."

"I'm real sleepy," I said, letting my eyelids flutter. Then I crossed my hands over my heart, as if I had only hours to live, the victim of a rare and deadly spider bite. I was relieved when Dwayne announced that visiting hours were over.

"So *soon*?" complained Minerva, gathering her knitting.

"Give us just a few more minutes," said Eleanor.

"I'm sorry," said Dwayne. "Rules are rules."

"Bye-bye, honey," said Eleanor. "Sleep tight. Scream at those nurses if your cardiac monitor stops beeping."

"She will," said Dwayne, waving at them.

"Isn't it time for that cute doctor?" I said.

"Which one?" Dwayne raised his eyebrows. "Dr. Granstead or Dr. Lambert?"

"Lambert," I said.

"Him?" Dwayne snorted. "Forget it. He's only been married a year or so."

"Good." I smiled to myself. "Then he's broke in."

"He loves his wife."

"That's okay. I like a challenge."

"Honey, worry about yourself, not the married doctors." He bustled around my bed, tucking in sheets, adjusting machines. Then he stuck a thermometer in my mouth. "I heard about your edible basket, sugarpie."

"If my hip wasn't screwed to Teflon," I said around the thermometer, balling up my fist, "I'd show you what edible is."

"Honey," he told me, "if you weren't screwed to something, you'd be dangerous."

FREDDIE

My plane landed in Nashville Sunday afternoon. I shuffled down the drafty tunnel, swinging my duffel bag. I had packed light—I didn't own very much that I cared about—but I was ill-equipped for Tennessee: shorts, bathing suits, cutoff jeans. I had bought a batik shawl in Tijuana, because desert nights could be cool and windy, but I'd left it draped over a chair at the Mirabel.

When I stepped into the terminal, I blinked. The light was thin and wintry, streaking tentatively through the glass, hitting rows of empty blue chairs. The terminal was mostly empty. What a strange word, I thought. *Terminal.* And how inaccurate. Endings, the termination of a journey. What if you were starting out or just making a pit stop? Why not call this huge, glassy wing a way station?

I followed the signs to the escalator. Not too far from the baggage terminal, I found the information desk. A woman at the Hertz window directed me to the Mid-State Limousine Service—nothing more than a fleet of Chrysler minivans. I bought a ticket, then searched along the curb for a white van. There were only about a hundred. The next to the last one was mine. Without saying a word, the driver took my bag and squeezed it into this incredibly tiny space. I climbed through the open doors, sitting down in the third row, behind two rumpled businessmen who were reading the *Wall Street Journal*, and two sunburned women, one blond, one brunette. Both ladies were anchored with gold jewelry—earrings, bracelets, thick herring-bone necklaces. They were talking about the casinos at Freeport and the slimy-looking men who inhabit them. The blonde looked back at me and smiled. Her eyes were ringed with white, in the shape of cat's-eye sunglasses.

"Hi," she said cheerfully, tossing back her bangs. Her dark blue eyes were outlined in kohl. "You been on vacation?"

Vacation? I thought. In the strictest sense of the word, I hadn't been on a holiday in my entire life; but I had vacated an area. I had vacated my husband and my career, leaving both to the devil. And I knew I looked weird, with my ugly haircut, thong sandals, ripped jeans, and short-sleeved T-shirt that said SAVE THE WHALES. I looked as if I was returning from a budget beach trip to Panama City, a week in a sleazy, bay-side motel. A mite underdressed, Jo-Nell would say, considering the weather. It had to be at least 32 degrees outside, because all the cars in the long-term parking lot had frosty windshields.

"No, not a vacation," I told the blonde, then glanced down at my jeans. I had always looked wrong—the Queen of Inappropriate. If everyone else was wearing black-tie, I'd show up in flats and a cotton dress. Invite me to a pool party, and I'd come in a swimsuit, then pretend not to be shocked to see the other guests wearing caftans, shorts, and slacks. I could see it now: The pool was empty. The hostess rushes up, saying she's sorry, perhaps the invitation was misleading, it is a metaphori-cal swim party. Get it? But since you're dressed for the occasion, by all means take a dip. Don't be shy, no one's looking.

"Well, *I've* been on a vacation. I just thought maybe you were, too." The blonde smiled at me, showing slightly crooked teeth. She shifted in her seat, stirring up a wave of perfume, jonquils, and vanilla beans. "So where're you coming from?"

"The West Coast." I hesitated, trying to decide how much to divulge. If the blonde thrived on tragedy, the way some

Southern women do, then she'd ask questions the whole way to Tallulah.

"Oh," said the blonde, raising her eyebrows. The white rings elongated. She glanced at her companion, a chubby brunette who narrowed her eyes at me. She appeared to be the smarter of the two.

"Is that in California?" asked the brunette.

"Yes, but I've been working in Baja," I said.

"Is that a beach in L.A. or is it further south?" said the blonde.

"Baja, Mexico," I said, running my fingers through my hair.

"I always get that confused." The blonde laughed. "Are you one of those, oh, what are they called nowadays—not missionaries but something else?" She turned to her companion. "What're they called, Brenda?"

"I don't know," said Brenda. "But my church has a whole group that witnessed to the aborigines in Jamaica."

I stopped playing with my hair. I blinked at the women. "The *what*?" I said.

"Aborigines," said Brenda. "You do know they worship black roosters over there? It's a disgrace." She gave the blonde a knowing look, then turned back to me. "So, have you been witnessing?"

"Hmm," I said. All I could think of was the federal witness protection program. Then it hit me: *Witness, as in gimme that old-time religion, there's room for many-a-more.* I'd been gone from the South too long; I was losing the language. Now that I lived in California, I believed that all of the land south of the Mason Dixon was a mythical place, existing largely in the minds of scholars, souvenir salesmen, and old, yellowed ladies who believed the exaggerated stories of their childhoods. God, I must have been crazy.

I smiled at the women and said, "No, I haven't been witnessing. I've been picking fruit." Then I cringed. The businessmen in the second row lowered their newspapers and briefly stared.

One was extremely handsome, with a thick mustache and sharp blue eyes.

"Fruit?" said the blonde, turning her head slightly, as if she had misunderstood me.

"Well, that's just wonderful," said the brunette quickly, giving me a strained smile. "I buy fruit all the time at Winn-Dixie, but I never thought I'd get to meet an actual picker."

"Me, neither," said the blonde. She nodded to her friend. "It's like I always said, picking fruit is a worthy occupation. And one that's needed in this world. It's nice, isn't it, Brenda?"

"Oh, yes. Very nice indeed."

"What kind of fruit do you pick?"

"Passion," I said. "Passion fruit."

From the front of the van, the businessmen stirred, shaking out their papers.

"Well, goodness. That sounds so exotic," said the blonde, nudging her friend. "We sure don't get anything like that at Winn-Dixie. Do we, Brenda?"

"No, we're lucky to get parsley."

"We're lucky to get fresh thyme."

"I envy you," said Brenda, puckering her lips. "If you're going to pick fruits, you might as well pick passionate ones."

"I'll second *that*," said the blonde. She smiled sweetly at me. "And I'll bet picking is the i-deal way to get a good suntan. Because you sure do have a good one, honey."

"An occupational hazard." I glanced down at my bare arms and shrugged.

"It's a beautiful tan," said Brenda, nodding eagerly. She held up one sunburned arm. "Me, I just fry in the heat. Fry then peel like an onion."

"Me, too, Brenda." The blonde sighed. "But *she* looks like an ad for Hawaiian Tropic."

"I sure hope you don't get skin cancer," said Brenda.

I knew I was supposed to say thank you—anything to let

those ladies know I was one of them, that I appreciated their compliments. This was another thing I had forgotten about the South: It was the one place on earth where an unsuspecting person could get killed by kindness.

My silence seemed to offend the women. They opened their pocketbooks and pretended to fish for something. The van's tires made a shrill, humming sound until the driver changed lanes. The scenery on Interstate 40 flowed by, gray and industrial. It seemed to me that we were moving through time—whether forward or backward, I couldn't say. The van passed through a hollow limestone ridge, the rough sides encased with transparent icicles; when it reached Percy Priest Dam, I thought of Dewey, California, and the house on Tomales Bay. In the summer it shines like polished metal. From the third floor of that house, a rickety staircase leads to a cupola. On a clear day you can see the ocean, the distant wedge glittering. The season for whale-watching at Point Reyes, which was just up the road, was mid-December through March—naturally when we were gone. The first thing we did when we got back to Dewey was to visit the lighthouse, walking from the cliff tops down hundreds of steps. Sometimes we would see whales on the northward migration—once, Sam spotted anchovies and plankton floating in an enormous, watery cloud. For five hours, we watched the feeding strategies of three whales as they plowed up and down in the blue water.

I suddenly felt so homesick, I thought I might cry. Right now it was wool-shirt weather in Dewey, a Western version of Down East Maine—with a twist. I missed the herd dogs rounding up Mr. Espy's lambs. The hills were like green whales, the land yielding luxuriant grass for livestock. I missed the windbreaks of cypress and the scattered groves of sycamores and oaks. I told myself that I'd be back in Dewey before I knew it. I knew Sam missed it as much as I did. Twice a week we'd drive over to Point Reyes, stopping at the Station House Cafe—chocolate cake for me, Tofu Salad Supreme for Sam, while the waitress hottened up our coffee throughout the meal. We could look forward to another foggy summer, with brisk winds at Drake's Beach, with the buoys clanging loudly. We would dive for abalone, sail in the bay, go surf fishing, wade through tidepools at Duxberry Reef, collect glossy agates and jade pebbles after a storm, drive to Limatour Beach for a vegan picnic—blackberry mineral water, cucumber sandwiches, organic sunflower seeds, chopped zucchini, asparagus, and tomato salad with a balsamic vinaigrette.

I deeply believed that a town's character was formed by its food. I loved living in a place with fish and cheese stores; where the roadside vegetable stand offered comice pears, red huckleberries, Walla Walla onions, chanterelle mushrooms, and orange pippin apples; where bakeries sold scones and chocolate croissants; where coffee shop menus promised *Omelettes, Name Your Filling—jalapeños, caviar, avocados, organic tomatoes, shiitake mushrooms*. The Honeydew Market offered gourmet picnic foods—imported cheeses, fancy crackers, eleven mustards, *pain de mie*, and crème fraîche in quart jars. All of this in a town of twelve hundred souls, set on a high bluff overlooking the ocean.

Dewey was laid out in a grid, with numbered streets running north/south, parallel to the water, and the lettered streets ran east/west. For years it was a typical small town, consisting of little more than a grocery/post office, gas station, and a few ranches. During the seventies, a small tourist trade had started up. The town sprouted a bed-and-breakfast, yacht club, a few bars and restaurants. The proximity to San Francisco lured a few adventuresome writers and artists, and soon the newspapers were calling Dewey the Left Bank of California. Now the tiny downtown was lined with trees, awnings, outdoor cafes, boutiques full of pottery, copper weathervanes, and original watercolors. If you decided to dine out, the whole world was your oyster. At Chez Madeline, the owner played classical flute;

at Manka's, the cuisine was Czech, with a fireplace that smelled poignantly of piñon; at Stinson Beach Grill, the menu was nouvelle cuisine, and the background music was barking sea lions.

When I first met Mr. Espy, he said that Dewey had a Mediterranean climate. At the time I hadn't been to Europe, but I wasn't a total hick—I had taken world geography in college. I asked if he meant Spain, Southern France, Italy, Greece, the Holy Lands, or North Africa. Mr. Espy smiled and said it depended on your perspective. After Tennessee, northern California seemed exotic and unusual, with its dazzling sunshine, low humidity, and rugged headlands that plunged into the sea. The water was almost too blue, as if the sky had flooded it. If you didn't count the town, the lighthouse at Point Reyes, and the winding road connecting them, the land was largely wilderness. The mouth of Tomales Bay was reputed to be a breeding ground for the great white shark. The bay was also notoriously foggy and windy. It was long and narrow, thirteen miles long, and the San Andreas Fault ran right down the middle of it. Mr. Espy said that two things kept the land open—the violent weather and shaky ground. Whatever the reasons, I always hated leaving our ranch—the high, grassy hill where the ewes grazed, with the whole, polished bay reflecting everything. I know I'm going on and on about it, but I thought the West was my country. Although I was born and raised in Tennessee, I thought of myself as a confirmed Californian, native as a grape.

Now I opened my eyes, taking in the depressing scenery on Interstate 40. The van shot past a scattering of brick houses, all protected from the road by a tall chain-link fence. I studied the backs of the women's heads. They seem so trusting, so polite. I hated to lie, it went against my grain. The blond woman must have sensed I was staring. She turned slightly and smiled, her eyes crinkling in the corners. "You sure do look familiar. Haven't we met somewhere?"

"No," I said and shut my eyes. According to local standards, it was rude, but I was exhausted. I didn't know what made me say I'd picked fruit, except that it was easier than explaining about the whales, Jo-Nell, and the train wreck. Besides, I was utterly convinced that my sister was dead. I didn't see how a Volkswagen had a chance against a train.

Once the van passed the Hermitage exit, I curled up into a ball and pretended to sleep, using my hand as a pillow. The women started chatting about their sunburns, losses at the casinos, and souvenirs they wished they'd bought. In the very front of the van, the driver fiddled with the radio, switching the dial to WLAC. "Anybody mind if I listen to talk shows?" he asked, looking into his rearview mirror.

"*Nooo*," said Brenda, flipping her hand. "You go right ahead."

"We'll listen to anything," called the blonde. The businessmen looked at each other and shrugged. From the radio came a soothing, masculine voice. "This is Eddie Duggan, your host, and your calls are welcome. The subject is earthquakes, specifically the New Madrid Fault line."

A woman with a nasal accent called in to complain. "I'm sick and tired of predictions," she said. "All I hear, day in and day out, is disaster and weirdness. Last week it was crop circles and alien visitations, and the week before that it was ozone. It's making me a nervous wreck. I mean, really. Listen to yourself, Eddie. One minute you say the Southeast is overdue for a major quake and the next you say it's baloney."

"No, ma'am, what I was trying to say—"

"Don't you interrupt me, boy. I just want to know my chances, if the quake will hit Nashville in my lifetime. This is *all*. Because I'm sick and tired of packing and unpacking my Hummels. Sick of taking Prozac and hoarding bottled water and me on a fixed income. I tell you, I can't take these talk shows of yours *anymore*. Why can't you do garden pests? No, you have to do earthquakes, with after-Christmas sales going on and I'm already afraid to drive to the malls. I'm sick of your thises and your thats, your poltergeists, your human vampires in downtown Nashville."

"Ma'am?" said Eddie Duggan. "Are you finished?"

"No!" The woman began weeping, her voice climbing higher and higher. "It's every bit your fault. Do you hear me, Eddie Duggan? I can't take these guests of yours *another second*, always preaching one calamity after the next. Personally, I'd rather not know. Maybe you would, but I wouldn't. My blood pressure is already sky-high, thanks to you. Day after day you're the voice of doom. So let me tell *you* something for a change. If the quake comes and my house goes down in flames, yours will, too. I know where you live. Why, you're nothing but a—"

Eddie Duggan disconnected her, and a reassuring dial tone purred out over the air waves. After a brief silence, a Budweiser commercial started playing. In the front seat, the driver snorted, then leaned toward the radio. "Miss Whoever You Are," he said, "if you can't take it, then listen to WPLN."

I gave up trying to sleep. Instead, I watched the hazy blue mountains in the distance, arranged like stepping stones that rose up and out, into low clouds—foothills of the Appalachians. I knew Sam could never ever live in a landlocked place like Tennessee, even with Center Hill Lake and the Caney Fork. Fresh water had no effect on the man. The ocean was different—salt acted like a chemical, making him daring and spontaneous. I had a picture of him riding on the fin of a sixty-foot whale shark. Sam looked like a piece of seaweed hooked to the fish's overwhelming girth—it was roughly the size of a reef, supporting a chain of animal life. He liked being adrift in living water. The ocean was my element, too, and just for a moment, I was furious with Jo-Nell for crashing into that train—furious that my attachment to her was larger than my need to stay in Baja, watching over Sam and the whales. It seemed senseless to love someone that much, for the pull of family to be stronger than gravity.

JO-NELL

I was dreaming about Freddie, that she was heading toward Tallulah in a hot air balloon. God, it was so real. When I opened my eyes, I half-expected to see her emptying sandbags. Instead, I saw Dr. Lambert standing at the foot of my bed, turning pages of my chart. He looked up, saw me staring, and shut the chart.

"Good, you're awake," he said. His lips parted, showing movie-star teeth. "How are you feeling?"

"Like I've been hit by a train," I said.

He smiled, nodding. "I mean other than that."

"Sore. And I have a funny taste in my mouth."

"Do you remember the accident?"

"Yes." I shut my eyes, saw the engineer's startled face and the spinning ground. When the car door came off, it hit my head. Then I fell.

"Do you remember what you were doing on that road so late?"

"Sure," I said, then racked my brain for a decent lie. "I was coming home from a girlfriend's house. She's got leukemia? I'd brought her supper and everything. Then we just sat around watching old movies. I guess I got sleepy and didn't see the train."

"My goodness." He pulled up a metal chair and sat down. "It's a miracle you survived."

"That's what I hear."

"Did you have on a seatbelt?"

"My Volkswagen didn't have any."

"Well, then you really are lucky." He cleared his throat. "Mind if I ask a few more questions?"

"About the accident?"

"Actually, I need to get a medical history. It's routine, Miss McBroom. Are you up to it?"

"I don't know, are you?" I gave him a full-dimpled smile. "And it's Jo-Nell."

The questions were doctorly, not as personal as I would have liked. I kept staring into his eyes—they were metallic gray. I wondered if Dwayne had told the truth, that Dr. Lambert was practically a newlywed.

"Do you smoke, Jo-Nell?" he asked. "Any history of cancer?"

I shook my head to everything. I'd never had trouble hooking a man, but reeling him in was a pain. Usually I'd pull too hard, and he'd wriggle free. I knew all this, even as I did it, but I couldn't stop myself. I always tried to play it cool, but I was a red-hot woman. I was feminine and dainty-boned, with the morals of Sharon Stone. I just hoped he was married to somebody big and mannish, her hair cut so short you could see wrinkles on the back of her neck.

"Are you sexually active?" He blinked.

I thought about saying, Are you? He wasn't no gynecologist; if he was an internist, like he said, then he didn't need to know about my private parts. Still, I wanted to make a good impression. I knew I had to be careful, choosing the exact right words.

"No," I said.

He fixed me with his most penetrating stare. "When was your last menstrual period?"

"Gosh, I don't even know what day it is." I laughed, trying to aim for a lighter tone.

"It's Sunday, December thirty-first."

"Are you going to a New Year's Eve party tonight?" I said in a little-girl voice, hoping to change the subject.

"Well, not really." He lifted one hand. "Just to the country club."

"Oh, that's right." I smiled. "They always throw a party."

"You're a member?" He gave me a doubtful look.

"I've heard about the parties," I said. "Me, I just don't get out much."

"Really?" he said, and I knew I'd gotten his attention.

"See, I come from a bookish family. My sister's a marine biologist in California? And when we were growing up, we used to lie around the house on New Year's Eve, reading library books. We had to use a wheelbarrow to return them. I don't know how I ended up being a gourmet baker, but that's exactly what I am."

"So what kind of gourmet things do you bake?" Dr. Lambert smiled, and I knew he was starting to like me—a girl who read books and didn't screw around.

"Well, that depends." I let my hand trail along the sheet, so he could see my pretty fingernails. They were painted Adobe Brick Red. "What do you like?"

FREDDIE

The van was turning off I-40, curving back toward Tallulah. Here, on the outskirts of town, very little had changed. I recognized the old, corrugated tobacco barn, Snow White Dairy Queen, and Geneva's House of Hair. The van curved around a two-lane road, past a trailer park and a bait-and-tackle shop. Through bare trees, I saw the dull green Cumberland River and the sharper, mint-green of the bridge. The van stopped at a flashing red light, then turned. As we drove over the bridge, I stared into the water. Up close it was muddy gray, the current heaving, as if it were pushed along by unstoppable urges.

One block from the bridge, the street became a four-lane, South Washington Avenue. I didn't recognize it. All those years ago, when I'd left Tennessee for good, this street had been a two-lane that led into town, circling back again to the bridge. It had sported a single Exxon station, boot outlet, and a summer vegetable stand. Now four concrete lanes were hemmed in by McDonald's, self-service gas stations, and used car lots. All the streets were still decorated with fuzzy Christmas bells and candles. Then it suddenly hit me—today was New Year's Eve, and I felt more depressed than ever.

"Tallulah, Tennessee," said the driver proudly, waving his hand at a strip shopping center. "It's tiny, but it's home of a right nice college, not to mention the fourth-biggest Wal-Mart in Tennessee."

I tried not to smile, because the man's comment was obviously directed at me. After all, I was the only passenger getting off. I thought about telling him that I knew plenty about little towns; that places smaller than Tallulah existed in the extreme West, yet there was nothing small and Wal-Martish about them. Why, Dewey was smaller than Tallulah, but it seemed larger and faster. There was a tiny town on the Mendocino Cape that only had a gas station/post office with a plank floor; if you wanted to see a movie, you had to drive fifty miles north to Fortuna. High school students were boarded with families in Ferndale, also forty-five miles north. Even so, sometimes the smallest town in the West is larger than a major Southern city.

When the sunburned ladies heard me stirring in the backseat, they smiled. They told me they sure hoped I enjoyed my stay in Tallulah. "Do you have family here?" said Brenda, arching one thin eyebrow.

"Not really." I shook my head. Once you started lying, you couldn't stop. Which was why I rarely did it.

"Oh? Well, I thought I might know them," the woman persisted. "I live on down the road, in Baxter. I know lots and lots of people 'cause I went to college in Tallulah."

"Actually, I'm from San Francisco," I lied.

"I thought you said Mexico."

"No, I work there."

"With all the fruits," said Brenda, then she looked horrified. "No, I meant—" She slumped in her seat and put one hand over her mouth. She didn't say another word until the van pulled into a paved lot, past a sign that said CUMBERLAND TRANSIT—LIMOUSINE SERVICE.

"Bye-bye, now," called the women as I made my way down the narrow aisle. The driver dragged open the doors, and I jumped out into the chilly air. In the distance I saw a line of scratchy trees and smudged mountains. Here, the sky seemed lower, or perhaps the trees were taller. It was the landscape of my childhood, yet it gave me a strange sense of dislocation. It was hard to believe that I'd been swimming in the Pacific less than forty-eight hours ago.

The driver was fishing for my duffle bag. He pulled it out, slapping it onto the pavement, then stared down at it as if to say, Is this *all*? While he waited for me to say something, his breath rose up behind him, hanging in the air.

"Thanks," I said, handing him a dollar. He stared at it, and I wondered if I'd violated some limousine service rule—no tipping. Or perhaps a dollar was insulting. From the van windows, the women were staring. I rubbed my bare arms, feeling rough bumps, like orange peeling. I was icing over, I could feel my blood chilling. If I didn't start walking, the McBroom clan would be faced with a second tragedy—they'd find me frozen stiff. There was nothing warm in my bag—all my thermal underwear and flannel shirts were back in Dewey. Aside from a muslin dress, which had about a million wrinkles, I was wearing my best outfit.

"Got everything?" the driver said, tucking the dollar into his pocket.

"Yah," I said.

"Excuse me?" The driver scratched his head.

"Yes," I told him. Then I turned all the way around, hoping he'd get the message and drive off. In spite of the views, which I should have known by heart, I was still confused by the town. Across the street was a new Cracker Barrel, Executive Inn, Wendy's, and a Git-and-Go market with a pay telephone.

"Somebody coming to meet you, miss?" The driver asked. "Or can I carry you someplace? I don't mind."

"No, thanks." I lifted the bag.

"Town's that way." The driver pointed north, toward a hilly road.

"Right." I started walking. If I knew my local geography, the town square was about five blocks away. I remembered that

Fred's Doughnuts was situated on a side road, North Jefferson, which gave way to River Street. Our house stood at the end of this road; it faced a limestone bluff, and in the gorge beneath it, the dusky river ran on. I like to imagine that the water was a tunnel to the real world, carrying everything away, even the things we wanted to keep. A great tunnel of love and home and summers past. A little further east, I could see the clock tower of the college. Way in the distance, I made out the white cupola of the chemistry building, with its aged, copper wind vane, although it was impossible to tell which way the wind was blowing. I began walking briskly toward the square.

Two blocks later, a long green station wagon pulled up beside me. It was an ancient car, with wooden panels on the sides. A woman rolled down the window and stuck out her head. She had dull brown hair, all slicked back with a dingy terry-cloth headband, and her face was covered with freckles. She wore reading glasses, which magnified her yellow eyes. In the backseat were two old ladies, who were leaning forward, staring at me.

"Freddie!" cried the yellow-eyed woman. The station wagon stopped about an inch from the curb. "Thank *heavens* I found you!"

"Eleanor?" I said, taking a step forward. In the backseat, the old ladies began whispering.

"Don't tell me you don't recognize me!" She laughed, turning up her flat face. The family always swore that Eleanor had fallen on her nose at an early age, thus rearranging her features, but facial flatness was a McBroom trait, one that had skipped both me and Jo-Nell. "Well, I guess it's catching," Eleanor said, squinting up at me. "'Cause I barely recognize you. Lord, your hair is short."

"What? Oh." I ran my fingers through my bangs, briefly touching my scab. "How's Jo-Nell?"

"She's awake," said Eleanor, "and already in a bad mood. I

told her you were coming and all. Then Minerva found out I'd made you take the shuttle, and she got me all paranoid. I thought, Goodness, what if Freddie takes the wrong shuttle? What if something bad happens? I even turned on CNN to see if there'd been any major plane crashes, but there wasn't."

I just stared.

"Honey, you're going to catch pneumonia out here. It's freezing cold, and you aren't even wearing a coat." Eleanor climbed out of the station wagon, leaving her door ajar. She hugged me, then stepped back and looked at my hair again. I gaped up at her, wondering if she'd always been this tall. Out in the road, cars swerved around the station wagon, honking.

"Well, I guess we'd better scoot." She reached down with her bony freckled hands and lifted my bag. With a little grunt, she tossed it into the front seat. I stepped down from the curb, waiting for a break in the traffic, and then dashed over to the passenger door. I climbed into the station wagon and slid across the dark vinyl seat, which looked and smelled like fried eggplants. That was the thing I remembered best about Minerva and Eleanor— the way food scents always seemed to cling to their clothes and hair, the way French perfume and tobacco hung around other women. I shifted in the seat, nodding to the old ladies. They had curly white hair and humpbacks. I would have taken them for identical twins, but one lady was taller, with filmy blue eyes.

"I'm Freddie, Eleanor's sister," I said.

"Sweetheart, we know all about you," said the blue-eyed woman, extending one hand. The skin was taut and shiny, spattered with brown spots. "My name is Winnie Daniels. I'm friends with your grandmother. I guess you know she's the vice president of the Tallulah Widows' Club. I myself am the recording secretary."

"And I am Matilda Lancaster," said the shorter woman, shaking my hand. She wore a gray felt hat, which rakishly askew. "I'm a new member of the club."

"She means she's a fresh widow," said Winnie Daniels in a conspiratorial tone, leaning toward the front seat. "They're the worst kind. They'll cry at the drop of a hat."

"I do *not*," snapped Matilda, her eyes flashing.

"We're on our way to the Senior Citizens." Winnie peered at a diamond wristwatch. "We always have bingo on New Year's Eve."

"Eleanor offered to take us," said Matilda. "She drives us everywhere, since Minerva got those cataracts."

"The poor thing's blind as a bat." Winnie nodded, then she looked stricken. "You won't tell her I said that, will you?"

"No, ma'am," I said. "I wouldn't dream of it."

I squinted out the window. Eleanor was standing on the sidewalk, talking to a policewoman and gesturing at the car. My sister looked dumpy in her long beige sweater, the sleeves hanging over her wrists. Her navy plaid skirt was hemmed unevenly, and she wore high-top tennis shoes and purple socks. She had always worn weird outfits. Some people thought she was eccentric, but I knew better—my sister dressed for comfort, not color coordination. The policewoman held up her hand, indicating she'd heard enough. Eleanor scurried back to the station wagon and lunged inside, hunching over the wheel. "I almost got a ticket!" she hissed. Her cheeks were the color of blood oranges. "Illegal parking, my foot! Why can't the law chase after real criminals?"

"Forget the criminals. Let's get cracking, child," said Winnie Daniels. "I don't want to be the last one to walk into Senior Citizens."

I settled back against the vinyl seat. From the radio, the talk show was still playing, with Eddie Duggan taking more calls about earthquakes. "Last summer—maybe it was August, yes, I think it was August—anyhow, a earthquake hit Dyersburg," reported a man with an Alabama accent. "It cracked my durn driveway."

"I remember that," said Eddie Duggan. "It registered 3.2."

Eleanor started fiddling with knobs, adjusting the heat. She flipped one hand toward the backseat. "I guess I ought to introduce everybody."

"We've met." I smiled at the widows.

"Well, hold on, girls." Eleanor gripped the steering wheel with her big hands. Then she stepped on the gas, and the station wagon lurched into traffic. The old ladies gasped; I propped one hand against the purple dashboard. After the ride in the Cessna, I was ready for anything. A red-and-white truck swerved and honked. "Okay, okay. I see you," Eleanor said impatiently. She slouched over the wheel, staring at the road through those huge eyeglasses.

"How is Minerva bearing up?" I asked.

"Better than me." Eleanor snorted. "Lord, that woman's strong. She always did like hospitals and sick people, you know. Baking food like there's no tomorrow. For a minute, I thought she would bake her own self a pound cake, but she didn't."

I smiled. In the backseat, the widows chuckled.

"I've just been out of my head worrying about Jo-Nell." Eleanor flicked down the sun visor, blocking out a wedge of wintry sun. Then she honked at a green Jeep, slapping one hand against the steering wheel. "Did you see that? Pulled out in front of me and nearly caused a wreck. I swear, they shouldn't let teenagers drive."

"That wasn't a teenager," I said, staring back at the Jeep. "It was a middle-aged man."

"Is it?" Eleanor squinted. "Well, I guess I need new glasses."

From the backseat, Matilda said, "Don't we all, honey."

"Not me," said Winnie. "I've got the eyes of a forty-year-old."

"My eyes went out at thirty-nine." Matilda sighed.

"So, is Jo-Nell still in ICU?" I prompted.

"Mmmhum. Hooked up to these monitors and machines. Remember that old TV show we used to watch, *The Six-Million*

Dollar Man? That's what it reminds me of. I had this gosh-awful nightmare that the doctors cut off Jo-Nell's real leg and sewed on a bionic one. For all I know, that's what happened." Eleanor's eyes filled, and she rubbed her bottom lids with her thumbs.

From the backseat came soft clucking sounds as the widows comforted Eleanor. "It's all right, honey," they said, reaching up to pat her shoulders.

"No, it's not," she said, wiping her nose on her sleeve. "It's really not." She turned down Profit Street and stopped in front of a clay-colored house, where a wooden sign said SENIOR CITIZENS.

"Here we are, ladies," said Eleanor, smiling at the widows. "Just in time for your bingo game."

"You're such a dear," said Matilda, gathering up her purse and gloves. "Isn't she a dear, Winnie?"

"A saint," said Winnie, nodding at me. "I don't know what I'd do without her."

Eleanor got out of the car and guided the women up the sidewalk, gripping their bony elbows. On the radio, Eddie Duggan was arguing with another caller about the possibility of fault lines in middle Tennessee. I reached out and punched the FM dial, landing smack in the middle of an Aaron Neville song, "Tell It Like It Is."

I stared out the window, but once again, I didn't recognize anything. How could a town change this much in eight years? Or maybe it hadn't. Maybe my memory was faulty. I had tried hard to blot out everything about Tallulah. When Mama was married to Wyatt Pennington, his mother, Money, felt it was her civic duty to enlighten us three girls about Tallulah's history. "It's an old Tennessee town," she'd tell us, waving her hands wildly, causing her diamonds to flash. "Forged out of the wilderness by sturdy Scots-Irish stock."

Like we cared. Now I saw that the town was like Money and

all the Penningtons, made of things that persisted: steep limestone hills, grained with coal; the sage green cedars, biting
deeply into the thin topsoil; waves of mountains rising at a slant
toward the east. I leaned against the window, looking at everything. The houses around the square had been built in the days
of craftsmen, with heart-of-pine floors, lathe-and-plaster walls,
oak beams, and rock foundations. Money had died the day her
son was buried at City Cemetery, but I could still hear her
twangy nasal voice telling me how these houses were in no
hurry to deteriorate.

Straight ahead, I saw the bell tower at the courthouse and the
stores around the square, the flat, tar roofs where pigeons were
lined up. I recognized a few buildings, despite their altered
facades—the old, white Standard station was now painted
Williamsburg blue, with a sign proclaiming BOBBY JO'S AUTO
REPAIR. There was the brick armory, where I used to roller skate
before the rink was built, with its chain-link windows and
empty flagpole; a sign out front said TALLULAH ANTIQUE MALL—
37 DEALERS UNDER ONE ROOF. The Princess Theater had been
turned into a used-furniture store, with the marquee spelling
out X-MAS SALE in crooked black letters. Everything about the
town seemed sad and shabby, homely rather than homey. It was
how I'd always imagined the town would age.

"You want to go home first or the hospital?" Eleanor asked.

"The hospital."

Eleanor glanced at her watch, a battered Timex with a black
leather strap. "Visiting hours aren't for forty-five minutes."

"I could talk to Minerva."

"She's at home cooking."

"She's not at the hospital?"

"You know how she is when company's coming. Anyhow,
they won't let us hang around the ICU. So do you want to go
there or what?" She raised her skinny eyebrows, making me
think she'd just asked a trick question—will Freddie, the long-

lost sister, pick home, which indicates selfishness, or will she pick the hospital, which means sisterly love and concern?

"Home, if Minerva's there." I glanced down at my bare arms. "I need to find some warm clothes before I freeze."

"Warm clothes! Didn't you bring none?"

"No." I shrugged. "Don't have any."

"Oh, that's right. I keep forgetting that you live in the tropics."

"Only for a couple of months a year."

"You can probably fit into Jo-Nell's things," Eleanor barreled on. "She's got enough to open a used-clothes store. In fact, she turned the spare bedroom into a giant closet. You know the one Mama used to keep birds in? Anyhow, we'll find you something to wear." Eleanor pursed her lips, then glanced up and down the road. When the light turned green, she hit the accelerator with her toes, and the station wagon jerked forward, deeper onto Broad Street. I noticed that many of the old stores were gone—Grady's Dry Goods, Bob's Shop for Men, Ensor's Stationery, Kuhn's 5 & 10. The whole downtown had been remodeled. In place of the old dime store was a restaurant with colonial-paned windows, its name spelled out in curvy letters, CHOICES. Along one side of the street stood a string of gift shops and boutiques, the windows full of dresses and brass lamps. Even the old Salvation Army was gone, replaced by a funky little place called Rags to Riches.

On the corner of Broad and North Jefferson, Eleanor turned left. When we passed Fred's Doughnuts, I turned all the way around to stare. A red sign hung on the door, YES! WE'RE OPEN! Deeper inside, I caught a glimpse of the wooden chairs with red plastic seats. A woman pointed to a glass case, while a thin, gray-haired lady pulled out trays of doughnuts.

"I've got a woman helping me run the place, but I worry that she steals. You know me. I can't mix business and tragedies at the same time. Listen, I know you're cold and all, but I want to show you something."

"What?"

"The crime scene." Eleanor blinked. "Where our sister almost lost her life."

"Getting hit by a train isn't a crime."

"Maybe I should say accident scene. Whatever it is, that L&N should've seen Jo-Nell coming." Eleanor lifted her chin. She turned onto a highway, pressing her foot to the accelerator. "And speaking of crimes, not two miles from here on this very same road, an old woman stopped to pick up a girl hitchhiker and you know what happened? The hitchhiker beat the old woman to death with a hairbrush. A hairbrush, can you imagine? The woman must've had a very fragile skull, like a ripe bell pepper. Anyhow, the teenager got rid of the body and drove to Memphis in the stolen car. I just don't know what the world is coming to."

I just stared.

"Next I want to drive by Jimmy Purcell's junkyard," Eleanor said. "So you can see her Volkswagen."

"Do we have to?"

"I haven't even been to see these things my own self. But now that you're here, I think I can stand to do it."

The station wagon passed a bait-and-tackle shop. Way off in the distance I could see the green bridge and a wedge of the Cumberland River. As we left the city limits, we passed trailer parks, an upholstery shop, and yet another bait-and-tackle shop that appeared to be boarded up for the winter.

Eleanor slammed on the brake, knocking me into the dash. When I looked up, she had stopped in front of a squatty building. "It all started here," she said.

"What did?" I peered out the window. On top of the building, a neon sign spelled out STARLIGHT. In addition to a string of colored lights, someone had strung up green and silver tinsel around the door, framing a handmade sign that said HO-HO-HO! HA-HA-HA! The gravel parking lot was empty, except for a red pickup and a black Bronco.

"The beginning of the end." Eleanor sighed. "Jo-Nell stopped here before the accident."

"She did?" I eyed the building. "Didn't Wyatt Pennington do some serious drinking here?"

"Oh, I've tried to forget about him."

"I think he hung out here." I turned all the way around to stare at the Starlight.

"And look what-all happened to him. Dead before the age of thirty-eight. If Jo-Nell hadn't come here, she wouldn't be in a fix."

I just stared through the window. A sign said OPEN 24 HOURS. It was easy to imagine Jo-Nell in a place like this. A thin plume of smoke rose from a vent on the Starlight's roof.

"I think she was drinking," Eleanor said, her voice barely audible. "Why am I whispering? Jo-Nell was drunk as a skunk. And it's not one-hundred-percent her fault. Look how trashy this joint is. All those burned-out Christmas lights. Nobody's bothered to change them in years. You can imagine the clientele they attract. Come sundown, it'll be packed with criminals."

"Let's go home," I said, touching her arm. "I want to see Minerva."

"Just one more minute. The train tracks are dead ahead. We can't go this far without seeing the actual spot where it happened." She narrowed her eyes, then pressed her foot to the accelerator. The station wagon shot around the curve, stirring up old leaves. I turned, watching them waft down, the color of sweet potatoes, hanging in the light, falling any which way.

MINERVA PRAY

I couldn't remember the last time we had company—maybe back when Freddie was in medical school. Whenever she came home, I'd do fifty things at once. Strip the beds, clean out the refrigerator, fry chicken, wipe down the counters, bake a peach cobbler, and then iron me a fresh dress, one all decorated with teeny green umbrellas. Today, I wasn't going to dig through my freezers. No, froze-ahead food might be fine for a funeral, but it wasn't okay for my Freddie. I knew how she set a store on freshness—because she'd been to medical school and knew all the doctoring secrets of good health, and because she lived in California. Her homecoming was a occasion.

You might say feeding people is a hobby with me.

I stopped by the Ash Street Piggly Wiggly so I could buy a decent meal. I bought three T-bones, romaine lettuce, green onions, two loaves French bread, Irish potatoes, store-bought red wine vinegar, and some of that bright orange Kraft dressing that Eleanor loves. I didn't know if Freddie would want pie or fruit, so I just got vanilla ice cream and some froze strawberries. I could always dig in the freezer for a vanilla pound cake.

Soon as I got home, I headed to the kitchen. I was happy to be alone—tearing lettuce, chopping onions, cubing French bread for croutons. There was so many things I wanted to fix for her! Then it hit me: Wasn't Freddie one of them vegetariums, or maybe it's veterinarians, what don't eat meat? She had told us all about that boy she married. Sam was a finicky eater—he didn't eat no meat or eggs. He must've been hard to cook for. I couldn't help but think of all the foods he would never get to taste—bacon deviled eggs and Lane Cake (the icing alone calls for twelve egg yolks). I didn't know what you'd feed a man like that—lettuce, sliced peaches, ice water? I worried that his crazy diet had rubbed off on Freddie. So I made extra salad, just in case she couldn't eat the T-bone. I wasn't worried about the waste because Eleanor would eat the leftovers. She always did. For a big woman, she carried her weight good, even though she'd got too stout for regular pantyhose.

When I heard the old station wagon turn into the drive, I was already in the hall, opening the door, running down the porch steps with my arms open wide. The first thing I noticed was her hair—short as a boy's. It made her eyes look too big and brown, like Ruthie's. She was no bigger than a twelve-year-old child, far littler than I'd remembered. And she looked, I don't know, seedy. Patched jeans, tennis shoes, and a short-sleeve shirt.

"Minerva!" Freddie ran across the grass, just a-squealing, and threw herself into my arms. She leaned back to stare at me. "You've gotten shorter!"

"And you're so thin!" I grasped her hands. "I've got salad and fresh, seared T-bones for supper. Do you still eat meat?"

"Sure." She grinned and ran her fingers through that cropped hair. I was so relieved that I dragged her into the house, elbowing past Eleanor. In the kitchen, I parked her at the oak table. "Eat, child," I said, scurrying from the counter to the table, setting out bowls.

"Did you know it's New Year's Eve?" Freddie said.

"Thanks for reminding me." I put my hands on her shoulders, feeling the little bones. "I'll cook us a pot of black-eyed peas for luck."

"Lord knows we need some," said Eleanor.

*   *   *

After they went to the hospital to see Jo-Nell, I put on my coat,
gathered up my bag of flowers, and walked over to the cemetery. It was late in the afternoon, nearly sundown, with a cold
wind blowing from the northwest. I walked toward the square.
Some folks was proud of the way Tallulah had got so modern,
with its tanning beds and video stores and Chinese takeout. But
I couldn't see that we were so stylish. Just because a place
changed didn't mean it wasn't the same, deep down. That
sycamore in front of City Hall was 115 years old, and seven people was hanged on it in 1902—in this century, mind you. Video
Express use to be Kuhn's 5 & 10. Four Seasons Tanning Salon
was Sears Roebuck. Dr. Chili Manning's old clinic is now a furniture store. If you get sick nowadays, you go to the emergency
room or the Redi-Med clinic on Carthage Highway. At the Redi-
Med you get a different doctor every day, none of them local.
Which makes you wonder what they did wrong in another
state.

The cemetery sat high on a hill, surrounded by hazy blue
mountains and deep, weedy ravines. For many years after
Amos died, I would climb up this hill, moving at a slant away
from the square, until I reached the grassy plateau of the cemetery. I'd pass through the creaky iron gates, curving around
stones that dated from the late seventeen hundreds. I would
look down into the deep bowl of the town, with the dirty green
river making endless S-curves, and the scratchy mountains rising higher and higher toward the east. The trees were mostly
bare, thin and starved. Ruthie and Amos was buried near a
stand of maples, which gave off cool green shade in the summer; in autumn the leaves would drop down in red drifts, and
in winter, the limbs were laid bare, but you could see for miles—
beyond the town, the only sign of life was the wood smoke curling up into the clouds. As much as I missed Texas, I didn't think
Tallulah was all bad—there had to be goodness in a place with

a place like City Cemetery. In the old days, by the time I'd set out my flowers and walked back home, I had a different view of things.

I walked stiff-legged up the gravel path, then cut across a slew of Crenshaws and Penningtons, to the Pray headstone—the only one in the entire cemetery. "Afternoon, Amos," I said, then knelt down, brushing leaves off the headstone. My name was carved up there, too, Minerva Pray, without no death date. I didn't mind. It was the only time I'd ever saw my name in print. I gathered up the old plastic spray that had been scattered by the wind. Then I reached in my bag and pulled out the plastic roses, what I bought by the gross at Big Lot's. I arranged them in the granite vase. Then I scrambled to my feet and stepped over to Ruthie's grave. I had wanted to bury her close to her daddy, and I got lucky—back in 1975, the cemetery wasn't this crowded. I took up her poinsettias—they were a bit faded from all the ice and rain—and then I set out the roses. I stepped back to admire my handiwork. Some of the fancier graves—and I don't mean the fresh ones—had live wreaths left over from Christmas. White pine and cedar all tied up with red bows. That sure looked festive. Next year, Lord willing, I would try to remember to decorate the headstones with a long garland, dotted with candy canes. Jo-Nell was egging me to string up lights—she said they came battery-operated now—but folks might think this hill was haunted.

There was plenty I could do this afternoon—winter always makes the graves look sad and shaggy—but I was give out. That is just the price of old age. When you are young, even middle-aged, you never imagine it will come to this—getting too old to seek out your pleasures. Now look what I have: too many heart-breaks, graves with too many weeds. The wind whipped around my legs, flapping my coat. The cold seeped into my bones, turning my fingers into claws. I looked up at the sky—it was pearl-gray, with a shimmery haze over the trees. I headed

toward the gravel path, digging my hands in my pockets, turning back a time or two to stare at Amos and Ruthie.

"See you all later," I said. "And Happy New Year." It was a
shame how some people left up poinsettias till Easter. I guess
they was just busy. And there's nothing like a Tennessee winter
to keep you indoors. My favorite graveyard season was summer. I liked how the town was hemmed in by rivers and mountains, the thick blue haze of summer, and a pink organdy sky all
ruffled with clouds. I saw the prettiest sunsets up there. Some
people took irises and planted them along the graves, like a
forked green border, but I never did. Me, I liked the change of
seasons. I liked digging weeds, feeling the sun beat into my
back. In the cool morning hours of June, after I'd finish with
Amos and Ruthie, I'd move on down to a stranger's grave, one
that needed tending. Seemed like I got to know the dead better
than the living.

Come summer, I would tend these graves like they was
flower gardens. First, I'd pack me a sandwich, a Mason jar full
of sweet tea, and a basket of roses or delphiniums from the garden. Then I'd start at one end, hacking at weeds that were
strewed with blackberries and wild daisies. When I'd get hungry I'd sit down under a oak tree, the one where the red bird
nests every year, and I'd nibble my sandwich. Sometimes I
brought tuna, sometimes I brought egg salad. I'd take my sweet
time, looking down into the bowl of the little town, the tall
white steeples and the rough-roofed houses and cars moving
like bumblebees down Washington Avenue. My graveyard days
was wide and deep. I could be alone with my thoughts, yet feel
the ghosts walk through me. No, I couldn't wait till spring. On
my way down the hill, I heard an oriole from high up in one of
the oaks. I had not heard an oriole since I was a girl in Mount
Olive, and it soothed me. It seemed like a Sign—whether good
or bad, I just couldn't say.

FREDDIE

The moment I stepped inside Tallulah General, I wished I had never stolen those organs in Memphis. Eleanor walked straight to the elevator, but I stood in the lobby, nodding at a gray-haired clerk from admissions, listening to the purring of the electric doors. Behind a glass wall, a dot-matrix printer erupted, racing back and forth across the paper. Phones rang on and on, with a dozen voices answering at different times, so that the room held a perpetual echo. I crossed the lobby, passing through layers of noises from outpatient admissions. *I'm sorry, but we'll need your insurance card before we can—*

Your full name, please.

Will this hurt? Will I feel any pain?

Please have a seat until someone calls your name.

While Eleanor and I waited for the elevator, the operator's voice constantly pleaded to the doctors, emanating from the acoustic ceiling. *Dr. Jamison, call ICU. Dr. Trammel, call extension 6919. Dr. Granstead, call surgery.* I had forgotten the authoritarian posture of a hospital. Once you become a patient you relinquish yourself utterly into the hands of strangers—nurses, technicians, dietitians, phlebotomists. The imbalance of control always annoyed me; not for the first time I wondered if I'd stolen the organs because I wanted to get caught, knowing full well it would derail my medical career. If it was true, if I was that weak, then maybe medicine wasn't the only thing I'd been trying to quit—maybe I'd been finished with Memphis, and with the love of my life, Jackson Manning. We had met in college, with plans of becoming vascular surgeons. I don't remember feeling discouraged or trapped; I was working much too hard, existing on far too little sleep to hatch out a plan this complicated. But of course that's the exact function of the subconscious.

The ICU nurse let us see Jo-Nell, but she was sleeping. Her room was partially glassed-in; the air was cold and smelled sour. There was a metal strip of instruments behind her bed: Oxygen, Medi-Vac, sphygmomanometer. Her IV dripped into a calibrated machine, which periodically squawked, as if a parrot were trapped inside. It seemed to me that all intensive care departments were the same—the season was always winter, full of snow, ice, coma.

"We'll come back," Eleanor whispered to the nurse, who shrugged and went back to reading a chart. The intensive care waiting room was in a new, brick wing of the hospital. It smelled vaguely spicy, as if potpourri was being pumped through the heating system. I hadn't been in a hospital since medical school, and I wondered when they'd stopped smelling medicinal; or maybe it was just Tallulah General—this wing, this floor, this crazy town.

I glanced around the room; it was packed with unfamiliar faces, all staring at me and Eleanor. I sat down in a straight-backed chair, then tipped back my head, briefly closing my eyes. I heard the operator bleat out Jackson Manning's name, imploring him to call pediatrics. I couldn't help but wonder how different my life would have been if I hadn't stolen those organs in Memphis. I imagined my own name drifting from the ceiling speakers—*Dr. McBroom, call surgery.* I would have worn a starched lab coat with my name stitched on the pocket, a black stethoscope entwined around my neck. My handwriting would be slanted, unreadable as hieroglyphics. I saw myself walking down these long, windowless halls, which resembled the interior of a battleship. My sensible shoes would clap on the tile, reassuring the patients as I hurried by.

My real life couldn't have been more different. I worked in a wet suit, breathing oxygen from an elaborate coil of tubes. The regulator's rubber seal always reminds me of the masks in surgery, smelling vaguely of general anesthesia, the sweet, dizzy air pouring through, filling my lungs and rendering me weightless. Falling backward into the water is like falling into a controlled, medicinal sleep, with everything dizzy and upside-down. Then the world rights itself. The sun is above, with the dusky blue dropping off into some further darkness which seems bottomless.

When I was in graduate school, I spent two weeks off the coast of Ecuador with some friends who were looking for sperm whales, those huge toothed carnivores. Afraid the Aqua-Lung would frighten them, we put on snorkels and slipped underwater to film them. They were extremely curious, sonaring like a dolphin—with loud clicks and creaks, like a cat dancing on cellophane. I could feel it moving through me. I have also braved the protected, shallow waters north of the Dominican Republic, where wintering humpbacks breed, singing long, intense mating songs to their prospective mates. Near Santa Catalina Island, Sam and I spotted three blue whales, the largest mammal on earth, with a heart like a red Volkswagen. After you've been swimming with creatures larger than a dinosaur—with brains larger than your own—it changes your perspective. I would have made a pathetic MD, but I was a half-decent biologist.

"Freddie? *Freddie McBroom!* I can't believe my eyes." A stout woman with gray braided hair was standing over me. She wore black stirrup pants and a baggy sweater with a missing button. "You are the spitting image of your mama."

"She sure is," says Eleanor, looking up from the newspaper.

The woman leaned over and hugged me, lifting me out of my chair. Then she leaned back and stared, wobbling slightly. "You don't remember me, do you, child?"

"No, I'm sorry," I said, looking at Eleanor for help.

"I'm Clara! Clara Mae Sanders. I used to work at the bakery after, well you know, after your mama passed."

"You remember Miss Clara, don't you," prodded Eleanor.

"Of course," I said politely.

"You was like one of my own. Here, do you want to see pictures of my younguns? I've got three grandbabies, though everybody swears I look too young." She patted her hair. "I'm here with my mother-in-law. You all remember her, don't you? Willene Gibson from City Hall? She had a stroke two weeks ago last Tuesday. She was bending down to put a cake in the oven, and she just keeled over. The batter ended up in her hair."

"Did they let you wash it?" Eleanor leaned forward.

"I never even asked," said Clara. "Do you think I should?"

"It's worth a try," said Eleanor. "The nurses in ICU won't let me get near Jo-Nell's hair with a ten-foot pole."

"Did she get cake batter in it, too?" Clara's eyes widened.

"Actually, it was blood," said Eleanor.

"Oh, my," said Clara, laying one hand on her cheek. "What happened?"

"You didn't hear?" Eleanor rolled her eyes. "She got hit by a train."

"No!"

"It's the gospel."

"Child, I heard somebody got hit by the L&N, but I never dreamed it was little Jo-Nell," said Clara, her voice perfectly heartbroken. "Why, that's just a shame. I wish I'd known, but you see I been cooped up in this durn waiting room night and day. You'd think a hospital would be the best place for gossip, but everybody's so down in the mouth. Too depressed to talk, much less slander. I don't hear nothing juicy, and you know what? It's getting me down."

While Eleanor slept, I took the elevator to the first floor. A row of vending machines stood against a wall, in a room adjacent to the cafeteria. I reached in my pocket for a dollar, pressed out the rumples, and then fed the bill into the machine. A woman approached me from behind, tapping my shoulder. "Well, Freddie McBroom!" she cried. "Or do you go by something else these days?"

I blinked. Before I could answer, the woman threw her arms around me, knocking me slightly off-balance. "Just look at yourself! You look like a country music star!"

"Me?" I didn't know whether to be flattered or offended. I glanced doubtfully at my dress—I'd found it in Jo-Nell's closet, a brown wool number that was a mite too short.

"You look sensational," the woman said. Her voice was raspy, ruined by cigarettes. I had absolutely no idea who she was, and it was unnerving. "Shoot, even with that hair you look good. It takes good bone structure to carry off a hairdo like that. I couldn't do it."

I blinked, and the woman's smile dimmed; I realized, too late, that I should have said, Don't be silly. You look fantastic. I didn't care; I was tired of politeness. I looked at the woman—her bright green eyes fanned by squint lines, her reddish-brown hair falling around her shoulders in loose curls, her wide, smeared mouth. She was wearing a pale pink uniform with VOL-UNTEER embroidered on the pocket. I didn't see a name tag.

"I was just *stunned* to hear about your sister." The woman shook her head. "She *did* survive the crash, didn't she?"

"Yes."

"Well, tell her I said hi."

"I'm sorry," I said. "I don't remember your name."

"Well, you *should*!" She smiled a little too brightly. "I'm Mary

June Carrigan. We *only* went through elementary, junior and senior high, and kindergarten, too."

"Oh," I said.

"It's true." Her eyebrows lifted, and she gave me a scornful gaze, as if she'd put her finger on all that was wrong with the McBroom women.

"It's been a while," I said, watching her light a cigarette. Now I was embarrassed. When I'd known Mary June she was a straight-A student, captain of the cheerleaders, class beauty, and was secretly, violently in love with a troubled Vietnam veteran, Eddie Starnes. He was much older than Mary June, but I barely remembered him. All through school, she had ignored me. Her parents had belonged to the country club and owned real estate downtown. As I recalled, her father had an office at Carrigan Motors, but it was all show. He never sold any cars. He lived off his inheritance. As Mother was fond of saying, "Horace Carrigan never worked a day in his life."

"Didn't you marry Eddie Starnes?" I asked.

"Oh, God." She held up two fingers, making a crucifix. "Don't mention that bastard's name. I divorced him a million years ago. Now I'm married to Benny Harrison—he works for Daddy. But he's studying for his real estate license. No, I divorced Eddie. I think he smoked too much marijuana. I just wouldn't put up with it. At least, something screwed him up." She made a fist and coughed into it. "I heard you're a psychologist. Somebody said you were doing research or some such about people who cry and wail?"

I waited for her to laugh, to show she was teasing, but her expression never changed. "No, I'm a cetalogist," I said. "I study whales."

"Say what?" Her forehead puckered.

"Whales." I spelled it. "Grey whales."

"Good Lord. How'd you end up doing *that*?"

"Well, it's kind of a long and boring story."

"I can just imagine." She lit another cigarette.

"So, tell me about yourself, Mary June," I said. "What are you doing these days?"

"About what?" She blew out a smoke ring, then smashed her cigarette in an ashtray. "Well, of course I'm a volunteer. I'm thinking about taking a correspondence course in interior design—everybody says I ought to. But I don't want to be tied down with a career. The Tallulah Woman's Club satisfies all my creative urges. We're involved in the restoration of an antebellum house on the Cumberland River, Belle View. You ought to come see it. It only costs three dollars, and the club gets all the proceeds. In fact, maybe I can give you a tour while you're in town?"

"Sure, sounds good," I lied.

"How long *will* you be here?"

"I don't know."

"I'm sure our paths will cross again. Right now, though, I've got to get back to volunteering."

"See you," I said, flooded with relief.

"Bye-bye," she said, waving three fingers. She drifted out into the hall, then turned a corner.

It was a little after ten o'clock, and every bone in my body ached. I'd divided the day between sitting with Jo-Nell and helping Minerva deliver an entire meal to someone named Etta P. Vaughn—a recent widow. "Thanks for all this food," Etta told Minerva, "even though I can't eat a bite. With Purvis gone, I may never eat again."

"Oh, honey, you will," Minerva said, lifting Saran Wrap from a chocolate Bundt cake. "I promise you will. It just takes a while. Grieving can feel so crazy."

After we got home, Minerva said she sure hoped I didn't mind, but she was too pooped to cook. I fixed a damp spinach salad with chopped scallions and homemade garlic croutons. Eleanor made poppyseed dressing. Later, while we washed the dishes, Minerva went to bed, saying she was tee-totally exhausted; she had this sad look in her eyes, and I couldn't help but wonder if all this death-monging sometimes backfired on her—dredging up the past.

I dried my hands, then sat down at the table. I picked up a Tallulah *Gazette*. Every page had mysterious gaping holes— squares and rectangles—making it impossible to read a complete article. "Just look at this mess," I told Eleanor.

"It's for my scrapbook." She pointed to the counter, where a two-inch pile of clippings lay. "See, I'm keeping track of things."

"What things?" I blinked.

"All kinds." Her eyebrows drew together. "It's hard to explain, so don't you bug me."

"But you've mutilated the newspaper." I held up the local news section, poking my fingers through the holes. "Let me see those clippings."

"Just wait till I've glued them in my scrapbook." She patted the black-and-white papers, aligning the jagged edges.

I leaned across the table and stared at the pile, skimming a few headlines: DRUG BUST AT THE CECIL G. DAVENPORT HOUSING PROJECT NETS 10 ARRESTS. DOOLITTLE'S MARKET ROBBED AT GUNPOINT. KMART MUGGER CLAIMS FOURTH POCKETBOOK. TEN-CAR PILE-UP ON I–65 KILLS 1, INJURES 3.

"This is weird subject matter, Eleanor," I said.

"It isn't!" Her face turned red. "I'm keeping track of trends? There's fashions and trends in crime, just like in clothes?"

I had forgotten her habit of croaking upward at the end of a sentence, turning it into a question. I sat there, shaking my head, trying to absorb what she'd just told me. "Why don't you collect recipes instead?"

"Why don't you shut up?" She glared. "I mean, it's not like I'm the only worry-wart in this family."

Behind me, the wall phone rang. I leaped up, sloshing coffee from my mug.

"Hello?" I said, barely moving my lips. Eleanor's news stories had set me on edge.

"You sound funny," said Sam—not hello, not I miss you, but you sound funny.

"I do?" I smiled and leaned against the counter, watching Eleanor gather up her clippings. Glancing at me sideways, she darted out of the room.

"How's Jo-Nell?" asked Sam.

"Lucky to be alive. Her spleen ruptured, and she's not exactly ambulatory, but that's temporary. She looks pretty good. The nurses said they're moving her out of ICU in a few days."

"That's good news. So, when can you come back to me?"

"Soon." I fingered the telephone cord, wrapping it around my wrist. "What's going on in Baja?"

"Here? Things are pretty calm, actually. About fifteen new cows arrived since you left." He paused. "Tomorrow I thought I'd drive up to Santa Rosalía and have dinner at Las Brisas."

"Nina, too?" I held my breath. Whenever Sam and I were in Baja, it was a tradition to drive up to Las Brisas.

"Yes," he said.

"I see." I felt very sad. I chewed my lip to keep from shouting, That's not fair!

"I wanted to go diving in Mulegé, but Nina was in the mood for Mexican food. So that's where we're going."

"She must be a persuasive lady." I wondered where he was sleeping these days. I pictured him at the Hotel Mirabel, separated from Nina by six doors and a courtyard full of prickly pears—or worse, perhaps they were sleeping on the boat, my namesake, separated by nothing more than a lightweight summer blanket.

"*Any*way, we'll be back tomorrow. I just hope none of the whales calve while we're gone."

"Wouldn't that be terrible," I said through my teeth. I was thinking that this would make a good story, how Sam and Nina were in Santa Rosalía while all the pregnant whales in Baja simultaneously calved. To comfort themselves, they'd get a room at La Pinta Guerrero Negro, staying in one of the twenty-nine colonial-style rooms on the beach, with the walls featuring paintings by Mexican artisans. While they made ferocious love, the pictures would bang against the walls, causing the management to ring the room, saying, "*Por favor*, can you please keep it *down*, señor?" Sam would say, "*Perdóneme*, but the lady prefers the other direction, *up*."

As I imagined this, my eyes burned. My imagination had always been vivid in a cruel way. Finally I said, "Well, it sounds like fun." Then I bit the back of my hand to keep from weeping. I fingered the spiral telephone cord, as if I could feel Sam's voice moving through the black wires.

"I'd much rather be with you," he said.

But you aren't, I wanted to blurt. That seemed like an important distinction—our dislocations. We had never spent time apart, except during our brief separation, when Sam was smitten by the lactovegetarian painter. I thought back to our first winter in Baja. We had driven down to Punta Prieta, where we set up an overnight camp. It was hard to sleep, with the whales breathing, coyotes yipping, and frogs singing their nightly chorus. I fell in love with San Ignacio, with its ponds and groves of date palms, and sour grape vines. When I was learning how to sight whales, Sam taught me to watch the water. Even though you don't always see the whales, there are dead giveaways to their presence. First, you look for the "blow"—this is just condensation that's formed when the whale's warm breath collides with the sea air. Accompanying each spout is an explosive *whoosh*—an eerie sound as evening descends. Next, you look for what appear to be oil slicks—these are made by the flukes as they disturb the water. Now I began wondering what sort of signs I had overlooked between Sam and Nina. I felt very sad.

After a minute he said, "Freddie, you aren't very talkative."

"Should I be?"

"You aren't upset?"

"Me? Why?" I laughed. "You're merely taking your blond researcher out to dinner. Why should I be upset?"

Now it was his turn to be silent. "It's just dinner," he said.

"*Just*," I mimicked.

"I won't go if it's going to up*set* you."

"No, go. Have fun." I bit my thumb.

"It's not going to be that kind of dinner."

"Of course not."

We sat there, silently connected by the phone line, our thoughts spiraling in separate directions. It occurred to me that it was senseless to have an argument at international rates. While I was considering what to say, Sam coughed and cleared his throat. I repressed an urge to ask if he was getting sick.

"The other day, off Isla Natividad, I didn't see a shark," I said in a confessional tone. "It was a whale."

"A grey?"

"Yes."

There was a long silence. "It hit you?"

"No, just a power surge from the flukes. But still."

"I didn't see it breach."

"Maybe you weren't looking at the water."

There was another silence. "Why didn't you tell me?"

"Because Nina was harassing me."

"Was she?"

"See? You are so oblivious. I *hate* that quality in a man."

"I am not oblivious. You're the one who ran into a whale."

"Yes, but you're the one who'll end up beached."

"Huh?"

"Forget it."

"No, you're upset."

"I am not."

"Don't be, honey."

"I'd better go," I said.

"Wait! I'll call you tomorrow."

"From Santa Rosalía?" I said sarcastically.

"Wherever I am, I'll call." He sounded tired, or maybe he was disgusted. Without seeing his face, it was impossible to tell. This time of year a persistent wind pushes down from the northwest, blowing until sunset, working on the eyes and nerves. I thought of the Santa Ana winds that sweep through the southern California passes, sometimes at hurricane gales. They were the hot winds of late summer and fall, but I've been told they can materialize in January. Sam told me about the winter of 1967, months before the Summer of Love, when those malevolent winds started a death fire in the San Gabriel Mountains. Now I couldn't help but wonder if they were starting up in the canyons, blowing toward Baja and breaking my heart.

I tossed my coffee into the sink. From the living room, I could hear Eleanor cutting out more headlines. Her scissors made a rasping sound, interspersed with periods of silence—no doubt she was pasting items into her scrapbook. The noise began grating on me, so I went upstairs.

I turned into Jo-Nell's old room. Here, the walls were painted sage-green, with matchstick blinds on the windows. Her iron bed was painted white, and a poufy striped spread was heaped in the middle, as if she'd just pulled it back. Clothes were heaped on chairs and the exercise bicycle. Piles of *Gourmet* were strewn about, among Diet Coke cans. A trail of silk panties led to the closet, which bulged with dresses and sweaters, the colors slapped together like a sweet pepper sandwich. A boom box sat on the floor, surrounded by hundreds of CDs.

I walked over to the marble dresser. An address book stood open, and I ran my finger down the *B*'s: Eddie Bascum, Ronnie Bell, Carl Bowman, Joe Ray Brown. The rest of the names were scratched out with purple ink. I ran my hands along the marble top. Trapped between bottles of nail polish and tubes of blush was a large wineglass. I picked it up. Inside was a frilly goldfish, swimming in circles. This was just like Jo-Nell, trapping some poor creature. She'd started out with fireflies in old mayonnaise jars, but now she was capturing men. Unfortunately they were like the bugs—they either escaped or died. I held the wineglass up to the light. It was shaped like a tulip; I didn't see how the fish had survived. I looked around for a bowl—anything large—but I didn't see one. Muttering to myself about crazy sisters, I carried the glass to my bedroom, where an ancient aquarium churned on a black iron stand. It looked as if it had been bubbling for a hundred years, a kind of weird cauldron. I had set it up a decade ago, so it wasn't surprising that algae had taken over, clumped thickly on the glass walls. From the murky depths, a treasure chest opened and closed like a clamshell, releasing a string of bubbles. I lowered the wineglass into the water, and the fish swam off.

I pulled on one of Minerva's old flannel gowns—pale cream with violet flowers. My old bedroom was exactly as I'd left it. A couple of biology texts jutted from a pine bookcase. The walls were bare, no posters or framed prints. Two dingleball lamps stood on either side of the cherry spool bed. The double windows overlooked River Street—no draperies to frame the view, just dusty Venetian blinds. Sam would call it the room of a Buddhist.

As I settled back in the feather bed, I felt lonesome for him. I told myself that the cold, mountain air was working on me— maybe it was a kissing cousin to the Santa Ana winds. I longed to call Baja; just hearing Sam's voice would remind me that a larger world than Tallulah existed.

I fixed my mind on northern California. It was my mantra; thinking of Dewey was the same as chanting ohm. It was a climate of violent extremes—wet winters, windy, foggy summers—and every season was punctuated by shaky ground. But I liked storms, and bad weather of all types. Then I had an excuse to stay in bed, reading mystery and espionage, dozing in the window seat and listening to the wind. Sometimes, the beams and hidden studs squeaked and quivered, until I was reminded of the *Miss Freddie* and the long voyage south.

Mr. Espy's ranch forked out near the Pacific cliffs. You could walk down a grassy, half-mile path to the boathouse, where we docked a cigar boat, kayak, and a sailboat. On foggy mornings, while counting sheep on horseback with Mr. Espy, I could hear barking sea lions.

My thoughts veered back to Sam and Baja. Right about now he would be at the lagoon, observing pregnant cows. In the early evening the whales swam right up to the shore, as if they were people-watching. From almost any direction you could stand on the dunes with binoculars, or climb the observation tower, and see their broad, glossy backs creasing the water. Sometimes young bulls breached, cavorting around unmated females. Water spouts erupted like geysers, accompanied by explosive *swoosh*es. As dusk washed over the lagoon, staining the water purple, the whale noises rose up, familiar and eerie all at once.

I felt very sad. Here I was in Tallulah, and my sweetheart was a million miles away. A whole country lay between us. A helpless feeling swept through me. I couldn't think of returning to Baja while Jo-Nell's prognosis was uncertain. I loved my family. While I had physically left home, I was still tied to it in all sorts of complex ways. Yet the biggest part of my life also seemed like the most recent.

Now, from Minerva's room, I heard a rasping sound, like a cloth ripped in half. I threw back the covers and tiptoed down the hall; outside her bedroom door, I gripped the glass doorknob. It was cold, and my fingers fit into the indentions. The ripping sounds stopped and a long moan began. It was an eerie sound, like something from a black-and-white horror movie. For just a moment I felt paralyzed—unable to knock, unable to leave. The only thing I could do was lean against the wall, slowly inching down until I was crouching. For a second, I thought I'd cry along with Minerva, but it was just easier to sit here and listen. It seemed to me that everything crumbled. Walls, foundations, plaster. All matter eventually broke down and dissolved—Daddy, Mother, Wyatt Pennington and his mother. Even our old yellow house on River Street had fallen into disrepair. Time was wounding every single thing in my life; I couldn't stop it, and it was senseless to try.

After a minute, I stood up and walked back to my bedroom. As I climbed back into bed, I couldn't get Sam out of my mind. I kept seeing him in Las Brisas with Nina. I wanted to think he missed me, too, but he was probably thrilled to be free of my gloomy, fretful nature. For once he could dive in dangerous currents, swim with sharks, maroon the *Miss Freddie* on a sandbar. No one would be there to say I told you so. Nina would probably egg him on—Go for it, she'd say. She'll never find out.

When Nina joined the *Miss Freddie* in San Diego, she made a bee-line for me. "You must be Sam Espy's wife," she said. She clasped my hand and vigorously pumped it. Then she glanced up at my short, shaggy hair. "Welcome aboard," I said. I felt ragged in my plaid shorts and wine-stained T-shirt that said COWGIRLS LOOKING FOR TROUBLE. My owl sunglasses were ineptly held together with electrical tape. "It's a real honor to be Sam's research assistant," Nina said, and I blinked. Twice now, she'd called my husband *Sam*, as opposed to the more formal Dr. Espy. (I was keeping track.) I took it as an ominous sign, along with her perfect smile. Her teeth looked manufactured, something a dentist had painstakingly created from porcelain. She wore white canvas boating shoes and short white socks, the flaps folded down twice. Her cutoff jeans were just a hair too short, but her T-shirt was printed with MENSA CONVENTION: 1994.

Our first week in Baja, Nina urged Sam to take the *Miss Freddie* into deep waters. For miles, we didn't see a single whale.

Most of the greys were in the lagoons, cavorting with babies and mates. Nina and I sat starboard, drinking Sidrals. Sam cut the engines, reached into the ice chest, and pulled out a beer. After a few swigs, he began talking about other researchers we knew—husband-and-wife teams—who had been coming to Scammon's for years. Most all of them had vanished. Sam counted on his fingers, giving a where-are-they-now tally. One was in the Bay of Fundy, studying the soon-to-be-extinct right whale. Another was in the Caribbean, not researching whales at all, but measuring plankton at certain tide levels. Yet another was dead—a cerebral aneurysm at the age of forty.

While he rattled on, I laid down my *People* magazine and gazed at him. His subject matter had caught my attention. It had caught Nina's, too. She discreetly pretended to read a battered Audubon shell guide. She never turned a page, but it was clear that she was listening.

"People lose interest," I said lightly. "They also lose grants."

"I guess," said Sam.

"Not to change the subject," Nina said, lowering the book, "but I'm just dying to see a pair of forty-foot whales screw. Think I ever will, Sam?"

"If you're observant."

"Oh, I *am*." She pushed back a lock of hair, then smiled. "Have you seen it?"

"Only from a boat." He laughed. "It's hard to get close, with all that thrashing."

"Oh, I could." Nina leaned across the table, her hair brushing forward. "One thing puzzles me, though. The researchers down here are into baby whales, yet no one seems to have any kids of their own. That's really weird. But they could, I guess."

"Could what?" Sam said.

"Have kids. Although I don't suppose you could bring one here." She pushed the hair from her face. Blond strands were caught in her gold earring, and she hooked a finger to unthread them. "If I ever have a baby, it's coming with me. I'll be the Jane Goodall of Baja. With a little naked Grub toddling in the dunes. Do you guys have any?"

"No," Sam said. He tapped his fingers together, then briefly looked at me.

"I'm going to have at least four or five," said Nina. "And a full-time nanny."

I didn't know what Sam was thinking, but I was picturing Nina traipsing out of the lagoon, followed by a half-dozen babies, white-blond like ducks. I wanted to say that careers and children didn't mix, but what did I know? It seemed strange that my life's work centered around whales and their breeding habits, when I myself was childless. Normally I didn't think about children: You can't miss what you've never had. I'd suffered three miscarriages, the last one dying inside me slowly, like an overwatered alfalfa sprout. The ultrasound showed an embryo without a heartbeat, a placenta that kept pumping out hormones. One day I spotted blood; the next my breasts swelled up like eggplants, bruised and mushy. I was pregnant, yet I wasn't. A missed abortion, the doctor called it, a term that no one in Tallulah, Tennessee, would have understood. They would have seized on the word *abortion* and called me a baby killer. And in a way I was—my body just refused to bear life. It was more competent at holding on to death.

After each obstetrical disaster, I checked into the hospital and the doctor scraped me out. I pictured Halloween pumpkins: my mother's spoon rasping inside the melon, digging up seeds and membranes and strings. It had seemed like a kind thing to do for children—carve out a funny face—but now I wondered if it was a portent. For some odd reason, my sisters were just as barren as me. The McBroom clan was dying out, and there was nothing we could do to stop it.

The next evening we were sitting in the deserted courtyard of the Malarrimo Restaurant and Trailer Court, drinking tequila. It was a starless, windy night, and the almond tree kept dropping leaves. I leaned against Sam, into the deep C of his arms, hoping that Nina was paying attention. She was gossiping about a lady we'd seen a few days ago at Scammon's Lagoon, a tall brunette named Callie Something; she'd left her husband and children to work for Biological Journeys, a company that catered to eco-tourists—a big business in this part of the world.

"She's from Atlanta," Nina said, as if that explained the woman's behavior. Nina had dressed for dinner—a short, blue-jean skirt that showed off her marvelous legs. Her breasts bobbed beneath a sheer yellow tank top. She kept fingering her earlobes, rubbing the tiny gold hoops. She picked up a lime, took a bite, and her eyes filled poignantly with tears.

"I guess I ought to say *Hotlanta*?" She laughed. "Aren't Southern girls supposed to be hell at night?"

"Absolutely," said Sam. He lifted his glass in a mock salute.

"You say that like you know." Nina quirked one blond eyebrow.

"I do. Freddie's from the South."

"Well, I'll be damned," Nina said. She grinned at me. "Where?"

"Tennessee," I said, a little grudgingly.

She smiled and shook her head, pointing one finger at me. "I knew you had a funny accent."

"Me?"

"I couldn't place it till now." She tilted her head. "Doesn't it bother you to sound, uh, less than intelligent. I mean, I know you're smart, but god, that accent."

"Does it bother you to sound so blond?" I said. Sam squeezed my knee. I squeezed back, a little harder, digging my fingernail into his thigh to let him know I was furious; he didn't flinch, and I wondered if the tequila had left his leg numb, along with the rest of his body.

Nina chose to ignore my comment. She licked the back of her

hand and sprinkled it with salt. I watched, fascinated, as she sucked the lime, her chin jutting out. She swallowed a shot of tequila, and then licked more salt. I hoped her blood dried out; I hoped she turned into Lot's wife. Once I saw her jogging in the dunes, her ponytail damp and swinging, arms folded tightly against her rib cage. She looked very young and very self-assured, and I had a sinking feeling.

"I used to know a guy from the South," Nina said. "I think he was from Louisiana, or maybe it was Kentucky. Cute, but I never could understand a word he said."

"So how did you communicate?" asked Sam.

"Sign language." Nina gave him an alarmingly seductive look. Then she faced me. "So, how did you end up in Baja?"

"The whales." I shrugged.

"She followed me." Sam smiled.

"Interesting." Nina covered her mouth with her hands, as if hiding a smile. Beyond the courtyard, the sun was going down, the December afternoon dissolving into evening. Over the stucco wall, the sky was violet, streaked with orange. Nina was still smiling into her hand. "So Sam followed the whales, and you followed him?" she said, lifting one eyebrow.

"It's more complicated than that." I rubbed one finger along the rim of my glass.

"I'm sure." She bit into another lime, then frowned. Two creases appeared on her forehead. "Maybe you can teach me to talk Southern?"

I'll just be honest. I'm the last person in the world who would ever defend a place I hated, and I honestly hated Tallulah, but my heart started thumping. I looked at Sam, thinking that he must hear it, too. I was outraged—not because of any regional loyalty but because I myself was a little drunk. Instead of slapping her, which would have felt wonderful, I tossed my head. In an exaggerated accent I said, "Sorry, darlin', you got to be a native."

"Are you blushing?" She smiled, her lips slightly parted, showing perfectly straight incisors. "Is this, like, a maidenly thing, or have I hit a nerve?"

"When you do, I'll let you know."

"And she will." Sam burped, and Nina laughed.

"Now *that* sounds Southern," she said, nudging his hand, spilling tequila.

"Oops." He set down his glass, licking the back of his wrist. He eased away from me, rising unsteadily to his feet, then veered off into the dusky courtyard. I heard the pattering of urine against the almond tree, accompanied by soft sighing sounds as he relieved himself. Nina tilted her head, smiling to herself. This was where I drew the line—between sociology and physiology. It just didn't seem right, listening to Sam pee in the presence of another woman.

"Do you have a boyfriend in LaJolla?" I asked Nina. My voice was deliberately loud, without a trace of an accent.

"I *did*, but it's kaput." Nina shook the tequila bottle. It was empty. She cut her blue eyes toward the courtyard, where my sweetheart was stumbling out of the shadows, zipping his jeans.

"We're out of tequila," she said, handing him the empty bottle. "But look, I saved the worm for you."

ELEANOR

When Freddie and I stepped into the ICU, the nurses were lifting Jo-Nell by her armpits, forcing her to stand. "But it *hurts*,"
she cried. "Honest to god it does."

"It'll keep you from getting complications," said Dwayne,
the male nurse. He had pointy ears and slanted green eyes.
Put a felt hat on him and he could pass for the Keebler cookie
elf.

"I thrive on complications," said Jo-Nell.

This was true. She was always working herself into some
new calamity. She looped her elbow under Dwayne's neck, then
squeezed hard. He made a strangling noise. In a Donald Duck
voice he said, "Stop it, stop it!"

"No more walking," she said.

"For god's sake," he quacked to the other nurse. "Put her
back to bed!"

"Careful now," I warned the nurses as they staggered over. I
threw out my hands, as if I could stop any malpractice before it
started.

"God, I'm wasted," said Jo-Nell, falling back against her pillow, her eyes at half-mast. As the nurses stepped back, I had a
full view of my baby sister. Her hair was dull blond and matted,
like tomcat fur, one that's been in too many bloody fights. "Is
there any way I can wash her hair?" I asked Dwayne.

"Not in my ICU," he snapped. He squatted down, adjusting the bed rail.

"Well, how about if I just do a French braid?"

"I wouldn't advise it," Dwayne said.

"Why don't you just ask the doctor and see if it's okay?" Freddie suggested. She had the sweetest, softest voice; I thought it was wasted on those whales. She would have made a good doctor.

"This is not a beauty salon," Dwayne said. "It's a hospital. And you simply *can't* fool with her hair. She has too many tubes, and you might dislodge one. Okay?"

"What if she gets bugs?" I drew my fingers into claws.

"Bugs!" Dwayne and Jo-Nell cried. Freddie pressed two fingers to her lips, like she was trying to hold back from laughing.

"Listen up," I told them. "I know what I'm talking about. I once heard of a woman who wore her hair in a beehive so long that she attracted roaches. All that dandruff and sticky-sweet hair spray was the culprit, I guess. After some blood trickled down her forehead, they took down her hair, but it was too late. The roaches had eaten all the way to her brain."

Jo-Nell snorted, and Freddie said, "That's just a stupid myth."

"It's not. It's the gospel. And even if you don't believe me, you can't go around with dirty hair."

"Is it that bad?" Jo-Nell's face crumpled in, almost as flat as mine. She reached up and patted her bangs.

"Hmm, maybe you're right." Dwayne laid one manicured finger against his chin. "Since I don't have a before picture, I really can't comment; but I do get your drift. Her hair really *does* look a bit stringy. And all those snarls and dried blood don't help one bit."

"No," I agreed. "Limp, greasy dirty hair is not her style."

"She can always shave it," Dwayne said under his breath. "I would."

"You leave my hair out of this," said Jo-Nell.

"Honey, I'm not criticizing." I started to touch her hair, then I thought better of it. "Anyway, hair isn't important."

"Shave it and I promise it'll grow back." Dwayne straightened up. He put one palm on Jo-Nell's bed. "Anyway, it's not like you've got any admirers."

"I do so!" Jo-Nell raised her chin, scowling at him. "I've got plenty."

"So do I." He winked.

"Shut up, Dwayne."

"Well, you started it," he reminded her. He propped his hands against his lower back, his elbows jutting out like chicken wings. Then he sashayed out of the room.

"Thank god," said Jo-Nell.

"I think he's nice," I told her.

"You would."

We fell silent. Freddie was over by the window, looking down into the parking lot. I caught Jo-Nell eyeballing at me.

"What?" I jutted out my chin.

"You're dressed funny. Look at her, Freddie. A brown wool jumper, navy leotards, and black penny loafers."

"So?" I glanced down at my shoes, then back at her.

"You don't match."

"I'm not a china pattern."

"You look pitiful."

"I'm just a little eccentric is all." I shrugged.

"A *little*?" Jo-Nell snorted. "I wouldn't brag about it."

"I know *just* what we need here," Freddie said in a rushed voice, trying to smooth things over.

"What?" Jo-Nell curled her upper lip. A thin string of saliva fell down, breaking apart like a spider web.

"Chess. We can play chess."

"I don't know how."

"I'll teach you."

"I don't feel like using my brain. Is it harder than checkers?" Jo-Nell arched one eyebrow.

"Not really."

"You would say that." Jo-Nell grinned, then shifted her eyes at me. "Eleanor, why don't you run over to Kmart and buy a chess game?"

"Me?" I was startled. I didn't like her tone, ordering me around like I was nothing. Hadn't Minerva preached that we were equals? "Isn't chess a game for smart people? I'm sure they don't sell it at Kmart."

"Then get Wheel of Fortune," begged Jo-Nell.

"Or Scrabble," said Freddie.

"It was your idea." I blinked at her. "So *you* go."

"I don't even know where Kmart is."

"I'll draw you a map." I opened my pocketbook and began sifting thorough papers. As I scraped my fingers along the silk lining, loose pennies jingled. I wondered how much—if any-thing—Jo-Nell suspected about me. For the longest time now, my world had been shrinking. I wouldn't drive to Nashville because I could just see the station wagon breaking down. It was old, with a finicky starter. Besides, I hated to drive past that curve in the road where Daddy died; his van slid on ice and tumbled down an embankment.

"I'd go," Freddie said, "but I'm exhausted. I've got jet lag."

"I'm tired, too," I said, trying to change the subject. "We can get the games later. We need to be leaving anyway. Minerva's making chicken and dumplings."

"For who?" Jo-Nell teased, but there was a sting in her voice. "You or some dead person?"

"For *us*, me and Freddie. And do you go making fun of poor old Minerva. She's worried sick over you, young lady."

"Don't call me young lady." Jo-Nell gave me a pale, glassy stare.

Again, I was shocked by her tone. I knew if I could get her off track, she'd forget all about that chess game. "You're right," I said, cutting my eyes at her. "You're not young. And you've never been what I'd call a lady."

"Don't you dare pass judgment on me."

"Well, you *aren't* so very young anymore."

"I am too young!"

"Please don't fight," said Freddie. "Stop it."

"You've got the IQ of a soap dish," said Jo-Nell. "And the hips of a heifer."

I chose to ignore this, even though sweat was gathering at the nape of my neck. I just wanted to get out of there. "We're going to be late for Minerva's supper."

"I just hope she fixes you a salad," said Jo-Nell. "A salad with lots and lots of vinegar. Because you need it bad."

"Why do I need vinegar?"

"To pickle the bug up your ass."

The next morning, as I circled the Kmart parking lot, I noticed what the police call a suspicious character. He was wearing an orange knit cap and a camouflage jacket. As he lit a cigarette, smoke drifted up, like it was streaming from his ears. I had a feeling in the pit of my stomach, although it could have been indigestion. I'd eaten green onions and turnip greens for a snack. Anyhow, I wasn't really in the mood to go shopping by myself. It was evermore fun with a bunch of women. They shore me up, but also there's safety in numbers. Also, ten pairs of eyes can spot bargains a lot quicker than just one.

I drove away from the shopping center, down South Washington, and turned right on Profit Street. When I reached the Senior Citizens, I parked by the curb. Then I darted inside. All the little ladies rushed over to me, asking about Jo-Nell and the train wreck. They all talked at once, and I held up my hand to show I wanted to speak.

"Jo-Nell is fine," I told them. "In fact, I'm on my way to Kmart to buy her some goodies. Anybody want to come along?"

FREDDIE

The goldfish was dead, floating sideways in the dirty aquarium. I dipped it out with one of Jo-Nell's teasing combs, then I flushed the poor thing down the toilet. I paused in the hall, staring down at the phone. On impulse I called the Magdalena Cafe and the Hotel Mirabel, leaving messages for Señor Espy. I worried about my Spanish—what if I'd said Don't ever call, rather than Call whenever. On my first trip to Baja, Sam gave me a crash course in Spanish. He said if we ever encountered guerrillas, I was supposed to say, *"No disparen! Somos los Beatles!"*

"What?" I said.

"Don't shoot! We are rock stars." He laughed. "And sear this into your memory. *Yo tengo un amigo importante en la embajada de los Estados Unidos.*"

"I have an important friend—" I broke off, shaking my head.

"I have a powerful friend at the American embassy," he said.

Now I wrote him a letter, explaining that Jo-Nell was on the mend, and I hoped to see him in a week or two. In the back of my mind was Nina. I wondered if she traipsed around in her string bikini. Maybe she knocked on his door at three A.M. I can't sleep, she'd tell him, holding up a bottle of tequila. How about a nightcap?

Sometimes I saw him turning her down flat; other times he'd step back and open the door. If I were alone with someone who adored me, I didn't know if I could resist. I hated leaving him alone with her, even though they weren't exactly isolated. Other scientists were camped at the lagoons. There were marine archaeologists, and some colleagues from Scripps who were studying whale lice; a husband-and-wife team from San Diego were implanting radio-equipped tags in the whales' blubber, to be monitored by satellite; researchers from U.C. Davis were tagging brown pelicans; cetalogists from Vancouver had followed a pod of orcas from the Johnstone Strait. With all this activity around the lagoons, I had hoped Nina would fall for some boy-adventurer and leave mine alone.

I knew she hoped to meet someone—once, she'd left her purse in the rubber Zodiac, and I shamelessly looked inside: eel-skin wallet, sunscreen, Spanish-American dictionary, tampon, condoms, sunglasses, bottle of Lomotil. *Condoms?* I thought, panicking, then scooped them into the bottom of my sneaker, just in case she had designs on Sam. As if my theft could prevent anything.

Nina had expressed considerable scorn for all of the unattached researchers in Guerrero Negro and San Ignacio, if not all of Baja. I'd had high hopes of introducing her to a blue-eyed ornithologist from Coos Bay, Oregon, but Nina let him know she was strictly into whales. "There are all types of migration," he told her. He was studying a type of sea goose, the Brant, that nests from Siberia to the northwest coast of Canada—quite a range when you think about it. Every autumn the Brants gather on the Alaskan Peninsula, and by early November they are ready to fly down to the bays and lagoons of Baja. When the wind sheer is exactly right, all of the geese rise up into the dark sky and begin their three-thousand-mile journey.

"Wow." Nina lifted her eyebrows and stared imploringly at me, as if to say, Now look what you've started. When the ornithologist left, she curled her lip and said, "What a fucking nerd. And god, he's knock-kneed."

"So's Sam," I pointed out.

"Yeah?" She shrugged. "But on him it looks good."

She walked off, leaving me to puzzle out the rules of attraction: Why do whales swim from the Bering Sea to Baja and back again, a round trip of more than ten thousand miles; what makes the Brant rise into the chilly dark, pouring into the sky and never filling it; what drives a man to kiss a woman's neck, moving urgently against her, entering her body as if tunneling a path home? Sam would say it's animal instinct, the will to survive. That made sense to me—all those creatures seeking beautiful, desolate places. All those journeys ending and beginning again.

Deep attraction was something I had only experienced twice in my life. Once with Sam and once when I was a senior in college. My first real love was Jackson Manning, and I met him in a zoology course. I say met, but that really isn't true. We had gone to high school together, but I don't think he'd ever noticed me. I was short and myopic, the sort of girl who slips through the cracks of any high school, until the grades are tabulated for graduation. I was valedictorian, but I didn't get to attend the ceremony. A severe case of poison ivy prevented me from claiming my prize.

Jackson was my lab partner in cell biology, and I feared that he would distract me. He had thick wavy black hair and indigo irises. He possessed two very kissable dimples. More to the point, his father was Chili Manning, our family doctor, which meant he knew all about my strange family history, or at least the highlights—my grandfather's electrocution, my father's car accident, my stepfather's abandonment/death, and my mother's suicide. As much as I disliked the hoity-toitys of Tallulah, I really didn't think Jackson would say anything rude, because he knew about tragedy. In 1968, his six-year-old sister, Kelly, drowned at the country club pool while playing a breath-holding game called tea party. A decade later his mother, Miss Martha, died with breast cancer.

Jackson didn't recognize me until the professor called roll. I knew he was staring, but I refused to make eye contact, giving the professor my undivided attention as he handed out syllabuses. Jackson shifted in his seat. He opened a package of gum and offered me a piece. I wondered if this was a trick question—a piece of gum, a piece of me.

"No, thanks," I said. A minute later the smell of sour apple drifted over. I decided that he was my lab partner, not a roommate. He wasn't worth distracting me from my goal: vascular surgery. I wasn't too worried—he was involved with a long-legged strawberry-blonde named Mary Elizabeth, but everyone called her Muffin. She wore 24-karat gold barrettes, and her father was a proctologist in Cookeville.

All through September, Jackson and I shared a microscope, studying fruit flies that were infected with syphilis. I let him borrow my notes, and he repaid me with a bouquet of tiny wildflowers. They were neon yellow, and each petal was curved like an eyelash. He admitted that he'd stolen them from the botanical display in the adjacent biology building, but I was charmed. After class he opened my textbook and pressed them between chapters five and six.

"For luck," he said, looking deeply into my eyes.

"Can't have too much of that," I said. Even though I had a 98 average, I worried that I'd slip up and make a C. When I got home I set the flowers on my desk. It was not like me to hoard things, partly because I didn't like clutter and partly because I didn't like to form attachments. I hated to lose things. A little while later Jo-Nell came into my room, holding her chemistry book. While I balanced equations, she sat on my desk and painted her toenails a violent shade of purple. After she left the flowers were gone. Thinking they'd fallen behind the desk, I got down on my hands and knees, but I only found a few crushed petals.

The next afternoon I went to the zoology building, hoping I'd have the lab to myself. Jackson was sitting at our desk, examining slides under a microscope. Before I could back out of the room, he looked up. He was all backlit by the casement windows. The light fell around him in deep baskets of gold. "I'm worried about the midterm," he confessed. "If I don't get into med school, my dad will kill me."

"Oh, I doubt that," I said, walking up to the desk. I picked up a slide and held it up to the light. "Your dad seems sweet-natured. Did you know he's my grandmother's doctor?"

Jackson got up from his desk, then walked around and put his hands around my waist. He cupped my face in his hands. "What?" I said, pretending not to understand.

"I like you, Freddie," he said, rubbing his nose against my chin. "I like you a lot. In fact, I'm crazy about you."

"Me? I thought you were crazy about Muffin."

"I'm not seeing her anymore."

"Why not?"

"Because I want to see you."

Once we started kissing, we couldn't stop. We stumbled backward, knocking over three chairs. Then we sank down to the tile floor, sending up a cloud of chalk dust.

The phone rang, and I just knew it was Sam. "Hi, sweetie," I said, cradling the receiver.

"Sorry to disappoint you." It was a woman's voice. "I was trying to reach Freddie McBroom."

"Speaking."

"Well, hi! This is Cissy Alsup, used to be Cissy Browning? We were in the Glee Club at Tallulah High?"

"What can I do for you?" I wondered if I sounded as unfriendly as I felt. Cissy Browning hadn't spoken five words to me in high school. She had been one of those wild, popular girls who managed to keep her reputation—if not her hymen—

intact. I had been bookish, without any extra money to buy Bobbie Brooks skirt-and-sweater sets.

"I heard you were in town," Cissy rushed on, practically cooing into the phone. "Mary June told me that she saw you at the hospital. My husband's a doctor there, you know. Dr. Bill Alsup. So I said to myself, Cissy, you've just got to call. I heard all about your sister's little mishap. Bill told me she'd been admitted."

"I thought you married Jimbo Shrimplett," I said, then mentally added, *A month after high school graduation, in a double ring ceremony at First Presbyterian.*

"No, I divorced Jimbo seven years ago. Or was it six? Anyhow, the reason I'm calling is I'm having a party this Saturday night. I know it's right on the heels of New Year's, but it's been so cold, and I was in the mood for some fun. Oh, it's not a big party or anything. In fact, my house is a wreck. I haven't even taken down my Christmas decorations. It's such a pain, and my housekeeper has been out with a hysterectomy. Anyway, I want you to come. Jackson Manning will be there."

"Excuse me?"

"Jackson Manning, the pediatrician. I know you all used to date. He's divorced now."

"Oh, I didn't know."

"He was married to this simply *gorgeous* woman from Memphis. Isabelle Something-or-other. Have you heard of her? She was a model, I think. Anyhow, this dirty little rumor got started about Jackson and a pediatric nurse. True or not, Isabelle just up and left. Since then, Jackson has gone through women the way a monkey eats bananas. You know, take one bite, throw the rest away."

"He didn't remarry?" I cringed after I said this.

"No, but he's been through lots and lots of bananas. His last girlfriend was a real estate agent, a member of the million-dollar club. Julianna Howell. She's divorced with one kid. A boy, I think. Anyway, she can be a bit pushy—you know realtors. And she's from, shall we say, the wrong side of Tallulah. Her daddy worked at a gas station. Not quite up to the Mannings. But you've got to give Julianna credit. A million dollars is a million dollars. I thought for sure he'd marry her. But some men are just impossible to second guess. Still, I try. I swear I try."

I was trying to think of an excuse to get away, but she said, "So, tell me; what have you been up to all this time?"

"Me? My life is fairly quiet."

"You call a train wreck quiet?" Cissy laughed. "We all heard how you were studying whales and living in California. I just think it's real exciting. That's why I called you up. I thought you might like to come to my party and tell everybody about your adventures. You know how it is in Tallulah—boring. Everybody's always doing the same old things—you know, doing unto others before they can do unto you."

I didn't answer; I was thinking about Sam and Nina, trying to unravel the time difference between Tennessee and Baja. If I called now he'd probably be at the lagoon.

"So do you think you can come?" she asked, bringing me back.

"Come where?"

"To my party! It's at seven o'clock. My address is 502 Appomattox, but I can pick you up."

"Well, I don't really—"

"No! I just won't take no for an answer. You've got to come and that's all there is to it."

"I'll try," I lied. My hand was resting on the receiver, ready to disconnect. "Listen, thanks for calling, but I'm expecting a long-distance call from Mexico."

"From your mysterious sweetie?" She laughed.

"Yes, my husband," I said, steeling myself for another barrage.

"Well, that's nice. Don't you forget my party, now!"

"I won't." Before she could say anything else, I hung up. I had no intention of going to her party or any other party in Tallulah. I just wasn't that kind of girl.

JO-NELL

It was dinnertime, and I could hear the food trays being pushed up and down the halls. The wheels creaked, which grated on my nerves, and the smells were awful: overcooked roast beef and canned gravy, the type they serve in school lunchrooms. "Hey," I called to Dwayne, who was out in the hall. "When can I eat me some decent food?"

"How about something indecent, love?" Dwayne's head popped into my glass room.

"What did you have in mind?" I said, wiggling my eyebrows.

"I can't *wait* to write this down in your chart. The doctor will be *so* pleased."

"Why?" I sniffed the air again, and this time I smelled applesauce cake, one of Minerva's famous standbys. I wondered if this cake had caramel icing or just a dusting of powdered sugar.

"Be*cause*, dearie," said Dwayne. "Interest in food means you're going to live."

"What the hell do you know?" I said, knitting my eyebrows together.

"More than you."

"Eat shit, Dwayne."

"Darling, don't tempt me."

"I mean it! Go eat some doody!"

"I will. Just as soon as I can get down to the cafeteria. It's all

they serve here." He stuck a hypodermic needle into my IV.
"But now, it's time for your afternoon cocktail. Sweet dreams."

"But I don't want it."

"You need all the beauty sleep you can get." He winked.
"Maybe you'll dream of me."

"That'd be a nightmare."

"Think of it as intravenous Bud Lite. Oops, an air bubble," he
said, tapping the tube with his thumb and forefinger.

"Get it out or I'm fucked!" I yelled. I couldn't see any bubbles
in the IV, but then, I wasn't a trained nurse. (I wasn't sure
Dwayne was, either.)

"Oh, darn. I'm too late. It's halfway to your brain. You'll hear
the blowout in a minute."

I opened my mouth to scream, then he started laughing.

"Just kidding," said Dwayne. He sashayed over to the curtain, yanking it back. I could see the U-shaped nurses station
and the wall of monitors. "Toodle-do," he said, wiggling two
fingers.

"Toodle-do yourself," I said.

"When you wake up," he whispered, "I won't be here."

"Neither will I," I said, or thought I said. Whatever he'd put
in my IV was stronger than a Bud Lite. It was more like Bud Lite
and Valium. I had a drunk sensation, as if I was laying in the
Gulf of Mexico, in the real green, shallow water. I stretched out
my arms as the waves broke over me, foaming over my toes. I
let the current pull me to and fro, with my hair fanned out like
a jellyfish. I shut my eyes against the hard sun and drifted.

Back toward the beach, a man was calling my name, Jo-Nell?
Hey, can you hear me, gal?

I tried to open my eyes, but the Bud Lite had waterlogged my
lids. I swam out of the ocean, backstroking all the way to
Tallulah General. First, I heard the squeak of nurses' shoes, then
a sharp, nasal voice asked, Can I help you, sir? It belonged to
one of the RNs, a gal with short black hair and a mustache. She

was from Up North, Detroit or someplace, and she seemed mighty pissed off to be in Tennessee.

I just come to see Jo-Nell McBroom, said the man. Jo-Nell, honey? You awake? I brought you some flowers. Little orange sweetheart roses from the icebox at Winn-Dixie.

Sir, visiting hours are over, snapped Ms. Detroit.

I just wanted to see her for a second, said the man. Just for a second is all.

Are you immediate family?

Well, not exactly . . .

Then I'm afraid you'll have to leave, sir.

Oh, please. Can't I see her? It's important.

Sorry, she's resting now.

Is she gone be okay?

Sorry, you'll have to talk to her doctor.

Will you tell her I was here? And give her these flowers?

There was a deep sigh, then a shuffling noise. Footsteps clapped across the tile floor. Sir? I thought. Come and swim with me, sugarpie. Come on, the water's warm, it's like lying in a hot bath. I willed my eyes to open, and honest to God, I saw the back of that cowboy's head, little old Jesse from the Starlight. He walked out over the water, straight into the sunset.

Then the nurse shut the double doors, and he was gone. She walked over to a trash barrel and threw away the roses.

"Hey, you!" I yelled. "Yankee nurse!"

Ms. Detroit turned, one eyebrow raised. "Yes?" she said.

"Who was that man?" I said.

"He didn't say."

"I want my flowers. I saw what you did with them."

"Sorry, it's against hospital regulations," she snapped and yanked my curtain, pulling it across the glass wall. The hooks made a screaking sound. If I hadn't been drinking, I would have taken those regulations, maybe the sweetheart roses, too, and shoved them up her ass. Honest to God.

FREDDIE

Saturday afternoon, I was in the kitchen with Minerva, helping her make giant batches of chicken pot pie. My jeans were splattered with all-purpose flour; half-moons of chicken fat were lodged under my fingernails. Eleanor sat on a tall stool, crimping dough with her fingertips. Minerva had a plan to bake each pie in miniature aluminum tins, just like the frozen variety at Winn-Dixie. Then she planned to distribute them to the shut-ins of greater Tallulah. Anything left over would be labeled and frozen, stashed in one of her many freezers—the funeral freezers, we used to call them.

"A lot of people think chicken pot pie ain't fancy enough for a funeral," she told me, "but it sure warms the soul on a cold night."

I agreed. Her crust was flaky, with a buttery depth that I've never been able to duplicate (not that I'm handy in a kitchen, you understand). She boiled her hens in chicken stock, along with fresh onions, parsley, celery, bell peppers, and a single bay leaf. When I tried to pin her down about a recipe, she just shrugged and said, "Oh, I don't know how much garlic—a half teaspoon? But I've been known to use a tablespoon. It just depends on what I'm making. Chicken soups ain't created equal, you see. There's chicken soups for flu and colds, chicken soups for the brokenhearted. The garlic is adjustable."

The doorbell rang its two short notes, and Eleanor let out a long sigh. "Coming!" she called, lumbering into the hall. A minute later I heard a giggly, feminine voice. It bounced down the hall, into the kitchen. I looked up and saw a short, squatty blonde totter into the room, wearing a red plaid skirt, the pleats stretching over her wide hips. Her head was enormous, like an overinflated balloon. She wore two inches of mascara, gold rope chains, and poufy, teased hair—the total effect seemed to play up the incipient hydrocephali.

"Hey, girl!" she cried, grinning up at me. Behind her, Eleanor was lifting her hands and shrugging, as if to say, I tried to stop her!

"Hey," I said coolly, trying to place her. I honestly couldn't.

"It's me," she cried, reaching out for my hand with red plastic fingernails. "Cissy!"

"Of course," I said. To tell the truth, I would never have recognized her. To keep her from swarming over me, I held up my sticky palms. "I'd shake hands, but I'm covered in dough."

"Hello, Cissy," said Minerva, adjusting her eyeglasses with one floury hand. "You look mighty festive."

"Why, you cute thing you." Cissy turned on Minerva with a claustrophobic hug. "You're always just a-cooking!"

"It's what I do," Minerva said.

"Has somebody died?" Cissy's eyebrows drew together.

"Not as I know," said Minerva.

"My husband says you're a fixture at the hospital." Cissy let go of Minerva, then turned back to me. "You've been a bad, bad girl. Cooking and not paying any attention to my party."

"Party?" I let my hands fall.

"Shame on you, girl. It's tonight." She waved one finger at me. "But that's okay. No harm done. Just throw on a dress and run a comb through that hair and we'll take off."

"Take off?" said Eleanor, tilting her head. "Where?"

"Why, to my Christmas party!" Cissy clapped her hands.

"Why else do you think I was at your bakery today, picking up all those tassies and cheese straws and kiwi tarts?"

"I'm not going to any party," said Eleanor. Two spots of color appeared on her cheeks.

Cissy looked at me. "I hate to rush, but can you be ready in five minutes? Or should I run a few errands first and pick you up later? Say, around five or five-thirty?"

"Cissy, I can't come to your party," I said.

"Why not?" Her eyes blinked open wide; she clasped her hands under her chin.

"I just can't."

"But you promised!"

"I've got a million things to do," I said, feeling obscurely bullied.

"Well, I'm not leaving without you." She climbed up on a stool and crossed her legs. Her knee made a swishing sound under the taffeta plaid. "I won't take no for an answer. You're practically my guest of honor. And if you won't come to my party, then I'll bring it to you."

"Don't do *that*," said Eleanor.

"It's up to Freddie." Cissy's eyes glinted. "What's it gonna be, girl? Your place or mine?"

"That's blackmail," I said.

"Yes, and I am an expert in it, a black belt." Cissy grinned. "Or is that in karate? I never can get that right."

After Cissy disappeared into her bedroom, I roamed around her house, dodging a little tan Chihuahua that kept darting under chairs and sofas. The rooms were decorated in a curious, almost baroque style—lots of reproduction cherry veneer tables. The windows were swathed in lace and taffeta. Every room had been stamped with Christmas cheer. I counted six artificial Christmas trees, each one with a theme: In the kitchen, the tree was covered with preserved orange and lemon slices, gadgets, and shortbread cookies. A seashell tree stood in the Florida room; magnolias and floral bows in the living room; a tree for each child. There was even a pint-sized tree for the Chihuahua (it featured mini–dog biscuits, cleverly dangled out of the little snapper's reach).

Cissy's house was jarring, with its crystal angels and nativity scenes. I didn't blame her for leaving up the decorations. The removal could take six months. Since Sam and I spent every Christmas in Baja, we more or less avoided the season—it was like escaping a whole month of guilt. We missed Sam's dad—he was the last of the north coast cowboys, and he spent Christmas morning rounding up his sheep. He always said we went to Baja so we wouldn't have to bother with setting up a tree. In truth, we liked the idea of escaping the crowded stores in San Francisco and Petaluma. In Baja, we worked eighteen-hour days—taking photographs, compiling data, comparing nearly a decade's worth of research. Sometimes we would be eating in Guerrero Negro, and the jukebox would start playing "Feliz Navidad," and we'd say to each other, "My god, it's Christmas." We would order Ensalada de Noche Buena and Mexican chocolate. We just weren't into religion, but we admired the purity of the celebrations in Guerrero Negro, where Christmas Day marked the end of a week-long *posadas*, with children dressed up like Mary and Joseph, reenacting the journey to Bethlehem. We enjoyed the piñatas full of candy and the red and green salsas that the cafes served.

By seven o'clock, Cissy still hadn't materialized, but her husband, Dr. Bob, cornered me in the kitchen. He pressed me against the speckled granite counter and dangled a piece of mistletoe over my head. "Just one little kiss."

I ducked under his arm, and slipped into the dining room. A chubby caterer was arranging silver trays on the table. A waiter was pouring champagne into tall flutes. I lifted one in the V of my fingers, then fled into the marble hall. Through the glass doors, guests were coming up the driveway. Dr. Bob breezed in, opening the door with a flourish. He winked at me. "I'll get that kiss yet, sugar," he said.

Me, I would just as soon kiss the Chihuahua. I ducked into a large, jade-and-apricot room that was lined with books and sat down in a corner. According to the mantel clock, it was five till seven. I felt trapped, and I wished I'd brought the station wagon. I told myself I'd stay thirty minutes, then call Eleanor. Until then, I'd mill around—my standard behavior at parties and fund-raisers. The house was filling with women's voices, perfume, and the sound of exploding champagne corks. The little Chihuahua zigzagged around tables, yelping when a guest accidentally stepped on its paw.

As I passed through the library, I overheard three women discussing Cissy's decor. "It *should* look good," said a brunette with wide hips and chunky legs. "She had a decorator."

"That's no big deal," said a blonde with long burgundy fingernails. "Ethan Allen supplies them for free."

"Cissy shops every day in Nashville," snapped a woman with capped teeth. "I run into her constantly in Green Hills."

"Say what you want," said the wide-hipped brunette, fingering the green plaid draperies, "But this fabric isn't from Ethan Allen. It's Cowtan and Tout, two hundred dollars a yard. And not just any decorator can get it."

"Two hundred dollars a yard!" cried the blonde. "She must be crazy."

"No, just another miserable doctor's wife."

"Well, I'm married to a dermatologist," said the blonde, "and I'm not miserable."

"A different breed of doctor." The wide-hipped woman sighed. "Cissy's married to an ear, nose, and throat. The bastard has put tubes in every ear in Tallulah. He's made more money than Ricky Skaggs."

"Did you know her husband is sleeping with a twenty-five-year-old recovery room nurse?"

"Oh, everybody knows that."

"Everybody but Cissy."

"If she wasn't such a bitch, I'd feel sorry for her."

"Will you look at this painting? I saw it in Green Hills for fifteen hundred dollars."

I ducked out of the room, giving the women a wide berth, and turned into the kitchen.

Cissy was sitting on the granite counter, sipping eggnog. I turned, thinking I'd double back to the dining room, when I spotted Jackson Manning. He was standing in a group of people, paying attention to a redhead in a low-cut green dress. His eyes were still the same shade of indigo, set into an older face. I felt a blush tingle along my neck, rising toward my jaw. I turned abruptly away, heading for the dining room, but it was too late.

"Freddie?" he called, shouldering his way through the crowd, saying, "Excuse me, oops, sorry 'bout that, excuse me."

I stopped, then leaned back against a counter. "Hi, Jackson."

"Is that all?" He grinned. "'Hi, Jackson'?"

"Well, I guess I could say, *Buenas noches. Cómo está usted?*" A waiter came by with a tray of champagne. I picked up a fresh flute, took a sip, then smiled up at Jackson.

"*Muy bien, gracias,*" he said. "How do you say I want a kiss, in Spanish?"

"I don't know," I said. "But I could teach you how to communicate with Mexican doctors." I kept sipping champagne, holding the glass with both hands to keep from running my hands through my hair. I knew I looked wrong and haphazard, and it wasn't just the haircut. I was wearing one of Jo-Nell's dresses, black wool, real short, with little gold buttons down the front; all the other women were wearing long velvet skirts and frilly blouses.

"Okay," he said, smiling. "I'm game."

I took another sip of champagne and said, "*Al demonio con su jura mento! Tengo bichos adentro que necesitan ser matados.*"

"And that means?" He raised both eyebrows.

"Damn your oath! I've got things inside me that need to be killed!"

He laughed. "How long will you be in Tallulah?"

"That depends on Jo-Nell."

"God, that's right. I heard about the wreck. How's she doing?"

"Well, she's alive. She had a total hip and a splenectomy."

"That's *all*?"

"Yes; but she's still in ICU."

"I would think so. God, hit by a train. I'm ashamed that I haven't been to see her. I never seem to get beyond the pediatric floor. The only gossip I hear is pint-sized." He looked down at his shoes, then glanced up. He chewed one edge of his lip. He seemed unable to say anything else. Then he said, "Gosh, it's been a long time. You look great. I guess California agrees with you?"

"Seems to." I felt a little disappointed. So that was it, no going over the last eight years, no filling in details. Back in Dewey, whenever I called long distance, my sisters never mentioned him. They were loyal, but they also knew it was a sore subject. I had no idea what he knew about me.

"I see your grandmother at the hospital now and then visiting sick people. She keeps me updated about your adventures."

"Well, you know Minerva. She exaggerates."

"Then you don't study whales?"

"Yes. I do." I smiled, feeling very happy all of a sudden. I took another sip of champagne. "The California grey."

"Sounds pretty exciting to me."

"Oh, not really," I said, but the truth was my career bowled me over. I couldn't believe my incredible luck—I'd started out as a skinny little kid who was afraid of water; I couldn't even dog paddle. The year I graduated college, Jackson and his father taught me to swim at Center Hill Lake, and life was never the same. It was ironic—the Manning men were responsible for my career. I suddenly remembered diving off Cortez, descending into a school of hammerheads. I'd worn a rebreather so I wouldn't frighten the sharks with bubbles. And one time in Lorento, a manta ray floated by, belly up, and I hitched a ride. Just thinking about the ocean made me homesick, and I wondered if it showed.

"While you're here," Jackson was saying, "I mean, if you have time, I'd really like to see you. Maybe take you to dinner?"

"Sure," I said, thinking of Sam and Nina at Las Brisas. My heart levitated, pressing against my ribs. A blonde in a brown taffeta dress walked up to Jackson, taking care not to spill her eggnog. Up close, I noticed that she wore tinted turquoise contact lenses, and she was about five inches taller than me. Her hair was swept over to one side, calling attention to long, dangly earrings that looked vaguely Egyptian. "Sweetie," she said, sipping eggnog. "I'm surprised to see you here. I thought you hated parties."

"I do." Jackson smiled. "Sold any houses lately?"

"Not a one, and it's breaking my heart. Well, my mama always said to pray for what you want, and work for what you need. If you hear of anyone wanting to buy or sell, let me know." The blonde smiled at me, waiting for me to introduce myself. When I didn't say anything, her eyes swept up to my hair. She wrinkled her nose. I leaned against the counter, drinking the last of my champagne. It felt warm against the back of my throat. The blonde took another long drink of eggnog. When she lowered the cup, her upper lip was smeared with whipped cream.

"Actually," said Jackson, "Cissy Alsup bullied me into coming."

"Cissy did?" The blonde laughed. "In what way?"

"She said she'd move the party to my place if I didn't come."

"She said the same thing to me," I said.

"Really?" Jackson shook his head and laughed. The blonde looked at me. She seemed only mildly curious.

"Yeah," I said. "She dragged me out of the house."

"Cissy *dragged* you here?" said the blonde.

"Yes." I looked toward the kitchen. Our hostess was still sitting on the counter, watching the three of us with an amused expression, and I saw that she'd set us up.

"I'm sorry, I don't know you." The blonde smiled down at me. "Have we met or . . ."

"Did you know you have eggnog on your lip?" Jackson pointed.

"I do?" She rubbed her fingers over her mouth. Keeping her eyes on me, she said, "I didn't catch your name."

"Freddie," Jackson and I said at the same time. We looked at each other and laughed.

"What an interesting name for a woman. Are you new in town? I haven't seen you around. Oh, wait a second." She gave me a swift, suspicious look. "Are you the whale lady?"

"I study them, yes." I reached behind me and set down the champagne flute.

"And you guys used to date, right?"

"We were engaged," said Jackson.

"Fascinating. Well, I've got to circulate." She handed Jackson her empty cup. As she sifted through the crowd, smiling and waving at people, it occurred to me that I hadn't asked her name. She disappeared into the jade-and-apricot room, into a throng of women wearing party dresses and diamonds.

"Who was that?" I asked. I was thinking that I could be driven to extremes.

"Julianna Howell," he said. "She's a realtor, but I guess you figured that out?"

I nodded.

"She sold me a farm—that's where I live now. It's just an old farmhouse on Tater Peel Road, with dogs, outbuildings, and a summer garden. Forty-two acres. We dated about three months. She wanted to get married."

"And you didn't?"

"No, I'll never remarry." He set down his glass. "I think I've had enough of Cissy's hospitality. You want to leave? "

"Sure." The champagne was starting to bubble toward my brain. "This isn't a pickup, is it?"

"I hope so." He pointed. "Did you want to say good-bye to Cissy?"

"No, I don't have any manners."

"Me, either. I'll bring my truck around to the front. It's dark gold and looks like it's got muscles."

"What kind of truck do you have?"

"An antique one. A '52 Chevy. You watch for me, okay?"

"No need for that. I'll go with you."

"But it's parked way down the road. It's 38 degrees and pouring rain."

"That's okay. After Baja, rain is a novelty."

"Well, come on, then." He took my arm. "Let's get the hell out of here."

MINERVA PRAY

I lay there listening to the rain, worried sick that Freddie was having a bad time at that party. She had never been sociable. One time Ruthie took her to a birthday party, and she hid in the backseat. She was a first grader, I think—around the time her daddy died. Ruthie took one leg and I took the other. We made her go to that party, but I can't say it was the right thing to do.

From the other side of the wall, I could hear Eleanor getting ready for her bath—running water, lifting glass jars from the shelves, creaking open the hamper. Then I heard her splashing in the tub. She always did have an attraction to bathrooms. I wondered if all those family tragedies had took a toll. She was another one who didn't like to party. "Don't you slip and fall," I hollered.

"If I do," Eleanor called back, "it's Brother Stowe's fault. He's watching every move I make."

"Then take the picture down, honey."

"You take it down."

"Now?"

"No! I'm naked!"

Sometimes I just didn't know about Eleanor. She couldn't wipe her own rear end until she was five years old. One time she insisted on going by herself to the bathroom at Cain-Sloan in downtown Nashville. Wouldn't let us set foot in the ladies

room. Made us stand in the shoe department. Ruthie was pushing Freddie in a stroller, and her nerves were frayed. "Oh, go
ahead," she told Eleanor. "But you'll be sorry."

In those days, Ruthie was still a pretty woman. Straight, chin-
length brown hair, the bangs held back with tortoiseshell pins.
She had big brown eyes, and a heart-shaped face. She had a
habit of sucking in her cheeks, so she would look thinner. When
Eleanor did not come out of the ladies room, we began to fear
the worst. Ruthie said one of us would have to go in after her.
Finally the child popped out, just a-smiling. She proudly told us
she'd done Number Two, which had never happened in public.
"But who wiped you?" Ruthie asked.

"I got me a stranger to do it," Eleanor said.

"Tell me you didn't!" Ruthie groaned, and I knew it would be
a long time before she let Eleanor out in public again, not until
she was capable of wiping herself.

"I did, too. And there she is." Eleanor pointed to a redheaded
clerk in the ready-to-wear.

"Quick, let's go before she sees us," Ruthie said, aiming the
stroller toward the elevator.

"Wait!" I hollered. "Where are you going?"

"Across the street to Harvey's," she said over her shoulder.
"Where nobody knows us."

They say that bad luck comes in threes, like deaths and plane
crashes, but sometimes it comes in sixes. That is when it turns
into a full-fledged curse. Now, this was something I never
understood—how tragedies got attracted to a particular family.
Hard luck and heartbreak seemed to roost in the same old
places. Like pigeons, once troubles got used to you, they kept
coming back. It wasn't much different from the way a cat
pooped in a sandbox. Tragedy got used to the scent of a place.

When I first came to Tallulah, I truly believed that me and
Amos had outfoxed death. I'd cursed God and got away with it.

Amos thought we had suffered more than our share, that God, or whoever doled out tests of faith, was letting us rest for a spell. From our sorghum, we had laid by enough cash to buy us a little farm on Church Creek, about seven miles from town. In the olden days, there was a church, Hurricane Baptist, that was set high on the cliffs, over the exact spot where the creek emptied into the Cumberland River. During the Civil War it was known as Observation Point. The Confederates used the church as a hospital, but no Union troops ever braved that river. Tallulah was too far off the beaten path, and the Federals had no intention of occupying it. Still, the Baptists kept watch, and the tradition lingered into the next century. Even now, long before you reached Tallulah, half the town knew you were coming. They'd either see you following the river on Highway 70, a road that was carved out of limestone, or they'd see you crossing the green bridge.

At Church Creek, me and Amos grew us a little corn and sorghum. We had us a tobacco allotment from the government. I was scared to go back to Texas, afraid of what-all I'd stir up. Meanwhile, I tried to live my life as best I could. On Sunday mornings I dressed my baby and carried her to Hurricane Baptist. On sunny afternoons, I laid her on a blanket and planted daffodils along my front walkway. When Ruthie got older, Amos rigged her up a tire swing. After a hard rain, I would stand in the corn, just listening to the water sifting down, counting all my blessings. The soil smelled of iron, and it gurgled fast, soaking up the moisture. Kneeling by the creek, digging up wild ferns with a tablespoon, I felt like a young girl.

In 1957, Ruthie took a hankering after Fred McBroom. She was sixteen years old. Before I knew it, she was planning a big wedding at Hurricane Baptist. Amos and I thought it was a good match. The McBrooms went all the way back to Scottish kings, Ruthie told us. Nowadays, they ran the doughnut shop on North Jefferson, one block off the square. The shop sat in the shade of a hackberry tree. When you opened the door, a little bell jingled. Inside were three glass cases, shaped into a giant upside-down U. A few metal tables were scattered about. On Saturdays, before Winn-Dixie began selling doughnuts by the dozen, people had to take a number and wait their turn. They'd set in those metal chairs or gaze into the cases. The doughnuts came in chocolate, caramel, brown sugar, and cinnamon. Some oozed red jam or pale yellow cream. There was a shelf of pastel petit fours, powdery wedding cakes, walnut brownies. A book filled with pictures of wedding cakes stood on a little easel.

Ruthie and Fred got married, and they moved into the yellow clapboard house on River Street. Mr. McBroom was a widower, and he liked having the young people around. The house had two big porches, with fine views of the Cumberland River. Ruthie loved being a wife. She swept the wood floors and polished the silver. In the attic, she found a whole set of Limoges china—each dish was decorated with fishes. On Saturdays, she helped out at the bakery, bagging the pastries or helping housewives make up their minds. Sometimes she helped old Mr. McBroom in the kitchen, frosting cakes with butter cream. She learned to tint small batches and stuff it into pastry bags. Mr. McBroom had a box of metal tips. He showed her how to pipe out pink roses and rumpled green leaves. Flowers on birthday cakes was popular in Tallulah—everybody wanted white sheet cakes with either pink or blue icing, depending if it was for a boy or a girl.

Eleanor was born in 1958. Three years later, when Ruthie was pregnant with Freddie, Mr. McBroom took a wasting disease. In no time flat, he shriveled up to nothing. Me and Amos came every day to help out. We'd watch after little Eleanor or fix Mr. McBroom something soft to eat, like poached eggs. Amos would read him the newspaper. The poor old thing didn't last no time. His skin hung from the bones and the whites of his eyes turned yellow. His face looked like it had been washed with egg yolks. His passing was slow and hard—back then you died at home. A hundred times a day me and Ruthie washed Mr. McBroom's feet and changed his linens. His stools were the color of dry mustard, with a little water mixed in. The pain drew him into knots, and he'd moan so loud that little Eleanor moaned along with him. I hate to say this, but it was a relief when he finally died.

The next death came in August 1966. Amos and Eleanor were walking to town, headed to Mr. Harris's fruit stand on Freeze Street. Ruthie was pregnant again, this time with Jo-Nell, and she had a craving for peach ice cream. She was seven months along. Humming in the kitchen. Making shortbread cookies. Freddie, who couldn't have been more than four, stood on a chair, making a mess creaming butter and sugar. I was dragging out the ice cream maker, slapping cobwebs with a rag. Hunting for rock salt in the pantry. Meanwhile, Amos and Eleanor turned onto Freeze Street. I knew, because Mr. Harris told me all about it. He said the sky lit up with lightning, and then it thundered. A light rain began falling. Eleanor skipped ahead, waiting in the fruit stand for her granddaddy. Mr. Harris reached down and gave her a ripe plum. She called out to Amos, hurry up, she said. A big crooked bolt of lightning came down. It knocked Amos into the road—knocked his shoes right off his feet and burnt every hair on his head, fraying them like copper wires. He was dead before he hit the ground, said Mr. Harris.

They sent Ruthie's pastor to break the news. He was a young man, fresh out of the Baptist seminary. By the time he knocked at the back door, it was raining hard—one solid noise on the roof, like a fifty-pound sack of corn had busted in the sky. Freddie slid off her stool and unlatched the screen door. The pastor just stood there. His hair was slicked down, and his chin was dripping water. He wore a short-sleeve white shirt, and it was so wet, it looked transparent, with his pink skin shining through. Ruthie was taking her shortbread from the oven. She laid it on the counter, rubbed her back, and slogged toward the door.

"Why, Brother Pearson, you're just drenched!" She reached out to pull him into her kitchen. Through the open door, the rain hissed louder. I saw a low gray sky, heard a crackle of lightning. In the distance, trees were smeary green, swaying back and forth. It looked to me like a set-in rain. I grabbed the tail of Freddie's dress and told her to fly to the bathroom and fetch towels for the preacher. She took off running, while me and Ruthie tried to dry him with dishcloths. We didn't have a inkling nothing was wrong, even though it wasn't every day you had a dripping wet preacher in your kitchen.

It had been a long time since I had to pick out a coffin, but Fred and Ruthie went with me to the funeral home. It was still pouring rain, and the radio was warning about flash floods.

The undertaker, Mr. Eubanks, took us down creaky basement stairs, where the caskets were strewn about on the concrete floor. A bare light bulb dangled from the rafters. The walls were made of gray cement blocks, turning darker in spots from the seeping rain. I drew in a deep breath—this was going to be hard. The air smelled musty, and I realized we were deep in the ground. I could almost hear the rain collecting behind the cement walls.

Ruthie walked between the coffin rows, her hands holding up her belly. Her eyelids were swollen double, and she hadn't eaten all day. I was scared the shock would bring on the baby. She picked up a brochure and showed it to me. All of the coffins cost a arm and a leg, more than a set of bedroom furniture. Included in the cost (according to the brochure) were things that money couldn't buy, like ten free copies of the death certificate, sympathy notes, printed obituary booklets, and notification to Social Security and the U.S. government for tax purposes.

Mr. Eubanks told me to pick out what I wanted. Since he'd known Amos and liked him so much, I was getting a discount,

ten percent. "We can set you up a payment plan," he explained.
You can pay this off in thirty easy monthly installments."

As I studied all the coffins, my heart beat hard, like a storm
was going on inside me, too. I pictured hail, thunderclaps. I did
not believe, not for one second, that Amos would know or care
which model I picked. I thought he was somewhere I could not
see or reach, plowing up the corn or digging wild ferns along
the creek. Still, I hated to put his sweet body in a cheap coffin. It
seemed like a lack of respect for all he'd been.

Ruthie liked a gray polished model with a tufted blue lining,
and we picked that. On the way out of the basement, Fred saw
a big pine box under the staircase. "Is that a chicken coop?" he
asked.

"Nearbouts," said Mr. Eubanks, laughing into his cupped
hand. "That's for the most shiftless of all niggers, for no-good
white trash that their own people don't claim."

"It seems real practical," said Fred, squatting down for a better look. "When my time comes, Ruthie, put me in this."

"Why, she wouldn't dare! I'd sell it over my dead body." Mr.
Eubanks flushed, and sweat broke out across his forehead. He
headed up the stairs, into the first floor's gloomy light. The next
day, the Tallulah *Gazette* ran a story about Amos, calling it an
irony: MAN STRUCK BY LIGHTNING ON FREEZE STREET.

Two years later, Mr. Eubanks had passed to his own reward,
and so had Fred McBroom. It was late January 1968, and Fred
had been driving home from Nashville in a ice storm. He had
gone to a big wholesale store to buy baking pans and whole
wheat flour—it was the latest rage with the college people; they
wanted everything natural. The storm had come up all of a sudden, within hours, and the temperature dropped from 40
degrees to 28. It started raining, but in spite of the temperature,
it never changed to snow—the ground was too warm. Ice
encased all the trees and bushes, and the roads were a clear,
glossy black.

On curvy, treacherous Highway 70, Fred's van skidded on the ice, broke through a guard rail, and tumbled down a steep holler. The van mowed down cedar saplings, snapping them off at the ground. The Civil Defense later said it looked like a machete had swept through, chopping down the trees at random. Fred McBroom was dead on arrival at Tallulah General. It just didn't seem fair—to die when you were only twenty-eight years old. He'd left behind a wife, three little daughters, and a secret recipe for the best doughnuts in town.

Once again me and Ruthie climbed down the stairs to the basement of the funeral home, weaving through the coffins, listening to Carl E. Eubanks Jr. praise each one's failings and virtues. Since our last visit, prices had creeped up. Business was brisk, said Junior, thanks to the Vietnam War. The Eubanks Funeral Home was the first in Tennessee to offer a patriotic model—a red, white, and blue casket; full flag drape; a patriotic musical selection, including a Sousa march, to be played by musicians from the college—either at the funeral home or the cemetery, take your pick.

Ruthie was weeping into a balled-up Kleenex. She had baby Jo-Nell on her hip—she was two years old—and she kept reaching out to grab Junior's eyeglasses. "You're a little firecracker," said Junior, trying to sound friendly, but it was real clear that he didn't like children. I thought back to what Fred had told us about the pine box, and I wondered if we'd have the courage to do it. Ruthie was only twenty-seven years old, too young to be a widow. I myself knew about living alone—how crazy it can make you if you don't stay busy. I still had my house at Church Creek, and not a day went by that I didn't think Amos would walk up the back steps, open the door, and ask me when supper was going to be ready. I'd be half-asleep, and I'd hear him call my name—*Minerva*? I'd wake up, my heart pounding, and I'd swear that I could smell him.

In 1970, she began courting a rich boy. His name was Wyatt

Pennington, the only child of Money and Alfred, who owned the woolen mill on Sycamore Road. Money, who had a teaching certificate from George Peabody College, had fancy ideas for her boy. They did not include a widow with three children. When the engagement was announced, Money took to her bed. She considered herself a local monarch—the county had been named after her husband's people. On her side of the family, the Havilands, she claimed that one of her forebears had signed the Magna Carta. It disgusted her that Wyatt had picked a commoner. Me and Amos weren't even locals, you see, and that seemed to eat away at the Penningtons.

"Texans!" cried Money, wrinkling her nose. "Why, that's in another state!"

I couldn't deny it. We had come up from Texas, and nobody cared if we'd been well-to-do, comfortable, or trash. My people had been wildcatters, and the Amos's people were ranchers. It didn't matter that a Pray had come within a hair of dying at the Alamo. These crazy Tennesseans had their own histories and genealogies—especially Money. She didn't have room for anybody else's legends. I didn't waste my time talking about Texas or our ranch with the cattle and the peach orchard. I could tell the Penningtons had already made their minds up about us. That's what small towns do: close ranks against you.

A lot of people have asked me why Ruthie married Wyatt Pennington. Was it the money? Was it the glory of marrying into the Magna Carta? No, I can't say as it was, seeing as she'd already married into Scottish kings. To tell the truth, Ruthie was a simple girl. Happy to sweep floors, knead bread dough, and set out her tomato plants of a spring morning. She had four dresses in her closet, which I thought was a disgrace, and her only jewelry was a gold cross her daddy give her one Christmas. In another place and time, she would have made a good lady's maid, or else a nun, but in Tallulah, Tennessee, she was destined to be the bride of a spoiled rich man.

Money did what she could to draw things to a halt, but the nuptials took place as planned. After the honeymoon, Money started harassing her boy to get a job. "You could help me at the doughnut shop," Ruthie said, trying to help.

"I don't like the smell of yeast," said Wyatt.

"Well, *learn!*" Money stamped her foot.

"It gags me." He made a face.

"What would you prefer?" asked Money, dead serious. "You can work in a men's shop. You're good at matching ties to pin-striped suits. Or I could set you up in the insurance business."

"I don't know what I want to do." Wyatt examined his fingernails. "There's nothing I like."

"Son, you aren't supposed to *like* what you do. Do you think your daddy *likes* running the woolen mill?"

"Oh, Daddy doesn't run anything. He plays thirty-six holes of golf every day."

"Don't you dare criticize your daddy. Why, you little family black sheep," Money yelled. "I should cut you out of the will."

"Baa-baa," replied Wyatt, then lowered his head, inviting a motherly pat.

Money came over every Sunday afternoon, the only day Ruthie didn't work, and rearranged all the furniture. She told me I should stop visiting so much, to leave the honeymooners alone. She was always begging Ruthie to let the three girls sleep over at her house. It will be a treat for me, she'd say, pushing the girls out the door. They'd look back at me, begging with their eyes. Eleanor was twelve, Freddie was eight, and Jo-Nell was four.

It got to where Jo-Nell would hide when she heard Money's voice. You'd call and call, but that child never answered. She did not talk plain for her age, but there wasn't nothing wrong with her hearing. She was just babified. One morning in late February, I found her hiding behind the bookcase—I saw these two blue eyes just a-watching me. I said, "It's all right, baby. Money is gone."

At this, Jo-Nell squeezed out. "Me firsty," she said.

"Then let's go down to the kitchen, and I'll fix you some hot chocolate."

After I got her settled at the table, she picked up her mug and took a dainty sip. Then she set it down. "Hock," she explained.

"Jo-Nell, baby," I said. "Why don't you like Money?"

"N-munna," she said.

"Em Unna?" I was confused.

"No, N-M-Uhh," she said. "Hut Lownell."

Lownell was what she called herself, and *hut* stood for *hurt*. "She hurt you, baby?" I kept my voice low, so I wouldn't scare her.

She nodded.

"How?"

"N-M-Uh," she kept saying. Then she reached under her dress and pointed to her privates. I didn't know what an *N-M-Uh* was, but I knew it was bad. Still, Money was the president of the garden club. It was hard to believe she'd hurt a child. When I told Ruthie, she said she'd get to the bottom of it. Well, one thing or another cropped up. Eleanor got to where she couldn't see the blackboard at school, and it turned out she needed glasses. Freddie won a statewide science contest. Jo-Nell got real sick with a lung ailment, something called histoplasmosis, what nearly everybody in middle Tennessee gets, and she spent one whole summer in bed.

Two years later Wyatt fell in love with a go-go dancer. Naturally Ruthie didn't have a clue. To tell the truth, it came as a shock to me. You would think a marriage would last in a house full of chess pies and cinnamon twist-aparts; in a bedroom with a dual-controlled electric blanket and white Priscilla curtains on the windows, with the Venetian blinds heaved all the way up to let in the smell of the river. But only the Lord knows what would have made Wyatt Pennington happy.

It was the summer of 1972, and I'll never forget because Ruthie and I were in the kitchen chopping onions and celery for

potato salad. Wyatt flung open the back door, all flushed and
wall-eyed. I could tell he'd been drinking. Ruthie was too busy
chopping to notice. She looked up, tears streaming down her
cheeks from the onions. Then she lifted the knife and waved it,
as if to say hello, but Wyatt must have misunderstood. He ran
out of the kitchen. Ruthie gave me a look, then laid down the
knife. She ran upstairs after him. After a minute, I went, too.

She was standing in the doorway, watching Wyatt pack his
clothes. He walked back and forth from the dresser to the bed. I
didn't know where he was going, but I knew it would take him
a longish time to fill the suitcases because he loved fine clothes.
Twice a year Money paid a tailor to hand-sew him suits and
shirts and vests. Even his ties came from New York City. "Talk
to me, Wyatt," begged Ruthie. "Why are you packing?"

"Don't you know?" He swung around, staring at her. "I
mean, you were crying and waving that knife at me."

"I was chopping onions," she said.

"I see." He opened his underwear drawer and took out a
clean, white stack, smoothing it with his hand.

"Wyatt, look at me. What don't I know?"

"I'm leaving."

"I can see that; but where are you going?" said Ruthie. From
the look on her face, I could tell she was hoping he was going to
Atlanta to see the Braves—an overnight trip.

"Nashville," he said, scooping out jockey shorts.

There was a thrumming silence, as if he'd said a bad word.
"Why are you going there?" she asked.

"Because I'm in love with Betty June Price."

"Excuse me?" Ruthie's eyes popped wide open.

"She's a twenty-nine-year-old dancer," he explained.

"Twenty-nine? Maybe in dog years," scoffed Ruthie. "I'll just
bet she's lying."

Wyatt stopped packing. He looked up at Ruthie. "You haven't
seen her."

"Oh, I can imagine." Ruthie crossed her arms.

"Her age doesn't matter. She's beautiful." Wyatt shut his powder-blue Samsonite cases, clicking the latch. "And that's all that counts with me."

"But you said I was beautiful." Ruthie's eyes were bulging with tears.

"*Was*," he said, blinking at her. "That's the key word."

He drove to Nashville in his brand-new lizard-green New Yorker, with the dancer riding shotgun. Even for Tallulah, it was tacky. A few weeks later we heard that he choked to death on his own vomit. Everyone in Tallulah wanted to know the dirty details—had Wyatt Pennington died in his sweetheart's arms? Had they been having an orgy, as rumored, or did he eat too much roast beef at the Belle Meade Cafe? Some people said murder. Nobody ever found out, because the dancer was never seen again. She'd left them poor children of hers back in Tallulah with a teenage baby-sitter. Finally, some relatives were located in Ohio, and the kids was sent up north on a Greyhound.

The morning Wyatt was buried, it came a hard thunderstorm. An hour before the funeral, both the toilets in Ruthie's house stopped up and ran over, and the tub filled with chopped onions and urine. "What have I done to deserve this?" cried Ruthie, madly plunging the toilet. "Is the Lord trying to tell me something?"

"It's the curse," I said. "Nothing but a curse."

A neighbor-man came over with a box of sulfur acid. He poured it down the drain, filling the house with a putrid smell. "You need a plumber," said the neighbor. "It'll have to wait," Ruthie told him, herding the girls out the front door. "We're late for the funeral."

All during the eulogy people kept sniffing. It shocked me that this many folks were heartbroke over Wyatt. Then a small boy hollered, "Mama, what stinks so bad?" "Shhh, shhh," said the mother, but it was too late. I realized that we carried the smell of the neighbor-man's drain cleaner. Across the aisle, Money fixed her eyes on me and Ruthie, as if to say, This is a funeral. You could have at least bathed.

On her way out of the cemetery, Money's black spectator pumps skidded in mud, and she fell sideways in the gravel road. Her pocketbook slid under the hearse. The moment she went to reach for it, the undertaker got into the hearse and took off driving. The hubcap snagged Money's lace blouse, dragging her all the way to Broad Street. She was buried in the Pennington family plot, between her husband and son.

Church ladies brought chicken casseroles in Corningware dishes, the party kind with cheddar cheese, slivered almonds, and crushed potato chips. We'd each take a spoon and go sit on the sofa that Wyatt bought before he left—tan Naugahyde with big saddlebag pillows. While the television flickered, casting red and blue light on the walls, we watched the Democratic Convention. All the stars in California were coming out for McGovern, but in my heart I knew he was doomed. I could see it in his eyes, all slanted down in the corners. We passed the Corning bowl back and forth, dipping out hunks and licking our spoons.

Even with the casseroles, Ruthie lost so much weight that her wedding rings fell off and slid down the kitchen drain. She walked into the plate-glass window at Citizen's Bank and broke her nose. Everybody in town predicted that she would not last the year. She was pasty-white, as if she'd powdered her face and limbs with all-purpose flour. Sometimes she would cook all night long, with the radio station playing polkas in the background.

Around this time she started drinking on the sly. She favored Jack Daniels and Wild Turkey, slipping it into her iced tea. One time Freddie accidentally picked up her mama's glass, and you would have thought she'd broke into Fort Knox. "Give me that!" Ruthie cried, lunging for the striped tumbler, but the girl was too fast.

"What's in this?" Freddie lowered her nose to the rim.

"Nothing but tea and cough syrup," Ruthie said, snatching up the glass. I would have worried, but she didn't drink every night, just when the blues hit. Then she'd lock herself in the bedroom, crying and drinking and listening to Frank Sinatra records.

A few years later, the drinking stopped, and Ruthie started courting Mr. Peter Crenshaw. He ran the dime store on the square, the Eagle 5 & 10, which was in head-to-head competition with Kuhn's. It all started when Ruthie bought a blue parakeet. Mr. Crenshaw was just tickled to death. He helped her pick out a cage, birdseed, and a cuttlebone. He even threw in a bird mirror. Ruthie said he followed her clear out to the sidewalk. Even some of the customers stopped to watch him moon after her. He was a widower, a past president of Rotary—a little old for my Ruthie, but who was counting?

She went back the next day, picking out a green parakeet. That girl must have bought seven birds before Mr. Crenshaw got the nerve to call her up. They had supper at the boat dock, then came back to the house for fresh-squeezed lemonade (the girls had made it, along with a platter of peanut butter cookies). It did my heart good to see Ruthie all perked up. Mr. Crenshaw brought her little presents—chocolate-covered peanuts from his candy counter, plastic coin holders, smelly blue bottles of My Sin. The three girls liked having the older man around, especially since he owned a dime store. Jo-Nell would climb in his lap, begging him to make his Adam's apple bob up and down. Sometimes he pulled quarters out of his right ear, tossing them to Freddie and Eleanor. Best of all, he owned a little half-boxer dog that followed him everywhere. Rebel Rouser was his name, and he had a great big black spot around his right eye. Like Mr. Crenshaw, the dog could also perform tricks—he could shake hands, play dead, and howl to the tune of "Oh, Susannah."

Ruthie said he wanted to marry her, but he had a grown daughter in Oak Ridge. He was afraid she might disapprove.

"This sounds like trouble," I told her. He was closer to my age than hers.

"Don't you worry. I can deal with the daughter." Ruthie winked. "I've got me a secret weapon."

"You and Nixon would make a fine pair," I said, laughing.

"No, I mean it."

"Then you'd better explain."

"Let me put it this way. Do you know the strongest fiber on earth? Well, it's pussy hair."

"Ruthie!"

"If I can get him in bed, he'll forget about our ages."

"Don't you *dare* have relations with that man!" The blood pounded in my ears.

"Mama, I'm not exactly a virgin. I know what I'm doing."

"I can't listen to another word." I cupped my hands over my ears. Eleven weeks later, Mr. Crenshaw sold his store and moved to Oak Ridge. Ruthie not only stopped eating, she gave up cooking. I brought hen soup, meat loaf, salmon patties, and lasagne, but she wouldn't eat a bite. Her shoulder blades jutted out like gull wings. For days on end, she sat in her dark bedroom, fingering a dime store scarf and listening to Sinatra. Liquor bottles showed up in the garbage. She began hoarding all sorts of crazy things, like relish jars, newspapers, tin cans, old *Redbook*s. The mess filled up the kitchen, spreading into the dining room, hallway, and front parlor.

"Why are you saving all this?" I asked.

"Because I just can't stand to throw it away," she told me, fingering a French's mustard jar. "I may need it someday."

Next, she turned the parakeets loose, letting them fly around in the spare bedroom. All the saved newspapers went on the floor, catching seeds and doody. "You all could get bird diseases," I said. "Ain't there laws against letting them fly loose in a house?"

"There ought to be laws against keeping them caged," she said. "It's cruel."

I feared the worst—pregnancy—but she wasn't carrying no baby, she was carrying grief, and it was eating her alive. A year to the day that Mr. Crenshaw left town, Ruthie hanged herself on the Venetian blinds in her bedroom. I hadn't expected this. She did not leave no note, so I was left to wonder. The worst part is Eleanor found her—just came home from school and there was her mama, dangling.

By this time I was practically an expert on funerals. When I went down to see Mr. Eubanks, he clapped me on the back and said, "Minerva, I'm giving you a fifteen percent discount. You take the award for picking out the most coffins."

I was tired of well-meaning folks, telling me it was time I got over being heartbroke. When somebody tells you that, a little bell ought to ding in your mind. Some people don't know grief from garlic grits. There's some things a body ain't meant to get over. Now I am not suggesting you wallow in sorrow, or let it drag on; no, I am just saying that it never really goes away. A death in the family is like having a pile of rocks dumped in your front yard. Every day you walk out and see them rocks. They're sharp and ugly and heavy. You just learn to live around them the best way you can. Some people plant moss or ivy; some leave it be. Some folks take the rocks, one by one, and build a wall.

I closed up my house at Church Creek and moved in with the girls. First thing, I trapped them parakeets and gave them to the elementary school, cages and all. Next, I rolled up my sleeves and cleaned the house. It took me three months to haul out the jars, papers, and tin cans. Sometimes I'd fall into bed, too tired to sleep. All during the night I'd hear one of the girls crying. I wasn't sure if it was the right thing to do, but I drove to the nursery and bought a pink hydrangea. Then I told each girl to sit down and write their mama a letter. "Write down everything you meant to say," I suggested. Next, we went out into the yard, and they watched while I dug a hole. I let the girls drop in their letters. The four of us planted that hydrangea. It took hold in the soil—sometimes blooming cream, sometimes pink. That whole summer, it gave us cut flowers but mostly it gave us hope.

All them years I kept right busy raising and lowering things—cakes, yeast, oven doors, children. I began to use the doughnut shop as a giant kitchen. There was a long marble counter where I kneaded sourbread dough (from Annette Donnell's starter). Four ovens baked a month's worth of apple spice cake. Every single Wednesday, I searched the newspapers for recipes. Whole years went by, and it seemed like all I did was bake, label, and freeze. Inside the deep freeze, I stashed peach and pecan pies, chocolate layer cakes, banana nut bread. Pot roast, vegetable soup, spaghetti, stew, chili. If it froze good, I made it. Whenever I heard tell of somebody keeling over in their garden or growing a tumor in their brain, I went into the freezers, sifted through the foil-wrapped containers, and drove over to the house of the bereaved. I always took a entire meal if I could. Later, after Jo-Nell got me hooked on garage sales, I bought two used upright freezers and set them up in the garage. With so much extra room, I branched out, taking cakes and roasts to the sick and injured. If you lived in Tallulah and you had anything from a kidney stone to liver cancer, I would be there.

I taped my name to the bottom of plates and pans. I wouldn't have cared if my dishes got back to me or not—plates is cheap, child. I wondered if I needed to put my mark anywhere at all, so's the folks could have a new cake plate or sandwich tray. I thought the true spirit of giving didn't have no name tag. Yet I couldn't break myself from labeling. I guess I kindly wanted people to know I'd cared enough to bring a apple pie or frozen cherry salad. Here, my pie or roast would say. It's me, Minerva Pray. Take a load off, come set awhile. Put your feet up and eat you a bite. Now there, ain't that better?

I thought I had it all under control—this curse-and-death

business. Have casserole will travel. That was me. As if food could heal all the hurt parts of the self. I suspected that it took more than turkey divan to heal your sorrows. So I took to setting all day with sick folks so the wife (or husband) could get a bite to eat or run a load of laundry. I liked the hospital best, because I could tell at a glance how many people were needy. If the patient was in a coma, I'd take my knitting and set by the window. For the wide-awake, I'd fetch ice or talk about what's going on at Senior Citizens; or I'd read them the newspaper. "You are an angel, Minerva Pray," people told me. "You are a godsend."

Well, maybe I was to them, but not to my granddaughters. They did not like my little hobby. They each one had something smart to say about it. You should be a nurse and get paid for it, but I didn't care. As the years wore on, they seemed embarrassed to have an old granny running the show. Opening the door to boys and hollering up the stairs in my creaky, wavy voice, *Jo-Nell?* or *Freddie?* Then, to the boys, I'd say, "You be sure and be back here at eleven."

I was at the tail end of my life, or nearbouts, and they was just starting out. Eleanor was a natural-born cook, Freddie was always winning them awards at school, but Jo-Nell was boy-crazy. She passed herself to men like she was a Whitman Sampler—she let them take little nibbles, squeezing out her good stuff.

I knowed all along what she was doing.

If only I could have been the granny I'd always dreamed. Not the dating police, not the one who made them clean their closets and go to church. No, I wanted to be the kindly, pie-baking grandma whose sole purpose in life was to be a comfort. No, I had to be Mother, Daddy, and Minerva, all rolled up into one. There wasn't no choice. When they all pulled away from me— in different directions, to be sure—I guess I made up my mind to be granny to the world. It was a unusual hobby, but it was the only thing I knew to do. If Ruthie knew what-all was going on, she'd roll over in the grave. I called up Hattie and said, "I've let down my granddaughters."

"No, you haven't," she said. "These days all the young people is running wild. They've got too many hormones, but they'll simmer down. You just wait and see."

"You really think so?" I asked. After all day of setting with these strange, sick Tennesseans—folks who were, after all, not so very different from the ones back in Mount Olive—it was Hattie's sweet voice that comforted me. It was far better than a sheet cake with pink icing and strawberries.

"I do," she said. We fell silent for a spell. In the background I heard the sink running, and I knew she was watering her sweet potato vines.

"Hattie? Do you think we're put on this earth to help each other?" I asked after a while.

"Why, sure," she said.

"The girls say I help too much, that I give and give until I'm empty."

"Don't they mean you give until your freezer is empty?" She laughed.

"I don't know what they mean."

"Well, they probably don't, either. They're just busy with their lives is all. And, Minerva, they're so young. Their bones are still growing. They'll get some sense later on down the road."

"Is that what we have?" I laughed. "Sense?"

"Minnie, girl," she said. "Ain't that enough, child?"

Jo-Nell got married in 1984, the day after she finished high school. I hate to say this, but in a way it was a relief to have her gone. I didn't have to sit up at night, wondering where she was—if she was hurt or in trouble. She and Bobby Hill rented a two-bedroom house by the college and bought a beagle puppy. He put up a clothesline in the backyard, and she roasted chickens. Three months after the wedding, Bobby drove his convertible into the back of a produce truck, causing an avalanche of Texas watermelons. The Highway Patrol said it wouldn't have mattered if the top had been up on the convertible, the boy would have been crushed just the same.

"I am doomed," said Jo-Nell at the funeral home, and everyone agreed. She cried so hard that her eyes swelled shut. Over the next few years, we got hit by a rash of troubles, like when a peeping Tom caught Eleanor stepping out of the bathtub and *he* screamed first; or when Freddie got kicked out of medical school; or when Jo-Nell's third husband gave her crabs. Yet I couldn't rightly say that we'd suffered any tragedies, other than Bobby Hill's death. I wondered if it was possible for a curse to end.

Now Eleanor let the water out of the tub. It sucked down the drain, making a gagging noise. The bathroom door opened, and a wedge of light fell into the hall. She padded into my room, all splay-footed and flat-faced, wearing pink sponge curlers and her daddy's old purple plaid robe. Outside, a car pulled into the driveway, scattering gravel. I heard two doors slam, then two sets of footsteps.

"That must be Freddie," I said.

"Well, it's about time." Eleanor crept over to the window. She pinched back the blinds, the same ones her mama hung herself from. Voices floated up to us, and I strained to listen.

"Thanks for the ride," said Freddie. The front door creaked open, then slammed shut. Eleanor kept on peeking through the blinds, twisting her body around. "Why, it's that old Jackson Manning," she hissed.

"Chili's boy?" I said.

"Mmmhum. Picking right up where he left off. And she's married! Why, she's starting to date and carry on like Jo-Nell. It must be something in the air."

"It sounds like a ride home," I said. "Not hanky-panky."

"Ha, that's how it starts." Eleanor snorted. "Next thing you know, she'll be in a dirty little love triangle."

"Oh, I doubt it." I sighed, wishing I lived in Texas. Oh, you just had to wonder. You raise them half-decent, and they grow up and leave. They move to Miami or California—someplace with gourmet groceries and nude beaches because you've reared them to cook good and be liberal-minded. It's just the opposite with your failures—them kids stick to your tail like a cocklebur. You'd think it would be the other way around, but it's not. No matter how old I get, this will always amaze me.

JO-NELL

The Yankee nurse came in with a pain shot. I wasn't hurting anywhere, but I needed to chill out. So I rolled over and let her stab it into my ass. It's bruised to high heaven—yellow, green, purple, black. Like spoiled fruit. I was in my new room on the medical-surgical floor, and a potted amaryllis was sitting in the window. The card was signed, *Thinking of you, Dr. Jay Lambert.* Next to the amaryllis were two vases of roses. One was from the ambulance driver; the other was from a local politician I used to see. He'd signed the card *BD*. He had high hopes of rising to power in the Tennessee Republican Party, so he had to give me up. A fern basket sat on the floor—a present from the gang at Billy Ray's Tire and Alignment.

As I stared at my flowers, the colors ran together. I felt dizzy-headed, so I closed my eyes and drifted.

When I was growing up I not only dreamed in color, I sleep-walked. Once I got all the way down to the street. I was wearing a purple shortie nightgown that I'd got for my birthday. Minerva opened the front door and hollered, "Jo-Nell! You get back in this house!" I ran inside screaming, and to this day I don't remember anything but Minerva standing on the porch, yelling at me.

Sometimes I dreamed about driving in the car with Mama and my sisters, long before she died. She was singing along with the radio. "American Pie" and "MacArthur Park." Mama just loved food songs. I dreamed we were all coming out of the funeral home, wearing white gloves and hand-smocked dresses, and people said, Poor little motherless things. I dreamed that it was graveyard day, and we were helping Minerva pick flowers, and there were always red bugs and seed ticks in the honeysuckle and Queen Anne's lace. I dreamed we were eating pecan and lemon chess pies, drinking iced tea with fresh mint leaves. I dreamed of long, hot summer afternoons, sitting in the kitchen making terrariums while Freddie sunned herself in the backyard, stretched out on a quilt, her transistor radio playing "You're So Vain" and "Bad, Bad Leroy Brown."

I dreamed further into the past, in pure Technicolor, back to when Mama was married to that no-good Wyatt Pennington. I dreamed that I was raised by Money and Dr. Spock. *A* for *accidents* and *adenoids*; *B* for *balkiness* and *bowel movements*; *C* for *colic* and *constipation*; *D* for *discipline* and *dog bites*; *E* for *eczema, earache,* and *enema.* It was the same nightmare I'd had for years and years—so clear and true, it felt more like a memory.

In this dream there was a red plastic bag hanging behind Money's bathroom door, like a long, plucked goose. The tube was long and flexible, attached to a white nozzle. First, she would get rid of my sisters. Then she'd go into one of the empty bedrooms and lay out a waterproof sheet, all covered with thick towels. "Jo-Nell?" she'd call out, her voice sweet.

I was just a little girl, but I wasn't stupid. The way she stretched out my name like that, I knew she wanted to hurt me. I hid in the back of her closet, where it smelled of leather and sweaty feet. I pressed myself flat against the wall. *N-M-Uh*, I thought.

"Jo-Nell? Sweetheart? Don't make this hard on Grandmother, please."

She wasn't my grandmother, but I knew she'd catch me. No matter how hard I kicked, even if I sank my teeth into her arm, she'd chase me out of the closet with a belt. Then she'd wrestle me to the bed and pull my butt apart, jabbing me with the enema. It had a hard tip that was smeared with Pond's Cold Cream. Sometimes she'd hold the bag high, and my insides would cramp. I'd claw at her face, but she'd only lift the bag higher. She wore a grim expression, like a miner boring deep into a vein of ore, a mustache of sweat on her upper lip. But her eyes glittered. She made a sound in between laughing and crying.

"Do *not* kick," she warned and whacked my leg with the belt. Each time I wiggled or screamed, I'd get another slap. "Hold it in," she commanded.

The enema dreams were all different. Sometimes nothing came out, as if my insides were perforated like a colander. That made me happy. I wanted it to disappear and make her wonder. She'd make me lie there for thirty minutes; then she'd push the potty under me. If she wasn't satisfied, she'd dip the bag in the pail of milky water and give me another enema. She had an old chart on the bathroom wall, penned in her loopy handwriting: "½ cup = small infant, 1 cup = 1 yr. old child, 1 pint = up to 5 yrs."

In those nightmares, there were two Jo-Nells, the one who caught june bugs with her sisters and the one who got enemas. I dreaded the sound of my name and the way water dripped into a pail and how she smelled of Pond's and how cool her fingers felt against my skin. She didn't even seem aware of me unless I arched my back and screamed. I'd just blank out, which was worse than a nightmare.

One enema dream happened on a cloudy afternoon. The sky was getting dark. A storm was building to the west, but it was hours away from us. I was visiting Money, but I managed to escape. I'd gone to play at the water's edge with two boys from Second Avenue. We started a fire with Money's charcoal bricks, then roasted marshmallows until they flamed and turned crispy black. The boys kept poking twigs into the spent charcoal. The coals were gray and powdery, with orange centers.

"Don't do that," I warned, and they stared, rocking on the balls of their feet. I was older, and I liked to boss them. Still, the second I turned away, they jabbed the sticks, breaking open the soft, flaming coals. Money must have spotted me from the upstairs windows, and she came flying out of the house in her apron, pausing to snap off a slender branch from the hackberry tree. She stripped off all the leaves, then slogged down to the water. She switched me all the way to her house, while I danced in front of her. Once she got me inside, she chased me upstairs, where I threw myself onto the bed. The hackberry switch kept stinging my arms, legs, and back. With each blow she said, "Mustn't play with fire! Mustn't play with fire!"

She threw down the hackberry limb and abruptly left the room. I leaned over, snatched up the switch, and tossed it out the window. From downstairs I heard her rummaging around in the bathroom. Then she came upstairs, carrying a sloshing, steaming bowl. The enema bag was looped around her neck. I fought hard, kicking her in the titties, but she was stronger. First, she probed with her fingers, same as always.

"Just making sure I've got the right place," she said. "I don't want water squirting out your ears." She stuck the nozzle up me, and I felt the warm liquid seep into my bowels. I didn't even try to hold it in. I just let it flow onto the waterproof sheet, until it pattered against the floor. I screamed until the blood rushed into my head. Then I kicked her in the stomach, hard.

"Ooof!" she cried.

"N-M-Uh!" I yelled.

"Stop it, now. You stop it!" Money held the bag above her head, stretching the tube.

When she was finished with me, she calmly opened the door and fluttered out. I was lying on my side, hiccuping, trying to catch my breath. A little while later, the old black maid, Bernice, came into the room. She tried to help me stand up and pull up my panties; soapy water trickled down my leg. I heard the front door slam. Bernice and I looked out the window and saw Money on the front walk, sweeping in the dark. Car lights swept by, briefly illuminating her, but she kept swinging the broom like she was a regular person.

"She nuts," said Bernice.

"I hate her."

"Most peoples do."

"At least she doesn't put water up you." I sagged back to the bed and shut my eyes.

"No," said Bernice. "But I got to put up with her shit just the same."

Later, Money came back inside, still holding the broom, and opened my door. "Are you calm now?" she asked. "Would you like a meat loaf sandwich?"

"No." I pulled the quilt up to my chin.

"What were you and Bernice talking about?"

"You."

"Oh." She squeezed the doorknob. "And what did you all say?"

"That I'm sick and tired of getting enemas!" I shouted, feeling the veins stand out on my neck. It hurt. "You don't give them to anyone else but me. Why? Why!"

"Because you are constipated. They aren't. And if you ever tell anybody, I'll break your little neck. I'll burn your house down." She went over to the window and looked out. I could see dirty clouds heaped over the bluff, the same color as the river. Lightning flashed, a hairline crack, followed by a rumbling. A mild wind blew into the room, riffling the trees.

"There goes our nice night." Money sighed and shut the window.

JACKSON

I bought a bouquet at Flower Power—the florist knows what I like, coral roses, tiger lilies, bird of paradise. Then I drove up to the cemetery. I parked my truck next to the Confederate Dead monument and walked six rows east to the Manning plot. Kelly had a cherub on her stone, but the little wings had chipped off in places. Mother's was sleek rose granite, carved Martha Jackson Manning. She was supposed to be related to Andrew Jackson, but Daddy never believed it. He never believed her about anything, even when she got that lump in her breast. "For God's sake, Martha," he said, in an exasperated tone, "it's fibro-cystic disease."

"Just feel it," Mother said, reaching for his stubby hand.

"Martha, I feel women's breasts all day long. A man likes to rest when he gets home."

She asked me to feel it, too, but I declined. Seven months later she was dead. The cancer was a rare, inflammatory sort—like a firecracker going off, sending down sparks to her liver, brain, bone, and lungs.

Not too long afterward, I met Freddie. One chilly fall night she offered to cook supper at my apartment. I'd uncorked a bottle of Beaujolais, and she carried it into the little kitchen. Said she thought she'd poach our pears. I was impressed—a gourmet cook, I thought. I was a culinary idiot; I didn't know that something other than eggs could be poached. Much later, after I'd gorged myself on a pecan cheese ball and Wheat Thins, my tipsy darling emerged with the pears. She was completely nude, carrying a pottery tray with the fruits sticking up. She had forgotten to broil the salmon, forgotten to toss the salad or butter the rolls, but by God, we had pears. We ate them in bed, feeding bits of lemon zest to each other. It was, I thought, an auspicious beginning.

Before we went to medical school, I took my mother's two-carat diamond out of the lock box and had the jeweler set it in white gold—I just knew I had to marry Freddie McBroom. I even had it cut down to fit her finger. She was not a jewelry person, but she loved that ring. We had planned a long engagement, mainly because my daddy said that medical school marriages never lasted. Freddie didn't care. She had a room at the dorm, but she practically lived with me in Midtown. After she was kicked out of school, I couldn't understand it; I never dreamed she needed money—it wasn't like Freddie had a whole lot of wants. I groaned and blustered. "I can't *believe* this. Are you expelled, like, forever or can you reapply?"

"I don't know," she said. She was lying on the sofa, flossing her teeth.

"You don't know?" I yelled. "How can you not know?"

"Look," she said, "it's not you. It's me."

"It's the same thing. What happens to you, happens to me."

"That's not true."

"Yes! It is!"

"What, are you *ashamed* of me? Is that it?"

I just stared. I knew what she thought—ever since our days in cell biology, she'd described our relationship as the doctor's son cavorting with the baker's daughter. She swore it was a recipe for disaster. "I just can't believe it," I said. I began pacing our small living room. "You stole a fucking heart."

"It wasn't just a heart. It was a gallbladder, too. Anyway, I needed the cash. I was broke."

"I have money," I said, beating my chest. I reached out and grabbed her shoulders. "You could have come to me!"

"You aren't my keeper."

"No, just some idiot who loves you. Or at least I did."

She walked into the bedroom and started throwing clothes into paper sacks. She had never owned a lot; she said she didn't want to own anything she couldn't bear to lose. While she packed, I pretended to watch the ten o'clock news, my feet propped on the glass coffee table. I couldn't help but think of the dead Egyptians, carrying fruit and flowers from the pyramids to the next world, only Freddie was bringing everything to her childhood bedroom on River Street. After she'd filled two duffel bags, she stood in the doorway and said she was leaving. "Bye," I said, keeping my eyes on the television. She pulled off the diamond ring. It clinked in a glass ashtray. The door slammed, and she stepped out, into the muggy delta night.

There are a thousand details you discover about a person when you live with them, but I had a hard time decoding Freddie. Her hair was her most revealing feature—it smelled like freshly ironed linen napkins. She had no belongings—no furniture, no posters, no nothing, except a toothbrush, textbooks, and a few seedy clothes. There was nothing to hint at her real self. No habits, like chewing pencils or shredding Kleenex. No favorite foods, like olives and cream cheese. Even in motel rooms a person makes their mark, but Freddie was a minimalist. If she made a salami sandwich, she cleaned up after herself—not a stray crumb on the counter.

My ex-wife was just the opposite. You could size up Isabelle in five minutes, maybe less. Scattered about the house were copies of *Vogue*, *Gourmet*, and *Architectural Digest*. She also subscribed to *Women's Wear Daily*. The bathroom was filled with shells she'd picked up in Bermuda and little oil bottles, all tinted different colors, from a bath shop in Midtown. On her desk was a fat calendar opened to every day of her life—tennis, manicure, leg waxing, body sculpting class, herbalist, shrink, Junior League, power luncheons with Julie Fay of Fashions by Julie Fay. Tickets to the symphony were sticking out of the latest Tom Clancy novel. All over the house were nail files, Estée Lauder polish, recipes from the *Commercial-News*. A jar of capers on the counter, with a silver spoon sticking out of it. This was only the tip of Isabelle's iceberg, but still, you knew what waited below the surface.

After Freddie left me, I spent the night searching the apartment. She had left nothing behind, except two bobby pins stuck way back in a drawer, two long strands of brown hair, curled up in the shower drain, and a lemon zester. To this day I still have that zester, although the hair and pins have long since vanished. By the time I tracked her down in Tallulah, she was already living in California. The following year, my dad's wife (I forget which one) sent me a two-line notice in the Tallulah *Gazette* about Freddie's marriage to Sam Espy, Ph.D., another sort of doctor.

When I married Isabelle, I gave her a plain gold band—cried poor-mouth. She believed me. I was a poor pediatric student, with a year left in my training. All the while Freddie's ring was sitting in a box at Liberty Bank and Trust. It's still there. I never bought my wife a diamond, and I wonder if it's because I knew, even then, that we would fail each other. She was a blond goddess, a model for the trendiest boutique in Memphis and Germantown. I thought I loved her, but now I see that I wanted to be married. I think Isabelle wanted a doctor. I had planned to become a vascular surgeon, but I wasn't accepted into the residency. I matched up with pediatrics, my last choice. It was a worthy branch of medicine, to be sure, but it felt like a penance—spending the rest of my life examining screaming infants, listening to a litany of symptoms from overwrought mothers. I have since learned that the challenge lies in the boredom—not letting the one, true sick child go untreated. The baby with lymphocytic leukemia, meningitis, diabetes.

The money didn't suit Isabelle. She tried to keep up with the wives of cardiologists, orthopedic surgeons, obstetricians, anesthesiologists—the lucrative fields. Even if there had been more money, the town of Tallulah disappointed her. She hated the old red-brick facades around the square. The dress shops that still sold penny loafers and gored skirts and old-lady crepe. She pointed out the absence of a ballet, symphony, or tea room. The doughnut shop was, according to my wife, an abomination. Even a decent jewelry store eluded her. She drove to Nashville every day, as if it were her job to shop in Green Hills and Belle Meade.

At the end of two years, I was flat broke. My banker, George Carmichael, said it was impossible—I hadn't made stupid investments, bought luxury condominiums, or built a million-dollar house. Nevertheless, I was busted. When I explained this to my wife, she cried and fumed. The next day she went out and charged a five-thousand-dollar silver fox jacket. She began lunching with a shark realtor. Together they picked out two houses in the two-million-dollar range—a fifteen-room log "cabin" on two hundred acres and a replica of Tara on a half-acre lot.

A man has his ways of coping. I am ashamed to admit this, but I began seeing a pediatric nurse-practitioner—a cute, bouncy, big-cheeked girl who put me in mind of the Flying Nun.

It took about seven minutes for Isabelle to find out. When she did, she chased me around the house with a battery-operated carving knife. After the divorce, there was nothing left. No house, no car, not even a chair or a lamp. Both the wife and the Flying Nun were gone. I felt as if I'd been picked clean by vultures.

I thought of Freddie and her spare, low-maintenance life. It was liberating to have nothing—burglars wouldn't plague you, colleagues wouldn't be envious, and housekeeping was a snap. The thing was, I didn't have Freddie, just a ruptured bank account, a pile of debts, and a career that was dependent upon the sickness of children. I thought about leaving—going out to California and begging Freddie to take me back. I even went to Fred's Doughnuts and sidled up to Jo-Nell. "Show you the cream puffs?" she said. She was a blond, blue-eyed version of Freddie, with bigger hips and breasts. They had the same kind of smile, I noticed, with small white teeth.

"Sure," I said. "Uh, what do you hear from Freddie these day?" (Subtlety was never my forte.)

"She's getting a second master's degree," Jo-Nell said, hunkering down, sliding out a tray of pastries.

"Oh?" I said. I didn't know she had the first degree. The newspaper in Tallulah was usually fastidious about printing all the accomplishments and accolades of the locals. When there were omissions, it could be chalked up to two reasons—either the society editor, Miss Phyllis Gossett, didn't know about your recent coup, or she claimed not to know about it, which amounted to the same thing: exclusion. In Phyllis Gossett's eyes, the world was divided into people who mattered and people who did not. She adored social climbing, riding the coattails of various well-heeled citizens. She preyed upon people who could help her get what she wanted—she was a user. She had worshiped at the shrine of all the Penningtons, but she had no use for anyone named Pray or McBroom.

"I called it into the paper," Jo-Nell was saying, "but it was never printed. I told Phyllis Gossett that Freddie was swimming with whales. I mean, in the water with them. She said, 'My goodness, I hope one doesn't swallow her.' Isn't that bitchy? And jealous-hearted, too."

"Sounds like vintage Phyllis Gossett," I said. I was really mad—working up a sweat over this. "Trying to punish someone for achieving what she couldn't."

"She's hateful."

"Full of sour grapes."

"Full of shit, too." Jo-Nell pulled out another tray of doughnuts. "Freddie thinks it's funny. She's, like, respected everywhere *but* Tallulah. Minerva said, 'Don't you fret, Freddie. Even
Jesus wasn't accepted in His hometown.' Me, I hope Miss
Gossett never writes for anything better than the *Gazette*."

"I'm sure she won't." I was trying to figure out a way to work
the conversation back to Freddie, but Jo-Nell had a way of dom-
inating all situations. I bought a dozen cream puffs, cinnamon
swirls, jelly doughnuts, and a box of brownies. I took everything to the pediatric nurses station and left it on the counter.
On a prescription pad I wrote, *Enjoy—Dr. J. Manning*.

It proved to be a kind of turning point, because from that day
forward I was knee-deep in nurses. This was not bragging, just
the truth. Another divorced colleague, Dave Williams, a gas-
troenterologist, told me it's an occupational hazard—it has
nothing to do with good looks or ugliness, our riches or our
deficits. "It's that red *D* on your chest," Dave explained. "A
divorced doctor is like being in the ocean with a bleeding
femoral artery—it's just a matter of time before you start attracting sharks." I bled for years, but the wound never scabbed over.

After I ran into Freddie again at Cissy's party, I asked if she
needed a ride home. She said yes, and I thought my luck was
changing. I didn't know anything about her situation in
California. I only knew that I was still attracted to her—I was
glad for the darkness of the truck, so she couldn't see my erec-
tion. If she had casually rubbed against me, I thought I might
explode. I wanted to take her home and slowly unbutton her
blouse. I would have been happy just to sit in the truck and
smell her hair; it was all cut off, sexy as hell, and it still smelled
of ironed linen. Still, I was afraid. The slightest hesitation on her
part would have daunted me considerably. When I turned onto
River Street, I took a deep breath and plunged ahead. "You want
to go to my farm and have a beer?"

"Beer?" she said, looking at me sideways.

"Or we could have wine, Kool-Aid, or filtered water," I said, trying to joke.

She laughed. "It's tempting."

"You want to come, then?" My heart beat like a tapped watermelon—hollow and ripe, full of sweet sticky stuff.

"I should go home."

"But it's early."

"I know; I'm just tired."

"Parties will do that," I said, but I knew she was lying. In the dusky light of the truck, her eyes took on depth. The pupils seemed to open up, drawing me inside her. I knew her eyes so well, they could have been my own eyes.

The next day I drove down the gravel alley behind her house. She was in the backyard, gathering broken tree branches and throwing them into a wheelbarrow. She wore an old sweatshirt, a couple of sizes too big. It was hooded, with SAN FRANCISCO STATE across the chest. I left before she spotted my truck. I wondered whose shirt she was wearing—her husband's? But the next day I was back, trying to see into her backyard or into the windows of her house. I knew this was not normal, but I couldn't seem to stop myself.

One afternoon I spotted her in the hospital cafeteria, and I walked over with my tray. "Can I join you?" I asked, praying she'd say yes.

"Sure," she said, waving at the empty chair. I sat down. I couldn't think of anything to say. I remembered the hooded sweatshirt she'd worn, and I asked where she'd gotten her master's degrees.

"Scripps," she said, licking her spoon. She liked her coffee sugary, I seemed to recall, with lots of cream.

"Did your husband go there, too?" I asked, thinking how smooth and clever that came out—like I was getting a patient's medical and social history.

"Yes. But he did his undergraduate work at San Francisco State. He was, like, totally radical. He still is in some ways." She pointed to my tuna salad sandwich. "He wouldn't approve of your lunch."

"Why not?" I blinked at my tray, a little sorry I'd brought up the subject of her husband.

"Fish and eggs." She shrugged, smiling a secretive smile. "Sam's a vegan."

"From the Planet Vega?" I teased.

"No, it's a type of vegetarian. He doesn't eat any meat or—"

"I know what a vegan is," I said, but still, I felt stupid. The remains of a salad were scattered across her plate. "Are you one, too?"

"Me?" She smiled. "No way."

"Prove it." I tore my sandwich in half, handing one wedge to her. She ate every crumb, then licked her fingers.

"God, that was good," she said, smiling into her hand. "I was really hungry."

"You want the other half?" I held it up, but she shook her head. The vegan husband seemed like a minor technicality. Something bloomed inside me—I caught the scent of hope and lust, maybe. It was laced through me like strong curry and garlic. I wondered if I had a chance with her, or if she'd gone too far into the Wild, Wild West.

"Now that you've passed my litmus test, let's have a truly nonvegan dinner this Friday," I said lightly, folding my hands on the table. "A disgusting, artery-clogging fish fry, with hush puppies, slaw, and potatoes a la Buddy."

"Then you can only mean one place," she said, one eyebrow slightly raised. "Center Hill Lake."

"That's right," I said. "Buddy's Restaurant and Boat Dock."

"I don't know." She bit one finger, as if she were genuinely anguished—over the cholesterol or the company, I couldn't tell. Except when it came to certain medical conditions, like sniffing out strep throat or tracing the root of a strange purpuric rash, I had never possessed one shred of intuition—especially with women. She continued to gnaw her finger.

"Freddie?" I said. "How 'bout it?"

"Sure. It's been a long time since I've eaten Buddy's fish." She ran one hand through her cropped hair—the style was sheer Freddie, the ultimate no-nonsense approach to beauty.

After I left the hospital, I drove up to the cemetery. I liked it best in the winter—it was a cold, windswept hilltop with 360-degree views. No one ever asked why I came here, but if they did I'd say, Look, I'm a Southern boy, and all Southerners worship their ancestors. *Ancestors?* they'd think, imagining whole generations of Mannings and Jacksons. Until my daddy moved to Florida, I had assumed he would be buried here, too. Now I see how impossible that would have been, with all of his wives. When it came to Daddy, my mother was doomed. He just never wanted to be with her. When I was old enough for kindergarten, she let me stay home. She took me on long walks. Sometimes we came up to this cemetery and looked at the old stones. We would see Miss Minerva and the McBroom girls, weeding and setting out flowers in JFG coffee cans, the bottoms weighed down with rocks.

Even then, Mother was into death, but she also had a pretty good grasp of life, too. She let me adopt stray cats, a cockatiel with a paralyzed claw, box turtles who ate raw tomatoes, frogs that hopped out of their shoe box and trilled all summer long under the kitchen sink. After Kelly died, there was only the three of us, Chili, Martha, and me. Now I'm the only Manning in the Tallulah phone book. I feel like an orphan, even though Daddy calls once a month from Tampa. All winter long he sends crates of oranges and tangerines, with the green crinkly paper sticking out. What I'm missing, I think, is kinfolk, but that's something you can't manufacture. You either have aunts and cousins or you don't.

Now, over by the trees, I spotted a woman wearing a tan coat and a red scarf. Her back looked boneless, a humped shape like the back of a whale. When she straightened up, I saw that it was Minerva Pray. I sprinted over a dozen foot stones, breathless by the time I reached her. She looked up, startled to see me. "Miss Minerva!" I cried. "I thought that was you."

"It's me, all right." She thrust one hand into her pocket, bringing up cotton gloves. "Just checking to see if the wind blew over Amos's flowers. But they were fine."

"You look frozen," I said. "Can I give you a ride home?"

"Oh, that'd be nice." She pulled on the gloves. "I'd appreciate it."

I held out my arm, and she took it. Even through the gloves, her hands felt like defrosted chicken breasts, limp and bone-damp.

"You here to see your mama?" she asked.

"Yes, ma'am."

"That's mighty good of you, Jackson. Young people don't put much stock in the dead nowadays."

"No, ma'am."

We walked in silence for a minute. Then she said, "I've got me some fresh chocolate pie at the house. Do you like chocolate, Jackson?"

"Oh, yes, ma'am. I sure do."

"Well, how about me fixing you a slice. And a nice, hot cup of coffee, too. The pie is a new recipe I got out of the *Banner*. Wednesday is *the* day for clipping recipes. But you have to test them first."

"I'd be happy to try out your pie," I said. My heart lurched at the thought of seeing Freddie again—twice in one day. I hoped she wouldn't think I was chasing her, but I was too lovesick to care. Even if I didn't get to see her, I would be eating from a fork she might have touched.

FREDDIE

When Jackson invited me to dinner at Center Hill Lake, I almost declined. It certainly wasn't because of the restaurant, which is a sort of Tallulah legend—a glass-and-cedar building that seemed to float over the water, connected to the marina by pilings and a maze of docks and boathouses with corrugated tin roofs. The food was four-star, written up in travel magazines. Everything on their menu was Southern fried and ambrosial. Hush puppies with the right proportions of minced onion and cornmeal. Slaw that's crunchy, sweet, tart. Grilled, corn-fed beef, marinated in Buddy's secret sauce. Fresh bass, trout, perch—fried, broiled, stuffed, or sauteed in butter and lemon. Potatoes fried with onions and garlic. The secret at Buddy's was fresh ingredients and experienced cooks—older women who were intimately familiar with the local bounty. It was served up with a sassy, almost corny ambiance by wide-hipped waitresses who dyed their hair a shade too black.

Still, the lure of Buddy's fried catfish was not enough to soothe me. I had mixed feelings about the lake, and I was trying to ration the bad ones. I had spent one of the worst nights of my life at Center Hill, but I'd also learned to swim here. I told myself it was nothing more than a body of fresh water—not a repository of joys and sorrows.

When we reached the boat dock, Jackson parked on a hill. We

walked down about a hundred concrete steps to the boat dock, crossing a swinging rope bridge. It was freezing, and I had dressed inappropriately, a short plaid dress, navy hose, and heels, all from Jo-Nell's bulging closet. I shivered, hugging myself. January evenings in Tennessee could be painful—just one more thing I'd forgotten about the place. Jackson draped one arm around me. The sun was dropping behind the trees, and the moon was already on the rise. We walked past the boats, our shoes clapping loudly on the wooden boards. Beneath us the water made soft, slapping sounds. A man in a waterproof vest stood at the end of the dock, washing down the side of his boat with a mop. From a portable radio, over the static, an oldie was playing—Journey was singing "Girl Can't Help It."

The Penningtons had been boating enthusiasts, and during my mother's brief marriage to Wyatt, we'd come down to the dock at Silver Point, to make sure vandals hadn't stolen anything from their cabin cruiser. We never did any actual boating. Since we couldn't swim—not even a successful dog paddle—Wyatt wouldn't even start up the engine. He would let us sit on the dock, dangling our feet into the green water. I remembered staring enviously as Jackson and Chili Manning cruised up to the dock, all sunburned and radiant after a day of skiing. What I would have given to have lived with such abandon.

"Your father had his boat over there, didn't he?" I nodded toward one of the tin buildings. I was really wondering if Jackson had a boat—he wasn't the type to own a lowly kayak, but something grand and speedy. I assumed his life was crammed with expensive toys, typical of most small-town doctors, yet he drove a battered gold truck. I pictured the blond real estate agent lying on the bow of a speedboat, her legs sheathed in oil, her shoulders turning pink in the midday sun, as if she'd rubbed herself with raspberries.

"Long time ago," Jackson said. "Remember when Daddy and I taught you how to swim?"

"I sure do." It had changed my life. They had anchored the boat in a cove and gently lowered me into the warm green water. Jackson got behind me, holding me up with his knees. From the boat, Chili clapped, urging me to take a few strokes. "Pretend you're part of the water, Freddie," Jackson said in my ear. "Pretend I'm the sky, and you're swimming straight to me."

"I can't!" I cried. I was really scared; but I was also embarrassed. I was the only girl Jackson had ever dated who couldn't swim. I pushed off from his leg and spread out my arms, as if I were gathering up pale green leaves. I drew my legs up like a frog, just as Chili had instructed, and kicked toward the boat.

"She swims!" said Jackson, throwing back his head, letting out a Rebel yell. "Do it again, baby! Do it again!"

Now he was pulling me toward the restaurant. "We used to fish every Sunday," he was saying. "Mother would get so pissed. She wanted Daddy to be like other men. You know, in church every Sunday, mowing the lawn, raking leaves, changing light bulbs. He just didn't care about that stuff." He glanced down the length of the boathouse. Light hit the water, casting eerie, rippling shadows on the tin ceiling. He squeezed my shoulder, guiding me toward the restaurant. "God, I love this place, don't you? I wish I had a boat. I'd take you fishing this spring."

Come spring, I didn't think I'd be around, but anything was possible. As Minerva always said, disasters in our family tended to come in sixes, not threes. There was just no telling what calamity would keep me stuck in Tennessee. Also, the lake was working on my nerves. Not too far from here, in an old aluminum boat, I'd lost my virginity to Jimbo Shrimplett, Cissy Alsup's ex-husband. I had just graduated from high school. Cissy had left with a group of girls for a vacation in Panama City, leaving behind a bereaved and horny Jimbo Shrimplett. One night he passed my house in his lime-green Cougar. He slowed down when he saw me sitting in the glider. He stopped and asked if I wanted to go to Center Hill. Flattered, I said yes. I ran inside to tell Minerva, then darted back out to Jimbo. We went to the Cliffs—a secluded, rocky spot at the lake where people mainly went skinny-dipping. Jimbo had a silver canoe, and before I knew what was happening, he had filled me with beer, then lured me into the boat. The whole time he was touching me, peeling off my clothes, I imagined I was a gigantic boiled shrimp, my inner skin pink and glistening. Then he shoved himself into me, hard, and I stopped thinking. He would not stop pushing into me, even when I yelled and beat on the sides of the boat. When I finally stood up, blood streamed down between my legs. Since I didn't know how to swim, I was trapped. If I jumped, I'd sink straight to the bottom. I'd be an item on the evening news—*Divers are combing the lake for eighteen-year-old Freddie McBroom, a Tallulah girl, who was reported missing by a friend.* That night I saw the necessity of swimming, but I never worked up my nerve to learn until Jackson came into my life.

"Come here," he was saying, pulling off his coat, draping it around my shoulders. "You're just freezing to death, aren't you."

"I should've brought a coat."

"You can keep mine." He pulled open the glass door, and we stepped inside. It was dark, and candles burned on every table, the flames reflecting against the windows. From hidden speakers came Roy Orbison's voice, singing "Dream Baby." Through the windows, the water held a broad streak of light, fading into a gloomy brown. On the opposite shore, a peninsula of cedars ended in a rocky point, where a herd of goats loped off into the trees. I gazed back at the restaurant. As my eyes adjusted to the gloom, I noticed trophy fish were mounted on the walls, poised as if to swim away—large and small mouth bass, crappie, and whiskery catfish. A waitress with green eyelids appeared from the shadows, clutching calendar-sized menus all sheathed in burgundy plastic.

"Two?" She smiled, showing a gap between her front teeth. Her hair was teased three inches from her scalp.

"Yes."

She walked ahead of us, her wide hips blending into the darkness. We fumbled behind her, skirting tables with families, dodging waitresses bearing huge trays of fried fish, hush puppies, sizzling steaks. The waitress stopped at a table in front of the window, then laid down the menus. She stepped back, still smiling, and vanished. Jackson was holding out my chair. When I sat down, his hands slid up to my shoulders, briefly squeezing them. "You warmed up yet?" he said into my ear.

I tilted up my face. "Yes. Thanks." I was still wearing his jacket. I started to hand it back, but he draped it over the back of my chair.

"You hang on to it," he said, then walked around to his chair. He was backlit by copper water. From the speakers, U2 began singing "One." I ran my fingers through my hair. A witchy-looking, mahogany-haired waitress appeared and took our orders. Then she snatched up the menus. For a winter evening, even though it was Friday, the place was packed. Jackson told me it had been the most popular restaurant in the area for half a century.

"That long?" I said. "I didn't know that."

"See?" He pretended to leer at me. "Middle Tennessee is full of undiscovered pleasures."

This, I sincerely doubted. Our waitress materialized from the shadows and set down two glasses of sweet tea, bobbing with huge lemon wedges. This was one habit I had given up—tea drinking. The people around here, Jackson included, drank it iced year-round. In Mexico I drank Sidral, tequila, or bottled water; the rest of the year, in California, I lived on espresso, Evian, or my father-in-law's famous limeade. Aside from a battered tin of Lapsang Souchong, which I sometimes made for breakfast, I don't think we ever drank cold tea.

"After Mother died, Daddy used to bring his dates here," Jackson said, running his hands over the candle. Behind him the sky had turned cobalt, the water a shade darker.

"Did he ever remarry?" While I couldn't recall his marital history, I saw Dr. Manning plainly. His hair was buzzed off so short, the transparent hairs sparkled like filaments of glass. He always wore an oversized, white lab coat that fell past his knees, hiding his massive abdomen. He had a thick mustache and round, wire-rimmed bifocals that always made me think of Teddy Roosevelt.

"Oh, God, yes." Jackson shook his head, then leaned back in his chair. "A couple of times. Let's see, there was his office nurse. Fae, spelled with an *E*. She drank herself to death. Then there was Pamela, the cardiac care nurse, who ended up in rehab."

"For?"

"An addiction to prescription drugs—courtesy of Daddy, of course. Mostly Valium and Percodan. They were divorced in, let's see, was it '89? No, '90. Seven months later he married Sallie, spelled with an *I-E*, not a *Y*. I think he met her at the hospital, too. She's my age, with two grown daughters. Sallie-with-an-*I-E* is into diamonds, condos, luxury cars, and cruises. They're still married. Two years ago, they moved to Tampa. Dear old Daddy. The love junkie."

"How old is he now?" I kept picking up my iced tea glass, making wet rings on the table.

"Seventy-one."

"He's spry, then."

"All that testosterone, I guess. Although he's gotten a bit too old to chase nurses." He reached across the table and tapped the back of my hand. "He's got a bad heart. In fact, he barely has any heart tissue left at all. He had a triple bypass last year; but if you ask me, Daddy just wore that sucker out."

I didn't know how to answer. I stared down at his hands, the flat pink nails and whorls of hair on the backs of his fingers, just like Chili Manning's. I was thinking that genes were stronger than most people realized—maybe Jackson loved the ladies, too.

"Daddy always chased women," Jackson said, as if reading my mind. He circled my wrist with his thumb and forefinger. "I think it was one reason Mother just gave up and didn't try to fight the breast cancer."

"Do you blame him?" I said suddenly, looking at him sideways. I hadn't meant to be so blunt, but now that I'd started, I felt compelled to continue. "I mean, do you think the stress of all his women brought on the cancer?"

"I don't know." His brow creased. "Looking back, it's real clear that she was a troubled woman. Unhappy. She could have left him, I guess. But women in her generation just didn't do that. I loved her more than anything in the world, but I don't think Daddy did."

Once again, I couldn't answer him. I was thinking that she *had* left Dr. Manning—death being the ultimate kiss-off; but I didn't want to get philosophical about family members or obituaries. It occurred to me that the only men I'd ever loved were motherless. Also, they'd never left home. That said more about me than the men. Finally I glanced up. "Sam's mother is dead, too. She drowned in Tomales Bay."

"Sam?" Jackson looked puzzled. "Your husband?"

I nodded, and Jackson looked away. I felt suddenly chatty about Mrs. Espy, but I held back. She had died long before I ever met Sam, but he told me she'd earned an Olympic bronze medal in the late 1940s—a champion swimmer. She was also something of a Girl Scout. She never lied; she was renowned in Dewey for uttering brutal truths to her friends—"Yes," she'd say, "You *do* look fat in that dress." If she made a vow, she kept it—from a daily swim to forsaking all others, till death do us part. She drowned in the bay during one of her morning swims.

She had believed in keeping trim for Mr. Espy, although God knows he wasn't the sort to fool around. She just wasn't taking any chances. Since her body was never found, the Espys assumed a current had swept it out to the Pacific, into the heart of the notorious Red Triangle, where white sharks regularly bite surfers and kayakers.

Jackson looked relieved when our waitress appeared, holding a huge tray. The plates steamed as she set them down. Charbroiled trout, headless, with the stiff tails curling inward, garnished with parsley and carrot curls. Green salad with pale, winter tomatoes, drizzled with French dressing. Baked potatoes, the feathery insides erupting, with butter and sour cream pouring over the edges. Next to Jackson's elbow, she parked a red plastic basket filled with rolls and cornbread.

"Coffee?" she asked Jackson, and he looked at me, raising his eyes. I smiled and nodded.

"Yes, please. Two coffees."

The waitress briefly disappeared. Then she returned and plunked down two cups, rattling the saucers. The coffee glittered rich-brown into the white china, steam curling above it. "I think Daddy was a product of that same generation," Jackson said. "He practiced medicine in pre-Medicare days. Way back when doctors could do anything and no one asked questions. When he was in medical school, the nursing students at General were taught to stand at attention and salute the doctors." He laughed, then leaned back in his chair.

I began opening little buckets of cream. In all fairness to Jackson, his father was an oblivious man. Years of ministering to the ill and incapacitated had blunted his senses, like someone who had lost their sense of smell and taste and used enormous quantities of salt and sugar to make up for it. It took something excessive to get his attention. Something more than discrete blotches of color in an already perfect room. Miss Martha had been a classic beauty. I remembered seeing her in the library, checking out best-sellers. She had an etched widow's peak and high cheekbones and her blond pageboy and her reading glasses. She wore a thin gold wristwatch set ten minutes fast. Her closet was full of linen dresses in wheats and creamy beiges that wrinkled when she sat down. It seemed to me that Chili Manning had married elegance, but deep down he preferred cheap women: platinum-blonds with plucked eyebrows and capped teeth; women who wore parakeet-green suits and matching eye shadow and way too much mascara; women who wore hairpieces and drugstore perfume. Deep down he lusted after women who made expensive jewelry look like the stuff you'd win at the fair, jewelry that turned your fingers green.

"So," Jackson said. He picked up his fork. "How much longer will you be in town?"

"Maybe forever," I said gloomily. "I spent the whole morning talking to the local travel agent. They can get me to La Paz but not Guerrero Negro. It's a lot easier to arrange a charter from the Baja end."

"I can imagine. In Mexico, it's not what you know but who you know. I was in Mexico City once, and I—" Suddenly his face changed. He looked past me, slowly rising from his chair.

"Jackson?" I said. He was already running over to the table behind us, where a balding man in a red sweater was clutching his throat. The man's face was rapidly turning bluish-gray. A half-eaten steak was on his plate, the red juice running under the fried potatoes. A woman with white, shellacked hair stood behind him, pounding his shoulders.

"Cough it up, Walter," she commanded. "Just cough it up."

I stood, and my napkin fell down the front of my dress. Jackson rushed up to the man, then whacked him between the shoulder blades. Nothing came up. The man stared, all bug-eyed, reaching around to clutch his wife's arm, clawing at her sleeve. Jackson put his arms around the man's stomach, as if to hug or restrain him, and made a fist under the man's breastbone. He jerked up. At first nothing happened. The man's face had turned an intense gray, and his lips were blue. Jackson's hands jerked upward again. I heard a pop, and a chunk of steak flew out of the man's mouth.

"Good Lord," said the wife, watching the object arc across the room. A few tables over, a waitress squatted and picked up the meat, staring at it. The man wheezed, drawing in a long, jagged breath. He shut his eyes and put his hand over his heart. He was still gray, but his cheeks were rapidly turning pink. The restaurant was hushed, almost churchlike. A crowd had gathered around the table, their faces drawn in tight concern. Someone said, "Jackson?"

A trim brunette stepped out of the crowd, looking curiously at him. She was wearing a navy wool dress, with a paisley scarf draped around her throat. From the chair, the bald-headed man blinked at her, then shot an adoring look at Jackson.

"I'm alive," he croaked.

"Why, you certainly are," said the brunette. She smiled, then gave Jackson a knowing look. "Lucky for you that a doctor was eating here tonight."

"Doctor?" croaked the man, his eyebrow twisting up.

"Dr. Jackson Manning," said the brunette. "A pediatrician in Tallulah, but so what? They can save us big folks, too."

Jackson walked back to our table, trailed by the brunette. I was still standing. She peered at me, then reached out and shook my hand. "Hi, I'm Ann Presley. I don't believe we've met?"

Her fingers felt limp and cold, like chilled crab legs. I wasn't about to introduce myself, so I stepped back, hugging my elbows. She started to say something, but the bald-headed man was trying to get Jackson's attention.

"How much do I owe you?" he barked. His face was bright pink. Aside from a slight wheeze, he seemed to be breathing normally.

"Yes, how much?" said the white-haired wife. She already had her purse open and was pulling out a checkbook.

"Absolutely nothing." Jackson held up both hands.

"Well, at least let us buy your dinner," said the wife. "I insist."

"No, ma'am, it's unethical," Jackson said, trying not to smile. "But thank you anyway."

"You should let them, Jackson," said Ann Presley. Then she gave him a shrewd look. "So, fancy seeing you here. I guess it *is* a small world."

"Well, that depends," Jackson said politely. "Sometimes it's so big you can lose people."

"Oh, I don't know about that." Ann Presley laughed nervously. "I've never lost anyone."

"Hope you enjoy your dinner, Ann." Jackson reached for his wallet. He dropped a wad of bills on the table—a tip for the waitress, I supposed. Then he took my elbow, helping me out of my chair, leading me toward the front door. When he stopped at the counter to settle our bill with the cashier, I glanced back at our table. Ann Presley was still watching. I wondered who she was—a friend of Cissy's? One of Jackson's old lovers? The mother of one of his patients? I realized with a start that she could have been all of the above. Also: It didn't really matter.

"Ready?" said Jackson. He slid his arm around me. With his free hand he pushed open the door. A bell jingled above us.

"That lady is still looking at us," I said.

"Let her." Jackson planted a wet kiss on my lips. Behind us, the door *whoosh*ed shut, the bell making a muffled sound. He took my hand and we stepped out into the cold night.

JO-NELL

When my stepdaddy ran off with the go-go dancer, he told me
to remember three things. First, he was sorry. Second, I should
mind my mama, and third, to remember that joy didn't occur
without consequence. I didn't know what the hell he meant. I
was just a little kid. A few days later, he choked on puke and
died, and that was the end of my stepdaddy. Now I think he
was trying to say that what comes around, goes around, and
then it bites you on the ass. I started to ask Freddie what she
thought it meant, but I changed my mind. I had more important
questions.

"So how was your date with Jackson?" I asked her. I was trying to play chess, my first game, but I couldn't keep all the
moves and people straight—knights, bishops, pawns, and these
little columns, I forget what they're called. The object is to kill
the king. I was black, Freddie was white.

"It wasn't a date." Freddie looked up, rolling a bishop
between her palms. It made me think of rolling out biscuit
dough, of rolling a man's thingamajig between my oiled palms.

"But you *did* go out with him."

"It was dinner, not adultery." She lowered her eyebrows.
"You've got a dirty mind."

"True." I really did have a dirty mind, but I couldn't seem to
stop it. When I baked, I wanted to screw; and when I screwed, I

wanted to bake. It was like one action fed and fueled the other. Go figure. "And then what happened?"

"He took me home."

"That's *all*?"

"All."

"You didn't feel anything for him—a smoldering spark? A twinge in the old twat?"

"If I did, would I tell you?"

"You should. Confession's good for the soul. It also passes the time."

"It's your move." She nodded at the board.

"Move my horse two spaces up, over to the right."

"A knight," she said. I watched her move the piece.

"There," I said. "Thanks. Ain't that checkmate?"

"No, check."

"Shit. I quit."

"No, wait."

"I don't see the point." I sighed deeply, looking around for a way to kill her queen, but I was bottlenecked with my own freaking pawns. I toyed with the strap of my pale pink nightgown—one of my more sedate numbers, Frederick's of Hollywood, bought for practically nothing at a garage sale. My specialty was crotchless panties, but I couldn't wear any in the hospital. My hip felt all grown together, like somebody else's leg bone had been rooted.

"You're not concentrating," she said.

"Look, this game sucks." I wished we were playing Wheel of Fortune. We could buy vowels for G- F-ck Y-urs-lf.

"Don't be vulgar, Jo-Nell."

"But I'm so good at it." I reached out and patted her hair. "So, what's going on with that Nina woman?"

"I don't know." She moved her queen, killing my horse.

"You did that on purpose." I laughed. "I myself have good news. Since my little Volkswagen was totaled, the insurance company is giving me money for a new car."

"What kind are you getting?" she asked.

"I'd like a Lexus, but that's a pie in the sky. I'll probably get a Camaro. Or even a Ford Explorer. I can do a lot of garage saling with that."

"Get something with air bags," she said in a motherly tone.

"Freddie?"

"Yes?"

"Do you ever think you'll, you know, have a baby?"

"I don't think so."

"Me, either." Although I did not like to think about it, I had bad endometriosis. Inside, I was all scarred up like a ruined CD. At the music store they'll give you your money back or else let you have a new CD, but you can't get new female parts.

After she left, I pulled up the sheet, pretending to sleep. This was a ploy I'd learned to throw off the nurses. God, they were mean. After ICU, where I had Dwayne wrapped around my little finger, I'd kind of gotten spoiled. Here on the regular floor, the nurses wouldn't even change your sheets, much less give you a sponge bath. On the other hand, they loved to poke me with needles and make me walk up and down the hall—anything to cause pain and suffering. That was them, all right.

While I lay there thinking of ways to revolt, I heard somebody call my name. First thing, I thought of the green-eyed cowboy, Jesse. My heart started roaring like a lawn mower.

"Mmmhum." I opened my eyes and saw Jackson Manning. He sat down on the far corner of my bed. I was real touched. It had been a long time since I'd had me a genuine man on a freaking mattress. Just for the record, I had never been faintly attracted to the guy, but famine's famine. A starving woman don't ask no questions. Even so, I knew he wasn't here to see me.

"It's about Freddie," he said, staring at me with those Manning-blue eyes.

"What about her?" I said.

"Do I have a chance with her?"

"You don't beat around the bush, do you?" I smiled.

"There's no time for that. I'm afraid she'll be leaving soon."

"Then you have your answer." I lifted my hands. "Why start something you can't finish?"

"Because I have a feeling about her. She's different—not like other women."

"Is that good or bad?" I said, laughing.

"I have this overwhelming urge to hold her and love her and make babies with her."

I blinked.

"I really do love her, Jo-Nell. It's so strong. She's bound to feel it, too."

I kept on staring.

"What?" His eyes widened. "Did I say something wrong?"

"No. I was just thinking how much I could use a lovestruck man." I grinned. "My sister's lucky. But she's also married."

"Happily?" His eyebrows raised into upside-down *V*'s. He lowered his hand and sighed.

"How should I know?" I raised one shoulder. As if on cue, my pale pink nightgown strap slid down. I ignored it, but I wondered if he would. "She's not a blabbermouth. She's a clam."

"She seems . . . distant." He rubbed his chin, staring right through me. I might as well have been wearing flannel. This was a man in love, I thought. It did not make me happy.

"Maybe she misses Sam," I said, watching his face.

"Could be. Even when we're talking, she's far away."

"You're just worked up because she won't grease your pole."

"What?"

"You know, fuck you."

"I wouldn't put it that way."

"I would."

"I wouldn't."

We seemed to be stuck.

"Couldn't you talk to her?" Jackson said.

"And say what?"

"That I'm crazy about her."

"Is that all?"

"Tell her I'm on my knees."

"That's better." I smiled. "You're getting the hang of it. Keep trying."

"You're making light of this. I'm serious."

"And she is married, like I said."

"I know it." He put one hand on top of his head.

"Look," I said. "I'm no marriage counselor; although a lot of people say I'd be a natural. You know how it is—your own life's a mess, but you know how to fix everybody else's? Anyhow, it seems to me that you've got an age-old problem here. Even if she fell madly in love with you and left Sam, you'd still have problems. There aren't no whales in Tennessee."

"I see what you're getting at."

"You don't have anything on the line. It's so easy for you to say you want a stab at her, but you aren't married. You don't have a job that requires salt water. I mean, really. You can't take a fish out of a pond and expect it to say, 'Whew! Just what I needed. Thank you so much!' If your patients were baby whales, wouldn't you feel terrible if you had to give them up?"

"Of course I would." He put his hands under his chin. His eyes switched back and forth.

"If you start romancing my sister, just be careful. You may think you're giving her a new lease on love, but you're liable to steal something away, too. But why take anything? Any way you look at it, she's making all the sacrifices. I don't think that's fair. Do you?"

"No, of course not."

"My advice is, don't romance her if you can't stand to lose her."

He looked confused, and that made me feel smart—like I

could hang out my shingle and charge fifty dollars an hour. Men would be my specialty. They were just like onions—in order to reach the good stuff, you had to weep. It was best to peel them slowly, savoring their rings and layers, taking care to cut around the rotten places. If I ever got out of this goddamn hospital, I was heading down to Texas and find me a decent man. (A state that big was bound to be good on people's reputations.) I'd move into Hattie's old house and start me a catering business. I didn't know if a town as small as Mount Olive had any use for hors d'oeuvres, but I could always advertise in Austin or San Antonio. I'd spend the rest of my days dispensing advice and chicken salad sandwiches. I would make it with seedless grapes and toasted pecans. Sometimes I would try curry mayo. From where I sat at Tallulah General, all broke up like a box of dog biscuits, Texas seemed like a right good life. It was the land of crude oil and cowboys—and both of them seemed to grow right out of the ground.

I have thought about it a lot, and I've got this theory that men try too goddamn hard to *be* hard. It just makes them soft in the wrong ways. They are raised by women, so they spend the rest of their lives trying to be like Daddy. And Lord, the daddies of the world were raised by women. That ought to tell you something. I believe with all my heart that men would be perfect if they weren't scared shitless of their X chromosome. It's the Y that causes all the trouble, the yin/yang of the gender. The long, dangling Y, hanging down like a limp penis. I've seen plenty of them, in my young life, and at the rate I'm going, I'm bound to see more. It's enough to give a girl an honest-to-god conniption fit.

ELEANOR

A man from Federal Express came to the front door and knocked. I was all alone in the house—Freddie was at the hospital, and Minerva was delivering baked spaghetti to Matilda Lancaster, who was down in her back. I ran upstairs, pushed open a window, and shouted down, "Can I help you?"

The man stepped back and gazed up at the house, his eyes switching back and forth, as if trying to figure which window the voice was coming from.

"Up here," I directed.

"Uh, yes, ma'am," he said, reaching in his pocket. "I need a signature for a delivery? It's for, let's see now, Ms. Jo-Nell McBroom?"

"I'm not her."

"Can you sign for it?"

"I've never had to before, and we get packages all the time."

"I don't make the rules, ma'am." He looked at his clipboard. "It says right here signature required."

I couldn't think what to do. The man seemed polite, and he wore a bona fide Federal Express shirt. Probably it was all right to sign, but I wasn't dressed. I ran around the bedroom, hunting for my orange sweat pants and the lime shirt. If Minerva was here I wouldn't think twice about going to the door. I'd just throw a trench coat over my nightgown. When I was by myself

I got jittery. I just didn't like to be alone, but nobody could ever say I was a loner like those postal clerks who shoot all their coworkers for no good reason, just pure craziness. She was nice, people would say later, but a loner. No, this was not me. I had parties galore for the senior citizens. Jo-Nell said this did not count. She thought my whole problem could be traced to my social life. I just didn't know a whole lot about men. The few times I had dates in high school, Jo-Nell would sit on the edge of the bathtub, watching me brush my teeth. She was nine or ten, real cute, with blond pigtails. When the doorbell rang, she'd go downstairs and check out the boy. Then she'd come back and tell me if I should wear heels or not. I was just so tall, like a praying mantis.

Not too long ago Jo-Nell told me that she was fixing me up with a blind date. "No!" I screeched, picturing somebody in sunglasses, holding on to a seeing-eye dog.

"He's a real sweet guy," Jo-Nell said. "A postman."

"No, thank you," I snapped.

"Men aren't *all* bad," she said, laughing. I just handed her my scrapbook.

"Ted Bundy was a man," I pointed out.

"No, he was a monster."

From the front yard, the delivery man called, "Ma'am? You still there?"

"Just one second!" I stepped into my pants, snapping the elastic waistband. I started for the stairs. Then I stopped cold. I remembered an *Oprah* show where she got a conman to trick a housewife with a dummy package. The woman opened the door wide. Later, Oprah brought in an expert who advised all women to be more suspicious, to keep their doors locked. "But isn't that taking things to extremes?" said Oprah, grimacing. "I'd feel foolish."

"Better to make a fool of yourself than to be a statistic," said the expert.

I went back to the window and told the man I was sorry. "I'm up here with a highly contagious disease," I hollered. "It's bulbar meningitis. I could infect you." (I didn't know if there was such a disease, but it sounded good to me.)

"Oh." The man stepped backward. "In that case I'll just leave this paper for you to sign and come back tomorrow, then."

"Fine." I watched him climb into his truck and drive off. Then I had a funny thought. What kind of package required a signature? Had Jo-Nell ordered more of those edible panties? They looked like Fruit Roll-ups, but the flavors were different—vanilla, cherry cola, butterscotch.

That was weird, but so was I. At this very moment, all over America, women were signing for packages. They were driving to shopping malls and even driving cross-country. Why was it so easy for them and so hard for me? Didn't they know what was going on in the world? I saw on the news where a teacher got kidnaped at a strip-shopping mall. She'd just stopped to buy a sandwich and a teenager snatched her. Then he took her to a remote place and strangled her. I told this to Freddie, and she just said, "That's awful."

"It's more than awful," I said. "If a woman isn't safe buying a sandwich, then what's the point of leaving home?"

Freddie just raised her eyebrows, like I was cuckoo or something. Living in California had numbed her to crime; but not me. When I was a little girl, no one in Tallulah locked their doors. Now everybody's got burglar alarms. You just had to wonder what the world was coming to.

Minerva thought my troubles began when I found Mama. It was late winter, pouring down rain. I was in Home Ec IV, smack dab in the middle of flipping pancakes, when I burned my hand on the griddle. The old maid teacher, Miss Mulligan, bandaged me up with butter and cheesecloth. "Eleanor, these are two kitchen staples you must never be without," she said.

I tried calling Mama to come pick me up, but there was no

answer at home or the doughnut shop. I told Miss Mulligan I'd just as soon walk home. Carrying a black umbrella, I cut through two dozen backyards, counting clotheslines as I went. When I reached our driveway, I noticed the station wagon in the garage. I stepped into the living room and yelled, "Mama?"

No answer. I thought, Good, she's gone. Now I can fix me a pitcher of Kool-Aid and eat a whole box of Mystic Mint cookies. Mama didn't like me to eat chocolate on account of my complexion. Although I was seventeen and five feet, eleven inches, my bones were still growing. And I had this great big appetite. It was like I had a starved place inside me that refused to be filled.

I fixed me a snack, turned on the TV, and watched *Guiding Light*. It wasn't my favorite show, but beggars couldn't be choosers. My hand got to throbbing, and I thought I better go upstairs and see if there was any ointment in the medicine cabinet. I passed by Mama's room and peeked inside. It was dark, full of a stuffy smell. The blinds were shut tight, with light spearing through the slats. Beside her bed, I saw the dingleball lamp, her eyeglasses, a box of chocolate-covered cherries, and a *Reader's Digest Condensed Book* (she'd been reading *Karen*). I started to back out of the room, but something caught my attention. I flipped on the light, looked at the window, and screamed. Mama was hanging from the Venetians. Her blue chenille robe gaped open, showing a nylon slip and her saggy breasts.

I screamed again, then rushed over to her, hoisting her up by the legs. Her head lolled on her chest. One of her arms swung down and smacked me. I thought maybe she was alive, so I raised her higher; if she had some slack, I thought she'd have room for air. The cord made a loop-de-loop above her head, but she was dead weight. Dear Lord, please. Make it all right. Look at me, Mama. It's me, Eleanor.

Next thing I knew Minerva was in the room, cutting Mama down with the sewing scissors. Outside, the rain was pouring down, gray and greasy like old dishwater. Mama fell on me, and I staggered back. "Let's get her on the bed," said Minerva, lifting her legs. It was no use. She was starting to get stiff. A long time later, when my sisters got home, I could hear Minerva telling them to come here, babies. Come here, chickens. Minerva's got some real, real bad news.

Next thing I knew, the three of us were vomiting in the same commode, heaving and spitting and carrying on. I thought every single thing we'd ever eaten was trying to come back up, all the way back to Mama's titty milk. I swore I could taste it, and Jo-Nell said she could, too. Once I banged heads with a sister, but I didn't even know which one. It didn't matter. We were like one puking body, three-headed twins with a single stomach.

Five years later, bad luck hit again. I was in the station wagon by myself, driving down I-40, singing along with the radio—three stations were playing Sting. From under the car came a loud pop. All of a sudden the steering wheel began to shake and wobble, and it took every drop of my strength to aim the car to the breakdown lane. It was a flat tire. Traffic whizzed by me. A Red Ball truck roared down the highway, blaring his horn. A brown Skylark angled into the breakdown lane, stopping in front of me. A man with a beer belly got out and walked over to me. I rolled down the window. "Looks like you got a busted tire," said the man. "Can I give you a ride anywhere?"

I said yes. Then I said no.

"You'd better make up your mind." The man laughed, showing a row of rotted teeth. "That tire ain't gone fix itself."

"Thanks anyway," I said, trying to be polite. "I'll just wait for a policeman to stop."

"You may be setting a spell."

"That's okay." I was starting to get scared.

"If I was you, I'd hate to be stuck here after dark."

"Well, you're not me," I said. "You're you."

"Why, you little bitch." He reached inside the car, but I was too fast. I rolled up the window, trapping his fingers. The man screamed, tugging backward. His fingers turned pink and swelled up like sausages. I cracked the window, and his hands fell out. He ran over to his Skylark and took off, spitting gravel. An hour later, a policeman stopped. He called a service station, who fixed the tire. When I just happened to mention the man in the Skylark, the police said I was real smart not to get in his car. He refused to elaborate, but I had an imagination.

It was a narrow escape. Which only meant that I'd increased my chances for another calamity. To my way of thinking, a person was born with only so much luck—once it's used up, it's one disaster after the other.

One time Jo-Nell got to drinking Pink Ladies—that is a concoction, not volunteers at the hospital. "If you think about it," she told me, stifling a burp, "it's no small wonder that we're the way we are, you and me. We've led hard lives."

I couldn't have agreed more.

"Men die," she said. "Men leave."

"And they rape, plunder, and beat women," I added.

"That wasn't exactly what I meant." She sipped her drink, leaving a pink mustache. "Daddy died, and I don't even remember him. Then Wyatt left us."

"And died," I reminded her.

"I don't think his leaving had anything to do with him choking to death."

"I do."

"No, it was fate."

"It was God."

"There isn't a God."

"Jo-Nell!" I looked around, as if God Himself might be standing in the corner, shaking His head at us. I reached out and poured myself a drink. I finished it off in three swallows—it was so cool and fruity. I liked the taste of Pink Ladies, and I was glad that there wasn't a drink called Pink Men. I would have been scared to taste it. Jo-Nell adored the fellows, but I couldn't think of one nice thing to say about them.

"A lot of the great chefs are male," Jo-Nell said, reading my mind. "I see them on PBS all the time, always chopping, whisking, beating, frying. Cooking is not effeminate like a lot of folks believe—it's violent."

"Women are the ones who have babies," I pointed out.

"Yeah, but not us." She drained her glass, then stared into the froth.

"We're still the sourdough of humanity."

Jo-Nell couldn't disagree. She couldn't name a single man who'd given birth. For once I'd won me an argument, and that is something when you think about it. The more I drank the more I wished I lived in a city of women. You'd drive by and see ladies in funny garden hats, tying up their tomatoes; you'd see women making corn relish in July, grape jam in August, chutney in September. Every month of every year, women would be hanging out cold, dripping wet sheets on the clothesline; they'd be sweeping, kneading, grating, polishing. Sometimes they'd just lay back with their feet up, reading the newspaper, while a five-pound chicken roasted in the oven, with carrots and potatoes. And there I'd be, right in the middle of everything—a piece of the pie, a small but necessary ingredient.

FREDDIE

It was a cold Monday night, with temperatures plunging into the low teens. Eleanor said she was afraid the pipes would freeze. While she and Minerva went around the house turning on the faucets I sat in the living room, watching David Letterman flirt with his perennial guest, Sarah Jessica Parker. I kept thinking about what Jo-Nell had said. Two days ago, Jackson had come to her hospital room and quizzed her about me.

"Me?" I said, flattered in spite of myself.

The next time he called, I invited him over for Eleanor's homemade caramel coffee cake. Then he took me to see a funky new vampire movie at the Princess Theater. I told myself that I wasn't doing anything wrong. When the phone rang, I leaped up, skidding into the kitchen on my sock-feet. I answered on the third ring.

"Freddie!" The moment I heard Sam's voice, I felt disappointed. Until now, I hadn't realized how much I'd wanted it to be Jackson. Then, almost immediately, I was overcome with guilt. I was a married lady. I had forfeited my right to yearn for another man.

"Hey!" I said, trying to sound enthusiastic.

"You've developed an accent already."

"I have?"

"Must be viral." He laughed. "Is it?"

"Could be." All at once I saw him clearly: He wore a ragged Hard Rock Cafe T-shirt and cutoff jeans. One sockless foot was jiggling on his knee. The soles of his feet were white and peeling.

"No, you sound great," he said. "I miss you."

"Where are you calling from?" I put one finger in my ear. "There's lots of background noise."

"The Magdalena."

"Why aren't you at the Mirabel?"

"Because I happened to be here, and I had this urge to hear your voice."

"Oh." I pictured him at the ancient black phone, the cracked cement wall behind it. It was curry-colored, peeling off in places, with penciled-in numbers and Spanish graffiti. I pictured the long, dingy Formica counter at the cafe and the little wooden chairs that always wobbled. I heard a woman's high, twittery laugh ring out like a chipmunk's. "How's Nina working out?" I asked, a little breathlessly.

"Fine."

"Tell her I said hi."

"Freddie says hi," he called out, his voice muffled. Then, louder, he said, "She says hello, too. We're having a light dinner."

"I thought you two had dinner the other night."

"Yeah."

"Well, how was it?"

"It was okay."

"What did you order?"

"Order?"

"The food, Sam. What did you order?"

"You know the menu—a vegan's nightmare." He groaned. "But I like the atmosphere. I ended up eating rice. Nina had tequila-marinated abalone."

"Just what I would have ordered." Now that I had eaten a

genuine Southern-fried meal with Jackson, I felt benevolent
toward Sam and his Third World dinners.

"The rice had too much cilantro for my taste, but everyone
else ordered extra."

"Everyone else?"

"Did I mention that some people from the marine museum
went with us? Seven in all, I think."

"Sounds like you had a good time." I squeezed my eyes shut.

"The marine folks are always interesting. So how's your sister?"

"On the mend. Out of ICU and in a regular orthopedic room.
She's been using a walker."

"So she's ambulatory."

"A little. It just slays me the way she still flirts with the doctors."

"Slays you?" He laughed. "Is this Southern punk talk?"

"I don't know."

We fell quiet, and I heard static, like crinkled cellophane.

"Last night I had this awful nightmare about you," he said.
"You were with another man."

"Me?" I leaned against the counter, holding my breath.

"Yeah. You were fucking the hell out of him."

"What a funny dream."

"It was so real."

"Sounds like it."

"But I know you haven't."

"Haven't what?"

"Slept with anybody."

"Have you?"

"There's nothing going on with me and Nina, if that's what's
worrying you."

"I'm not worried. You're the one having weird dreams." I
tapped one fingernail against the receiver. "Did I tell you I had
dinner with Jackson Manning?"

"Wait a minute, is he that guy you were engaged to?"

"Mmmhum."

"I thought he was married."

"Divorced. But it was just a meal. Like your little outing with Nina and the museum people. What's the harm in a little dinner?"

"Not a thing." His voice seemed different, both alert and amused.

"We went to a boat dock. I ordered the Trout a la Buddy. It was char-grilled, caught that morning in the Caney Fork, but something didn't taste right. I think the cook used lard to fry the hush puppies."

"Not olive oil?"

"I don't think they sell olive oil in Pennington County."

"That's too bad." He laughed. "You hate lardy things."

"I miss you, baby." He drew in a long breath. "But stay as long as your sister needs you."

This wasn't what I wanted to hear, and I felt something fall inside my chest. I wanted him to say, I can smell you through the phone lines. I hear something in your voice. Come back, baby, and I'll never let you go again.

After we hung up, I thought back to the early days of our courtship, when Sam and I had taken his two-man kayak out into the Pacific. From the ocean, Highway 1 resembled a narrow thread, with cars and logging trucks weaving up and down. We paddled by a sea lion—it was draped over a rock like a limp sausage. It looked up, regarded us thoughtfully, then plunged into a wave. Out in deeper water, I noticed a bank of fog rolling in from the open ocean. I squinted and saw a fifteen-foot swell headed straight toward us. I shook Sam's shoulder. He turned, saw the wave, then he yelled, "Let's get to shore! Paddle hard!"

My arms had never moved that fast in my life, but it wasn't fast enough. A dark blue wall hit us, and we shot straight up, bouncing out of the water. Then I was paddling air. The kayak smacked down hard, into the next wave. The blow knocked out my breath, but still, I kept on paddling.

"I think I'm in love," Sam shouted, but I was never sure what he meant—did he love me or kayaking?

The next evening I couldn't get Sam off my mind, so I tried to call the hotel. "Let me get this straight," said the South Central Bell operator. "You want to place a person-to-person call *where*?"

"Guerrero Negro, the Hotel Mirabel," I said, suddenly tired. I was sitting on the kitchen counter, threading my toes through the loopy telephone cord. Then, for pure meanness, I added, *"Persona a persona."*

"Excuse me?" said the operator.

"Nothing."

There was a long silence. I heard a trilling sound, followed by snaps and buzzes. The hotel manager answered on the sixth ring. The operator spoke in an excruciatingly slow voice, asking for Seen-Your Sam SSS-pee's room.

"Okay," said the manager. The line made a series of flat beeps. Then a sleepy-voiced woman said, *"Bueno? Qué pasó?"*

What's up, my ass, I thought. It sounded like Nina, but I couldn't be sure. I didn't exactly remember her voice. The operator went through her litany again. The woman said, "Sorry, uh, he stepped out. But he'll be right back." There was a rustling sound, and I pictured bodies turning on a Mexican mattress.

"Thank you," the operator said crisply. Then, to me, she said, "Do you wish to place the call at another time?"

I hung up. Then I drew my knees to my chin. Maybe the manager connected the call to the wrong room. But no—the woman (Nina?) had said Sam would be right back. Surely there was a logical explanation. Nina was in Sam's room because ... Because her room had caught on fire. Because Sam was down the street buying Coronas and condoms. God, I didn't know. I stared out the kitchen window, blinking at the old magnolia. We had planted it one summer—me, Eleanor, and Jo-Nell. We had wanted to cheer up Mama after Wyatt's defection. His infidelity, as opposed to his death, had always seemed like the end-point of their relationship. The time line of his affair was, of course, unknown to us all. We hadn't even known the go-go dancer existed. I was a ten-year-old child; I didn't know that a stepfather could run away with another woman.

The night he left, I was in the kitchen, making a peanut butter and banana sandwich. The counters were messy, full of onions and boiled potatoes. From upstairs, I could hear Wyatt telling Mama he was going to Nashville. Eleanor was old enough to know what was happening. She was listening in the downstairs hall, tears streaking down her face. She had liked Wyatt. I remember looking down at my sandwich, thinking it was too big for my throat. Jo-Nell, who had just turned six, walked into the kitchen. She looked at my sandwich and I held it out. She ate it in three gulps, then held out her hand and said, "More, please."

The next day, Eleanor and I went to the nursery and picked out a magnolia. Although it was summer, not a good time to plant anything, we dug a hole and sprinkled it with magnesium sulfate, one of Minerva's garden c) curealls. Now, over twenty years later, I was sitting in the same kitchen, staring at the magnolia and wondering how in the world it had survived. The magnolia was taller than our house. It had outlived both Wyatt and Mother; perhaps it would outlast us all. I bit my knee. Thousands of miles away, another woman was sitting in my sweetheart's motel room. Did she know it was me on the phone? Would she even tell him I'd called? I tried to imagine the mind-set of a calculating woman. I thought about calling back, asking the operator to try again. This time I'd ask Nina what the hell she was doing in my husband's room. No matter what she said, I knew she wasn't responsible. In many ways he was more courtly and Southern than any man I'd ever known, but I also knew that he was capable of deceit—sleeping with me, sleeping with someone else.

Eleanor and Minerva walked into the kitchen with a box of Mason jars, complaining about the frigid temperatures. They unpacked the jars on the table—pints and quarts with curious diamond patterns, all filled with Minerva's famous chutney. She made it every fall, then put it in the pantry, where it bloomed and deepened into something celestial. "I just hate January," said Eleanor. She picked up a stack of labels and laid them out in a fan. "If it's going to be bitter cold, then I wish it would snow."

"I don't," said Minerva, taking the jars out of the box. "If it snowed, I could fall and break my hip."

"Gosh," I said. "Don't do that."

They looked up, surprised to see me sitting on the counter. "There you are," Minerva said brightly.

"Come help us," said Eleanor.

I exhaled slowly, relieved that my unhappiness had slipped right over their heads. Jo-Nell would have noticed my mood right away, but Eleanor was innocent in the ways of love. Minerva, thank heavens, had one thing on her mind—fitting circles of red calico and lace over the lids, secured by ribbons. I had promised to help her circulate them at the Senior Citizens tomorrow. I slid off the counter, sat cross-legged in an empty chair, and began writing out labels.

When the phone rang, I didn't rush to answer it. I just sat there, writing out CHUTNEY BY MIRANDA PRAY, but I was thinking: It's Sam, calling from the Mirabel, saying Nina has suffered a nervous breakdown, for me to meet him in Los Cabos in three days. Then I thought, It's Jackson asking me to run off to New Orleans for the weekend. Eleanor reached back with one long arm and picked up the phone. "Hello?" she said, narrowing her eyes suspiciously. Then she held out the receiver. "It's some man for you."

I took the phone, thinking that Nina had told Sam that I'd called. I felt surprised and relieved—I would have thought her to be more scheming—but it didn't explain what she was doing in his room. "Hey, Freddie," said Jackson. "Hope I'm not calling too late."

"You're not." I leaned back against the counter. Eleanor kept shooting poisonous glances at me, but Minerva was bent over the labels, writing in her spidery scrawl.

"Great." He made a sound that was something between a hum and a laugh, like when you taste something good. "Hey. You wouldn't like to go for a ride, would you?"

"Now?" I said. Both Eleanor and Minerva stared.

"Daddy still owns some land over on Calf Killer Road? It's got this California view in the wintertime, like what you see in the movies. An L.A. view. I thought you might like it. But we can do it another time. Or not at all. Whatever you want."

"An L.A. view, huh?" I tucked the receiver into my shoulder and smiled. He sounded so much like the old Jackson—boyish, sincere, eager to please—that I was touched. I didn't have the heart to tell him that I'd only been to L.A. five or six times, and all the famous views had been blotted out by smog. Twice the Santa Ana winds kicked up fires. It was bad luck, said our friends, bad timing.

"It won't take long," he said. "I promise you'll be home in time for *Letterman*. Sooner if you like."

"Okay," I said. Then I started trembling. I hung up and glanced at Minerva. "I'm going out for a bit. Do you need me to pick up anything—bread or milk?" I asked.

Minerva didn't answer. She just leaned forward, staring out the window, into the chilly dark.

"You're going out at *this* hour?" said Eleanor, blanching.

"It's not even nine o'clock." I shrugged.

"Yes," she said, almost strangling. "But Tallulah isn't like it used to be. There's a purse snatcher on the loose."

"Relax, I'm not going to Kmart."

"But nothing else is open except Git-and-Go and Wal-Mart. You aren't going all the way out there, are you?"

"No."

"Then, where?" Eleanor blinked, and her eyes resembled dark yellow lozenges.

"Jackson wants to show me something."

"Can't it wait? I really think you should stay here. It's supposed to rain."

"What, are you my mother?"

"You know I'm not." Eleanor snorted. "You aren't acting right."

"Yes, she is," said Minerva.

"No, she's not."

I stepped into the hall, trying to decide if I needed some perfume, maybe a little blush and lipstick. But it was all the way upstairs, in Jo-Nell's room. I picked up a blue jean jacket, felt in the pocket for ChapStick, and pulled it out. The waxy taste instantly made me think of Mama lining us three girls up in the kitchen, rubbing our lips in assembly-line fashion. I looked out the window, watching for Jackson's truck. About ten minutes later, it pulled into the drive. I ran out, skidding in the gravel, and opened the passenger door. When I slammed it, the door popped back open; I shut it again, but still, it refused to lock. Jackson leaned across the seat, pressing against my legs, and fingered the lock. He yanked the door, hard. I held my breath, waiting to see if it would hold; the door creaked open. I wondered what else was wrong, but I didn't say anything.

"Old cars take patience," Jackson said, reading my mind. He pulled the door, hard. This time I heard a click.

"It's fixed?" I said into the space over his head. He moved off my legs, and the upholstery springs squeaked.

"Just don't lean too hard on it. In fact, you might want to scoot a little toward the middle." He laughed, then lightly pinched my jacket.

"I won't fall out," I said, but I braced my hand against the dash. We drove in silence, passing into deeper country where the houses were more rustic, the road level with the tree line. It was a moonless night—cold and clear. The truck's headlights poured out into the darkness, dividing the road into two bowls of rough-paved concrete. Behind us the lights of Tallulah slipped further away, casting a pink haze up into the sky. The country looked dark and forbidding.

"We're almost there," said Jackson.

I studied his profile, willing him to face me, but he kept staring through the windshield. I briefly closed my eyes. In medical school I once read that optical images leave shadows on the retina for less than a second, but I could still see him. It was as if his face was etched behind my lids—the slope of his nose, the boyish, vulnerable curve of his throat. He turned down a gravel lane, and the truck shuddered up a steep hill. Weeds beat underneath the tires. At the top, he switched off the lights. Through the windshield, the winter moon reflected into an icy pond. All around us the land seemed to heave, falling in black waves, an ocean of hills. Way off in the distance, the lights of Tallulah burned. "Oh, Jackson," I said, leaning forward. "It's beautiful."

"I told you it was an L.A. view. Daddy bought this hill back in the sixties. He always planned to build up here."

I kept staring, trying to locate landmarks—the red blinking light from the radio station, WANT; the parallel rows of sulfur lights along South Jefferson Avenue; I could even see the Kmart sign, the red *K* and the blue *mart*. Jackson leaned across the seat and gently pushed back my bangs. I had often imagined myself in this situation—not with Jackson, exactly, but with some dark, faceless man who loved me. I believed in commitment. I always pictured myself as faithful, with a streak of prudery. Now I smiled at him, and he smiled back. My only worry was that he wouldn't kiss me, that he would be the one with scruples. He picked up my hand, uncurled my fingers, and kissed my open palm. It was such a tender gesture that I thought I might start crying. I closed my eyes and felt his lips travel to my wrist.

"This feels right to me," he said. He kissed me, wetting my upper lip. My fingers tangled in his hair, then dropped down to his neck. He moved up, shifting in the seat. His lips were utterly familiar, yet different from Sam's. I hadn't kissed another man since my wedding, but I remembered exactly what to do. I put my hand on his thigh, squeezing just above his knee. He pulled me across the seat, against his chest, and began unbuttoning my shirt. His fingers felt surprisingly cool, and when I shut my eyes, I had the curious sensation of being surrounded by water. His belt made a jingling sound, and his trousers slid down. I felt his breath on my face, his warm mouth, his hand circling the back of my neck.

"God, you're beautiful."

When a man says that, you may not believe him but still, you pay attention. It was easy pushing everything from my mind. I really did feel beautiful. And I had this need to feel him inside me. He was hard against my leg. I twisted away, digging into my purse, bringing up one of Nina's condoms. After so many years of monogamy, I'd forgotten the awkward negotiations: Did he have a prophylactic? He took it, holding it up to the moonlight. I held my breath, waiting for him to say something smart, but he ripped open the plastic cover with his teeth. Then he pushed down my jeans. I kicked them off, and they fell somewhere around the steering wheel. In one motion he fell back against the seat, pulling me on top of him. Using his chest for balance, I straddled him, gasping into his mouth when he pushed inside me. I moved back and forth, riding him like a wave, my bangs flipping into my eyes. I had a sensation of sinking through black water, with currents pounding me smooth as shells on the bottom of the ocean.

We made love as if we had been waiting our whole lives. When you sleep with someone, it lays bare all of your loves and losses, and all of the intervening years. I wondered if the time between Memphis and California was a sort of hibernation for us. We were waking up, starved for each other. It was over quickly, and I lay on top of him, my eyes shut, listening to his heart, listening to the rain that had suddenly started to fall. It drummed against the hood. I thought, Maybe this is how it is for a man, to give in to your passions, however fleeting, without remorse. Like a diver rising to the surface, I felt myself traveling toward light from someplace deep and blue and silent.

That night, I couldn't sleep. I lay on my side, in my childhood bed, watching rain pour down the wavy glass windows. I knew what Jo-Nell would say. Great sex, even if it occurred in a car, was a far cry from great love.

Don't think about it.

From the street, the mist rose up in waves, making me lone-some for California. Dewey was barely a wrinkle on the map, where steep arroyos and bluffs plunged into the Pacific. After a wet winter, the hills would be covered with luxuriant green turf, strewn with buttercups, daisies, and long-stemmed lavender lupine. When I squinted, the hills reminded me of green whales. Many evenings Sam and I drank wine in Mr. Espy's outdoor arbor, which featured a stone fireplace, barbecue pit, and a grapevine roof. From there, a footpath wound down the bluff to the rocky beach below. At the edge of the property, near the ocean, was Sam's old lookout tower. As a young man he'd watched the whale migrations, calling out numbers to his mother or Mr. Espy, who wrote them in a little notebook.

On Tomales Bay, the cold California current collides with the warm coastal air, creating foggy mornings and evenings. Right about now a thick fog would be pouring in from the open ocean, and all the lights in Mr. Espy's house would glow the deepest shade of gold—a beacon in the damp night, for what or whom, I couldn't know. I saw my father-in-law clearly—moving through the redwood-paneled rooms, shaking out Friskies for the tabby, dribbling a little water on my African violets, waiting for his housekeeper, Hoo Shee Laong, to announce supper. The air would be dense with aromas—fresh scallops baked in paper with saffron-infused polenta and roasted sweet peppers. Wild mushroom fettuccine with crushed chilies, garlic, and truffle oil. Or maybe Hoo Shee would prepare something lighter, a pear and goat cheese salad with warm pancetta and sherry vinaigrette.

I pictured the dining room table—a long, polished slab of rosewood, set for one, the mismatched flatware framing the old Ainsley china that Mrs. Espy had registered for in San Francisco many decades ago. The roses on the plates serve as a silent reminder of how much has been lost, how much it's still possible to lose. Mr. Espy always hinted that Sam was welcome to take up ranching, anything to keep him securely on dry land. All around us was the slender Tomales Bay, which traces the San Andreas Fault. It lies beneath everything, flooded by the sea, a great crack in the earth resting on nothing.

On the other side of the wall, I heard a crash. It rattled all the windowpanes. I sat up, thinking automatically of an earthquake; then I remembered where I was—flat-footed Tallulah, nestled in tons of limestone. I held my breath, poring over possibilities. I waited for another noise, but the only sound was the rain pattering over the leaf-clogged gutters, drizzling into the yews and boxwood. I worried that Minerva might have fallen out of bed; a woman her age could easily break a hip.

I eased out of bed, padded down the hall, and cracked open her door. A lamp was burning next to the bed, but the bed was empty, with the covers thrown back. Minerva was lying on the floor, halfway between the bed and dresser. I ran over to her and immediately felt for a pulse. It was weak and thready, but regular. Her pupils were equal, shrinking automatically when I pulled back the lids. My first thought was: Cardiac. Her color was ashy gray, and her whole body was dripping with perspiration.

"Minerva?" I said, grasping her hand. "If you can hear me, squeeze my fingers."

Nothing, not even a twitch. She was out cold. Reaching back toward the bed, I yanked the phone off the night table. It struck the floor, the bell trilling sharply. I dragged it by its cord, got a dial tone, and punched in 911. I told the operator that my grandmother was unconscious.

"Did she fall?" asked the operator.

"I don't know. I think so. Just send an ambulance to 201 River Street, the yellow house on the corner."

"We know where it is, honey bunch," said the operator, smacking gum loudly in my ear. "Just hang on, we'll be there in a heartbeat."

ELEANOR

Freddie drove to the hospital like a bank robber, causing the rubber to shriek on the station wagon's tires. "Just slow down!" I hollered, holding on to the dashboard. "The roads are wet. You're hydroplaning!"

"I just know it's her heart," Freddie kept saying. "A classic MI."

"MI?" I said, drawing back to stare.

"Myocardial infarction."

"I'm sure it's not," I said, but a chill went though me.

When she swerved into a no-parking zone, I could not contain myself another second. "You can't park here!"

"Why not?"

"It says Emergency Vehicles Only. They'll tow you off."

"This is an emergency."

"But you're not driving an ambulance."

"So let them tow me."

"But it's my car!"

"Then why don't you drive it?"

"Because it's night, and I'm scared!" I was practically screaming in her face. I wanted to say something on the order of, Look, I am scared of men—nothing but robbers and rapers and defilers of women. I didn't have time to collect my thoughts. She got out of the car and broke into a run, making me chase after her. Once we got inside the emergency department, I blinked. Freddie's hair was standing straight up, like fur that's been rubbed the wrong way. Her shirt gaped open, and I thought I saw a hickey on her neck. A nurse led us to a little cubicle. Minerva was lying on a cot, hooked up to machines and tubes.

"Now don't you girls fret," she said, opening one eye. "The emergency doctor says my heart is strong."

"It wasn't a heart attack, then?" I said, gulping air. "Freddie said it was."

"No, no. Just a little old fainting spell is all."

"I don't believe it," said Freddie. She looked at the heart monitor. "What kind of training does this doctor have?"

"Honey, he didn't say," Minerva said, but her voice sounded weak. "I'm fine, really. I just got up to go to the bathroom, and I must've passed out."

"When a person loses consciousness," said Freddie, standing on her toes to study the monitor, "it's either the heart or the brain."

"Then I guess it was my brain, honey. I never did have me a good one."

"Oh, you do, too," I said.

"Are you having any chest pain?" asked Freddie.

"Not a bit."

"Short of breath?"

"No."

"This is very strange." Freddie shifted her eyes at me.

"Don't look at me for answers." I held up my hands, as if to push her back. "I bake for a living. I don't know an MI from a pie."

"Well, I'm getting to the bottom of this." Freddie went out of the cubicle and found the ER doctor. She dragged him back to Minerva's bed. She began throwing out big words—cardiac caths, enzymes, PVCs. She insisted they call up a heart doctor or else.

"Once I saw Dr. Bernard," said Minerva, her voice real weak. "He treated my blood pressure, but he's a heart doctor."

"I'm afraid he's not on call," said the ER doctor. "But his new partner is."

"How new?" Freddie blinked.

"He's been in town six weeks."

"Who is this guy?" she asked the emergency doctor, folding her arms. "What do you know about him?"

"This *guy*," said the doctor, drawing back his upper lip, "is Dr. Starbuck, and he's board certified."

"What an odd name for a cardiologist," said Freddie. "Starbuck."

"He's brilliant," said the emergency doctor. "His credentials are impeccable."

"Then what's he doing here?" I snorted, but the emergency doctor ignored me.

"It's a large cardiology group," he told Freddie. "The best, the very best."

We waited for the young hotshot to show his face. About four hours later, he called us into the hall and pronounced Minerva as fit as a fiddle. He said she was suffering from something called malignant fainting.

"I've never heard of that," said Freddie.

"And she's a doctor, too," I said, nodding.

"Really." Dr. Starbuck didn't seem impressed. "Just because you haven't heard of it doesn't mean it doesn't exist. Malignant fainting won't kill your grandmother. But she'll probably lose consciousness from time to time. She might have to stop driving."

"Are you sure it's not her heart?" Freddie asked.

"Positive. But I want to keep her a few days to run tests."

"An arteriogram?"

"If it's indicated." Dr. Starbuck's eyes narrowed just the least. "Would you feel more comfortable if I consulted a neurologist?"

"If it's indicated," said Freddie, looking him square in the eye.

He snapped the chart shut, then turned down a hallway. We stepped back into Minerva's cubicle. "What do you think of that young doctor?" asked Minerva.

"I don't like him," Freddie said.

"Me, either," I said. "His eyes are beady."

"Well, I like him fine," Minerva said. "I think he's right cute."

They put her in something called the Cardiac Step-down Unit, which sounded like one of those aerobic programs on ESPN. She was hooked up to a heart monitor, IV drip, but no oxygen. She kept dozing off. "You all go back home," she told us, waving one wrinkly hand. It had an IV in it, hooked to a plastic bag. I was watching the tubes for air bubbles—those things can travel straight to the brain and kill you dead.

"She's right." I punched Freddie's arm. "Let's go."

"No. I want to be here when they run tests."

"Child, that's not till tomorrow," Minerva protested.

"I've got news for you, Minerva," said Freddie. "Tomorrow's here."

"Please go on home, girls. Get some rest. I ain't going nowhere. And I can't sleep with you two gibbering and jabbering." Her hair was pale and thin, and her skull seemed to shine through, a pearly shadow under the scalp. She looked old. I ached to cry, but I wanted to be strong.

After a while we left. As we walked out of the hospital, I tugged at Freddie's sleeve. Actually it was Jo-Nell's red wool coat from the junk store. My sister was a card-carrying member of the Goodwill Industries Preferred Customer Club. "You think Minerva'll be all right?" I said.

"I hope so." She glanced back at the hospital. "She's in their hands now."

"You think she's really got that malignant fainting?"

"No, I do *not*."

"Well? What, then?"

"I don't know. Maybe the tests will turn up something."

Soon as it got daylight, she called up old Jackson Manning, quizzing him up one side and down the other—and he was just a pediatrician. When she got off the phone, she looked at me and said, "He thinks it's a misdiagnosis—malignant fainting is asinine. And he doesn't know anything good or bad about Dr. Starbuck."

"What else?"

"When he gets to the hospital, he's going to look at Minerva's chart. Maybe he'll find out what's going on."

I wanted to say something on the order of, Isn't he a baby doctor? But I held my tongue. If she got mad, she might run off with old Jackson, leaving me all by my lonesome. I thought she had some nerve to have one man in Mexico and another in Tallulah. Day by day, she was getting more like Jo-Nell. I mean really—she goes out to dinner with him and comes home with wrinkled clothes. What's a sister supposed to think? Not that I blamed her, you understand. I thought about love and marriage, but I always saw myself with the children and no man. Just give me the ready-made baby and forget the peter part. Although I would never admit this to anyone, I didn't think I could have a bowel movement with a man in the house. It was bad enough to do my business with Brother Stowe's picture hanging on the wall.

After Freddie ran off to California, Jackson used to call the house and ask about her. "I don't know where she is," I'd tell him. It was the truth, sort of. I was just tired of him calling. Finally I just said, "Look, she's not coming home. You ought to go and find yourself a nice girlfriend." A few years later I read in the paper that he'd up and married a fashion model. She specialized in modeling hats (and, some folks said, lingerie). They said she could have been the Cindy Crawford of Memphis—a green-eyed blond version—but she gave it all up to marry

Jackson. Some called it Rebound, but I didn't. I wasn't surprised in the least. A good-looking fellow like Jackson. He was a catch, but he was also easy pickings. Two things don't grow on trees, doctors or money.

After Jackson finished school, he moved back to Tallulah and set up a practice. First time his wife set foot in the doughnut shop, I knew she was bad news. She walked up to the counter and asked if I had any madeleines.

"Madeleine?" I said, trying to be polite. "I don't know nobody by that name."

"No," she said, her voice all icy. "*Madeleines!* It's a sort of cookie."

"We don't have that, but we got some nice, fresh doughnut holes."

"What about Scottish shortbread?" She raised one brownish eyebrow, and I knew right then she wasn't a natural blonde.

"Miss," I said, "our shortbread is American—it's called short-ening bread, but I don't have much call for it."

"God, what kind of place is this?" She blinked. "Okay. One more time. Do you possibly have any hazelnut biscotti?"

"What you see is what you get." I was starting to get mad my own self. "If it's not here, then we don't have it."

"What kind of bakery doesn't have biscotti?" she cried.

"The Tallulah kind," I said. "Now. Do you want them dough-nut holes or not?"

"God, no," she said and ran out of the shop. Not too long after that, she left Jackson and went back to Memphis.

The next morning, on the way up to Minerva's room, we stopped in to see Jo-Nell to break the news. She was chipper, just in the best mood. Going on and on about getting out of the hospital and moving far, far away from Tallulah, where her name was *M-U-D*. We couldn't get a word in edgewise.

"Your name is fine," said Freddie.

"No, it's not." Jo-Nell shook her head. "Some men think I'm the Death Angel. Stick with me, kid, and you'll end up six feet under. And other men think I'm a slut—you know, a revolving door for a vagina. Now that I've survived a train wreck, I'll be an oddity. Somebody to talk about and look at, but avoid like the plague. Like bad luck is contagious, you know?"

"That's not true," said Freddie.

I cut my eyes at her. Lord, she made me sick, indulging Jo-Nell this way. I sat on the metal chair, my chin in my fists, thinking Jo-Nell was telling the truth—she had a terrible reputation. You just can't chase married men and expect to be received socially. Women will hate you. If Jo-Nell left Tallulah, she'd have to travel to a foreign country to escape her reputation. And once she got there, it would just be her luck to run into someone from Tallulah.

I had known this day would come—Jo-Nell getting a wild hair and trying to escape. I'd already started working on Freddie—trying to manipulate her into staying in Tallulah. "There's nothing more important than family," I told her the other night.

"No, there isn't," agreed Freddie. She was stretched out on the floral sofa, eating popcorn.

"More important than studying whales, even," I said.

"What?" Freddie blinked. She crunched down on a grain of popcorn.

"I just meant that there's plenty of other animals you can save."

"Excuse me?" Freddie's forehead wrinkled. She sat up, hugging the popcorn bowl.

"There's the African rhino, for example," I said. "Poachers are killing them for their horns. There isn't enough rhino police to go around. Isn't that awful? It gives me the chills."

"My field is whales," said Freddie.

"So? Change it!" I snapped my fingers. "Aren't you concerned that the national park in Africa, I forget the name, has less than thirty rhinos?"

"How do you know that?"

"I saw it on TV."

"Oh," said Freddie, peering into the popcorn bowl. "I don't have a TV in Dewey."

"Then how do you watch *Letterman*?"

"I don't usually."

"Well, you should get a nice little Sony," I said. "You've no idea what you're missing."

I was not one to talk about missing out on life, but she had no idea about my lists of safe and unsafe places. It was like that song, "It's a Small World." Sometimes I wondered if it was written just for people like me. I tilted my watch up to the light. We'd wasted fifteen minutes with Jo-Nell, and I felt like saying something on the order of this. I stood up and said, "We have some bad news, Jo-Nell."

"Let me guess," said Jo-Nell. "Freddie screwed Jackson."

"That's her bizwacks," I shouted. "Now, look, you crazy thing you. Something bad's happened. Minerva's in the hospital, up on the sixth floor."

"What!"

"She fainted," I said.

"Is she okay now?"

"The cardiologist seems to think so, but I'm not so sure," said Freddie. "They're running tests today."

"God, what's happening to this family?" said Jo-Nell.

"It's a curse," I whispered to myself. "Nothing but a curse."

Soon as I got Freddie alone in the elevator, I said, "So, are you and Jackson doing it?"

"What's it to you?"

"Just curious is all." I shrugged. "I can't help but wonder if you'll run out on him a-gain."

"Like you care."

"I do. I really do."

"Why?"

"Because Minerva's sick with Lord knows what, and Jo-Nell says she wants to move away and you don't know if you're coming or going. Meanwhile, I'm stuck in the same old place I've always been. I don't have a life."

"You're too scared."

"I am not!"

"Boo!" she cried, waving her arms. I screamed before I could stop myself, and I jumped against the back of the elevator.

"See?" she said.

"You just caught me off-guard." I straightened my skirt, brushing away the wrinkles.

"If you're scared of muggers," said Freddie, "then carry Mace."

"They don't sell that in Tallulah."

"That ought to tell you something."

The elevator doors opened with a *whoosh* and two nurses stood staring at us. I stepped out past Freddie, like she was the crazy one, into the chilled, germ-free air.

JO-NELL

Now that Minerva was in the hospital, my sisters took turns visiting me. While Freddie was upstairs, Eleanor sat with me—like I needed a baby-sitter, with all these cute doctors rushing in and out. When Dr. Jay Lambert stopped by, he kept watching Eleanor, who was cutting a *National Enquirer* to ribbons. He was, like, get me out of here! That woman is crazy. I was relieved when she went to the cafeteria for one of her pig-out snacks. Then Jay Lambert pulled the curtain and walked over to me, unzipping his trousers. "Be careful," I said, guarding my leg.

"I will, I will." He pulled back the sheet. "I don't have much time."

"That's all right; I do," I said, reaching for him. He was already hard in my hand.

After he left, I watched the soaps. It looked to me like my life was turning into one—without the clothes and pretty men. It was just a matter of time before Jay Lambert told me he had to slack off, that his wife was getting suspicious. If I had a dime for every suspicious woman in Tallulah, I could buy a Lexus. It didn't matter. In six weeks, I'd have a new zip code: Mount Olive, Texas.

Jay came by every morning just before *The Young and the Restless*, bringing me flowers, candy, and gold jewelry. My favorite was a frog stickpin. "I'm falling in love with you," he said. I didn't ask what his wife thought about it—my usual line.

"Well, that's nice," I told him, "just don't fall *too* hard."

"Why not?" His forehead scrunched up, and I thought he was going to break down and cry.

"Because, darlin'." I put my hands on his face. "Falling's never fun. It hurts."

Now I looked up and a man was standing in the door. His face looked awful familiar, and I said, "Hi, could I help you?"

"I am Brother Stowe," he said. Well, you could have knocked me over with a feather. He didn't look a thing like his picture— he was a lot older in real life. He was fifty-something, wearing a red V-neck sweater and dark blue pants. A big gray overcoat was folded in his arms. Still, I was real touched, seeing as I wasn't a Christian and all.

When Eleanor stepped into the room, she gasped. I could almost read her mind—here in the flesh was the bathroom preacher. "Why, Brother Stowe," she said, just as polite as you please. "How nice of you to come."

"Hello, there," he said, rising and extending his hand. "Have we met?"

"Not really," she said, all breathless.

"Then, how . . ."

"Minerva has got your picture over the toilet," I explained.

"Oh," said Brother Stowe.

"Not *over* the toilet," snapped Eleanor. "Across from it."

We looked at Brother Stowe. His cheeks puffed up, and sweat was starting to gather on his forehead. "Well, Minerva's a fine, fine woman," he said, but I could tell he wasn't too sure about us. "Whenever there's sickness or death, she's Johnny-on-the-spot with a casserole. I just came from seeing her, actually." He pointed to the ceiling, as if he'd just floated down from heaven. "She's chipper, in good spirits."

"She always is," said Eleanor.

"Yes." He rubbed a spot on his coat, then glanced over at me.

"Jo-Nell, she tells me you narrowly escaped death—a train wreck, was it?"

"Yes," I said, happy for the conversation to swing back to me. "I got the living hell knocked out of me. Actually, I was real lucky, Father Stowe."

"Brother," he said. "It's Brother Stowe. Not Father. That's with the Catholics."

"Well, I'm not real up on religion," I said, trying to be honest. After all, I didn't see the point of lying to a man of God. "I know I should be, like, grateful to Jesus or somebody for sparing me; but I've just been too fucking sore to get on my knees and pray. Besides, I'm not a believer."

"I had no idea," said Brother Stowe.

"That's okay." I smiled. "You're not psychic."

Over by the window, Eleanor made a strangling sound.

"Are you okay?" I asked her. She cupped one hand over her mouth and nose, like she was sniffing her breath.

"Well, I've to run," said Brother Stowe. "I've got a lot of stops to make."

"Come back anytime, Father." I watched him scuttle out the door, giving Eleanor a wide berth.

After he was gone, Eleanor narrowed her yellow eyes and said, "Well, aren't you ashamed?"

"Of what?"

"You said the F-word in front of Brother Stowe."

"I did?" Honest to god, I couldn't remember.

"Yes, you did."

"Well, I didn't mean to. It must've slipped out."

"You said hell, too."

"Well, don't you think he's kinda used to that word, Eleanor?" I shrugged. "Anyhow, he didn't make a big deal out of it."

"I guess he was too shocked." Eleanor sat down and peered up at the TV. "What's happening on my show?"

"Well, on the night before Christine's wedding to Paul, she got swept off her feet by Danny, her ex-husband."

"I know who Danny is."

"And Paul caught them—actually, I missed it that day. Anyhow, they broke up. Meanwhile Danny's other ex-wife, Phyllis, is plotting to get him back."

"Never mind her. What's happening with Nikki and Victor?"

That afternoon, Freddie came to visit me. Before she got good and settled, I blurted, "Was it good?"

"Was what good?" she said. She was sitting in the brown vinyl chair, her legs drawn up to her chin.

"Don't you play dumb with me." I laughed. "It's written all over you."

"What is?"

"Sex, you nitwit." See, when a woman's getting laid in the proper way, she glows. Her hair takes on a sheen. Her eyes are all lit up—and smile, Lord, you've never seen such a smile. "You never said—was it good?"

She shrugged, then bit her knee.

"Sex ain't everything," I reminded her. "And doctors are the worst in bed."

"I didn't say that." She lifted her chin, staring at me with those brown eyes.

"And what about Sam?"

She shrugged again. So, I thought. This is how it's going to be. She wasn't going to tell me shit. "All those stories you told me about him—going scuba diving with sharks, petting whales, fishing off the coast of Spain. It sounds to me like you and him have a pretty exciting life."

"I guess."

"Can you give that up?"

"I may not have a choice."

"Oh, I see. You're going to fuck him before he can fuck you.

He slept with a woman, but you didn't forget, didn't forgive. And all this time you're a nervous wreck, you're thinking he's going to do it again. So the first time you're apart, you get all paranoid about some blonde—"

"With some justification."

"—and you get caught in your own little web of passion."

"Well, that's your theory," she said. "You're forgetting I was vulnerable."

"And horny, don't *you* forget that."

"I've been sitting here thinking crazy things," she said.

"Orgasms can do that to you."

"Seriously, I've been thinking about staying."

"You mean, *here*?" I reached up and grabbed the trapeze bar, then shifted my legs. It didn't hurt to move, but I was afraid I'd jerk something loose. "In Tallulah?"

She nodded.

"Knock me over with a feather," I muttered. "But Freddie, that don't make sense."

"I know; that's why I said it was crazy."

"It sure is crazy. Honest-to-god crazy. I can understand the men, but you can't keep throwing away careers."

"I wouldn't necessarily give up the whales."

"In case you ain't noticed, the only waters in Tallulah is the river and Cissy Alsup's swimming pool. And speaking of Cissy, why on earth would you care to live in a place where she lives, after what she pulled? Throwing you with Jackson and that real estate woman. Trying to cause a cat fight."

"She doesn't have anything to do with me." Freddie gave me her most stubborn stare.

"If you move back here, she'll find a way."

"It's easy to avoid her kind."

"You think so? We're talking about *Cissy*."

"I won't ever call her."

"Don't you worry. She'll call you."

"So I'll get an answering machine." She shrugged. "I just won't return her calls. She'll get the hint."

"Look, forget Cissy. You can solve that problem with Caller ID. Let's talk about Jackson. Are you in love or what?"

"It hasn't been quite long enough for love."

"It's not like you're starting from scratch. It's kind of like those dehydrated porcino mushrooms the gourmet stores sell. Add a little water and the whole batch doubles in size."

She laughed.

"You lucky thing you. Two men on the line."

"I don't have two."

"Sure, you've got Sam and—"

"I called his motel room and his assistant answered."

"Oh, my god." I put my hand over my mouth. "He fucked her?"

"I don't know." She released a long sigh.

"So," I said, "tit for tat. You went and did it with old Jackson. You got even, just in case."

"No, I didn't." She frowned, picking at a scab on her arm. Then she looked up at me, her eyes shiny brown. "I guess I did. Maybe just a little."

"There you go." I flipped one hand.

"But like you said, I do have a long history with Jackson."

"You can fuck somebody for no reason, but still have a damn good time, you know. The thing is, it can turn on you."

"How?"

"You can make a real bad choice. Pick the wrong man. If you start to fall in love, it's a disaster."

"It's not like I have a choice here. If Sam's sleeping with Nina, I don't want him."

"You've got all kinds of choices. I thought you were crazy about Sam. The only man for you and so on."

"Yeah, right. I'm having a family crisis, and he's entertaining women at the Hotel Mirabel."

"It's just the one woman, right?"

"If he slept with her, after all I've been through, it's downright mean. It's like he's kicking me when I'm down."

"Look, you don't have X-ray vision. You didn't see inside that motel room. That Nina woman could've been there for an honest-to-god reason."

"Sure."

"You don't know. Instead, you think you've got it all figured out. So you go screw Jackson."

"It's a little more complicated than that." She sniffed.

"The hell it is. It sounds like something I'd do. But see, you aren't me. You do it with a guy, then start feeling all guilty. You can't fuck without marriage. Elizabeth Taylor has the same problem. She just can't have an affair and let it go. Well, take it from me, Freddie. Don't feel guilty. Just lay back and enjoy yourself."

"I don't know what I want."

"My advice is, don't spill your guts to Sam. Don't you dare tell him a thing. Because he won't understand. Men can screw anything they want, but their women have to stay true blue. What they don't know won't hurt them is my motto."

"I hate liars."

"Sometimes little white lies are necessary. Sometimes they save your ass. And speaking of honesty, do you really want a man who tells you everything?"

"Yeah."

"Then you'll be crazy in six months." I lifted one lock of my hair and sniffed it. It smelled like dirty feet. "I don't know if Jackson's big on honesty, but I know he's big on sports. He's eat up with SEC football, like all Southern men. I'll bet you money that he's got season tickets to the UT games." I waved my fist. "Go big Orange."

"So? You've gone to Knoxville plenty of times."

"Yes, but with *dates*. I had, like, a choice. I wasn't married to one of the fools. And I don't hate contact sports the way you do. The only thing I've seen you watch on TV is skiing on ESPN, or figure skating on Saturday afternoons. I'll bet you've never set foot in Candlestick Park."

"I have, too."

"Well, maybe so. But I'll bet if you opened Jackson's closet, you'd find two hundred sweaters, all ranging in colors from tangerine to muskmelon. How does that old joke go? Why is Tennessee so colorful in October? Because all the rednecks turn orange."

"So what if he likes football?" Freddie shrugged. "Sam's a 49ers fan."

"Look, he's down in Baja during the Sugar Bowl. That tells me everything I need to know about him and sports. You're not used to a fanatic."

"You don't know that Jackson's one."

"No, I don't. I'm just trying to say that sports has a way of separating two people. The way oil beads up in water. Half my ex-lovers wouldn't have needed me if their wives liked UT football, I swear."

"You're on the wrong track," she said. "My problem isn't sports."

"But it has to do with balls," I said. "Every problem known to women is centered around a man's balls—whether they're attached to his body or not."

She threw back her head and laughed. Then she hugged my neck. "Whatever would I have done without you?" she said.

"Not very much," I told her, then ran my fingers through her hair, messing it all up. "Not very much at all."

MINERVA PRAY

My room was at the farthest end of the little hall. It was known as the little CCU. The nurses perched in that station of theirs, clucking like pigeons, eating popcorn and bagged chips and pretending to be busy. I was real happy when Freddie wheeled Jo-Nell into my room, so we could all watch *One Life to Live*. All the nurses had signed Jo-Nell's air cast, making it look like a filthy rag. "Where's Eleanor?" I said.

"Shhh," said Jo-Nell. "If you say her name, she'll appear."

"She's at the doughnut shop," said Freddie.

"You'll never guess the latest," said Jo-Nell. "Freddie's thinking of staying in Tallulah."

"I am not," snapped Freddie. Her cheeks flamed red.

"You are, too."

"What brought this on?" I asked her.

"I just said I *might* stay." There, she'd spit it out. The truth was inside her all along, like a big egg stuck up a chicken's craw.

"I'll tell you who brought it on," said Jo-Nell. "Jackson did. And she called Sam's motel and a lady researcher answered."

"Shut up," said Freddie, her eyes burning holes into her sister.

"Freddie's a grown woman," I said. "She can make her own mind up."

"She's crazy as a bedbug," said Jo-Nell.

"Maybe I am."

"You'll be happy here, let's see, six months? A year? Three years? And all the while, you'll be dealing with the Cissys of Tallulah. The Christian Women's Club, Medical Auxiliary, Junior Wives Club—all those things you hate. Why, you wouldn't be caught dead at one of their meetings."

(I was thinking the same thing myself: she wouldn't like it.)

"I'm telling you, this is all there is in Tallulah, honey," said Jo-Nell. "Clubs and gossip and in between, a lot of fucking."

"Jo-Nell!" I said, trying to sit up, and my heart skipped a beat—a little red light flashed on the monitor. "Watch your mouth."

"Let's see how long it takes the nurse to get here," said Freddie, glancing at her watch, a black, no-nonsense number.

"The nurses don't come to my room," I said. "They've forgot I'm here. Ain't that a caution?"

"I just don't think it's fair," wailed Jo-Nell. "Freddie's coming back home just when I'm leaving."

"I never said I was coming back," said Freddie.

I didn't say a word, but I was worried. As much as I would have loved to be near Freddie, Tallulah was not made for her.

"You left this crappy town once on account of Jackson," said Jo-Nell. "Don't you forget that."

"It wasn't his fault. I screwed up. I was ashamed of what I'd done in Memphis."

"But you made a life for yourself in California."

"I thought I had." She looked down at her hands, the fingers were laced together. "And I think you're wrong about Tallulah. It's not that crappy."

"You're all the time bragging about that town you live in— what's it called?"

"Dewey."

"That's right. With the gourmet gas stations."

"Maybe I was just being finicky and critical," said Freddie.

"Sometimes it pays to be nonjudgmental. It's like finding a roach in your cheesecake and saying, I'll never eat cheesecake again."

"That's what Eleanor would do," I said. We all laughed, then hung our heads for making fun.

"See, I just don't get you," Jo-Nell told Freddie. "I feel like I've used up this town and all of its people. I don't have any secrets. In fact, I will John Brown guarantee you that more lies than truths are told in Tallulah."

"But that's anywhere," said Freddie.

"This is true," I said, thinking that people have different accents and tastes, but deep down, we're all the same. "Folks is folks, no matter where you go," I said, smoothing the covers. I glanced up at the monitor—my heartbeat was regular as a drippy faucet.

"Nothing but a pack of gossips in Tallulah," said Jo-Nell. She snorted. "Me, I'm blowing this rat hole. Soon's I'm able, I'm going."

"Where you going to, baby?" I asked her, real gentle-like.

"I don't know. I've been thinking about Texas."

"Mount Olive is smaller than Tallulah," said Freddie. "And you'll be the object of curiosity, because you're new and you're Hattie's grandniece."

"I'll be fine," Jo-Nell said. "Worry about yourself."

"You're in no shape to travel," said Freddie.

"We're looking at the world from two different hilltops. You see Tallulah and think, Hmm, maybe I was wrong. Maybe it's not so bad. Jackson's here, Minerva's here, you're ready to give it all another shot. Me, I'm ready to tear out my hair."

"It's good people that make up a good place, Jo-Nell," I said gently. "There are weeds in any garden."

"I know it," she said. "I'm just ready for some different weeds. I'm the one who was never free. I never even tried to leave home. And anyway, ain't Texas our original home?"

"It's not mine," Freddie said darkly.

"It's mine," I said, mulling it over. "The ranch belongs to us all. It might be good for Jo-Nell to go. With nobody living at Hattie's, it'll run to ruin. I can't take care of it from here."

"If I really do go to Texas," Jo-Nell said, "it'll be like making a big circle."

"Don't go anywhere just yet. Stay in Tallulah." Freddie tugged her sister's hand. "Remember how we used to go to garage sales?"

"You never bought a thing," said Jo-Nell.

"But I might now," said Freddie.

Me, I knew what she was saying. She was willing to take a chance, to give Tallulah another shot before she wrote it off forever. Lord knows, I never meant to stay here. But before I knew it, twenty-five years had passed. Then thirty. Then I was an old woman, and the next thing I knew, Tallulah was a comfort. It was the patchwork quilt I'd started in 1941, and now, all these years later, it was big enough to keep me warm. I used it night after night, each bright scrap was a separate memory. A toddler's watermelon dress. A man's plaid underwear. Maternity smock all covered with mustang grapes. It was mine, built square by square, stitch by stitch. Plenty of mistakes was made, don't you think they wasn't, but a flawed quilt warms you just the same as a perfect one. Anyhow, a perfect one scares you—what if you get it stained? Wrinkled? What if the cat lays on it? Sometimes you need imperfection to enjoy your life, not just to endure it.

"Wait and see, Cissy'll try to drag you into things," Jo-Nell warned. "Even if it's just to entertain herself. To fill up spaces in her datebook."

"I can't waste my time with all that. There's good women here. Women who grow their own tomatoes and irises. Why, like you, Minerva."

"Me?" I said, waving one hand.

"You have always found happiness in weird places."

"No place is weirder than Tallulah," said Jo-Nell, snorting again. "I wish you and Minerva would come with me to Mount Olive."

"Not me." I waved my hand. "I got too much to tend here, child."

"Count me out, too." Freddie shook her head.

"Damn, if he's that good in bed," Jo-Nell said, laughing, "then bring him along. Put him in the car and bring him along."

After the girls left, the little CCU was quiet. All by myself I sat and watched the TV, just a-wondering about things. My girls was at the crossroads. One was coming, one was going, and one was getting left behind. Jo-Nell was ready for a fresh start, she was looking toward the future, and Freddie was seeking old links—links to the past, her past. With just me to live with, poor old Eleanor would have herself a hissy fit. Like I told her, Ain't nothing left to do but get some courage, the nerve to shop at Winn-Dixie without frothing at the mouth. She did not like me saying that one bit, but it's the gospel.

Simple pleasures is the key to life, you see. Planting lettuce. Rooting wild violets. Making grape jelly in August. Growing your own parsley and thyme. Hanging wet sheets on the line, feeling them slap against your legs like your own personal breeze. Hearing your mama tell you about when she was a girl and when *her* mama was a girl, all the way back to Eve and the apple tree. Like I use to tell my Ruthie, While you're busy making your grocery lists and planning your schedules, real life is happening. And you know what, child? It sure enough is.

This is a hard lesson. Some folks never learn it. I knew me a lady who was building a house, and she drove herself crazy over doorknobs. She picked out ones shaped like eggs—pretty little things, I thought. She died thinking about them knobs, wishing she had picked some with fancy engraving. I have known women who dithered over paint samples—which exact shade of off-white? Their whole lives hinged on the raspberries in their sofa to match the apples in their throw pillows. Fruit's fruit, if you ask me. Red's red. I ain't blind—I know they's different shades. Pinky-reds and brown-reds and red-reds, but child, why put your stock in a color? It won't make you happy one iota. Better to plant you a row of daffodils or azaleas. Get down on your knees, reach into the cool mushy earth, and praise God that you're able.

ELEANOR

The newspaper said KMART MUGGER TAKES ANOTHER POCKETBOOK: VICTIM TREATED AT TALLULAH GENERAL FOR INJURIES. When I read this, Freddie and I were sitting at the kitchen table, eating chicken salad on whole wheat. I got out my scissors and snipped the article. Freddie just laughed. "Crime wave hits small-town America," she said.

"It's not funny."

"Eleanor, you can't live your life this way, waiting for some man to rob you."

"I'm not," I bristled. "But you can't deny that a mugger is loose in greater Tallulah."

"Then stop carrying a purse." She bit into her sandwich, crunching loudly on lettuce.

"I'd just as soon die." This was the truth. Everything was in my purse. My glasses, driver's license, family pictures, Rolaids, overdue bills, coupons, money, keys, hand lotion, to-do notes, a running grocery list, recipes, chewing gum, egg timer, thermometer, and Excedrin. (You never know when you'll get a tension headache.)

"I just wish you wouldn't keep that scrapbook." Freddie set down her sandwich. Her eyes drooped in the corners.

"I like it. It's my hobby."

"Get another."

"That's easy for you to say."

"I'm not criticizing you." She wiped her mouth with a napkin. These days she was wearing lipstick all the time, along with Jo-Nell's short plaid skirts and hair mousse. When a woman fixes up, a man is at the bottom of it.

"No?" I raised one eyebrow.

"I'm just saying you need a little more confidence. Why don't you take a self-defense course?"

"I don't need one."

"I took a class in San Francisco. It was near Haight-Ashbury. Kind of scary at night."

"You would pick something like that," I said.

"The instructor told us to fill our purses with rocks. If we got jumped from behind, we had a weapon."

"Did you pay good money to hear that?"

"No, it was free."

"Well, that's a good thing, because it's worthless advice."

After she went off with Jackson, smelling to high heaven of Estée Lauder perfume, I stepped out into the backyard. Then I searched through the old brick pile. Minerva had been saving them to border a herb garden. I lifted a great big red brick. It felt heavy, solid. I didn't know if it would fit in my purse, much less serve as a weapon. If anybody asked why I was carrying it around, I'd say it was a garlic smasher. As I toted it back into the house, I felt just a little more powerful. I told myself that a woman with a weapon was a woman to avoid, but I really didn't know.

Two days went by, and Minerva seemed to go downhill. When she got up to go to the bathroom, she was breathless. She clutched her green oxygen tube like it was a lifeline. Her skin was hot and dry, like she was running a fever, and her color was terrible—like dirty dishwater. We ran into Dr. Starbuck in the hall and pinned him down.

"I want to know what's going on with my grandmother," Freddie said. "You did every test but an arteriogram."

"I hate to put her through it," he said. "Her echo's fine; her enzymes are super; and I've got her attached to a Holter monitor. Her heart is fine. No chest pain, no arrhythmias to speak of. However, she seems to be running a low-grade temperature."

"From what?" I said.

"It could be viral," said the doctor.

"Then what's making her short of breath?" I asked.

"I've ordered a lung scan, to rule out a pulmonary embolus."

"A what?" I leaned forward.

"A blood clot in her lung," Freddie explained.

"I really doubt she has one." He shrugged. "However, I think the TB skin test might be revealing."

"A what?" Freddie laughed, but her eyes were dead-center on the doctor.

"A tuberculin skin—"

"That's ridiculous."

"Actually, it's not. You'd be surprised at the number of tubercular patients who present with dyspnea." The doctor looked at me—I could tell he figured me for the dumb one. "Dyspnea means short of breath."

"I knew that," I snapped, rubbing my purse, feeling the hard edges of the brick. If he messed with me, he'd be sorry.

MINERVA PRAY

Word spread like wildfire that I was at Tallulah General. I had so many visitors that the lady in B bed complained to the nurses. "She's got the window *and* a crowd. It's just not fair."

"You'll be fine," said the nurse, drawing the curtain around the woman's bed. "Try to get some rest and you'll be fine."

"I'm just so tired," I said. It was like I'd been pulling up bean-poles or digging wild ferns. This malignant fainting, or whatever they call it, was hard work. It sapped me dry. The nurse come back and put oxygen up my nose. I snatched on to it, holding the green tube.

"Does that help?" she asked.

It sure enough did, but a little later, I got so clogged I couldn't breathe. I thought I was coming down with a cold, but Freddie said no, it's the oxygen. It dries up your sinuses. She made the nurses hook up a water bottle. In a little while I wasn't snuffed up atall. That girl would have made a good doctor. And I myself would have made a good boat, just drifting free down the river.

When I opened my eyes again, Freddie was sitting in the window. Behind her, the light blazed pink and yellow. Eleanor was setting in the chair, working on a crossword puzzle. Before she saw me, I shut my eyes. Didn't mean to be rude, but I was past going. Freddie or Jo-Nell would just set with you, but not Eleanor. That girl was a born talker, and child, I was talked out.

If only I could catch me a good breath, I'd be fine.

I don't know how much time went by—maybe a second, maybe a entire afternoon. "Mrs. Pray?" someone said. (It sounded like that heart doctor, but I couldn't be sure.) "You seem to be running a FUO."

"FUO?" cried Eleanor (I knowed it was her; I'd know that voice anywhere). "This ain't *Star Trek,* so don't talk gibberish."

"Eleanor!" said Freddie.

"Uh, no," said the man. "FUO. A fever of unknown origin."

"Well, why didn't you just say so?" snapped Eleanor.

I started to tell her not to be so sassy, but when I finally opened my eyes, it was evening, and the granddaughters wasn't nowhere to be seen. (I knew how Eleanor hated to drive after dark—even if somebody else drove her.) The nurse brought my supper tray, but I never opened the lid. The smells kindly turned my stomach. I just drifted in and out of dingy white veils, or maybe it was cheesecloth. I just couldn't be sure. When you get this tired, it's hard to be sure of anything.

Freddie's old beau, Jackson Manning, came and sat on the bed. I stirred awake and seen that he'd brought me a little fern with a red bow on it. He reached over and set it in the sunny window. Said, "Miss Minerva, is there anything I can do for you?"

"Me?" I tried to think, but it was too hard. I liked to ask that question of people—get to the bottom of what sick or hurt folks needed. A fresh pitcher of ice water, an extry pillow, saltine crackers and buttermilk. You can get all that and more at a hospital, if you can get hold of the nurses. But I couldn't think for the life of me what I needed. I had this deep pain in my chest, up under my ribs, way deep in the back, but I'd already complained to that heart doctor a time or two, and he didn't seem worried. "You might have fractured a rib when you fell the other day," said Dr. Starbuck. "I'll order a lung scan." Child, I've been scanned half to death, and they ain't turned up nothing yet. I hated to keep on complaining. Pretty soon they'd run out of things to test. You wonder sometimes if they think it's all in your head.

I opened my eyes a little wider, and looked at the boy—nice blue eyes, just like his daddy's, and a cleft chin. "Just do right by my Freddie," I said. "That's what you can do for me. She's a good girl."

"Yes, ma'am. I know she is," he said, just a-patting my hand. Behind him, the sun streamed down. Then he leaned close to me. "I've always loved her, you know."

"I know."

"I'm going over to see her tonight."

"You do that, child." My voice was so faint, it squeaked. It tickled me. "I'd appreciate it if you'd tell her to bring me a fresh nightgown in the morning."

"Yes, ma'am." He got up. "I'll see you tomorrow."

"See you," I said.

FREDDIE

All my life I've tried to mimic the turtle—if I couldn't carry it on my back, it got left behind. I didn't collect cookbooks, glass animals, or the latest fashions. Now I knew why: I was lugging around all kinds of excess baggage—Jackson, Minerva, Jo-Nell, Sam, my lost career. The biggest load of all was free-floating worry—I couldn't relax, couldn't trust, couldn't live my life for the worries. Sometimes I thought I was living in a war zone. I wouldn't take any prisoners or souvenirs. I'd be lucky to get out unscathed. I saw that Eleanor was on the front lines with me, except she suffered from battle fatigue. She was an extreme example of unchecked worry. It must have been in our genes, an inherited trait, like dimples—dents somewhere in the personality.

I didn't know what prompted me to do it, but I called the house in Dewey. Mr. Espy answered on the fourth ring. He told me a storm was roaring through Tomales Bay, washing oysters to shore—January being an *R* month. I saw him sitting in the living room. The windows had tiny square panes of old glass, each one warped and bubbled. "Sam keeps me posted about you," he said. "I understand your sister is mending?"

"Yes, but now my grandmother is in the hospital. You remember me telling you about Minerva?"

"Yes, I do. And I'm so sorry to hear it. I spoke to Sam night before last, and he didn't mention it."

"I guess he doesn't know. I haven't talked to him." I chewed my thumb. "Missed connections. You know how it is in Baja."

"Oh, yes," he said. "That I do."

"Well, I hope the storm ends soon."

"Is anything else wrong?" he asked. "You don't sound like yourself, dear."

"No, I'm fine. I just wanted to call." I put two fingers between my eyes, but the tears leaked through, wetting my knuckles. After I hung up, I seemed to recall that Mrs. Espy had despised Dewey. Sam said she called it exile. Petaluma was the nearest "big" town, and the road to San Francisco was always being closed due to road slides. She was a Phoenix native, where the seasons were bone-dry, where you could plant your summer garden in February. Dewey's climate must have left her unsettled. In late August and early September, the fog blew away, leaving behind clear, warm days. This was only a reprieve. Soon the wintry rains hugged the coast, as if that whole part of the world needed a thorough cleansing, a kind of seasonal baptism.

While Eleanor was bathing, I heard a car turn into the driveway. Through a crack in the Venetians, I watched Jackson run up the flaking stone walkway, onto the porch. He knocked, but I just stood there, trying to decide if I should open the door or wait and see if he'd go away. I felt very wicked. The old brown station wagon was parked in the garage—he knew Eleanor didn't drive after dark, so the car was a dead giveaway that I was here. I wanted to see him, yet I didn't. I hadn't talked to Sam in days, and suddenly I understood why women took lovers. Disappointments gathered like water on a leaky roof. Before you knew it you didn't have a marriage—you had a bucketful of grievances.

"Coming," I said in a rushed voice, as if I'd been hurrying through a maze of rooms to reach him. I flung open the door. Cold air ruffled my nightgown. It was one of Eleanor's, pale yellow flannel stitched with baby chickens on the bib.

"You're dressed for bed." He gazed down at me, grinning.

"It's the latest style," I said, pirouetting on my toes. Then I stopped spinning. "Eleanor's upstairs bathing."

"Bad timing?" He looked agonized.

"Depends on what you had in mind." I drew him inside, kicking the door shut with my foot.

ELEANOR

Jo-Nell used to sneak men into the house, fixing them bourbon and branch, giggling at every stupid thing they said. Then she'd get them down on the floor and suck their toes until they hollered. It was a sight to behold: grown men rolling on the floor, begging for mercy. It never woke up Minerva, which was a good thing; if she'd come down the stairs to see what was going on, she would have tripped over me and broke her neck.

Now I was spying on Freddie and Jackson. Jo-Nell's CD player sat on the counter, plugged in next to the toaster. The music was horrible, a creepy-voiced man singing about big-leg women and how they didn't have souls. Freddie and Jackson weren't paying attention. They sat the kitchen table, sipping hot tea. Between them was a bottle of apple brandy. I told myself to be grateful to have a sister who could sit in a chair like a normal person. No Ravel's "Bolero" blaring from the stereo. No Reddi-Whip spewing out on naked body parts.

"There's got to be a way to work this out," Jackson was saying. He picked up his teacup, then blew on it, ruffling the liquid. "You could live here from March till late November, then fly down to Baja."

"I don't think Sam would agree."

"I thought he was so hip," said Jackson. "I thought he was a vegetarian."

"Vegan."

"That's right. I forgot." He set down his cup, fixing those purple-blue eyes on her. "There are other waters, Freddie. And other whales."

"But my life's work are the greys. I couldn't give them up any more than you could give up pediatrics."

"I might could." He took another sip of tea. "But you're not asking, are you?"

"I wouldn't. I couldn't." She reached across the table and squeezed his fingers. "The West is, I don't know, faster? Is that the word?"

"I know how it is, Freddie. I've been to medical conventions in Los Angeles and San Diego."

"Yeah, homogeneous conventions in homogenous hotels. It's not the real thing."

"So what are you saying? That I'm incapable of making it in the West? That I'm too much of a Southern male?"

"I didn't say that."

"But you were thinking it."

"No, I—"

"If you stayed here, would it be so awful?"

"It would be a disaster. I wouldn't wear the right clothes. I'd avoid the church ladies and the Tallulah-Nashville shopping club. I'd get a reputation for being unfriendly. People would ask when I was going back to California."

"What do you care? You've always marched to your own drummer. It worked for Thoreau."

"Yeah. But he's dead." Freddie sighed. Music streamed out of the boom box, about big-leg women who want to ball all day. Lord, Lord, Lord. It just made me want to vomit.

"I've been thinking about this," Freddie was saying. "In

order to fit, I'd have to change. I don't think I can."

"But I don't want you to change."

"No?" She gave him a funny look. "I don't even consider myself a Southerner."

"You were born and reared in the South. It's what you are."

"I was raised on white beans and ham, biscuits and sorghum. No one in my family fought in the Civil War. Even thought I had a relative who almost got killed at the Alamo. As far as I know, no Prays or McBrooms ever had a plantation or wore white robes."

"My daddy has a George Wallace clock," Jackson said. "We found it when he moved. And when Mother was alive, she had a tag sale. She sold Mr. Eubanks a box of junk for fifty cents. About an hour later, he came back with this funny white hood. 'Look what you sold me, Miss Margaret,' he said. 'A bona fide Klan hood.'"

"Was it?"

"Yes. Mother swore up and down she'd never seen it before. She thought it was already in the attic when we bought the house."

"Hmm," said Freddie.

"Don't you miss all this craziness?"

"Oh, sometimes." She smiled.

"Then stay with me, baby."

"I can't," she said. "I just can't." Then she fell into his arms. Oh, Lord, I thought, here we go again. Talk about wishy-washy. Talk about Ravel's "Bolero," *The Postman Only Rings Twice*, and *Last Tango in Paris*. Clear the table and get out the Land O' Lakes butter. I was thinking something on the order of, I have the most stupid sisters in the world. Their brains are between their legs. More smacking noises started up, disgusting sounds that had nothing to do with drinking tea.

This was getting real boring. After a lifetime of watching the soaps, I expected a little more. And it was making me hungry. I wouldn't have minded some decent background music, like Tracy Chapman or Wynonna; but I just didn't have the heart to spy any longer. I crept back to bed, piling the covers all around me. I myself wouldn't mind if Freddie stayed here. We could go grocery shopping. Jo-Nell was no fun at Winn-Dixie. She was scared of running into the wife of an old lover. It scared me, too, and I was innocent. Once, we were standing in the frozen foods, and she got slapped in the face. "Who was that?" I asked after the woman ran off.

"Don't ask," said Jo-Nell, holding a carton of Cool Whip against her cheek.

It would be refreshing to have a low-profile sister in this house. All I had left in the world was Minerva and Jo-Nell. I didn't even have a cat. That made up a durn small family, but it was all in the world I needed. Sure, us three girls had fought— the differences in our ages was enough to make us mortal enemies, but family's family. I closed my eyes, but it was a long, long time before I fell asleep.

MINERVA PRAY

When I opened my eyes again, it was pitch-black, and a brick was setting on my chest. I tried to set up, thinking I'd shake it off, but it was hard to move with all them wires. Lord, I thought, this brick. Someone had throwed a brick and hit me with it.

A nurse came running, squeaking her shoes on the tile. "Mrs. Pray," she said, "let's get back in bed."

"Child," I said, gaping up at her. "I didn't know I was out."

"Are you in any pain?" she asked.

"If you could just move this brick."

"Excuse me?"

"I don't feel right." This was true. I had a funny feeling in the pit of my stomach, like I was waiting for the oven buzzer to go off. If I didn't listen good, the cake would fall, and I wouldn't have anything fresh to offer.

"What's the matter?" said the nurse.

"I can't really say."

"Here, let's get you back in bed."

"If you could just call my granddaughter."

"Sure thing, hon. Sit right here and then swing your legs around."

She helped me into the bed, and I leaned back against the pillow—I'll just tell you, hospitals really skimp on blankets and pillows. Then everything kindly went dark.

Thank you for shutting off the light, I said, or thought I said. It was hurting my poor old eyes.

She must not have heard, because a second later, the lights came on in a flash—soft, warm light that put me in mind of deep April, when Amos and I use to dig up wild ferns and plant them alongside Church Creek. He is kneeling in the mossy woods. All around him the sun spears down through birch trees and the wild strawberries bloom and blue jays caw at the sky. Church Creek rushes by so fast, it seems to flow backward. I can hear the children calling out to each other—Ruthie, Josie, and Amos Jr. But that's not right, that can't be right; why, Josie can't speak a word, and Little Amos has been gone ... Lord, how many years has it been?

The children's laughter breaks over me like cool water. Up on the porch, I can see Mam and Papa waiting; Burl and Hattie are there, too. And behind them is the Pray kinfolk who narrowly escaped the Alamo. I have the feeling that they have been traveling through all the years of our lives, through wars and peaceable days, through births and deaths and all kinds of partings, traveling all the way to this moment in my backyard.

The sun beats down on my head, it soaks clear through to my soul. I hunker beside Amos. I can hear him breathing. Our thoughts rise up in a tangle, like butterflies. I reach into my deep pocket, take out a soup spoon, and commence to dig.

FREDDIE

I dreamed that I was living with Jackson in his farmhouse, only it was summer and hollyhocks were chest-high in the garden. On his screened porch, Minerva and I quilted. The fabric of our lives was woven by genuine people, not the brittle, artificial ones from Cissy's party. One day I hated Tallulah, the next I was thinking where I wanted to plant zinnias. Since I'd been here, I'd felt a sense of community, of people shoring other people up—of the satisfaction and security of people knowing you and your family from way back. Of having a place where you belong. Roots? I guess.

Sometime in the night, the hall phone started ringing. In my mind's eye, I moved toward it, wondering if Sam had forgotten about the time difference. He was the only one who'd call this late. I sat up and rubbed my eyes. The room was dark. From the hall, the phone kept on trilling. I heard Eleanor's door creak open, heard her scruffy footsteps move across the wood floor. "Hello?" she said. A few seconds passed, then she let out a wail. "What the hell happened?" she cried.

I threw back the covers and shot out of bed. I'd just made it to the door when she slammed down the phone. Her eyes were the strangest color, not yellow at all but dark, like brown sugar coming to a boil. She drew in a ragged sob, then backed up against the wall as if she were holding it up. "I think I'm going to vomit," she said, glancing down the hall, toward the bathroom. A nightlight burned over the sink, illuminating Brother Stowe's picture.

"What's the matter?" I said. "Who was that on the phone?"

Eleanor fixed her eyes on me and said, "They lost Minerva."

"Lost her? How?" I shook my head. I had visions of her sleepwalking, turning down corners, bumping into walls. When I was a medical student, we found a senile patient curled up in the linen closet at John Gaston Hospital, sleeping on a pile of lamb's wool blankets.

"She just died."

When we reached the hospital, Dr. Starbuck was waiting in the hall with a tired-looking nurse. "I'm sorry," he said, sounding anything but. "There was nothing I could do."

"But what happened!" I screamed, and Eleanor whimpered. I didn't care if I woke up the entire hospital. "I saw her a few hours ago. She was *fine*."

"It was a massive arrest," said Dr. Starbuck. "We need to know which funeral home to call."

"I want to see her."

He looked shocked, then nodded at the door. It was closed. I turned back to Eleanor, took her hand, and dragged her with me. Inside, the room was gray, except for a fluorescent light burning over her bed. The sheet was pulled up to her neck. Her eyes were closed, and she looked very alive to me—I'd seen her sleeping a thousand times. Eleanor dropped to the floor in a heap.

"Minerva?" I said, half-expecting her eyelids to flutter. "Min?"

I reached under the covers and felt her hand. She was warm. Just for a second I thought the doctor was mistaken—you couldn't be this warm and still be dead. Then I remembered the fever. Her windowsill was crammed with plants and get-well cards. In the three days she'd been ill, I hadn't brought anything—not a single flower. I felt as if I'd overlooked something important. My grandmother had been dying, and I'd been too stupid to see it. I would never forgive myself. As I stared at the cards, the air seemed to change in the room. The cards rattled, then blew over. I wondered if it was Minerva's soul, rushing out to scold me. I glanced at Eleanor to see if she'd noticed the wind, but she was sitting on the floor, her legs splayed.

"She just can't be gone," she said, looking up at me. "We'll never hear her voice again."

I crouched down. Then I put my arms around her and squeezed as hard as I could. We just sat there until I remembered Jo-Nell. We would have to tell her. It was nearly daybreak, and I hated to wake her up—it would be a long time, I knew, before any of us ever slept again.

"We should go," I said.

"I can't move," Eleanor said, but she got up, wobbling toward the door. We stepped out of Minerva's room, walked past the doctor, and took the stairs down to Jo-Nell.

JO-NELL

I had this god-awful dream that Minerva died, and I was at the mall with my sisters, buying black dresses. When we went up to the cash register, the machine spewed out a long paper. I snatched it up, thinking it was the bill, but it was a death certificate. The next morning, when Freddie told me what had happened, I said, "But I dreamed this. Honest to god."

"Do me a favor," said Eleanor, "and don't have any dreams about me."

I checked out of the hospital AMA—against medical advice. The nurses made me sign papers so I couldn't turn around and sue them. They'd seen the railroad men sniffing around my room, bringing me chocolates and carnations, buttering me up for the kill—older men in three-piece suits, with yellowed nails and bad breath. They came three days ago.

"Look, you sons of bitches," I told them. "Trash sues. I don't want a goddamn penny from the L&N. I'm a quality woman."

I picked up a vase of orange tiger lilies and threw it as hard as I could. Glass and water went everywhere. They ran out of the room. I knew I'd gone too far, but I was stressed out to the max. Truth be told, I was scared the men knew all about my accident—drinking tequila sunrises, not paying attention to my driving. I was scared shitless that they'd make *me* pay for damages to the railroad tracks, or even the locomotive. Later, I took a wheelchair ride up to Minerva's room. I cried on her shoulder, saying I'd lost my touch. I always said the wrong thing and made a bad situation worse. Minerva told me to give up Madonna as my role model and exchange her for Grace Kelly. "But she's dead," I told her. "No," Minerva said. "She's still alive in the old movies. Check her out at Video Express. Grace's got a real cute hairdo in *Rear Window*."

Now I looked at these leech nurses and tried to think what to do. I didn't know if I had it in me to be like Grace. I was more like Sheryl Crowe, all I wanted to do was have some fun, with one-night stands and beer buzzes. I went back and forth, between Sheryl and Grace. Finally, I decided to just be myself.

"My grandmother is dead," I told them. "Now, get out of my way."

They parted like the Red Sea, only it was more of a white one because they were wearing uniforms. "Get my walker and my pain pills, and I'm outta here," I demanded, thinking I would make one hell of an old lady someday.

Freddie drove us to the funeral home. It took me a long time to walk up the brick path, all humped over the walker, stepping sideways like a crab. It was a bitter cold morning, frost on the grass, icicles hanging from the gutters. The funeral home was two stories, red brick, with four square white columns on the porch. It was hard to believe this was a house of the dead, but all my family had been laid away here.

The undertaker was Mr. Carl Eubanks III. He was waiting in the lobby, or whatever the hell you call it—one broad, white hand holding back the door, letting us all step inside. "Come on in," he said. "Just come right on in."

My sisters walked beside me, as if holding me up. Eleanor had cried so much her eyelids were swelled up like banana peppers. On a mashed-in face, that tends to stand out. Freddie was pale and shiny-eyed, with a green ring around her mouth. All three of us had been vomiting our heads off. Me, I hadn't looked in a mirror, but I knew I was a wreck. For the first time in my natural-born life, I did not give a damn. I tried to think what Grace Kelly would do—a young, sleek Grace who was smooching with Jimmy Stewart in the wheelchair, spying on the neighbors, and heating up the brandy in the days before microwave ovens. I'm sure she would hold out one gloved hand and say, "Mr. Eubanks." That is all—his name and nothing else. Yet he'd feel as if she'd been talking fifteen full minutes.

As we stepped through the lobby/hall, Mr. Eubanks handed out individual packets of Kleenex, popping each one open at the seams. Since I couldn't make it down the basement stairs, his big-boned grandson, a lineman for the Tallulah Warriors, carried me down. Freddie brought my walker over to me. We shuffled around the coffins, taking in the colors and styles. I picked up a brochure for a funeral that cost $7,049.62. A wee bit pricey, even though I didn't know what the sixty-two cents was for. A top-of-the-line funeral cost $12,101.29.

Minerva had always said a pine box would suit her just fine—that's what they buried my daddy in, but I don't remember it. I picked up a booklet that said "Your Funeral and You: 101 Tips." Then I looked at a solid cherry model with a silver lining. It cost a whopping $8,000.02.

"You and me both are in the wrong profession," I told Freddie, jabbing her in the ribs. "Look at these prices. If we could open a funeral home, we could make a killing."

"Hush up," said Eleanor, elbowing me from behind. "That's plain ghoulish."

"Ha. It's more practical than doughnuts."

"Well, I'm sticking to baking." She blew her nose into a Kleenex. "It's a family tradition."

"Then you can do the cremations at my funeral home," I said. "Get it? Cream-ation?"

"That's not funny!" Eleanor turned a sickly green.

"I just can't believe she's dead," Freddie kept saying to the cherry coffin. She ran her fingers down the cold, glossy wood. It was pretty, but way out of our price range.

"I know," I said. All of a sudden, I felt weak-kneed. I leaned hard against the walker. Death was real hard on the living, but I knew from experience that it could be worse. As long as no one was getting hit by watermelons or hanging themselves on the Venetians, I felt blessed. Minerva's death, as much as it grieved me, was not weird or embarrassing. A heart attack required no unusual instructions to the undertaker, such as reconstruction or a closed casket.

"I can't believe it, either." Eleanor sighed, and mucus rattled in her nose. "They said heart attack, but how can you have a heart attack in the little CCU, when you are hooked up to a million wires? Weren't the nurses watching her monitor?"

"The cardiac monitors all have alarms," said Freddie.

"Maybe they were turned off," I suggested.

"Or broke," said Eleanor.

"We'll never know," Freddie said, as if to herself.

"I hate the idea of Mr. Eubanks III touching Miss Minerva's dead body," said Eleanor.

"Why did you have to say that?" I frowned. "God!"

"I can't help it." Eleanor blew her nose again. "I don't understand why there has to be this rigmarole over death. Why not just dig a hole and get it over with? At least have just one kind of coffin, and not have umpteen models."

"Right," I said. "It's a burial box, not a fashion statement."

"Me, I'd rather be cremated," Freddie said. "Just reduce my body to its lowest possible denominator. Sam can scatter me into the Pacific." She lifted one hand, staring at imaginary dust.

"Ashes, ashes," I sang. "All fall down."

"Why don't you shut up?" Eleanor narrowed her eyes. "Ashes, my foot. Why, you won't even clean the barbecue pit."

I let that pass. From long experience with death, I knew vicious outbursts were part of the grieving process. I remembered a funeral in Nashville on West End Avenue. It was at a synagogue—a friend of a lover had died of cancer, and I got to tag along. I liked the idea of prayers for the dead, and one basic casket with the Star of David. I decided then and there that if I ever got any religion, which wasn't likely, I would come back to that synagogue. It was the only funeral that made any sense—not this picking and choosing of cheap, spray-painted metal coffins, with assorted tufted linings that were straight out of a vampire movie. You could get a pink coffin with cheap embroidered roses on the lid, and a ruffled eyelet pillow. You could get an all-white model with chrome handles, sleek as a Frigidaire. I did not see the point of putting a family through this. The funeral business was a racket, and I hated the Eubankses for making a profit.

"Whatever happened to old family graveyards," said Freddie.

"Land got too expensive," said Eleanor. Like she knew.

"But it was a good idea, once upon a time," Freddie said. "Keeping everybody together." Freddie moved over to a speckled coffin—from a distance it looked like a great big Styrofoam ice chest. She gazed down at it with her arms folded. "Families should stick together."

"I couldn't agree more," said Eleanor, shooting me a hateful glance. She tossed her head. "So, are you still going to move to Texas?"

"Yes," I said, but I didn't know. To tell the truth, I had forgot all about it.

"When?" She looked heartbroken.

"Soon as I can drive."

"That won't be long." Her eyes teared up. She clasped my arm. "Please don't go. If you stay, I'll start making napoleons at the shop. I'll take out ads in the *Gazette*, I'll say we're changing over to a full-fledged bakery. We can put out that sign you wanted, AMERICAN PIE."

"Eleanor, don't," I said.

"We can buy us an espresso machine. We'll do savories—tomato pies, marinated goat cheeses. Just please, please don't leave. I can't take any more losses right now."

"You should revamp the shop anyway," I said. "Whether I stay or go."

"I'd never do it without you. Why, I wouldn't know how, or even care."

"Well, I'm going, so get used to it." I hobbled over to Freddie, leaving Eleanor with the expensive coffins.

"Traitor," she called. "Coward."

"Now if that ain't calling the pot black," I said to Freddie. "Do you think I'm crazy for picking up and leaving?"

"Me?" Freddie shifted her eyes. "You're talking to someone who drove to California in a 1961 Valiant."

"And you came back to Tennessee in a shuttle bus. I don't know if that's an improvement."

"I don't know, either." She ran one finger down the Styrofoam coffin. "I've just been standing here thinking how much it would hurt if I lost Sam. If I knew I couldn't ever see him again. Even though he's a vegan, he made me salami and mustard sandwiches. I'd eat them in bed."

"I bet you had salami breath in the morning," I teased.

"And he used to bring me caramel coffee in the morning, freshly ground beans," she said gloomily.

"What about the blonde?" I kept my eyes on the coffin. It had a fluffy pillow, all embroidered with lily of the valley. And a tag on the mattress claimed to be inner-spring, like a dead body needed good support.

"I can overlook her," Freddie said.

"Thanks to Jackson, huh?"

"Partly," she said, considering.

"And what about the good doctor? You going to leave him and break his heart again?" I cringed after I said this, but I couldn't help it; I had to know.

"Oh, God," she said, then pulled out her own personal Kleenex box. She wiped her eyes.

"Life sucks, don't it?" I put my arm around her, leaning my good hip against the walker.

"Yeah," she said, blowing her nose. "It does."

We all decided on Funeral #15, a walnut veneer coffin that we couldn't really afford until Mr. Eubanks pulled out his calculator and told us about his convenient payment plan. So we went whole hog with the coffin liner, too. Mr. Eubanks told us this was the most important part. A cheap liner let the water seep in, and we just couldn't have that happen to Minerva.

Mr. Eubanks's grandson carried me back up the stairs, but still, our ordeal was not over. A skinny woman with bug eyes directed us to a lounge that smelled of burned coffee and cigarette butts. She had a sheaf of papers and a checklist—we had to decide on the obituary, musical selections, pallbearers, minister. Thinking how much Minerva loved Sean Connery, I suggested bagpipes. I could just hear them playing "Amazing Grace."

"Bagpipes?" said the skinny woman. She drew back as if I'd suggested something offensive, like a farting contest.

"We're Scottish," I explained.

"I thought you were born right here in Tallulah," said the woman.

"She means of Scottish descent," Freddie explained.

"Minerva was a Texan," said Eleanor.

"I think she had some Scots in the woodpile," I said.

"Her maiden name was Murray," said Freddie.

"That reminds me." Eleanor stood up. "I need to send a telegram."

"To who?" I said. "There's no one left in Mount Olive."

"I'm going now," Eleanor said calmly. She picked up her purse, grunting a little, then she slogged out the door.

"How about some nice organ music?" suggested the bug-eyed woman, thinking she'd gotten us off track. "And we have some lovely taped selections. I'm pretty sure I can find 'Amazing Grace.'"

"No, I want bagpipes," I said. "I want a Scottish funeral with all the works."

"I'll certainly try my best, but it may cost extra." She shuffled her papers, indicating that our little meeting was over. "I'll just call up the college and see what they can dig up."

"Dig deep," I said, then snorted into my Kleenex. "It's what you people do best."

FREDDIE

At six o'clock the next night, we began the curious process of "receiving," one of Tallulah's all-purpose traditions—weddings, gift teas, cocktail parties. At a funeral, the family members tamp down their grief and greet old friends and strangers like it's a soiree. I was dreading it. Within an hour, the funeral home was packed with semifamiliar faces. They came in ones and twos, in old fox furs and netted hats, in patent-leather pocketbooks and lace-up orthopedic shoes. As the ladies drifted up to the coffin, either me or Eleanor went up to "receive" them. The coffin lid was open, like a hinged seashell. From the ceiling, a pink light discreetly lit up Minerva. It was the same kind of bulb they use over supermarket meat counters, enhancing the depth and color of rib roasts and ground round. Minerva wore pearl earbobs and her favorite Sunday dress—navy crepe with a white collar and cuffs. Even though she was a sporadic churchgoer, she always had casseroles to deliver, fresh widows to visit.

Powdery old women kept kissing my cheek, giving off gusts of Chanel and White Shoulders. It really was like a ladies' luncheon, minus the chicken salad and peppermints, where the guests sat around in metal chairs, trying to be polite and catch up on gossip at the same time. Everyone was friendly in a hushed, restrained sort of way, begging to hear all about the last decade of my life—medical school, Sam, the whales. They showed me pictures of their children and grandchildren, but my hands were empty. I hadn't carried a purse in years.

Eleanor sat in the front row, her head slightly bowed. Jo-Nell was marooned beside her, a metal walker propped over to the side. Her arms were saucily crossed, and she was chatting with one of her doctors. Before the next wave of old ladies engulfed me, I stepped around a potted fern, then slipped through the French doors. I looked up a forbidding, spiral staircase that curved into a gloomy second floor. This funeral home had been designed by the architect of the Hermitage, but it had fallen into ruin. The floors were covered with red shag carpet, and the wood beneath them creaked precariously. When I accidentally touched a wall, it felt soggy and moveable, as if the old, flocked wallpaper had been applied with buttermilk.

As I wandered toward the front door, the crowd kept pushing me back up to the casket. Along the way, I bumped into the aged librarian, Miss Wimberly, who censored the books I once checked out. I talked to the Holloway sisters, ages seventy-five and seventy-seven, who had lived near Minerva on Church Creek. They called each other darling and wore matching clothes. I spoke briefly to Georgia Ray Tolliver, who ran a gas and bait shop on Highway 70. She wore greasy overalls and a Skoals hat, with the bib turned around backward. The faces kept bearing down on me, some familiar, some strange.

"Minerva looks real good," said one.

"Peaceful," said another.

"And her color's good, too."

"You ain't burying her with them pearl earrings," said Georgia Ray Tolliver.

There is a small, good thing about grief—numbness. It hits you like a strong dose of Novocain. Yet sometimes I'd look down at Minerva and I'd think, I can't stand this. How can I live in this world when you are not here? Why didn't I know you were going to die?

One of our neighbors walked up, Felix Ferguson, a bow-legged, self-proclaimed anarchist and semiretired biology professor. I always thought Felix was a little in love with Minerva, but he was too much of a curmudgeon to ever let her know. "Your grandmother was a legend," he said in that strange, pseudo-British accent that's popular with certain Southern men—usually those who are trapped in small college towns. "I'd see her coming and going with her Pyrex dishes, taking food to the minions, sloshing through mud and show and rain. Honey, she put the U.S. Post Office to shame, and I mean *shame*."

"She was goodhearted," I said, edging a look into the coffin.

"They just don't make them like her anymore. She loved you children dearly, too. I'd see her out raking leaves, and she'd reach in her pocket and pull out one of your postcards from Baja. She was so proud of your whales, Freddie."

I ducked my head, wiping my eyes.

"And I'll tell you something else," he said, barreling on. "She not only loved you girls, she loved to cook. She was born to cook in *bulk*. I won't go as far as to say she had a mathematical mind, but no one, and I mean *no one*, could beat her tripling or quadrupling recipes."

He leaned toward me, shifting his eyes back to Eleanor. In a low, conspiratorial tone he said, "Do *not* quote me, but Minerva had misgivings about Eleanor's, shall we say, talents. She was concerned about the girl's carrot cake. 'It's too rich, Felix,' she told me. 'She needs to use light brown sugar. And her icing's runny, Felix. It's just too runny.'"

"Eleanor stole that recipe from *Gourmet*," I said.

"Then she should *sue*." He rolled his eyes. "At the very least, cancel her subscription."

He drifted over to Eleanor and Jo-Nell. I kept shaking hands and receiving. As the night wore on, people filled up the room, spilling out into a hall. At one point it got so hot and noisy, the funeral director, Mr. Eubanks, opened up the front door, letting

cold night air suck out the congestion. Mary June Carrigan
sidled up to me. She gazed thoughtfully down at Minerva, then
nodded at Jo-Nell. "That poor girl. And she used to be so pretty.
Will she ever walk again?"

"She already is."

"Yes, but without that metal thing?" Mary June leaned forward, frowning with concern. "I heard she drove her car into
that train on purpose, like that poor Russian lady, Anna Karen."

"Don't you mean Karenina?" Jackson said, walking up to us.

"Whatever," said Mary June.

"Anna Karenina threw herself in front of a train, I think," said
Jackson.

"Did you know her?" Mary June gaped up at him. I noticed
that she had small, low-set ears and a freckled neck.

"No, I didn't," said Jackson. There wasn't a drop of irony in
his voice. "But I read the book."

"She wrote a book?" Mary June lifted one hand. "There you
go. Everybody's writing autobiographies these days."

"Would you mind terribly if I borrowed Freddie?" said
Jackson. His tone was so kind and courtly that Mary June
appeared flattered.

"Why, no," she said, beaming up at him. "Not at *all*."

I followed him into the front hall, next to a window. Here, the
crowd was so thick that people were standing on the porch. A
chilly rain was falling, and fog was starting to gather in the
ditches. In the front room Mrs. Rubye Kieffer kept banging on
the yellowed piano, playing "Rock of Ages." Mrs. Kieffer was
also a Tallulah tradition—you couldn't marry or die without her
music. I glanced back at her, watching the skin on her upper
arms flutter like crepe. Up near the casket, Eleanor was surrounded by ladies. Jo-Nell was talking to her old volleyball
coach, a short redheaded woman with thick calves.

I sighed and turned back to the window. Jackson put his
hand against the small of my back. "I've never seen so many

people at a funeral," he said. "It's like when Beau Bailey died."

"Who's Beau Bailey?"

"A state senator who jumped off the Life & Casualty Building about four years ago."

"Why'd he do that?

"Back taxes," Jackson explained.

"Why not just pay what he owed?"

"I think it was something like five million."

"Oh, my."

"That's exactly what I said: oh, my. You might have to start a formal reception line, just to handle the crowd."

"I don't think Jo-Nell can stand for very long, and I can't leave her out."

"We'll get her a chair. Just tell me what you want." His hand moved up to my shoulder. I turned back to the window.

"The people are still coming," I said wearily, thinking that Minerva had delivered a lot more than casseroles over the years. A black Jeep parked at a slant on Dixie Avenue. A man wearing wire glasses and a hooded blue parka climbed out. He pushed back the blue hood, revealing close-cropped hair, the color of sherry. Shaking my head, I stepped away from Jackson, then ran my fingers through my hair. "It's Sam," I said.

"Are you sure?" He peered out the window, but I was already running out into the hall, pushing my way past two men in black suits, saying excuse me, excuse me.

"Freddie, wait," called Jackson, but I was out the door, running down the concrete steps. Sam was halfway up the brick sidewalk. He stopped, and I slammed into his arms. I smelled his smell—Aramis and sea water. He leaned back, lifting me into the air. I felt his breath on my face, his warm mouth, his hand circling my neck.

"Your sister Eleanor sent me a telegram," he said.

"Eleanor?" I leaned back, staring.

"I would have been here sooner. Why didn't you call?"

That was a good question. If I had any guts I would have told him the truth, that it was easier keeping a whole country between us. Instead I said, "I just assumed you couldn't leave. You have so much research, and I know how you hate funerals."

"Yes, but . . . I know what Minerva meant to you. I'd never let you go through something like this alone." He pulled me against him. "I'm so sorry."

"I wasn't expecting to lose her."

"No, of course not."

"You should have called. I would have picked you up at the airport." I ached to cry, but I drew in a deep breath. Rain was beading on his hair, shining like metallic confetti. He looked so out of context at Eubanks Funeral Home, in all of Tallulah for that matter, that I kept shaking my head. A mild breeze was blowing, whipping the parka. Behind him, the clouds washed low and the sky seemed to start just inches above the trees.

"I rented a Jeep. The traffic was horrible on the Interstate. It took forever." He kissed me, pressing his hand into the small of my back. "I've missed you."

"What about Nina?" I said, then looked back at the funeral home. Jackson was standing in the doorway, both hands braced against the frame. Our eyes briefly met, then he looked away, stepping backward through the crowd.

"Nina?" Sam said. He looked confused.

"Don't play dumb. I hate that."

"Have I missed something?" He wiped rain from his face, squinting at me. "I don't understand what she has to do with my missing you."

"I called the Mirabel a few nights ago. You weren't there. But Nina was. She said you'd just stepped out."

"No, that wasn't Nina. It was Tatiana."

"Who?"

"Tatiana Young. I'm sure you've heard of her. She's a pho-

tographer on assignment for *National Geographic*. We were view-
ing slides."

"Of what? We don't even own a projector."

"It was Tatiana's projector. She must have been setting it up
when you called. Nina was helping me carry in the slides. God,
there must have been fifty boxes."

"I don't believe you." My eyes were stinging.

"Well, it's true, Mrs. Espy." He stared at me a moment. Then
he took my hand and kissed it.

"You didn't sleep with her?" I was having trouble breathing.

"No." He wiped his forehead.

"Then it was all my imagination?"

"Not entirely." He glanced away. The rain was falling harder
now. "I'll say this for Nina. She's persistent."

"She made a pass?"

"About five hundred."

"And?"

"I told her the truth: that I love you."

Oh, god, I thought. What in the hell have I done? My knees
began shaking. I put my hand on his cheek. All this time I'd
hoped his character would rise to the surface, that he'd keep all
of his promises. I hadn't kept mine and it was killing me. "Can
we go sit inside that Jeep a minute?"

"Yes, but . . . why?"

"I have to tell you about Jackson Manning," I said.

"Tell me now." He gathered my hands.

"Let's just go to the car." I took a step toward the street, but
he pulled me back. My fist was pressed against his chest, caught
between us like a chunk of limestone.

"What is it, Freddie?"

"Or maybe we should go home."

"You slept with him." His eyes searched back and forth
between my pupils. "Didn't you?"

I shut my eyes, considering all possible answers. Then I

stepped back several inches, and my hand fell down against my hip. It was a full minute before I answered. "Yes," I said.

"Oh, god." Sam shook his head. His eyes were deep with tears. "Do you love him? I mean, because if you do—"

"I don't know." I narrowed my eyes. Suddenly I was furious. "Did you love that painter? You know, the yogurt lady."

"This is different."

"How?"

"I can't stand it." He looked around wildly. Then he took off walking.

"Sam?"

He ignored me, jumping over a puddle, into the street.

"You had an affair!" I called. He didn't respond to that. He walked past the Jeep, past a row of brick bungalows. The end of the street was one wash of gray. I turned back to the funeral home. In the doorway, a dozen or more old ladies were staring. I gave them a disgusted look, and they quickly shuffled inside. Then I turned back to the street. It had stopped raining, and the street was slick and shiny, reflecting a traffic light as it flashed yellow, then red. From far away I heard the thrumming noise of the highway and the closer hum of the organ music. Sam was at the end of Dixie Avenue now. He'd never been to Tallulah, so he couldn't know where he was going. I thought about running after him, but I didn't know what I'd say.

I imagined him turning right onto Tarver, past rows of white clapboards with screened front porches; then he'd turn left onto Spring, where the houses were a little grander, facing the college baseball field. He'd turn left again at Hatton, hurrying past a wrought-iron fence with all the fleur de lis tipped in gold. At the Tallulah Library, he'd run into Dixie Avenue again—a street named for the long-dead daughter of a long-dead politician, Dixie Hughes. I seemed to recall that she had been hit by a train one block from the college. According to local legends, she had been driving past the women's dorm. She turned to wave at a boy, and the train slammed into her car, dragging it seventy feet.

A chilly wind started up, but I was afraid to go inside. I looked down at Jo-Nell's dress—the wool was sopping wet, and I was afraid I'd ruined it. Way off in the distance I saw Sam's profile against the haze. His hands were stuffed into his pockets. When he reached the last brick bungalow, I walked to the end of the sidewalk. He had come full circle, but I was meeting him halfway.

JO-NELL

"I'm sick and tired of funerals," I hissed to Eleanor.

"Shhh."

"Well, I am." If you asked me, a funeral was nothing more than a great big party where the guest of honor was put on display like a honey-baked ham. A waxy, stiff piece of meat laid out between mums and a brass candelabra. No fucking way, I thought. When my time comes, I'll be in Texas. Just throw me in the ground and plant a tree.

"Look." Eleanor pointed, and I saw Jackson slipping out the back door. On his face was the biggest hang-dog look in the world. I didn't know what to make of it. Maybe Freddie had PMS, or maybe he had an emergency call. Or maybe he was overcome with severe stomach cramps. That happened to me one time at the Crow's Nest, a bar in the middle of nowhere, and I had to run out into the night.

"Why was that doctor paying so much attention to you?" Eleanor asked point-blank.

"Which one?" I said.

"You know who. Dr. Lambert."

"He says he loves me."

"But he's married—right?"

"He wants to leave her."

"Sure." Eleanor rolled those yellow eyes.

"See this frog pin?" I held out my jacket. "He gave it to me."

"It's darling!" She petted its head. "It looks twenty-four karat. Can I wear it sometimes?"

"It's going with me to Texas."

"What about loverboy?"

"He says he's coming to see me." I smiled into my hand, thinking about what we'd done earlier in the ladies room. (I'd left my walker outside, propped against the wall.) There was a terrible banging at the door, and when I finally opened it, there stood Cissy Alsup. She looked from me to Lambert, and her bottom jaw fell open, showing a row of silver fillings.

"I may be coming to Texas sooner than I'd planned," Lambert told me later.

Now Eleanor was shaking her head. "If he's so in love with you, I don't understand why you're leaving. I mean, this is what you always wanted."

"All that doesn't matter now. I'm happy about Texas."

"I'm not." Eleanor jabbed me with her elbow. "In fact, I think you've had brain damage."

A wave of old-lady whispering made its way to me, and I turned all the way around to stare.

"Who's that with the granddaughter?" hissed one of the widow ladies. "A relative?"

"He sure is handsome."

"Me, I *like* a redhead. And it goes good with his sunburn."

"Wonder if he works at a tanning booth."

"Somebody said he was from Mexico."

"Lord, is he a Spaniard?"

"He don't look foreign."

"Freddie married a foreigner, you say?"

"At least one of Minerva's girls snared a man."

These widows were like buzzards, with their long, wrinkled necks and feathery hats, yellow nails spread out like claws. I could tell them plenty about ensnaring. Then I got a good look at my sister. God, she looked awful. She was rain-drenched, and her hair was flat as a boy's. Coming down the aisle with her was the best-looking guy I'd seen in years. He was drenched, too, with real short coppery-brown hair. Although I couldn't be sure, from here his eyes looked blue-green. Why, he was kinfolk, my own freaking brother-in-law. I had never seen him in the flesh; the pictures Freddie had sent didn't do him justice. I knew he was a blue-eyed redhead, but because of the scuba shit, I always imagined him as a dead ringer for Lloyd Bridges, like when he starred in *Sea Hunt*. I didn't know about my sister, but men like Sam didn't grow on trees, at least not locally. If my hip hadn't been broke, I would have ran over to him and started flirting, making him fall in love with me. Well, I'm lying. I would never do such a thing, especially at a funeral home. In spite of what this town thinks, I do have my morals.

They went up to the casket and stared down at Minerva. When Freddie started crying a little, he put his arm around her. He had very nice hands, I noticed, large and muscular, stitched with blue veins. My first husband had hands like that, and for a second, I saw my old self sitting in this same funeral home, an eighteen-year-old bride keeping vigil on poor old Bobby Hill. It was a closed coffin—had to be on account of the watermelons— but I'd spent a fortune on a rose spray. Minerva and my sisters pooled their money and had the florist make a giant football out of mums. It was really bitching, the best arrangement I'd ever seen.

"Wonder where Jackson is?" I asked Eleanor. I was sad that I was going to Texas and wouldn't be around to comfort him.

"Shhh, you're talking and I can't stare at Freddie's husband." Eleanor gaped up at him. "I didn't know he was a redhead."

"Well, it's more auburn than red."

"Yes, it is." She squinted. "I see what you mean. He's cute. I mean, for a man."

"Ain't that the truth," I said, watching Sam step back, letting

Freddie lead him over to the front row. Behind us, the whispering had turned into a roar—all them old ladies having strokes,
afraid they were missing out on the Young and Restless McBroom
sisters.

"Jo-Nell, Eleanor," Freddie said, walking up to us. She
beamed up at the man. "I'd like you to meet my husband, Sam."

It rained during the funeral, tapering off to a drizzle after Brother
Stowe's eulogy. I stood under the big maroon tent, with EUBANKS
FUNERAL HOME stamped on the sides. I wore dark sunglasses and
a black wool dress—it was an oldie from Goodwill, the closest
thing I could get to a Grace Kelly look on my budget. My hair
was parted on the side, swooping down in a blond wave. I felt
separate from the other women in town, but it was worse with
Minerva gone. I stayed close to Freddie and Sam, listening to the
rain drum on the tent, listening to the pastor talk about what a
wonderful person Minerva was, and how she had gone to her
Reward. I spotted old Jackson, and I envied my sister for being
loved by two men. All last night I couldn't sleep, and I lay there
listening to the mattress springs squeak like a chorus of katydids—Sam and Freddie going at it. I got so worked up, I almost
called Lambert. I had to touch my own self, rubbing and circling
with my fingers until I fell back, shivering, breathing hard
against my pillow. I told myself to get used to it—a long, dry season was waiting for me in Texas, and I had to be strong. Once I
got to Mount Olive, I wasn't giving in to my hormones.

The temperature had risen during the night, and the rain was
making the ground muddy. My heels sank down in the soggy
grass. Still, the graveside was clogged with mourners, all clutching umbrellas. They spread out in the rain like colorful mushrooms, some harmless, some full of poison. You just had to
know which ones to pick and pray you didn't make the same
mistake twice. Me, I was going to take things real slow in Texas.
I couldn't leave for at least three weeks—both Dr. Granstead

and Jackson told me I couldn't go until my bones and blood count checked out. And Lambert said I shouldn't go at all. Back at home, I had maps of Tennessee, Arkansas, Oklahoma, and Texas. I'd drawn me a route with red ink.

Meanwhile, I had to burn all my bridges in Tallulah. I thought of all the things I had to do. My room was stuffed with clothes and costume jewelry and cosmetics and doodads. Me, I was the original material girl—a low-budget one, to be sure, but the end result is the same: The clutter builds up, whether it costs fifty cents or fifty dollars; but I'd made up my mind to get rid of almost everything. I was even giving Eleanor my secret recipe for key lime pie—she couldn't run the bakery without it. I was starting to think that after you died there was nothing—no hereafter, not even a fifth dimension where you could haunt people. All that was left of you were things—dresses, books, makeup, pantyhose. I liked the way Freddie approached life—if it couldn't fit in the car, she left it behind. With my insurance money, I'd bought me a Ford Explorer—a pretty red one.

After the preacher said amen, I stared down at the casket, which was poised over its hole by a hydraulic lift. "You ready to go?" asked Freddie.

"In a second," I said. "You go on."

"I'll wait with her," Sam said, and I thought, Honey, this is your lucky day. Outside the tent, the rain hammered against the mourners, falling in sharp slanted sheets. My eyes swept through the crowd again, skipping over faces. I nodded at Granstead and Lambert. When I came to a green-eyed man with curly blond hair, I liked to have died.

"Jesse?" I said, squinting.

"Hey, Jo-Nell," he said and walked through the puddles to reach me.

Soon as we got home, the house was bustling with old ladies. A half-dozen staked out the kitchen, washing glasses and silver forks like it was a tea party. Another group of women set out food on the cherry drop-leaf table. I heard someone say, "She put a Hershey's chocolate bar in this chili? But it *does* taste good, don't it?" The Holloway sisters stacked china, forks, spoons, knives, glasses, paper napkins. Freddie was standing at one end of the table, pouring iced tea. I saw Sam and Jackson moving at opposite ends of the room, eyeing each other cautiously. Me, I knew better than to do something like that. (I hadn't invited Lambert, but I'd given directions to Jesse.)

Georgia Ray Tolliver came up to me and Eleanor. She looked funny out of her greasy overalls, in a red cotton dress all patterned with sailboats. She wore white, open-toed shoes, straight out of the forties. It was a pitiful ensemble, probably the only dressy thing she owned.

Mrs. Constance Smythe came out of the kitchen carrying a steaming dish—her infamous seafood hash, she told us proudly. She wore a black dress and rustled like a magpie as she moved around the table. In minutes, the room smelled like a rotten can of cat food. It wasn't her fault—she was a natural-born Yankee, from either Maine or Massachusetts, and she didn't know shit about seafood. A bit of lemon juice and zest would have cut the stink, but you couldn't tell Constance anything—she knew it all and then some. The rumor was her people had been chased out of the North with a broom. (I believed it.)

From the kitchen, somebody hollered out that we were running out of dishes. "All this washing is for the birds," Georgia Ray Tolliver said, reaching in her pocket. "Eleanor, here's you twenty dollars. Run over to Winn-Dixie and buy some paper plates and cups."

"Me?" Eleanor was horrified. "I'm not going anywhere. I'm too grieved. Put me behind the wheel of a car, and I'm liable to wreck."

"It'll do you good to get out," said Georgia.

"No, it won't." Eleanor was turning pale.

"Here." Georgia held out the money.

"Put it away." Eleanor pushed it back. "I told you, I'm not leaving this house!"

"I'd go myself, but my truck's blocked. And your wagon is parked out front."

"Then you drive my car," Eleanor said.

"I'm heating chicken. And there's all these people to feed."

"Okay, okay." Eleanor sighed. "Jo-Nell? Come with me."

"Sweetie, look at me. I'm on a walker."

"You go on," said Georgia, pressing the money into Eleanor's hands. "The fresh air'll do you good."

"But it's raining," said Eleanor.

"Oh, hush up and go before I start using the good crystal."

After she left, dragging her big pocketbook behind her, I inched my way to the dining room. Listen, this is not easy with a walker. I sifted through the guests. It felt weird to open our house like this, but I acted nice. Minerva would have expected it. The cherry table was packed with food. I thought of everything in the freezers and wondered what Eleanor would do with it. I myself had no appetite, but I couldn't help but watch what everybody else was eating. When it came to men, my grandmother had one piece of advice: "Watch him eat, girls."

Jackson's plate was a mishmash—a chicken leg, fudge cake, deviled eggs, pot roast, kielbasa pasta salad, corn casserole, angel biscuits, hot curry fruit compote, potato salad, and the infamous seafood hash. Sam's plate had a pile of salad, lettuce and tomatoes with all the cheese picked out; marinated mushrooms; mandarin oranges; pink apple sauce; raw broccoli, carrots, and cauliflower; boiled new potatoes. I tried to draw me up a portrait of these two men—one was fussy, but consistent, probably a little predictable and set in his ways; the other was unpicky but would eat cat food.

The clincher came when Constance Smythe sidled up to Jackson. She had the gall to ask what he thought of her seafood hash. He glanced back at the dining table—the casserole had one missing scoop, which was still sitting on his plate. He stabbed it with his fork, popped it into his mouth, and raised his eyebrows.

"Just delicious, Constance," he said. He swallowed hard, then briefly shut his eyes.

"If there's any left over," Constance promised, "I'll give it to you."

"No, no," he said.

"I *insist*," Constance said in a grand voice. "It's too expensive to waste, and besides, I'd like a doctor to have it."

Serves you right, I thought. Raving about crappy food was deceitful. I just hoped Freddie wasn't too busy pouring tea to notice.

I pushed deeper into the living room, trying to escape the mingled odors of perfume, baked cheese, and the stench of scallops and crabmeat. Mary June Carrigan and Cissy Alsup were discussing liposuction. Jackson was asking Sam if he'd ever seen killer whales in Baja. Felix Ferguson was telling Georgia Ray Tolliver about an unusual earthworm he'd dug up in his compost pile. The Holloway sisters were giving Freddie a recipe for French Toast Grand Marnier. And the green-eyed cowboy was talking to me about Texas.

"I'm from Austin," he said. "I used to rodeo in Amarillo, too. Houston, Odessa, Denton. I know right where Mount Olive is."

"You do?" I said, feeling shy all of a sudden. I noticed his plate of food—chicken breast, potato salad, beans, two biscuits, slice of lemon pound cake.

"I may be making a big mistake," I said. "Going down there all by myself."

"If you need anybody to drive with you, what with your condition and all, I'd be happy to. My brother Gordon trains cutting horses near Waco. I could drop by and see him."

"Thanks, but I've got everything all planned. But if you ever pass through Mount Olive, come and see me."

"I'll just do that." His green eyes lit up, and my heart lurched.

"Gordon's been after me to help him out. I love cutting horses, and I sure do miss Texas." Beads of perspiration lined his forehead and upper lip. He dabbed at it with his napkin, looking sheepishly at me, to see if I'd noticed. My heart lurched again.

"I'll be living on a ranch," I said. "There's a peach orchard. I don't know what-all else."

"It's different down there," he said, forking up some potato salad. "But good. Real, real good."

"Tell me all about Texas," I said.

"What do you want to know?"

"Everything," I said, looking up at him, smiling.

ELEANOR

I pulled into the Winn-Dixie lot, but let the engine keep on running, in case I had to make a quick getaway. From the radio, Linda Ronstadt was singing "Poor Poor Pitiful Me." I thought that should be my theme song—women laying their heads on railroad tracks and men putting you into Waring blenders. Then again, it could've been Jo-Nell's song, too. Before I shut off the engine, I looked all around. I felt too sick-hearted to grocery shop, what with the funeral and all. I looked at the sidewalk. Women, children, and old people streamed in and out of Winn-Dixie. Over by Radio Shack, teenage girls were talking to boys in bomber jackets. The girls wore their hair in side-swept ponytails. It was just a gathering place, I told myself. In the olden days, folks gathered around the square. I remembered going to town with Mama and Minerva. We'd park in front of Kuhn's, and watch all of the people milling by. All day long ladies got in and out of our car, catching us up on who was sick and who was going crazy. Now, Winn-Dixie had become the main exchange—in one spot you could pick up fresh broccoli, a video rental, and the latest gossip.

This wasn't going to be easy. It had been a little while since I'd gone to the grocery by myself, like about seven years. I shut my eyes. "Minerva?" I prayed. "If you are up there, watching over me, give me a Sign. Amen." Then I got out of the station wagon, swinging my purse, like I'd seen the young girls do. It was heavy, on account of the brick, but I told myself it would just build me up some muscles. I walked fast, and for the first time I was happy I had long legs. Halfway to the electric doors, a hand clamped down on my arm. Then I was yanked backward so hard, I lost my balance. I jumped back, planted both feet on the ground, and the whirled around, staring face to face with my attacker. I recognized him at once—the man I'd spotted at Kmart. He wore the same dirty orange knit hat. He had two green eyes, a mustache, tousled blond hair, bad breath, and grubby fingers. I tried to memorize everything about him so I could give the police a description, like they tell you on *America's Most Wanted.*

"I got a gun," the man said, sticking one hand in his pocket. "Hand over your purse."

"No!" I took off running in a zigzag pattern, in case he decided to shoot.

"You fat bitch!"

"Help me!" I cried, then I remembered you weren't supposed to say that; you should yell fire or gas leak. I tripped over my own feet. I fell down and scraped my knee. My pocketbook banged against my hip. I glanced back and saw the man coming straight for me. I scrambled to my feet, then heaved my purse. I struck out blindly. I felt it hit the man's head with a sickening *thwack.* He staggered, then touched his face. One hand groped inside his jacket, searching for the gun. I just knew he was going to shoot me, but I'd be damned if I was leaving my sisters with another funeral to pay for.

"You!" I screeched. I slammed my purse against his arm. "You!"

The man squatted, and I swung again, clipping him under the chin. He fell over backward and hit the pavement. His eyelids fluttered, and he let out a moan. I leaned over and spit on top of his nose. Later, when the police came, I showed them my brick. It had broken clean in half. They told me I'd done good, that I was a hero. "Does this mean I get my picture in the paper?" I said.

After I got home and told everybody my news, I got all shaky. I spilled a glass of tea down the front of my dress, and the ladies bustled around me, blotting me with paper towels. It was like I'd just realized what I'd done—the bigness of being a local crime buster was more than I could stand. I gave Georgia Ray the paper plates and cups.

"Don't let that brick go to your head," she told me.

"Don't you let it go to yours, Georgia."

"Shoot, I've hit many a man upside the head. It don't take nothing but a little muscle is all—and some balls."

"I guess."

"I been watching your sister Freddie over yonder. When she was little, I just knew she was going to turn out ugly. But she's right cute. Got that tight little ass and tits that ride up under her sweater and big brown eyes like Mariah Carey. I listen to her on my radio all the time. Mariah Carey, not Freddie." She burped, and a couple of ladies raised their eyebrows. Georgia stared them down.

"What the hell are you vultures looking at?" she said.

They scurried off, carrying dishes to the kitchen, and Georgia belched again. "I hate Constance Smythe. She's rich, but she don't look it. We're talking money, old money. The kind that makes you shit green turds."

"She can't cook," I said.

"They's a lot she can't do." She narrowed her eyes. "What's this about little Jo-Nell going to Texas?"

"She's going," I said, then shrugged.

"I just can't believe it. What's the matter with her?"

"She's just sick of this town. She's tired of people spreading gossip on her." This was the truth. Just because my sister liked to paint her nails peculiar colors, like blue, people gossiped. And of course there was the married men.

"So she decided to overhaul her life?" Georgia looked horrified.

"I guess."

"Poor old thing. She puts me in mind of a used Ford—got a little too many miles, been handled rough, but her engine's running and her frame ain't bent." Georgia snorted. "Why, she can't go to Texas!"

I wanted to say something on the order of, Don't feel rained on. She's leaving me, too. They are all leaving me. I was flat-out exhausted from being a hero, so I excused myself and went upstairs to my room. I laid down on the bed and stared up at the ceiling. Minerva was dead, and my sisters were leaving town. Me, I wasn't going anywhere, but I was lucky: I had lots of friends. Most of them happened to be over the age of seventy, but that suited me fine. Maybe I could adopt a few (if they'd let me). Maybe I could fry chicken and take it to the shut-ins. I didn't think one little brick could change my life, but it was a start.

"Eleanor?" It was Georgia's voice. "Get your ass down here. The newspaper's here to take your picture."

I sat bolt upright. Then I ran out of my room, clunking down the stairs. Georgia was smiling, one hand draped over the banister. "You aren't teasing me, are you?" I said.

"Hell, no." She nodded toward the front door. "Don't make them wait."

I put one hand over my heart, then started walking down the hall.

"Eleanor?"

"What?" I turned.

"Just remember the little people," she said. "The ones who put up with your shit before you got famous."

"I will," I said, reaching out to hug her. "Don't you worry, I will."

FREDDIE

The day before I left Tallulah, Sam drove Eleanor to Ace Hardware. Not three minutes later, Jackson appeared on the front porch. He held out a bouquet of jonquils, all wrapped up in green florist's tissue. "Are you alone?" He glanced nervously around the room.

"No, Jo-Nell's upstairs." I smelled the flowers, then glanced toward the staircase. Her boom box was belting out Melissa Etheridge. Back in Dewey, I liked to listen to Vivaldi while I made crazy pasta salads—scallions, parsley, garlic, shiitake mushrooms, red peppers, all served over linguine.

"Actually, I know Sam's not here," Jackson said. "I parked up the street and waited for him to leave."

I stared.

"Before you get mad, just listen. I've been dying to see you; but there was no way. So I was reduced to staking out your house. How long will he be gone?"

"I don't know. He took Eleanor to the hardware store."

"Why?"

"She's a little nervous about living alone, so he's putting locks on the doors and windows."

"Alone? Is Jo-Nell getting her own place?"

"She's moving to Texas."

"Why?"

"We inherited a house in Mount Olive. It was Minerva's."

"What about you?" He gave me a long, searching look. "Are you packing, too?"

"Some. I'm taking back quilts, baby pictures. Minerva's striped jelly glasses. A whole set of Fiesta and green Depression glass. Even some of Jo-Nell's miniskirts." I knew I was talking too fast, but I couldn't stop. "Can you imagine me with bulging closets?"

"No." He laughed.

"Eleanor said she'd ship it UPS. You think that'll be all right? I hope nothing gets broken."

"It'll be fine."

"It's funny, but acquiring things is dangerous. The more you have, the more you worry." I shrugged. "It was easier to have nothing at all."

"And now you've got dishes and doodads." He took my hand and rubbed his thumb over my knuckles. "What's next?"

"I'm so sorry, Jackson."

"For what?" His eyes widened; then he shook his head. "Damn, don't say it. Don't you say it, Freddie."

I didn't know if I could speak. I looked past him, through the window. The sun was low and dazzling, glinting off the top of his truck. I loved him and I loved my husband. I was greedy; I didn't deserve either man. From upstairs, the music changed, and Gladys Knight and the Pips started singing "I Heard It Through the Grapevine"—a sign that Jo-Nell knew I wasn't alone. I imagined her sifting through the tapes and CDs, choreographing my conversation with Jackson. However, if she started playing "Na Na Hey Hey Kiss Him," I would be forced to go upstairs and throw the boom box out the window.

"Well, I guess I asked for it. I chased the hell out of you, girl." Jackson smiled a crooked smile, and he looked exactly like his father. "I knew this would probably happen. But still, I hoped. So, I guess you're going back? You're actually leaving the land of magnolia-scented douches?"

I ran my fingernails through my bangs, then nodded. But I was thinking, Jackson, stop this day from turning, keep the stars from shining, hold the sun tight and in place, don't let it go down. I wanted him to take away the past. Make it different, change it so I never went West and met Sam at Point Reyes.

"I wish to god you weren't going." He briefly shut his eyes. "You're leaving me for another man."

"But he's my husband."

"I always knew you were that sort of girl. Hey, does he know about me?"

"I told him."

"Damn!" He whistled, then glanced up at the staircase. "What did he say?"

"He wasn't happy," I said, remembering.

"I guess not," he said, shaking his head. "This is binding. Well, I guess this really is good-bye. *Again.*

"You know, I just realized that I started all of this." He tapped two fingers against his hand. "I was the one who taught you how to swim. You remember that? Damn, I wish I was a whale."

"Your heart's the size of one."

"And it's killing me." He drew me into his arms. I shuddered, as the pressure of his lips and the spice of his cologne reminded me of other things. My left knee kept collapsing, popping out of joint like an old Tinker Toy. When he let go, I reeled backward, tottering slightly, then catching myself on the banister. I wished with all my heart that I could have two lives, one in California and one in Tennessee. Already I missed my sisters and Minerva and Jackson; I even missed the way the air smelled near the river. Each loss was private, just one more piece of excess baggage.

"Don't you ever forget me, Freddie."

"You? No way." I folded my arms, hugging myself. My chest felt very fragile, as if my ribs were made of bamboo sticks. "Like you said, I'm not that kind of girl."

"Well, remember," he said. He touched my arm, then he turned, walking briskly out the door and across the porch, his shoes clapping on the wood. He turned down the flaky rock path and climbed up into his truck. And then he was gone.

We were somewhere west of the Pacific Ocean, when the Cessna shot out of the clouds. I peered through the dusty window. My heart started beating fast when I saw the Laguna Guerrero Negro and Scammon's. I always knew that the whales were larger than my life—they would tip the balance of everything. The water was choppy, not from any storm, but from the whales. Sam passed me the binoculars, and I started counting the bushy spouts. They erupted from the ocean like geysers. During our student days at Scripps, we would crawl on the steep shingled roof of Ritter Hall and count the migrating greys.

Whale-watching, like most everything in life, was not without its risks. A few years ago in San Ignacio, the whales had made the water boil with frenzied tail thrashing—all within a few yards of a photographer. Another time a flailing fluke accidentally cracked a diver's ribs, flinging him into the air like a piece of bait.

"Look at that, will you. Got to be hundreds of them." The pilot grunted, then scratched his crotch. He was American, a part-time employee of Aero California. "I been taking censuses on these creatures since the seventies, right after I got out of Vietnam," he told us. "Did you know that of all the animals in the Bible, whales are mentioned first?"

I wasn't sure if this was true, but I nodded. I could almost hear Minerva saying, Child, some things you don't question, you just accept. Jo-Nell would have said, Don't piss him off—after all, he's the pilot. He squinted through the water-speckled window, looking down at the rough blue water. "Which whales sing those songs? Do these?"

"No," said Sam. "Right whales sing to their young."

"Any of them down there?" The pilot stared, his mouth gaped open.

"No, they're practically extinct."

"Ain't that a pisser. If we can't save the whales, can we save anything?"

"I don't know," said Sam.

"The planet's going to hell in a hand basket," said the pilot, staring down at the water. "What about those humperdinks? Don't they sing, too?"

"Yes." Sam leaned forward and kissed the back of my neck. "Humpbacks sing to their mates."

"Don't see how they hear it," said the pilot. "All that water. Looks like they'd get confused. It's a big ocean out there."

"It sure is," I said, reaching back to touch Sam's knee. The sun was going down, staining the water a deep plum color. Sam's legs felt just right against my back, and I leaned against him. His hands slid down my shoulders. The ocean was enormous, but it wasn't limitless, as the old explorers had once imagined. In a funny way, it was like myths concerning the heart—both were mysterious and forbidding, full of perils and fault lines, irreplaceable and unimaginably precious.

The Cessna curved back toward the desert, circling over a paved airstrip, which dropped off abruptly into sand. In the moment before we landed, I saw everything: Mama dancing in her stocking feet, waiting for Mr. Crenshaw to come over, singing "That's Life"; Eleanor and the widows measuring cake flour, creaming butter and sugar, separating eggs into whites and yolks, locking all the doors and windows against the night; Jo-Nell crossing the Texas-Oklahoma state line, leaving her old life in the dust, with Minerva hovering in the clouds, watching over us all, her breath rising up like a soul. I saw Jackson standing at the boat dock, maybe thinking of nothing, maybe thinking of me. A mild wind caught the sleeve of his sweater and it rose like a finger.

Thousands of miles away I could hear, and would go on hearing, the beating of his heart. I heard all the mysterious rustlings and heavings of that dock, and all the anonymous sounds of the evening. He stood motionless, outlined against the blue, a chance meeting of sky and water, curving into a sudden vanishing point.

▦ Perennial

Books by Michael Lee West:

CRAZY LADIES
ISBN 0-06-097774-4
A lively, multigenerational tale of six charming, unforgettable Southern
women. This funny, poignant novel spans more than four decades as it vividly
recounts the universal loves, sorrows, and joys of women's lives.

"Gripping . . . Dazzling . . . Unforgettable . . . An absorbing, skillfully
woven mix of calamity and comedy." —*Atlanta Journal-Constitution*

SHE FLEW THE COOP
A Novel Concerning Life, Death, Sex, and Recipes in Limoges, Louisiana
ISBN 0-06-092620-1
Every day in Limoges, Louisiana, presents either some kind of dark calamity
or comedy. Told through the voices of its richly eccentric characters, it is an
entrancing picture of the gossip-mongering citizens and a beautifully rendered
portrait of a 1950s small-town life filled with humor and humanity.

"Destined to be a Southern classic." —*Orlando Sun-Sentinel*

AMERICAN PIE
ISBN 0-06-098433-3
When a freak accident brings three very different sisters together again, they
end up confronting their past, their future, and one another in this hilarious
and moving novel.

"[West's] observations about life and love are perceptive and her food
metaphors can be downright delicious!" —*Chicago Tribune*

CONSUMING PASSIONS
A Food-Obsessed Life
ISBN 0-06-018371-3
A delicious memoir of Michael Lee West's trials and tribulations as a Southern
woman who becomes an "accidental gourmet." Rich with gracious Southern
hospitality, it includes the recipes that have passed through generations of
her family.

Available at bookstores everywhere, or call 1-800-331-3761 to order.